PRELUDE IN PRAGUE

Borgo Press Books by S. Fowler Wright

Arresting Delia: An Inspector Cleveland Classic Crime Novel
The Attic Murder: An Inspector Combridge & Mr. Jellipot Classic Crime Novel
The Bell Street Murders: An Inspector Combridge & Mr. Jellipot Classic Crime Novel
Beyond the Rim: A Lost Race Fantasy
Black Widow: A Classic Crime Novel
The British Colonies: No Surrender to Nazi Germany!
The Capone Caper: Mr. Jellipot vs. the King of Crime: A Classic Crime Novel
Crime & Co.: An Inspector Cleveland Classic Crime Novel
Dawn: A Novel of Global Warming
Dead by Saturday: An Inspector Cleveland Classic Crime Novel
Dream; or, The Simian Maid: A Fantasy of Prehistory (Marguerite Cranleigh #1)
Elfwin: An Historical Novel of Anglo-Saxon Times
The End of the Mildew Gang: An Inspector Cauldron Classic Crime Novel (Mildew Gang
   #3)
Four Callers in Razor Street: An Inspector Combridge & Mr. Jellipot Classic Crime Novel
Four Days' War: The Alternate World War II, Book Two
The Hanging of Constance Hillier: An Inspector Cleveland Classic Crime Novel
The Hidden Tribe: A Lost Race Fantasy
The Jordans Murder: An Inspector Combridge & Mr. Jellipot Classic Crime Novel
The King Against Anne Bickerton: A Classic Crime Novel
Megiddo's Ridge: The Alternate World War II, Book Three
The Mildew Gang: An Inspector Cauldron Classic Crime Novel (Mildew Gang #1)
Murder in Bethnal Square: An Inspector Combridge & Mr. Jellipot Classic Crime Novel
The Police and the Public: Some Thoughts on the British System of Justice
Post-Mortem Evidence: An Inspector Combridge & Mr. Jellipot Classic Crime Novel
Prelude in Prague: The Alternate World War II, Book One
The Return of the Mildew Gang: An Inspector Cauldron Classic Crime Novel (Mildew
   Gang #2)
The Rissole Mystery: An Inspector Combridge & Mr. Jellipot Classic Crime Novel
The Screaming Lake: A Lost Race Fantasy
The Secret of the Screen: An Inspector Combridge & Mr. Jellipot Classic Crime Novel
Spiders' War: A Novel of the Far Future (Marguerite Cranleigh #3)
Three Witnesses: A Classic Crime Novel
Too Much for Mr. Jellipot: An Inspector Combridge & Mr. Jellipot Classic Crime Novel
The Vengeance of Gwa: A Fantasy of Prehistory (Marguerite Cranleigh #2)
Was Murder Done? A Classic Crime Novel
Who Murdered Reynard? A Classic Crime Novel
The Wills of Jane Kanwhistle: An Inspector Combridge & Mr. Jellipot Classic Crime Novel
With Cause Enough?: An Inspector Combridge & Mr. Jellipot Classic Crime Novel

PRELUDE IN PRAGUE

THE ALTERNATE WORLD WAR II

Book One

by

S. FOWLER WRIGHT

THE BORGO PRESS

An Imprint of Wildside Press LLC

MMIX

CHAPTER I.

IT was the morning of Friday, January 28th, 1938.

The long façade of the new ministry, stone-white in the winter sunshine, looked out on the breadth of the great square that was now mantled with salt-white snow.

It looked across at the Cathedral of St. Vitus at the Palace of Wallenstein, at the castle of ancient kings. It looked down on the black, twisting, bridge-barred ribbon of the ice-cold Moldau, and on the narrow, age-old streets, the rich antiquity of museum and church and palace, which were the priceless jewel of Prague.

"The big house for the little Minister," so the people had called it, as it had risen in solid assertion of the city's freedom from the old yoke of the Austrian's power.

They spoke half in pride, and half in envy, if not derision of him whom they placed so high. For was he not also a Czech, and of peasant blood? In their hearts they found it hard to suppose that a Czech could be worthy of such a power, or so lofty a state. The brand of long centuries of servitude was upon their race, and twenty years of half-frightened freedom had been insufficient to wear it off. It might have been different had they been hardly oppressed in the recent past, had there been scars of shackles upon their limbs. But they had been tolerated in the easy Austrian way; they had been allowed some measure of freedom, even to individual places of power. Only, it had been understood that, if they would stand well in the land, they must ape the Austrian ways, they must talk with the German tongue.

They had been tolerated by their Hapsburg lords: plainly too inferior for envy, obviously too weak to fear.

Now, if a stranger should ask them the way to the next street in the German tongue, they would reply with no more than a silent stare, though they knew it well. If he spoke no Czech, let him ask in French, which is a language for every land, or in English, of which they would have pride in showing any knowledge they had. But the German tongue, which they had learned in their younger days, was a sound they hated to hear. They might have been more generous in their moods had they been more sure of themselves, had they been more secure in a freedom that they had not been single to win.

But the new republic of Czechoslovakia was so young that it still walked on unsteady feet...and it was ringed about with covert or open foes.

It lay like a lamb surrounded by dogs which waited to share its limbs if their master's eye should be turned a moment aside; or like a well-cooked joint with those who hunger seated around.

And in the spacious dignity of the reception room of the new Ministry, the man who, except one only, had done most to steer the land to freedom and prosperous days through twenty perilous years stood listening, with a quiet expressionless face, to that which was not easy to take in a patient way.

They both stood, for the German Minister had disregarded the offered seat.

He was a tall, upright man, still exhibiting some military stiffness, though good living had hung much flesh on an ample frame. His face, and the folds of flesh that his collar creased, were of the pink of a sleep-flushed child.

His almost colourless hair was cropped so close, in the Prussian style, that it was not easy to see where his baldness ceased. He spoke in a somewhat guttural voice, but, so far, with a slow precision of chosen words, as one repeating a lesson already learned. Now he went on in a higher tone: "I have to inform Your Excellency that we do not seek proof, of which we already have more than enough. Had we been worse served by our own police, the plot could not have failed. There must have been such a crime as would have shocked the ears of the world, and stirred every German heart with a passion to take vengeance on those who had given shelter to men so base, in which to ripen their bloody schemes."

The Czech Minister was not quick to reply. He considered, behind expressionless eyes, that it was a real emotion which had raised the speaker's voice to that higher note. He must make allowance for that. He saw that the peace of Europe might be weighed in a scale which trembled to what they said.

The risk of assassination is ever present to all who rule. It is part of the price of power. Dr. Dollfuss—the Yugoslavian King—there had been many before them. Doubtless there would be others to come. But he saw that, to the German mind, there was a special sanctity in the person of the present head of their own state, a special horror in the idea of his violent end, causing them to regard it differently from that of another—himself, for instance—being the victim of knife or bomb.

"If you will supply us," he said slowly, "with the proofs that you say you have, you will not find us slack to search for the authors of such a plot, or tender to root them out."

"I must remind Your Excellency," the reply came, in a voice which had become formal again," that we have had such assurances more than once before."

"Which have been sincere. You cannot tell me you doubt—"

The German Minister avoided direct reply. "Yet this has happened again. We must be better assured that it is the last time."

"I have said that, so soon as the evidence is supplied—"

"I regret that it is a matter that cannot be longer left. We are too fully informed; and too firmly resolved that the nuisance be rooted out."

"Then what is it for which you ask?" The question was quietly put, but the Czech looked up as he spoke. The eyes of the two men met, and the German was aware that he was faced by a cold anger, hardly controlled. But his instructions were clear; his self-assurance remained.

"We ask," he said speaking with deliberate separate words, "for the expulsion from Czechoslovakia of all active Communists, whether of German or other alien blood, including any of your own citizens who are suspected of plotting against the peace of the German lands, within seven days of this date."

There was a long minute of silence before the reply came. "They have the sound of men whom we are not anxious to keep. It may not be more than we should be willing to do with goodwill, if you will leave it to me; or if you will make request in such a way that it is easy to grant."

The German did not respond. He said stiffly: "It is a matter on which we must be precise. I have a list here—"

He drew from his breast-pocket a folded foolscap paper. He opened it, showing many names.

It was accepted in a silence as hostile as any words could have been. The Czech Minister looked it down; he turned over the first sheet.

He said: "It is a long list."

"Its length is the measure of the grievance of which we have been too patient in our complaints. I do not call it complete."

"There are Germans here whom we could not expel, except to your own land."

"They are men we should not refuse to take."

The eyes of the two men met again, as the German went on: "We should require that they be put over the frontier in such a way that they will pass into the charge of our own police."

"If there be nothing against them that you can show?"

"It will be for us to decide."

"It is a request which, as you know, is beyond my own right to grant. You have my assurance that it shall be fully considered without delay. You can inform your Government that I am resolved that no reasonable satisfaction shall be denied."

The words might be variously taken. The voice was controlled to a toneless quality. The German Minister found the list returned to his hand, which he did not like.

His eyes turned to the window. Facing them were the four spires of the cathedral which King Wenceslaus may have commenced to build, when Prague was a city of royal power.

Three of them were Gothic. The fourth was incongruously in the Baroque style. It had been shot down, as they both knew, by German artillery, nearly two hundred years before, and rebuilt in the newer mode, and it had been a misunderstanding—no more—that had waked the guns.

"A mistake," he said, "is soon made; but its results are of longer date."

He found himself equalled in the reply: "It is the common weakness of men to teach that which they do not learn."

He went out with no more than the formal courtesy that the etiquette of his position required.

CHAPTER II.

IT was at the end of the same day that Caresse Langton lay awake in Lady Walford's flat, which had been lent to her for that night, so that she could meet Perdita there, and they would both be on the spot for the shopping they had to do on the following morning. They were leaving for Ostend by the night boat, for a holiday which was to be taken together, and was to be spent mainly in Prague.

Perdita had come up from her parents' home in Warwickshire on the previous day. Now she lay in the twin bed, divided by two feet of space and eight years of youth, and by the dovetailing differences of brain and temperament which made their friendship fit like a worn glove.

It was for Perdita's sake they were going to Prague. Lawrence Norton was First Secretary at the Legation there, and it was he whom Perdita Wyatt would marry, if her parents could have their will, with her own inclination supposed to follow the same track.

It had been arranged in an indirect, casual way. Caresse had written to Lawrence that she would be wandering east, as she might do (being five years married now) with no implication at all, she having known him in earlier years; and after that she had asked Perdita to come.

As she considered the matter now, she was less than clear as to the motive that had led her to fix it up. Was it a desire to do Perdita a friendly turn, or from her own wish to see Lawrence again? Was it she, or Perdita's mother, who had contrived it, in their oblique feminine ways?

Caresse had married Gerald Langton five years before, and it was an act she had no cause to regret, though he was her elder by eighteen years. He had, she knew, a responsible position in the Foreign Office at Whitehall, though it would have puzzled her to say just what it was. There were some things she understood very well in her vivid way, but there were boundaries to them beyond which her ideas were vague and unsure. She was one of those who go through life with no sense of direction. She seldom counted her change. She would not trouble to enquire when the boat-train would leave. There were always others who could be trusted to fuss over such matters as that—as she was trusting Perdita now.

They had been to dinner at the Framptons'. There had been talk at the meal—light, idle talk—about the danger of war which had lain over Europe for the past three years, a sombre shadow that would not lift. It was the growing intimacy of France and Italy—or was it the growing alienation? She was not sure which, nor did it seem a point deserving exactness of memory—that was the moment's concern. But such talk would change with the days. It was like the rumbling of subterraneous forces in a volcanic land, now here, now there, and none could say where the eruption would come at last, or that there might not be a century of uneasy peace.

But it was sure that Caresse would not have been kept awake by such thoughts as these. Her mind was seldom vexed by matters more distant than the next street.

She was too young to remember much of the last war that had shaken the world. Her one clear memory was of a night when she had been waked from sleep to sit with mother and aunt, and two nervously giggling maids, on the cellar steps. She could recall how obstinately she had refused her mother's urgency of command till she had slipped on the best dress she had, and straightened disordered hair to a style in which it would be seemly to die.

It was an episode that she had narrated at times in a jesting mood, but which she had learned of late to leave in silence with growing care, for it dated her now beyond the remedy of making herself younger each time that the tale was told. It gave her a sense of fretful annoyance that the war had occurred at all. Providence had been inconsiderate in an almost inexcusable way.

But it was not the thought of wars that kept her awake, whether of one that was distant now, or might be speedy to come. Nor (she would have said) was it the thought of seeing Lawrence Norton again. But it was a rough night, and an east wind swept through the trees of the Green Park, so that the upper part of the window rattled loudly to every gust. And so, being kept awake, she played with dangerous thoughts in a way she had, doing that in dreams which must be shunned in the waking day.

She had been near to indiscretion (or so she told herself as imagination reconstructed the past) with Lawrence Norton six years before. She did not think that she had ever told Gerald of that, although she knew she had moments of casual, incredible frankness, at which she would be annoyed with herself in the next hour. But yesterday, when they were near to parting, and she had thought him to be less concerned than her pride required, she had made an audacious, teasing remark, which he had taken with disconcerting gravity, not easy to smile away. That was how provoking Gerald could be.

So her thoughts wandered loose in the night, while Perdita slept, having few cares in a pleasant world. Had she made complaint, it would have been to call it one in which she waited for adventure which never came. Caresse had no such grievance as that, for adventure was poured for her from a full cup.

Even now, was she not kept awake by a creaking sash, so that she lost the sleep on which her looks might depend on the next day? What could be more momentous than that?

CHAPTER III.

A CLERK entered Gerald Langton's office. He placed a decoded telegram at his side.

"I thought, sir, you should see this at once."

Gerald considered it for a moment. He said, "Quite right, Beeston; you had better take it on to the Chief."

He initialled it, and handed it back.

When he was alone, his thoughts turned to Caresse. Trouble stirring in Prague...it would be a foolish, needless risk for her to go now. He had been watching the cauldron of Eastern Europe every day for the last three years, waiting for the moment when it would boil. Steele was not one to be easily scared. He would not warn them without evident cause. Caresse must be stopped. But how?

She would not cross till the night boat. There was ample time. But he saw that he was likely to be kept late. And that which he had reason to fear was not a matter to be spoken abroad, even to her. Still less could he telephone a warning of such a kind, or write in explicit words. Yet a note was the only way.

He remembered that it was her habit to lunch at Forster's when she was shopping in that neighbourhood, as she was almost certain to be today. A note would reach her there, if he lost no time. Yet what was there that he could say? He wrote hurriedly:

> Dearest,
>
> I hear that the weather is likely to be getting worse, and the crossing tonight may be very rough. Reports of conditions in Central Europe are very unsatisfactory. Will you ask Perdita to come home to Redlands with you tonight, and stay with us for a few days, till the prospect improves? *Please do this.* You know I wouldn't suggest it at the last moment without good reason.
>
> I will explain more when I see you.

Much love,

G.

They lunched at Forster's, as he had guessed that they would. Caresse had finished, and lit the cigarette for which she must find time though the heavens fell. Perdita was near the end of a better meal. She watched the clock, and the shortening length of the cigarette, so that she might not give excuse to her companion for lighting another. She knew Caresse to be indifferent to the procession of time, and that she would be unmoved by recitation of those things they still had to do.

As she ate, she discussed the intricacies of foreign coinage, concerning which she had been diligent to enquire.

Caresse listened, faintly interested, slightly amused, fully appreciative of the advantage that her companion's mental energy would be to her own comfort and purse, but with no idea that her digestion should be disturbed by a similar effort.

"It's no use trying to get me to understand such muddles as that," she said cheerfully. "I never should, and I should be silly to try. I know what a shilling is, and it's always the same. But if a franc's worth two-pence in one country, and twice as much in the next—well, why don't they take them all where they are worth more?"

"It's not quite as simple as that."

"I expect it's simple enough if you've got the sense not to let people muddle you up. It's like algebra, that they tried to teach me at school. You had X and Y, and at first no one knew what they were, and then it turned out that X had been a flock of sheep all the time, or the number of spadefuls of earth you'd need to bury a cow. I said, everyone knew X isn't a flock of sheep, and it never was, and I stuck there, and wouldn't move till they gave it up."

Caresse's lips curved to a faint reminiscent smile as she recalled the demonstration of blank stupidity with which she had foiled attempts to teach her that which she had thought useless for the prizes of life that she sought to win.

It seemed that a second pleasure of memory followed the first as she crushed down the stump of her cigarette and added: "They tried to teach me to sew."

She said in a brisker voice: "I suppose you'll want to go on," and as she rose a page-boy was at her side.

"I think this is for you, madam."

She opened Gerald's note carelessly, seeing by the writing from whom it came, and then exclaimed in startled surprise:

"Now, how absurd! Gerald doesn't want us to go—"

The words roused the younger girl from the half-attention that she had given to her friend's chatter before. She looked at her with amazed, incredulous eyes.

"*Doesn't want us to go?* Why on earth not?"

"He says he's heard that the sea's rough, and there's bad weather in Central Europe. What did he think January would be likely to be?"

As she answered, she saw the feebleness of the excuse, and the incredulity in Perdita's eyes. The shrewd clarity of her mind perceived that there must be more cause for the letter than it contained, and became active to guess the truth.

With a sharp annoyance she recalled the indiscreet audacious remark of the previous day. Had Gerald brooded on that? Had he been roused to a jealousy she had sometimes wished he had been quicker to show with a higher cause? Would he, perhaps, propose to get leave, and come with them on a later date?

She saw, as she thought, an explanation she could not give, and one which resolved her mind that their plans should not be so absurdly changed at the last hour.

"Oh," she said lightly, "it's how husbands fuss. You'll find it out soon enough. Of course, we can't put it off now. It wouldn't be fair to you. I'd better send him a note."

She went to the writing-room and scribbled a few half-loving, half-jesting lines, putting his request aside as one which he could not have thought seriously that she would obey.

He returned to his Surrey home to find that they were not there, and when Caresse's letter reached him by the next morning's post, she was looking down somewhat fretfully from the window of the breakfast-car of the smooth, swift, eastward train, on the sodden flatness of a Belgian landscape that she considered an inadequate recompense for the hardships of the previous night.

They had not reached the hill-country beyond Liège, now dressed with a thin garment of winter snow. They looked down on a level land, where rain fell on the red tiles of the narrow steep-roofed houses: on the muddy squalor of the farm-yards: on the wide monotony of the hedgeless fields.

"Considering," she said, "how much trouble it is to get here, I think they might have something more worth seeing when we arrive."

"I expect," Perdita answered cheerfully, "we shall see a lot of different things before we get back."

CHAPTER IV.

THEY stayed two nights in Berlin, which Caresse approved.

"I like it," she said, "better than Paris. Somehow it is—it is more like home. It is less foreign than France."

It was much praise, coming from one who was half French in her own blood, though of English birth, and who could speak the French tongue like her own.

Perdita, saying little and seeing much, agreed that there were some aspects of German life in which they are more akin to English ways than are those of the Latin lands.

But though they dined at the British Embassy, they heard no warning, no menace of coming doom.

Even in London, Gerald Langton's first anxiety had found little on which to thrive. It was public knowledge now that Germany had made complaint against the harbouring of Communist plotters in Prague, though its immediate cause—the plot against its President's life—had been closely concealed. But it was a satisfaction which (as was commonly thought) the Czech Government had not refused. England, being regarded at the moment as the one among the great Powers whose voice would be heard in Berlin, had been asked to mediate on its behalf, which it had been active to do.

The English Foreign Office had been able to assure the Czech Minister that it had information upon which it could safely rely that there were no preparations for punitive action in Germany. In particular, the great aerodrome at Nürnberg—large before, but enormously increased during the past two years—was quiet, and the number of men on leave was unusually large. It had urged that there should be a similar discretion on the Czech side. War may spring from so small a spark!

It received reassurances about that. Czechoslovakia had no wish to be the occasion of such a war as might soon spread through the breadth of the civilised world, nor would it do anything that could be misinterpreted thus. The German request, discourteous, and naturally resented as it had been, had not been weighted with any threat, such as an ultimatum will bear. Doubtless a formula would be found.

Gerald Langton, who had drafted a wire which would have reached Caresse on her arrival at Prague, and was intended to bring her back, considered it for a time, hesitated, and tore it up.

"I expect," he said to himself, "we get too easily scared, knowing what we do. Even the Stock Exchange hasn't taken alarm. And, anyway, I don't suppose she would have come, unless I said more than I ought."

CHAPTER V.

IT was on Wednesday morning they left Berlin. Caresse had destroyed unanswered a wire from Lawrence offering to meet them on their arrival at Prague.

"After that journey," she asked, "how does he suppose we shall look? We'd better leave him to guess when we shall get there, and ring him up from the hotel."

Perdita, to whom the objection might not have occurred, whether from greater indifference to her own appearance, or greater confidence in its ability to endure the ordeal of long hours in an overheated train, assented cheerfully.

"We can manage all right," she said, "if he won't think it rude not to reply."

Caresse had no concern on that score, being accustomed to her own way, and to put inconsistencies lightly aside with a smiling evasive word. "We can say," she answered, "that we weren't sure which train we should take."

Perdita did not discuss the inadequacy of this excuse for a journey of such length, being accustomed to observe her friend's triumphant rejection of inopportune fact in a comprehending silence.

The time of year was reason enough for the fewness of the passengers with which the Prague express left Berlin. The first-class coach was almost empty, and the hotel porter had no difficulty in finding an empty compartment in which to deposit their lighter luggage.

They were in the dining-car when the train steamed into Dresden station, and the somewhat obese gentleman, with the aspect of a prosperous business man, who mounted the train there, hesitated in the corridor between a vacant compartment and that in which their luggage was evident witness to its occupation. Then he stepped in, examined their luggage-labels, and took a vacant corner, depositing a heavy portfolio upon the opposite seat.

A moment later a tall and much thinner gentleman, with a more professional aspect of face and manner, followed him into the coach, and paused at the door of the same compartment.

There was no word or sign of recognition between them, but the first arrival lifted the portfolio, as though offering the seat on which it had lain, which was taken, though not without a glance of puzzled annoyance at the evidence of other occupation which had been left on the window-seats.

It was not till the train was moving again, and they were clear of any possible observation, that the second-comer remarked in Magyar, which he changed to German as the conversation proceeded: "I can't see why you came in here, when we could have been alone, probably all the way."

"*Nein?*" his companion replied. "Yet it may be that we shall find less hindrance than help. Have you seen of what nation they are?"

"English ladies?" he replied. "And what help is there in them?"

"Perhaps none. But it is wise to be ready for every chance. There will be a close search, and we shall do well if we get through."

"We?" The intonation of the word protested against being joined thus, either in personal intimacy, or as one concerned in a common risk. But his protest had its rebuke in the German's reply: "Count, you mean it is a risk which you do not share? But it is as much to your land as to mine that I do not fail. And I may yet ask your help; for you will be less suspected than I."

There was no answer to this, for the ticket-inspector was already at the door of the compartment. They gave each other no word or glance till he had passed on, and their conversations with him were in different tongues.

Then the Hungarian asked: "Do we speak English, or not?"

"It may be best that I should, if not you. But we must judge that when we see of what kind they are."

There was no time to say more, for those of whom they spoke came along the corridor at the same moment.

The German considered them with satisfaction. They were young, attractive, probably wealthy. Obviously English. Not in the least likely to be suspected as Nazi agents. He resolved, if the opportunity should come, that he would attempt that which he had done with success before, when the occasion had been less urgent, and the unconscious object less appropriate for his design.

He was in no haste to open conversation, being content to listen to the self-revealing chatter of the girls, but he knew that there was a potential importance in establishing such friendliness as the occasion allowed.

The ventilators, which had been closed when he entered the compartment, were an easy pretext. Would they like them opened? The English were notorious for their love of the outside air. And, in that case, the door closed?

The first question, asked in German, having been received with hesitation, he had turned to English, of which he had sufficient conversational knowledge. The exchanges proceeded smoothly. Central heating—English habits and hardihood—impressions of Germany—his own knowledge of London, which he had visited five years earlier. On pleasure? No. He was a manufacturer's agent. Johann Schmit. He offered a card in evidence. He travelled much. They were going to stay in Prague? They would find it very different there. A beautiful country? Yes. But different.

They had liked Germany? Mutual admirations followed. He praised London. Caresse was kind to Berlin. He mentioned, as though it would be a mitigation of the strangeness of Prague, that many Germans were still there.

But many others had left. He did not say in explicit words that they had been exiled by the hostilities of those who had usurped control of the land, but the implication was there. He mentioned the large number of his countrymen who still lived in the western part of the new republic. The Bavarian frontier, he said with some truth, was little more than a political fiction. "For they are friends on both sides."

Adroitly, he drew the fourth occupant of the compartment into the conversation. Speaking pure English, in slow, carefully chosen words, and with a better accent than the German could reach, the Hungarian admitted similar conditions at the farther end of the land. He spoke of villages which were alien alike from Slovak and Czech.

Quietly, faintly satirical, he concluded: "They speak Magyar still. It is the only language they know."

Together, they vaguely outlined a picture of political oppression, endured with patience, if not resignation, by those who had the better right to the land.

The conversation went on till a waiter opened the door, to announce the serving of tea. Should he bring trays? The German translated. Caresse said with decision: "No. We'll go along to the car."

"Rather," Perdita agreed. They were glad of the opportunity for movement and freshness of air. They went out at once.

When they were gone, Herr Schmit opened his portfolio, looking through the papers which it contained, without drawing them out.

"Count," he said, "would you mind strolling along the corridor, and letting me know if anyone's coming?"

The Hungarian looked doubtful. "You feel sure," he asked, "that it's the best way?"

"Yes. I was going to tell you that Hansel didn't get through last week. We don't know what's become of him. We don't know what they suspect, or what kind of search they're likely to make. But I can't risk having anything they're not meant to see. I was going to ask you to take charge of—"

The Hungarian made no further demur. Without waiting to hear the conclusion of the sentence, he rose, and stood looking out of the corridor window, his aspect that of one who smoked in a listless indolence, his senses alert for sound or sight of anyone approaching from either end.

The German selected a number of papers from the portfolio. He knew that one of the suitcases on the rack was unlocked, having seen Caresse open and close it carelessly, but there was another, more substantial, the contents of which were probably less likely to be turned over by its owner in the next hour. He found that its fastenings were somewhat complex, but it proved to be unlocked. After some patient manipulation, the latch sprang open.

Low down, among Perdita's most intimate garments, and carefully concealed from anything less than a detailed examination of the contents of the case, he inserted the papers, and closed it again.

CHAPTER VI.

"PASSPORTS ready, please. All passports ready." The cry announced that the frontier station was reached, and the elaborate formalities, hostile in implication and manner, which had been in regular practice for several years between the two countries, had commenced.

This first inspection was by two German officials. It was deliberately careful, but politely conducted towards those who were obviously neither Czechs nor Communist refugees.

They were followed by others, whom the English girls took to be customs officers till they were otherwise informed. They were Czech police, searching the train for German newspapers.

It was a futile gesture, significant of the bitterness between the two nations, which only fear or politic delay had held back from each other's throats during the past five years. The Germans responded by confiscating all Czech newspapers on the returning train. It was a mutual irritation, obviously barren of result. The frontiers were too long, the means of transit and concealment too numerous, for any newspaper to be excluded which there might be sufficient reason for smuggling over.

But they passed on with no more than a perfunctory glance at a compartment destined for different investigation, and were succeeded by another cry for passports to be in readiness, and more officials, this time of Czech nationality, were at the doors, and credentials must be scrutinised again from an opposite angle.

The English girls found their passports returned with no more than a casual-seeming glance, a polite word. The Magyar passport was examined with greater care, recognised as being that of a well-known member of the Hungarian Government, and returned with outward respect, if without cordiality.

That of Herr Schmit was examined, passed from hand to hand, and disappeared down the corridor. If its owner were surprised or perturbed at this, he concealed his feelings with an air of passive indifference.

Following the passport inspections, there was a fresh warning that customs officers were approaching.

Caresse, smilingly conscious that their own inquisition was of the lightest, so that she had a feeling of looking on at a scene which she did not share, asked "Do they never end?"

Herr Schmit did not appear to heed. He may have had mental occupation enough, without attending to idle words. The Hungarian shrugged his shoulders lightly. He answered with a slight, indifferent smile: "It is routine; it is always so."

He drew an attaché-case, which was all the hand-luggage he had, on to his knee, and unlocked it, in readiness to display its contents.

A customs officer entered, another standing watchfully at the door. The first man's hand dived into the Hungarian's case, his eyes keenly observant, his fingers moving rapidly. He asked a question in a strange tongue. Receiving a coldly polite reply, his inspection abruptly ended. His eyes went on to the occupants of the two window-seats, and the suitcases on the racks over their heads.

Perdita had risen, and was making a motion to pull one of them down. She asked: "I suppose you want to see these?"

He raised a restraining hand. He asked a question in three languages which she did not know. The Hungarian came to her aid: "He asks, have you anything to declare?"

"No. We've only got our own things, that we brought from England."

The reply, translated somewhat freely, was accepted as satisfactory. With a smiling word, a gesture of dismissal, the officer turned to Herr Schmit, whose effects were subjected to a very different ordeal. Every paper in the portfolio was scrutinised, and then passed as though with reluctance, if not surprise, that it should be of an innocent kind. Then a handbag, containing clothes and other articles, received an equally minute examination. Its contents were tumbled on to the seat, and finally left for its owner to repack, without even perfunctory apology for the treatment they had received.

But it was over at last. Slowly the heavy train commenced to move forward again. The frontier was crossed, and Germany left behind.

"It seems," Perdita said lightly, "that they've decided to let us through."

"It's a silly business," Caresse replied. "Why shouldn't people be friends?"

They had no personal unfriendliness of which to complain, either from Germans or Czechs, but the whole long-drawn episode had had an atmosphere of hostile tension, a complexion political rather than economic, through which it had been unpleasant to pass, even in a semi-detached way.

Their remarks were unheeded, if not unheard, by their male companions, on whom it seemed that an added gravity had descended. Once or twice, when the corridor was clear, they exchanged remarks in an unknown tongue. An hour went by, and a call that dinner was ready passed through the train.

The girls rose with alacrity, but the two men, who should have been more hungry than they, made no motion to follow. They sat still, the German looking at Perdita's suitcase with doubtful eyes.

It was the time at which he had planned to regain his property: the only opportunity he might have. But his passport had not been returned. What could be the significance of that? Perhaps nothing. At any moment it might be brought. After that, it would seem a less risk to have those papers back where they had first been. At the worst, might it not be possible to call on Perdita at her hotel, and confess as much as it would be necessary for her to know? The papers would be nothing to her. She could not read them. If he should tell her that his life hung on her silence, he was inclined to think that the risk would not be great. If he should attempt their recovery now, he would require the Count's help to watch, as he had done before. But the Hungarian made no motion to rise. He must have the same doubt.

So he had. The eyes of the two men met. The Hungarian said, in a low voice: "I should wait. There is time yet."

The sequel justified the delay. One of the customs officers came to the door. He asked: "You are Herr Schmit? Your passport has not been returned? If you will come with me, you can have it now."

The German rose, puzzled, uneasy, but self-controlled. He was ready to follow, but the man did not move. He said: "You should bring that which is yours." He looked down as he spoke.

Herr Schmit made no protest. What use could it have been? He might have received no more than friendly advice. Its significance was not easy to see. He put on hat and coat. He picked up his bags. He found himself being led to the rear of the train.

There was a van in the rear, in which was an armed guard of Czechs, who must have joined the train at the frontier station. Herr Schmit found himself in the hands of those who would not scruple in what they did. He was stripped to the skin, and his clothing searched. His baggage was examined again, even the linings being torn out of the bags. He protested with the more confidence because he knew that there was nothing that they could find. But they shook their heads, as at a language they did not know.

When he was allowed to resume his clothing, an officer addressed him who did not affect to be unable to speak his tongue. He asked: "Will you say where they are hidden? It will be much better for you."

He answered stubbornly: "I have nothing hidden. You can see that. You have examined everything that I have."

The officer said no more. He handed his passport back. He said: "I cannot let you go on. I have an order for your expulsion. You can take your bags if you will."

The train was slowing down as he spoke. As it stopped, Johann Schmit was hustled roughly toward the door. He faced a cold wind and a driving snow. He looked down to see that snow was deep on the track. He saw no lights through the gloom. A pine-forest bordered the line.

He said: "You cannot put me off here. The frontier is far behind."

The officer said coldly: "I have orders for what I do. You will have no trouble for that. We will set you on the right way."

They followed him into the snow—the officer and four men. The train remained still, blowing off steam.

When they had gone twenty yards from the track, along a path under the trees, the officer said: "I must halt here. Your way will be straight on."

Herr Schmit said nothing to that. What was the use? He went on through the snow. He was not ten yards away when he heard a sharp order to fire. It was the last sound that was destined to reach his ears.

CHAPTER VII.

THE dinner was well cooked and well served: the waiters deferential, smiling, eager to please: the shadow of the frontier was left behind. In less than two hours they would be in Prague, and the journey done.

Toward the end of the meal, the train stopped, and remained stationary long enough for them to become curious to enquire the cause. Their waiter, who had a little English, and better French, was vague but cheerful in his reply. Perhaps snow on the line. At this time of year…. Doubtless they would soon be going forward again.

But the train had not moved when the leisurely meal was done, and they returned to their own compartment, more relieved to observe that the ventilators had not been closed in their absence than concerned that Herr Schmit and his belongings had disappeared.

Caresse said: "We shall be late getting in. I wonder what's keeping us here?"

The tone was casual, unconcerned. She had just had an excellent meal. What did it matter when they arrived by an hour, either more or less?

The Hungarian did not reply, and the next moment there came the dull sound of a volley of rifle-shots, somewhat deadened by the snow, but at no great distance away.

With a quickened interest, Perdita asked "What was that?"

She had a thought of brigands attacking the train, as she had seen portrayed in a recent film, but it was too vague and unreal to occasion more than a faint, pleasant excitement. It was an idea which her mind entertained, refusing belief.

The Hungarian answered with a quiet gravity: "It is, I suppose, the death of a brave man."

The explanation was enigmatic, the tone chilled. He said no more, and Perdita became silent. Caresse was less willing to leave a mystery unprobed. She asked: "You mean someone's been killed?"

He was not quick to reply. When he did, it was little satisfaction to hear.

"I said more than I should. I know no more than yourselves. There may be things which it is imprudent to see or hear. You will remember that you are not in your own land."

A few minutes later, the train whistled and commenced to move forward again. In the rear coach there was now the body of a dead man. It was that of one who had been arrested on suspicion of being a German spy, and the official report would state that he had been shot while attempting escape. The German Government would be unlikely to make open trouble for that. On its own side of the frontier, it disposed of too many unwanted Czechs in the same way.

CHAPTER VIII.

AT the same time that the body of Johann Schmit sank in the reddened snow, the Ministers of Czechoslovakia were gathered in council in the President's private room in the Vladislavsky Palace at Prague.

The President spoke suavely, for he sought to bring peace among angry men. He said: "There is no question of acceding to the German demand in the form in which it was presented five days ago. We are, I think, so far agreed. But"—his voice took its most persuasive tone, and his eyes were directed upon the Minister of Defence, whose protest had stirred the storm—"there is a wide difference between that and the blunt rejection of a request which was rudely made."

The War Minister was a spare, elderly man, who had seen service in the Russian Army during the last war. He was of bellicose moods, and of a temper easily frayed. In his secret thoughts, he would sometimes count his advancing years, grudging the time that passed in an indecisive and restless peace. He had an army of 150,000 men trained and equipped as efficiently as any force of its size that Europe could array on a field of death, and his own fierce spirit had been a fire to exalt its ranks. It was a bitter thought that the war to which he looked as to an unavoidable end might come so late that he would not be at that army's head.

He looked back at the President now, and his anger did not abate.

"Those who seek," he said, "for courtesy in reply should cast their requests in the same mould. That should be the answer to give to them. Would they have spoken so to England or France? Are the Czechs dogs, to wag tails to a German kick?"

He looked round on men who either murmured approval or remained silent, and broke out again: "Do you think when your bellies have rubbed the dirt that you will stand erect again upon the next day? You will be the scorn alike of the Teutons whose boots you have bent to lick, and of every nation of Slavs who will be partners to share your shame."

The Air Minister, whose blunt pessimism had aroused his wrath, was the one man there who remained unexcited and unconvinced. He was not one whom it was easy to call a coward. He had escaped from Austria as a youth of eighteen, twenty-two years before, and enlisted in the Italian Air Force, where he had become famous as the twice-wounded victor of a score of duels among the clouds. At a later date, he had dragged a wounded comrade from a wrecked and burning plane, though his own face had been caught in a gust of flame, by which its left side was still scarred in an ugly way.

"Such words," he said, "are easy to speak, but they are foolish, unless we can make them good on the field of war. If we should be attacked, as might be in an hour's time, will you say how you would save Prague?"

"In an hour's time? And will you say how that could be, unless they would strike from the air alone, as it would be mere folly to do. I tell you they have not a division equipped to move."

"It is the air which you have reason to fear."

"Then it is your own charge, which you should be last to say is unequal or unprepared. Will you tell us you are unready in your defence?"

"I have been too cautious to move a plane, or to fill a tank. Would you show steel in a storm, to draw the lightning about your head?"

The War Minister looked at the younger man with an impatience hard to control.

"Janda," he said, "you are a brave man, as I do not doubt; but you are obsessed with the importance of that which yourself commands.

"Germany would not strike from the air alone, if she should take the hazard of war, but with all the strength that she has. We know that her armies are not called up, and, while that is so, we are secure from a blustering word, unless we be the fools of our needless fears.

"Can you think only of what they would do, rather than we?

"If their planes should come, would our guns be useless to bring them down? Would our own planes be impotent in the air? Why do you talk only of Prague? Is not Dresden as bare to a swift attack?

"At the worst, have we not trained our people that they shall be equal to such a day? They have masks to the last child. The shelters that have been built in the last two years are the best that Europe can boast. For what gain have we spent and trained, if we are to lie flat at the first sound of a rattled sword?"

He looked round for approval, which came in a murmur from many tongues.

"Janda, you forget that Europe would not stand by to see us destroyed."

"You forget the friendship of France."

"Germany would not dare to wake such a war."

"In ten years, perhaps. But not now."

"What would Yugoslavia have to say?"

"Even Poland might not endure to see us attacked on so light a cause."

"They have Russia always to fear."

But the Air Minister remained unshaken in his opinion amid the storm.

"Whom the gods would destroy," he quoted, "they first make mad."

The Minister of Justice, a small bald-headed man, with restless eyes, and hands that were seldom still, interposed before the War Minister could reply. "Gentlemen, I do not boast what is still to do. I had not meant to speak now. I am on the track of a Nazi plot, I will not say of what kind till the proofs are here, but I have a hope that such documents will be in our hands by tomorrow noon that Germany will have but one thought—to make sure that we do not publish them to the world."

His words had the effect of a diversion from that which had assumed the aspect of quarrel rather than of sober debate, and the President was adroit to seize the opportunity of breaking up the meeting.

"It appears," he said, "that the feeling is general that we must not fail to act with the dignity of a sovereign State. But, within that limit, I suppose we are all agreed that we should give Germany any satisfaction that she is entitled to claim. We need not forget that even now England is making representations on our behalf, which Berlin surely cannot ignore."

The President shook hands with the others as they went out, and asked the Air Minister to remain.

"Janda," he said, when they were alone, "do you wish me to think that Prague is without defence? That the Act of 1935, and all the expenditure which it entailed, are of no avail?"

"I said less than that. Against gas attacks I think you are well prepared. If only I could be sure that it is on gas-bombs that they depend! But suppose they should come dropping high-explosive bombs, or some of a nature we have not guessed, from five thousand planes?—hour after hour, every few minutes, a fleet of fifty out of the clouds?"

"And your own planes could not hold them back, nor your guns avail?"

"We might destroy scores—even five hundred planes. It would be a most sanguine guess. But it would still be the same end."

"It is clear that our Minister of Defence does not agree. Do you think him a fool?"

"Far from that. I should say that he is about equally able to win the last war or to lose the next. His eyes are good, but they are turned the wrong way."

"Then we must rely on pacific words, and on the support of the stronger Powers. Having the sympathy both of England and France "

"Both of whom, for the past two years, Germany has ceased to regard."

"You would not say that they are impotent too?"

"I could answer both no and yes. England desires peace. She is sincere. I will grant you that, and that there is none other of whom we are equally sure in the same way. If she be forced to war, and have time to collect her strength, she has always proved a most stubborn foe. But can we say that she is all that she was of old, when her outward ships were filled with cargoes of living men? Egypt—Ireland—India—one by one she lets them slip from her grasp, as from the hands of one who is growing weary of power. And her Air Force is no more than a gallant jest. Has it not always been her weakness to make a sport of the deadly business of war? To suppose that it will be played by the rules of an ordered game? If she should hear that the Germans were bombing Prague, would she not keep her planes closely at home, seeing that the peril of London is little less?"

"And of France?"

"Would Germany pause for her? Or could we trust what she would do at a sudden pass? Would she not have gone down in three months in the last war if England had not come to her aid—as she went down forty years before? Her Government is ever unstable, and half corrupt. Her population has ceased to grow. Has she not been sick of soul, between fear and greed, every day since the Versailles Treaty was signed? And now that her armies in Algiers and Syria are so largely engaged—"

The President looked thoughtfully at the youngest member of his Ministry—the only one who would not face this crisis with bold and confident words. He said mildly: "You have hard words for our friends."

"That is not how it is meant. I face facts. But there is another, which is of more moment for us. If they should come to our aid, as you hope they would, they would be too late. They would be no use to the dead."

"You have a most cheerful mind. But I would trust you to do your part, if the need should rise."

The President shook hands cordially, and was left alone. He felt as one shadowed by a very imminent cloud. But it was one that would be likely to pass, as so many had passed before.

CHAPTER IX.

COUNT GEYSA looked at his two travelling companions hesitating between silence and speech. In an hour they would reach Prague, and his chance of intervention be gone. His own destination was Buda-Pest. It was vital that he should communicate to his Government without delay the terms of a most secret agreement with Germany which he had signed less than twelve hours before.

That could be only verbally done. He had left the document at the Hungarian Legation in Berlin. It was not of such a nature that it would have been prudent to bring it the way he came.

As to this matter of Herr Schmit, and the papers now in Perdita's case, he recognised the importance of the event, but he felt that it was one in which he must not be further involved. His interference might do no good, and, if suspected, might jeopardise even greater things.

He could not tell what the consequences might be, even to himself, if he should become suspect of complicity in Herr Schmit's activities before he had passed the further frontier and regained the safety of Hungarian soil. He could make no more than a vague guess of what those documents were, or how much they told.

He knew that Johann Schmit had been used by the German Government for several years as a means of communication with its secret agents in foreign states, on occasional matters only, of too great importance to be entrusted to the ordinary channels.

He was a man well known, and of good repute in the world of commerce, with substantial business interests in several countries.

His movements had legitimate occasions, openly known. He appeared to have no political interests, beyond promoting the international commerce on which he thrived.

His services had been sparingly used, and it was believed that no suspicion had been aroused. Until now, at this moment of greatest need, there had been some indiscretion or more probable treachery, and his life had paid. And the documents for which he had died lay, unknown to any living, except Count Geysa himself, in the suitcase of the English girl.

How would they be discovered, by whom, or when? And what consequences would there be?

It was hard to guess, and it might be no more than fair to herself, and even decrease the probability that the documents should come into the hands of the Czech police, if she were given warning of what they were. But her reaction was difficult to foresee. She might insist on handing them over at once, either to himself, which he did not desire, or to the officials on the train, which would be the worst fate they could have.

He had that disposition which is inclined to do nothing when in a doubt, and his hesitation was justified by the event when two officials appeared at the door of the compartment, with a tale which he must not appear to doubt.

It appeared that the German gentleman had been taken ill, as was feared, of some infectious disease. There was a hint of plague, though the word itself was not said. It was imperative that the compartment should be fumigated at once. Would he be so kind as to explain to the English ladies, and in such a way that they would not be unduly alarmed? There were attendants at hand by whom their luggage would be removed to a further carriage with the minimum inconvenience to them.

Count Geysa considered with satisfaction that, had they known more, they might have received the news in a less natural way. Caresse, who had an active dread of infectious disease, was quick to rise, and Perdita showed no inclination to linger behind her.

Neither of them displayed any concern for the integrity of their luggage, which they appeared content to leave for the attendants to handle. The Count was not surprised when his own attaché-case was drawn from his hands with polite insistence. He yielded it readily to the attendant's obsequious urgency, and, as he expected would be the case, he had been seated for some minutes in his new location before he saw it again.

His surprise was that the baggage of the English ladies was not subjected to similar treatment, but the intelligent Czech police had rightly regarded them as outside suspicion. The whole object of the manœuvre had been to clear the compartment, so that it might be subjected to intensive search.

The suitcase in which the objects of all this trouble were hidden was handled with such expedition that when Perdita seated herself again, it was already on the rack over her head.

After that, the question of warning, or of request, had ceased to be a practical issue, for there were other occupants of the compartment.

With no more than the perfunctory courtesies of leave-taking which long-distance travelling companions will exchange, he watched the English ladies descend from the train. He observed their luggage pass into the hands of a hotel porter, who had obviously been watching for their arrival. They were lost in the crowd as he followed them to the platform, where he was met by a secretary from his own Legation.

The two men strolled along the platform, talking at first of matters of minor importance; but when he was assured that he was free from unwelcome observation, he changed to a lower and more serious tone.

"Anton," he said, "listen carefully, for I am telling you that on which your lives may depend. I believe His Excellency has a good car? Yes? It is one which would hold you all? That is well. You will inform His Excellency that he may receive a wire from our Foreign Office on Friday next. It may say other things which he will regard in a literal way, but if it should conclude with the words *we hear that flour is likely to rise*, then he will arrange to vacate Prague within six hours of the time that it will have been issued at Buda-Pest. He will not attempt to return there, nor will he delay to take formal leave of the President here. He will leave by car for the Bavarian frontier, where he will be expected and well received. If no such wire should arrive, you will forget that these words have been ever said. That is clear? Very well. There is a smaller matter. Our friends in Berlin sent a secret agent on this train, with instructions to the Nazi organisation here, as to what they shall do under certain circumstances which may occur in a few days. Two hours ago this agent was arrested and shot. But before that he had secreted the papers in the suitcase of an English lady, Miss Wyatt, one of two who are staying at the Ambassador Hotel. She does not know they are there. You must let this information reach those concerned in a secret way, without risk that we may be supposed to have knowledge thereof, or have intervened. Is that also clear? I must go."

He ended abruptly, for the train, half an hour late in its arrival, was already signalled to leave.

CHAPTER X.

CARESSE laid down the receiver of the bedside telephone with a puzzled frown. She said petulantly: "He wants to come tonight."

"And you told him not to, of course?"

"Yes, of course."

"Well, what's wrong about that?"

Perdita went on unpacking her suitcase the while she talked. She was in a cheerful mood, and she was accustomed to hear Caresse complain of the conduct of those around her with an unruffled serenity.

"Nothing. It was the way it was said. It sounded almost as though he wasn't glad we were here."

"Well, perhaps he isn't. But if he wanted to come at once? Perhaps he'd got someone with him."

"That may have been it."

"What was it he really said?"

"Nothing really…only he sounded—well, queer."

"Queer?" Perdita's voice had become toneless, as though her mind were on other things. She added: "Well, so's this." Herr Schmit's bundle of papers was in her hand. She looked at it with wondering eyes, and then threw it over on to the bed to which Caresse had retired.

"Can you tell me what that is?"

Caresse looked at the papers carelessly. "No. You know I can't read Czech, if that's what it is. It may be Russian for all I know. Anyway, it's not German. What's the bother?"

"Someone must have put it into my case."

"It doesn't sound likely. You must have pushed it in with other things by mistake."

"But I'm sure I didn't. I found it between these."

Perdita held up the articles among which Herr Schmit had inserted the documents. Caresse waked to a more vivid interest.

"You're quite sure you didn't pack it yourself?"

"Absolutely certain."

"It must be that liftman at the Central. I told you he'd gone so crazy about you he wouldn't sleep for a week. He seems to have a good deal to say."

"Don't be absurd."

"Well, then, give a better guess."

"I wish I could. The case hasn't been out of my sight except for about three minutes when the porter brought it up here. Oh, and when we were in the dining-car—"

Her voice paused as her mind went back to the events of the day, seeing them in a new and more sinister light. She remembered the chilling atmosphere of the frontier inspection, as of criminals in transit from jail to jail: the disappearance of Herr Schmit: the previous unmannerly way in which the contents of his bag had been turned out on the carriage seat: the gravity of the Hungarian's warning that they were not now in their own land, and that there were things which they should not see.

With a sudden intuitive perception she exclaimed: "I don't believe he was ill at all. They turned us out so that they could search again under the seats. I believe they killed him for these, because he wouldn't say where they were hid."

Caresse said: "What a dreadful idea! They wouldn't do a thing like that. They wouldn't be let."

But her tone was without conviction. The idea, being born in their minds, found the circumstances too consistent to be rejected lightly.

"They must be very important," Perdita said. "I don't feel over-safe while we have them here. I wish you'd ring up Mr. Norton again."

"I don't see why we should do that. They can't have guessed where they are, or they wouldn't have let us bring them away."

"If we knew who they are, or how many 'they's there may be, I should feel more sure about that."

"Well, if anyone wants them, we don't object. They're not ours. I think, if there were a good fire in the room—"

It was an impulse which, had there been means of fulfilling it, might have saved many lives on a later day; but the open grate has no place in the guest-room of a Prague hotel.

Perdita, holding to her point, said again: "I wish you'd ring Mr. Norton up. I expect he'd be able to read them, and he'd tell us what it would be safest to do."

Caresse did not accept this suggestion with alacrity. She considered the effort of dressing again; of how long it would take to prepare to her own satisfaction for such a meeting; she even considered (and rejected promptly) the idea of Perdita going down to see him alone. In the end her hand stretched out to the telephone.

"That you, Lawrence? Yes, it's Caresse again. You never know when your troubles end. We want you to come round tonight. Well, we've changed our minds. Women do. But not for half an hour—quite. Rather late, I know, but I don't suppose you'll mind that. Yes, of course. Thanks. You'll understand when we've explained."

"So that's that," she said, as she threw back the single quilted blanket, and her silk-pyjama'd legs came to the floor, "and I only hope that Lawrence won't think we've called him here for a child's game. I wish I knew just how silly we are."

CHAPTER XI.

HALF an hour? And the Ambassador Hotel was less than two miles away. Outside, there was no more than a light sprinkle of snow. There would be time to walk, which would suit his mood.

As he was crossing the river-bridge, a small shabby saloon-car drew up to the pavement, and the door swung open. A voice from the interior said: "Mr. Norton, sir, if you'd like a lift?"

The man who spoke was a hanger-on at the British Legation, engaged at times as a second chauffeur, or as a waiter when extra help was required, in which occupation he had a reputation for nervous awkwardness and the dropping of plates. He was of English birth, but had a female Czech cousin with whom he lodged. She kept a huckster's shop in the lower town. An insignificant man, over whom even the keen eyes of the Czech police might pass as of no account, and the Nazis would be unlikely to notice at all.

Lawrence hesitated. "I suppose you saw," he said, "that I was going the opposite way."

There was no reply, but the door remained open, and seeing that, he got in.

When the car started, the man spoke again. "I was coming to ask your help. I hope you've got the night free."

He spoke as an equal now, for Lawrence knew him as one of the foremost members of the British Intelligence Department—Secret Service Agent No. 973.

"I had an appointment with two ladies."

"I'm afraid they won't see you tonight."

"Urgent as that? Then you'd better pull up while I phone."

"Much better not. Listen to me. I was out last night, and I'm nearly sure that I've found one of the secret German aerodromes that we've suspected but couldn't prove. If the snow keeps off, I mean to see more tonight."

"Where do I come in?"

"I shall want the help of a better man than myself."

"Which you certainly haven't got."

"We won't argue that."

After this there was silence. The car may have needed all the driver's care on a slippery uphill road that climbed clear of the town; but Lawrence knew that Steele always hated to speak more than the fewest of unavoidable words. He knew that, in due time, he would be told anything that he needed to know.

Four miles out, the car stopped on a lonely road. There were no houses in sight. They were on high ground, level and bare.

From a clump of roadside bushes a Czech soldier stepped.

"All quiet, Karel?"

"Yes, sir. No one about."

The man swung open a field-gate at the roadside. The car turned in, and bumped along a rough path. It passed through a narrow fir-wood, and emerged to an open field.

The moon shone, cold and high, through the broken clouds, and showed the dark form of an aeroplane at the upper end of the field.

Lawrence approached it with some surprise. He said: "This isn't yours?"

He knew that, with the secret aid of the Czech Air Minister, Steele had been making a number of solitary night-flights over the German frontiers, using one of the newest patterns of frail, swallow-swift scouting planes, in which everything was sacrificed to silence, and a speed which claimed to be almost incredibly high.

"No, I've got to risk going slower tonight. Janda knows what I'm after. He promised to have this one flown here for me after dark tonight, and to have a silencer fixed on the engine. I'd got to have one able to carry three, which the scouts won't."

"Three?"

"That's the idea. You'll see when the time comes."

They climbed into the cockpit without further words, and the aeroplane rose smoothly into the night.

CHAPTER XII.

FOR two hours they flew steadily west. The pilot spoke no word, but Lawrence could guess, by the direction they took, and by the mountainous desolation of the moonlit landscape that showed through the snow-squalls' gaps, that they looked down on the bleak solitudes of the Rhöngebirge, a waste of high, flat-topped Bavarian mountains on which the snow lies unmelted for half the year.

So far, they had flown too high to be endangered by peak or cliff, even though they should be caught in a blinding squall, but now they began to slant down like a settling bird.

The snow-white summits rose up to meet them, and then, as Lawrence wondered what landing they would be likely to have, they dived into the murk of a narrow gorge.

Here they flew perilously, with little more, it seemed in the dim light, than wing-clearance on either side, and then came out to skirt the side of a black cliff with a far valley below, in which there was the twinkle of scattered lights. Then, banking sharply as they swung round, they turned, it seemed, into the very face of the cliff, and the next minute had come to ground on a level space in a recess of the mountain-side.

"And now," Lawrence said, when they had climbed stiffly out, and no sound of life had come to their listening ears, "perhaps you'll say what you want me to do."

No. 973 was concise and explicit in his reply.

"This," he said, "is supposed to be a Government mine. Cobalt—copper. Rich deposits recently discovered. Guarded by a ring of sentries five miles round. There's a village of miners down below. They're inside the ring. So are we.

"What I want to know is, why they can't mine for copper without out a platform two hundred yards long. And why the entrance to the mountain-side requires such enormous doors."

"The answer seems obvious."

"So it does; even without some other evidences that can be best seen in a better light. But details are what we want, and there's only one way we can get them."

"If you'd like to leave me here till tomorrow night—?"

"Thanks. It's a sporting offer, but too big a risk for anything you'd be likely to see without being seen yourself. I thought we'd do more by getting hold of someone who knows, and taking him back with us."

Lawrence looked round. He was aware of silence—solitude—snow. The valley-lights twinkled a thousand feet beneath.

"Kidnapping?" he said. "Well, I'm game for that. But I hope we haven't got to carry him up here, if he's over ten. Or perhaps you've got your eye on a girl?"

He spoke lightly, his spirits rising to the adventure, and the intoxication of the keen night air, but there was no answering levity in No. 973's reply.

"There's no need to go far. There's a hut at the dump-head where a man sleeps. He seems to be quite alone."

"Sleeps?"

"That's what he was doing last night."

Steele led the way down a path that was rough and steep, with wooden steps inserted at the sharpest declines. At their right hand, a few feet lower, there was a track with a single rail.

They came to a cliff-edge, where the trolleys would be tipped, and to a little hut at its side. They looked through a narrow pane, and saw a stove glow, and a half-dressed man sprawling asleep on a pallet bed.

He was of muscular build, largely made, and did not look an easy capture to make, unless taken at the disadvantage of sleep, and Lawrence saw that there had been reason to ask his aid. Had the door been barred— But No. 973 lifted a noiseless latch, and they went in quietly.

In fact, the man was not easy to wake, and when his senses returned he seemed to take their presence in a dull way, not simply to understand.

When told he must come with them, he made no demur, only asking if he could put on his coat and boots, which he was permitted to do, Lawrence covering him the while, and Steele standing by with a short rope which was intended to bind his hands. It was evident that the final trussing could not be done till he had been persuaded to climb into the plane.

Looking at his stolid, apathetic movements, which were without haste, but did not seem dilatory of design, even Steele did not guess that the man had pressed a bell as he took his coat from the wall. Yet he had a feeling of uneasiness in his mind. It all seemed too smooth in the way it went; too absurdly simple. And yet he had experienced before how much audacity may achieve, if it be sufficiently sure of itself. The searchlight moved steadily along the edge of the pit, and settled upon the hut.

It took but a second for No. 973 to see that the plan he had was a lost hope. To save themselves—to regain the plane—to take back word of what they had seen and found—must now be their utmost aims.

He felt that he could not kill an unresisting prisoner, neither could they now attempt to take him away.

"I will bind his hands," he said; "there's no time for more. They won't see us while we stay here."

In a moment the knot was tied. The next, they were outside, in the white glare of the light which had settled upon the hut, as though waiting for them to leave.

They were none too soon, for a patrol of soldiers, four or five, were already within the searchlight's range, advancing along the level edge on which the hut stood. Seeing the two emerge, they shouted and came on at a run.

"Halt!" they cried, "Halt!"

Steele said: "Quick, down here. They're going to fire." He jumped down to the rail level, with Lawrence a short second behind. The bullets passed harmlessly overhead.

If they raised their heads, they could see their pursuers, and the path from which they had jumped. If they stooped, they were safe from the following shots. The wooden sleepers, less then two feet apart, gave them firm footing up which to run.

It seemed that the first searchlight was unable to follow where they now were, but a second, at right angles to it, was feeling to pick them up.

In the moment's darkness, they raised themselves, and looked back. The soldiers were nearer, making better progress than they.

With a common purpose they pulled out their guns. They fired deliberately, taking steady aims. The soldiers halted, returning their fire, and the mountains became loud with the echoed shots.

They were two to five, but they had the advantage of light, and they were hidden except for their heads and their lifted hands. Soon, three of those who had pursued had fallen wounded or dead, and the other two had withdrawn to the best shelter they could obtain. When the second searchlight found them, they could run on again with the assurance that they had checked immediate pursuit.

"But for this cursed light," Steele began, and then went on in another tone, as one who saw hope recovered: "Lawrence, could you pilot the plane?"

"I suppose I could. Why?"

"Then, when they fire at us again, will you fall as though hurt? You can run on when I have led the light in another way."

"Do you mean I should go alone, leaving you here? I think not."

"Then you are unfit to have come. Do you think you play in a boys' game? It is the one way you can help. And I may contrive escape, as you could not do."

As he spoke, there was an outbreak of shots on their left, from some distance away. Steele's voice became urgent: "Now! Now!" He did not wait to see whether Lawrence would do that which he had proposed. He was slightly behind. He caught an ankle, pulling with so sudden and sharp a jerk that Lawrence slipped down for some feet. Steele went ahead, increasing his pace.

Lawrence half raised himself in a first impulse to refuse a part that he had not chosen or liked, and then thought of the stake beside which their lives were no more than a feather's weight, and lay still.

To those who watched him move thus in the searchlight's glare, it must have seemed the abortive struggle of a wounded man who saw his comrade leave him behind. The light hovered over him for one hesitant moment, and then followed the man who was still active to move.

A minute later Lawrence rose, and made his dark, unmolested way to the waiting plane...almost silently, unseen and unguessed, it glided upward into the night, while the searchlights played and shots still echoed among the hills.

CHAPTER XIII.

IN the lounge of the Ambassador Hotel, two impatient girls sat watching an entrance through which traffic had ceased to pass, in a gradually dying expectation of one who did not appear.

Not for the first time, Caresse was emphatic in denial of possibility that Lawrence had not had the name of the hotel with an unmistakable clarity, and in refusal to telephone again to enquire why he had not come.

"Well," Perdita said at last, "it's past midnight now. So if you won't, I will."

"Then, let's do it upstairs."

This being agreed, they returned to their own room, and rang up the British Legation, to be informed that Mr. Norton had gone out more than an hour ago, and had not returned.

"Then it's bed for us," Caresse said, yawning. "When he looks us up tomorrow, he'll have a bit to explain. You might open the window before you get in. Double windows? I wonder what for. Well, I suppose you can open both. I'm always frightened of burglars. Simply *terrified*. I don't suppose I shall sleep a wink. But I can't stand these heated rooms."

She fell asleep even before Perdita had ceased to look out on a street two stories beneath her, which was whitening under a thin indolent downfall of frozen snow, and opened her eyes again at a later hour, to gaze into those of a man who pushed the casement window somewhat farther aside as he entered the room.

He showed black against the faint diffused lights of the street beneath and the moon above, and she could see that he was a small man, but little more, for his face was shadowed. He flashed a torch round the room, and into her eyes. He said, in low careful English: "You will have no harm if no sound you make." He found the light, which he switched on.

Caresse, who had lain many times with a quick-beating heart and head under the clothes from no greater cause than a board's creak in the night, found that she was only faintly excited, and not frightened at all. She said: "You have no business here. What do you want?"

"I want nothing of yours."

He saw the suitcases, to which he went, disregarding some scattered jewellery on a table beside him. His object was beyond doubt, and while he subjected the cases to a rapid but thorough search she had time to consider what she should do.

Had the papers been where he looked, she would have been well content for him to take them and go, but she knew they were not. Perdita had put them under her own pillow, from an impulse no more definite in its origin than the thought that they had cost a man's life a few hours before, and must have a value she could not guess.

Caresse thought: "When he finds they are not where he thinks, he will search the room. He will wake Perdita. I cannot tell what she will do, or what violence may result." She lay turned away from the man, but there was a mirror through which she could watch every movement he made. He had a face which she did not like. In a hip-pocket, an evident weapon bulged.

There was a small disc on the bedside table with three bell-pushes, each marked with a figure of the attendant whom it would call. She did not know whether they would all be on duty during the night, but she took the chances she had. Noiselessly, deliberately, her hand went out, and pressed the three down. So she kept it for twenty seconds, and withdrew it unnoticed before she spoke: "If you don't want to get caught, you'd better clear out. I believe the porter's coming up now."

The man raised a scowling face from his futile search. He may not have understood what she said, and what he might have done on that realisation she was not destined to know, for at the same moment a whistle shrilled from the street.

Quick as a startled cat, the man made for the window, and scrambled out on to the ladder by which he had climbed. He did not pause to switch off the light.

There was the sound of a shot in the street below. A night-porter's voice came from outside the door: "Madam, did you ring?"

Perdita lifted a sleepy head from her pillow to ask: "Is anything wrong?"

She heard Caresse answer the porter rather than her: "Thank you, it's all right now." She watched her switch off the light.

Caresse said: "It's a row in the street."

There could be no doubt about that. The shots were more frequent now. A scream came, and was repeated, as though from unendurable pain. It fell to a lower note, gradually dying away.

Caresse, looking out from the window of the now-darkened room, saw the ladder being withdrawn, and guessed that the would-be robbers had held their own, at least long enough to remove the means by which the room had been reached. She closed the windows, securing them in indifference to whatever temperature might result.

As she did so, there was a fresh outburst of shots, this time from farther along the street, and less loud through the double glass of the casements.

Perdita's hand went under her pillow, where the causes of this uproar remained. "Cheerful place to be in," she said sleepily. They did not wake till the late February daylight had invaded the room.

CHAPTER XIV.

IT was half-past nine the next morning when Lawrence called at the Ambassador Hotel, and, on enquiring for Mrs. Langton and Miss Wyatt, was informed that the ladies were not yet down.

He thought: "Caresse is running true to form," and had a wish that the world's beds had been more equally occupied during the past night. He yawned with the good excuse of a man whose own night had been spent in a flight of some hundreds of miles, and a vigilance that must not relax for an instant's rest either of mind or eye. But there was no weariness in his voice as he answered: "Well, you might let them know I am here, and ask them how long they will be."

Caresse, sitting up in bed to consume rolls and coffee with excellent appetite, while she regaled Perdita with a picturesque account of the night's adventure, was just saying: "Frightened? I should think I was! Out of my wits. I thought you wouldn't wake if the ceiling fell," when the telephone bell rang at her bedside, and her voice went on: "Tell him to come up. Yes, at once." And then to Perdita's exclamation of startled protest: "Yes, it's Lawrence, of course. And about time, too. Yes, why not? It's not as though you're alone, or me either." She considered a bed-jacket that suited her too well to be seen by none but feminine eyes, and that the tale she was telling deserved a larger audience than it now had. A moment later, Lawrence Norton entered the room.

"Hello, Lawrence!" Caresse said cheerfully, "don't look so surprised. I suppose you thought we should still be waiting for you downstairs. We might have had a quieter night if we had. You don't want to be introduced? You've met Perdita before, although I daresay you'll say you've forgotten that."

Perdita said: "That was ages ago. I don't suppose he remembers me." She looked up, as she shook hands, at a man whom she remembered as largely made, but who seemed to have grown in bulk, and surely was of a gravity very different from her memory of him as a guest in her mother's house four years before. He had been twenty then, and she a girl of sixteen. He had been secret hero to her, but she supposed that to be a fact that she had not exposed, for she had always been reticent of her own emotions, more disposed to listen to others than to reveal her feelings to them.

He said: "I have not forgotten at all." Their eyes met in the old friendly way, but his went on to Caresse, as she exclaimed: "What's the matter, Lawrence? Anyone'd think you'd had no sleep for a week."

"I haven't had much. I went out with a friend."

"Did she keep you all night?"

A smile chased the weariness from his face. "It was not a she."

"Then it's more difficult to forgive."

He made no reply. The former gravity had come back to his eyes.

Perdita interrupted Caresse's persiflage in a more serious tone: "We phoned you last night because we were in a jam, and we thought you might help."

"That is," Caresse interposed, "if you can read Czech."

"Probably I can, if it's clearly written." It was proficiency in languages by which his position in the diplomatic service had been obtained, and the many tongues and hybrid dialects of Eastern Europe had been his special study during the two years that he had held his present appointment.

Perdita said: "They're not written, they're typed. We don't know that they're Czech. That's a guess. Mr. Norton, you might put this on the table."

"Lawrence, please."

"Very well; Lawrence."

As she spoke, she had passed him the breakfast-tray from her knees, and twisted round to draw the bundle of papers from under her pillow.

He took them casually, but as he saw what they were, his expression turned to an added gravity, and then to a puzzled frown. During the moment's silence, the telephone rang at Caresse's side. She said: "Telegram? Yes. Send it up." And then to Lawrence: "You're not going to tell us they're beating you?"

"The first sheets," he answered, "are plain enough, though what they mean is harder to say. They are lists of men, mostly German, to judge by their names, and all Nazis at a good guess, by a few I've heard of before. The other sheets, being written in cipher, may be Persian or Japanese for anything I could tell. But how, in God's name, did these things come into your hands? Did you find them here?"

They were interrupted by a page-boy's knock at the door. He gave a telegram to Caresse's hand.

She stared at it for a moment, and when she looked up Perdita had commenced the narrative of their adventures in the train, and during the night.

She did not interrupt except once or twice to give a more vivid tone to her friend's descriptions, and that was rather because Lawrence's eyes were on Perdita's face as she spoke, which she did not like, than that the younger girl failed to make the narrative clear. But when it came to the events of the night, Perdita said: "Caresse can tell you best about that. I just slept like a fool," and so Caresse took the stage's centre again, as it was normal for her to do.

When the tale was done, Lawrence said: "I want you both to go back by the next train. It is not only because of this. It's what I meant to say when I came in."

Perdita said: "We shouldn't like to do that. Not unless we know why."

Caresse laughed: "'Two minds with but a single thought.' Look at this." She passed over the telegram.

It read:

COME BACK NEXT POSSIBLE TRAIN VIA VIENNA GENOA NETHERLAND BOAT FROM THERE SERIOUS REASON DON'T FAIL LOVE GERALD.

Lawrence, reading it, showed no surprise. He said: "That about settles it. They often know more in London than we do here." He seemed to be thinking aloud, rather than talking to them.

Caresse said sharply: "It doesn't settle anything. Why, our tickets wouldn't be any use! Are we to throw them away? Perhaps you will tell us what you both mean."

"I don't think you ought to need telling more than you've seen for yourselves already. It's not a very safe time for foreigners to be here."

"I thought English people were liked in Prague?"

"So they are. But—"

"Then I think we've had enough of crossing frontiers for a few days. I don't see—"

"I'm afraid you'll have to."

He spoke curtly, and with a tone of command which she remembered of old, and half-resented and half-approved.

Perdita said: "I suppose you mean there'll be war." Her tone indicated a mild excitement rather than apprehension of any evil to fear.

"I have said nothing of such a kind. You must please be clear upon that. It is not our business to start scares and that is a word that is best unsaid. I say that conditions here are such that you should get home while you safely can."

"And you think crossing frontiers about twice a day—" Caresse began (was he likely to think of how many dresses were in her trunks, or that there are no hairdressers on the trains?), but she was interrupted by a light knock on the door.

The man who entered was dressed in civilian clothes, but his manner was military, both in speech and gesture. He spoke English well, with a German accent.

He said: "Pardon, ladies," in a tone that was brusque rather than apologetic, and then looked his surprise that there was another visitor in the room. The next instant his eyes fell on the papers that lay on Perdita's bed. "I see," he said, "you have found that which is mine."

Lawrence said: "Which shouldn't have been here."

"It is a trouble which I regret. But it is one that is ending now."

"Herr Müller, if you will take your hand from that gun, I will do the same. This is a matter which can be settled best in another way." The man drew his hand from the hip-pocket to which it had gone when he perceived that Lawrence was in the room, and Lawrence's own hand came from his jacket-pocket to which it had fallen in a careless-seeming movement, as instant as his.

"If you know who I am, you will know that I ask for that to which I have the best right."

"And if you know me, you will know that my first concern must be to avoid association with the intrigues of a country which is not mine. But I will neither yield to a threat, nor let it be said that I have been the medium of handing over those papers to you, which should not be here, and which we are unable to read. They are nothing to us. If you take them away, we shall neither hinder nor help."

The man came quickly across the room. He gathered up the papers, and went. Lawrence said: "You are well out of that. The man you saw is the secret head of the Nazi organisation here. That he should have come himself, and after he must have heard of Herr Schmit's fate, is an indication of how important they were. You are clear of them now, but I must still urge you to get out of Prague with the least delay."

Caresse gave no direct answer. "Suppose," she said, "to begin with, you get out of this room. And if you like to ask us to lunch—"

"To dinner, if you don't mind. The fact is, I've got to get a few hours sleep."

"I suppose it's no use asking why you don't sleep at the usual time?"

"Not the least. Suppose I call for you at six-thirty, and we fix up for you to leave tomorrow?"

"Six-thirty will do for us," Caresse replied, avoiding the larger issue.

Lawrence found the lift on the point of descending, and in a few seconds he was at the hotel door. But as the porter swung it open for him to leave, a page-boy was at his side.

"If you please, sir, Mrs. Langton wants to know if you can see her for a moment again."

He went back to find that the trouble with Herr Müller might be less completely over than he had supposed.

Perdita held out a sheet of paper. "If you know Mr. Müller's address," she said, "you can send him this."

"She found it under her pillow," Caresse explained, "when she was hopping out."

He took the sheet with an inward curse at the perversity of the event, and yet with a thought that it might be worth while to discover what secrets the cipher held.

CHAPTER XV.

No. 973 had a reputation for calculated audacities which was not excelled by that of any member of the service to which he belonged. It was a reputation of narrow bounds, for the secret agent must work without hope of public applause. He must live and die unknown to those for whom he goes in peril by night and day. He must avoid publicity as anxiously as it is sought by others, dodging it as he now twisted and paused and ran to escape the searchlights that chased him and did not tire; for if it find him, his use is done.

His first aim, as he left Lawrence, had been to divert attention from him, and from the path he meant to take to the waiting plane. But with this object achieved, his mind became active to save himself, and to contrive that he should not fail to take full advantage of the opportunity which had been forced upon him.

Yet, cool and active though he might be, and adroit to take any advantage that was offered by the nature of the ground over which he fled, it is improbable that he could have escaped the hunt that was converging from every side, or the bullets that were frequent and swifter in their pursuit, had not the two searchlights ceased to assist the chase.

As though tiring of so petty an occupation, they swung upward at the same moment, lifting parallel bars of light to the southern sky.

It was evident that they had abandoned him for an object of greater or more urgent importance, and if it implied no hope that his human foes would relax their efforts, it gave the moment's respite which the situation required.

He saw that his worst enemy was the snow, which lay deep on the open hills, and would delay every step he took and record it for the guidance of those who would be eager in his pursuit. There was the poor choice of so hard a flight, or else to keep his feet on the trodden paths where he could have little hope of avoiding those who would seek to bring him to capture and speedy death.

He had the hunted creature's instinct for flight, but he controlled it to the adoption of the second course, both because he judged it to be a slender chance against none, and because it would offer the better opportunities of the observation for which he came.

But he saw that, if he were to remain in this secret camp, a disguise was his vital need, and, as the searchlights ceased their pursuit, he was instant to double back to the one spot where he hoped that it might be found.

On the cliff-edge path, a hundred yards from the hut which was empty now, he came to a place where two dark shapes were fallen upon the snow. He did not need to risk flashing his torch to know that these sprawling forms would be useless to him. He was not a small man, but their uniforms would have hung upon him loosely enough to tickle a scarecrow's mirth.

He moved to the tumbled rocks that bordered the path, seeking a place where he could crouch await for any who should come single along: and, as he did so, his foot sank in that which was smooth and soft, and which gave way differently from the crunch of the frozen snow. Under his tread, a man squirmed with a coughing grunt.

No. 973 flashed his torch down on one whom his hand had shot in the last hour, and who had crawled there, and fainted from loss of blood.

The man asked, with a sharp doubt in his voice: "Who are you?" and not getting a quick reply, his hand moved to a pistol against his side. Steele had had time to see that his clothes were likely to be of the right size. He would not withdraw, nor could he let the man shoot, nor risk the noise of a shot from his own gun. Seeing the hand move, he threw himself forward upon one who was not too wounded or weak to make a fight for the life that is dear to all.

Steele's fingers were on his throat: he thrust his knee between the gun and the seeking hand. He knew that it must be a fight to the death, whether with weapons or naked hands.

He felt the man's hand struggling desperately to reach the pistol against his side, and he could oppose this only with the knee he had thrust between. He might have been able to wrest the gun from the weaker man, but it would have been useless to him, for it was on silence that he relied. To kill and run would have been no service to him. He must remain there unsuspected amidst those who were searching on every side.

The man twisted and strove, and struggled for failing breath until there came a doubt even to his assailant's resolute mind of whether his strength would be the longer to last. But against one so wounded and underneath there could be but one end. There came a time when the man must forget all else in futile efforts to tear off the hands that denied him breath. Breathless himself, No. 973 rose at last, as he withdrew his grasp from the throat of a strangled man.

The death of Johann Schmit was no more than one of those frontier incidents that had been constant in Eastern Europe since the

Trianon Treaties had kennelled discordant elements within boundaries that had no reality beyond that of the barbed wire and loaded rifles that held their lines. But the death of this German soldier cannot be placed in the same homicidal schedule.

The world slept unconscious of the shadow which advanced upon it, but, with the fall of this man, and his two comrades upon the path, it may be said that the War of 1938 had commenced.

No. 973's reputation for successful audacities had not been won by mere temerity in the taking of hazardous ways. To gain such a name and live, a man must be prudent and thorough to the last detail of all he does. As he had created the nervous, ineffectual personality of Richard Steele, the Legation hanger-on, with such artistic completeness that even the keen eyes of the Czech police had passed him over as not worthy of their regard, so now he was not content with any superficiality of disguise, but he must strip every article that the dead man wore, he must discard every possession he had himself, even to the torch which the contents of his new pockets did not replace.

In every detail he sought to adopt the identity of him whose uniform he had put on, and that which his pockets held must be the things that he needed now. Among these, he found an envelope which gave him the name that must now be his, and the regiment to which he belonged.

He lifted the stripped body of the man that his hands had killed, carried it across the path, and dropped it over the sheer side of the cliff. Listening for its fall, he thought he heard a cracking of boughs, as though it broke through bushes, or found its rest in a wooded place. Hoping that they would not be revealed with the coming day, he dropped his own clothes and possessions at the same spot. He searched the other two men, but took no more than some food that their pockets held. He stood up Eugene Gumpert, private in a Franconian infantry regiment.

While he had been busy in these ways, he had raised his eyes from time to time to observe the searchlights that remained motionless, pointed aloft to the southern sky. Down the dark lane between those channels of light, one by one, there came a succession of aeroplanes, which dropped out of his sight where he then stood, but which were obviously descending to enter the wide doors at the end of a long platform that opened into the mountain-side. They were guided by a great light which rose to meet them from a source that he could not see, but which he guessed correctly to come from the opened doors. If, he thought, he could get through them before they closed, if he could see what that subterranean cavern held? It was an attempt to be promptly made, if at all, for each plane that arrived might be the last to come, and the lights might be cut off, and the doors closed. So he stepped out from the shadow in which he had stood a moment to form his plans, with Eugene Gumpert's rifle under his arm, and was aware as he did so that a man came up the path in a hurried and furtive way rather than as one of those who searched for himself, or was otherwise there with a good cause.

He stepped boldly across the path.

"Halt!" he cried. "Who goes there?"

The man stopped abruptly. He faced the moonlight, which brightened as the clouds broke. He was unarmed, and wore the uniform of a pilot of the German Air Force.

He gave his name in a hurried way, as one who would be glad to be gone. He added: "It is all right. I had six hours' leave. I have been down in the camp."

He spoke nervously, making it seem probable that he lied, though less easy to guess what the lie might be.

Steele said boldly: "I do not know you. I know most who are stationed here."

"Neither do I know you."

"I am Eugene Gumpert, of the 22nd Franconian Infantry. Now will you say who you claim to be?"

"I only came yesterday. I am one of those who have been transferred from the Nürnberg corps."

That was easy to believe, and suggested explanation of why Nürnberg was said to be very quiet, and to have many away on leave. But it was Steele's posture to doubt. He said: "That may be true. But I am searching for two spies who have been seen during the night. You are strange to me, and it is a risk that I dare not take. You must come back with me."

The man expostulated in a way that showed the proposal to be unwelcome, from whatever cause. In fact, he had slipped down to the valley camp without leave, and would have been sooner back had he not thought it prudent to hide for a time when there had come a sudden clamour of cries and shots, and the searchlights had descended upon the road.

But he pleaded in vain. The only concession Eugene Gumpert would grant was that he would not take him to his own officer. He need not consider himself under arrest. Private Gumpert's military conscience would be satisfied if it saw him return to his proper station, and observed him to be recognised by his comrades. He said, "You can go first, but you will be wise if you do not hurry your pace; for if you run, I shall fire."

On this bargain, the man went ahead, feeling that it might be worse than it was, and that, with good luck for a friend, he might avoid the observation of those who would punish his fault.

No. 973 had secured both a guide into the aerodrome, and an excuse for his own entrance there which might otherwise have been hard to find.

CHAPTER XVI.

THE man looked up anxiously. He was naturally reluctant to run, with the muzzle of Eugene Gumpert's rifle about three feet from his back. He was only less urgently reluctant to be shut out, with the inevitable exposure which it entailed. He looked back to ask: "If I go on a bit faster, you won't think I'm running away?"

"I might make a mistake."

Steele thought that his prisoner was going fast enough now. The path was steep and rough, and the winter uniform and accoutrements of a private in the Franconian infantry were weighty arguments for a more leisurely pace.

Airman Witz did not like the reply, yet his pace hastened rather than slackened. He said: "I only want to get in."

Private Gumpert considered that there might be advantages in the man using his tongue more and his legs less. He asked: "What's the hurry now?"

Witz looked up again as he replied: "That's the last plane coming in."

No. 973 would have given more heed to the skies had he not needed his eyes for a path that he did not know. Now he looked up to see a large plane of the night-bomber type that glided smoothly down the dark lane between the searchlights' parallel beams. He asked: "That's a Zeus, isn't it?"

"Yes, of course," the airman answered. There was impatience in his tone, as of one who agrees to a thing too well understood for the waste of words. He came back to that which engaged his own mind: "In two minutes, they'll have it in."

"And when that happens, you're anxious to be inside? Well, go ahead."

The man went on at a pace that was not favourable to further words. Private Gumpert made no demur, for he was equally anxious not to be shut out. He saw that there might be even more to learn than he had supposed a moment before.

It was a Zeus, "of course," that came down from the sky. And the whole world had known that Germany had abandoned the manufacture of that type of plane nearly two years ago! And yet, he remembered, the German Government had made no such assertion. They had even gone the length of officially denying the rumours of the unsatisfactory performance which had been whispered through the world of aviation regarding the new night-bombers which they had commenced to manufacture so largely after their open denunciation, in the spring of 1935, of the disarmament clauses of the Versailles Treaty.

But they had allowed it to be one of those secrets which all men know that they had turned to the manufacture of the new Vogel type of night-bombers, of which six hundred had been employed in the aerial manœuvres of 1937, at which attachés of other governments had been present, according to the custom of outward frankness which now prevailed.

The German Government was said to consider the Vogel to be equal to the newest type on which the British relied, or to any of the patterns which had been produced by the fertile genius of French engineers, and which were sufficiently numerous to make a fleet of samples of the great Air Force of France. But it was an opinion with which aviators outside Germany were not disposed to agree. They said the Vogel was heavy, powerful, but rather slow.

Now, he wondered, were the Vogels little more than a monstrous bluff, or a second line? Had the rumours of bad performance on the part of the Zeus pattern been deliberately set afloat? Had the formal denial of the German Government been no more than a clever ruse that was to succeed by its simple truth, which those who read it would be too shrewd to believe? Especially when they heard that a new type had been put in hand.

He had always been sceptical of the rumours of a huge subterranean German aerodrome which had been circulated during the past year. Not that he doubted the existence of such retreats. More or less, they had been openly known. Subterranean petrol reservoirs, and even aerodromes that would take in a substantial number of planes, had been known to exist for the past three years. That was the point. They had been known. The secret one, constructed on a scale that would be of military importance, had seemed too difficult to believe. The extent of the required excavations—other more technical difficulties—these still remained. But he saw that there might be more to discover than he had feared, or expected, to find.

It had become of tenfold importance that he should not fail to enter those open doors, of tenfold importance also that he should not be detected in what he did. But on that point he had some confidence in himself; and, at the worst, he did not run quite the danger that might appear. He had good reason to hope that, even if he were discovered for what he was, he might have something to put forward which would protect him from condemnation to instant death.

With these thoughts in his mind, he hurried on, making no further protest against the pace that his companion set. They were side by side, in a final spurt, when they joined the miscellaneous group of soldiers, airmen, and artisans who were gathered round the aerodrome entrance. As they passed through them, the great doors were already commencing to move together along their smooth oiled grooves.

Private Gumpert, still keeping his eyes upon the man who must be the explanation of his presence there, was yet vaguely aware of a cavern, vast in extent, though not in height, sufficiently lit by arc-lamps that hung above, and with a floor covered with heavy night-bombing planes, as though a horde of gigantic beetles had settled with open or folded wings.

It was with a natural satisfaction that he looked round and observed the absence of any who wore the uniform of the regiment that he had so recently joined. He supposed himself to be secure from detection for a few hours, if he could avoid meeting with those who would have learnt to attach his name to another man, and providing that he could give sufficient explanation of why he was in a place where he had no evident business to be.

But while the absence of other members of his battalion made the detection of his personation less probable, it rendered his uniform sufficiently conspicuous to make it a poor hope that his presence would pass unnoticed.

Deciding, therefore, that the bolder course was the safer, he approached an officer whose eyes he observed to be already directed upon him, drawing forward the reluctant Witz.

He saluted, and with the brevity that the occasion required, and a Bavarian accent worthy of his new nationality, he stated the duty on which he had been engaged, and the doubt that had brought him there.

"I suppose him to be whom he says," he concluded, "but he was a man whom I did not know. Having been ordered to watch for spies...."

"Did you see anything of those spies?"

"I saw two men run, with whom we exchanged shots. Two of my comrades were killed. I followed those who ran, till the search-lights lifted, and they made off in the dark. I think that I hit one."

"You have done well." The officer gave instructions to one of his own men to accompany Airman Witz, and to verify whom he was. He appeared to regard the incident as complete, but Private Gumpert saluted again to ask: "Herr Captain, have I your leave to return?"

It was a bold risk, but it could be seen that the great doors were closed, and they were not likely to be reopened for him. While he wore the uniform of Private Gumpert, he must act as that man would have been likely to do. And he saw that his position would be improved if he could obtain a direct authority for remaining within the aerodrome during the night.

The officer was decided in his reply. No one could leave till the next day, now that the doors had been closed. But he was considerate to one whose conduct he thought worthy of praise. He ordered that a message explaining his absence should be telephoned to the military barracks in the valley below. He gave instructions for his accommodation in the meantime.

CHAPTER XVII.

PRIVATE GUMPERT was soon seated among a group of airmen who were to go on duty during the night (though night and day were alike to them, where the sunlight would never reach, and work went on unceasingly under the arc-lamps' glare). They sat round a long table eating what was breakfast to them. As they ate they talked, and he found that he could learn much, even without speaking himself.

He saw Witz take a seat nearly opposite himself, at which he was less than pleased, though he thought that there could be little danger from him. The man appeared to have been able to slip back into his place without incurring the censure of his superior officers. Doubtless, he would wish it to be supposed that, like his comrades around him, he had been asleep in the last hours.

The talk of airmen naturally centres round that with which their own lives are concerned. These men had been recently drafted from different camps, of which they exchanged news. Much was naturally left unsaid, as being commonly known. Often more could be learnt by inference than by actual statement. Among idle chatter, badinage, and trivial gossip, there were allusions to the recent movement during the night of a large air force from the Baltic coast, to reinforce the great Sakrow aerodrome near Berlin. Exact numbers were not mentioned, but the impression given was of the movement of many hundreds of planes.

There was a joking allusion to the time, three years before, when the German Government had half flouted, half bamboozled Europe with the Lufthansa training of naval pilots, and the innocent activities of the Air Sport League. It appeared that the "Air Sport League" was still used as a jesting name for the greatest of the military air forces which the nations of Europe had contrived grotesquely for their own destruction.

The one fact of supreme importance which was implicit in the remarks around him was that this was only one of a number of secret subterranean aerodromes, though he could learn nothing of how many there were without a question too direct to be risked. But this was No. 7. There might be no more than six others. There might be twenty. He had already formed a vague guess that the vast cavern held not less than two hundred planes. The difficulty he had always felt in imagining a secret depot large enough to accommodate a great fleet was resolved in this way. The depots were not one but many. The secret air fleet might amount to several thousand planes, in addition to those that were openly known, and which were considered equal in themselves to any air force which the world held, excepting only that of the United States.

And it appeared that these concealed planes were all of a single pattern—the Zeus night-bombers.

The Zeus was not adapted to carry so heavy a load as could several of the patterns of bombers which the nations of Europe built with grim haste that their children might go to death by a shortened road. Its distinctive features were great speed and defensive strength. It was a streamlined, all-metal monoplane, with folding wings and retractile wheels. It had a crew of two only. Its bombs were dropped by the pilot, by a lever which his foot moved. It had the usual gun-ring, but no turret. Its four engines were of a design which was the most closely guarded secret of all. Its speed was 330 miles per hour, and its range, with a full load, about 1,200 miles. Against these qualities, what disadvantage was it that the single machines carried a lighter load than those of the latest designs of either England or France?

In building a great fleet of single pattern, the German Air Ministry had pursued the same policy which had guided the construction of the air fleet which it openly showed. It had observed the principle, long recognised by naval commanders, but not yet equally appreciated in the air, that a fleet can be manœuvred to better purpose, either for attack or defence, if its units be equal in strength and speed.

Private Gumpert listened and learned. He might have avoided trouble, had he not been drawn into the talk by an allusion which Witz made to the Hanover petrol depot, which he did not follow, and of which he would have been glad to hear more. He spoke in a natural way, and all would have been well had not Witz used his name when he replied.

When he did it a second time, another man said: "Gumpert? This isn't Gumpert. You give our friend the wrong name."

Steele smiled easily, it being a trouble he had feared, and which he met with a ready mind. He asked the last speaker: "Whom do you think I am?"

"I don't know that. I only know you're not Eugene Gumpert."

"You're wrong there. It must be my cousin you know. We happen to have the same names. It's the only point on which we're not about as different as any two people are."

The man agreed that the difference was not small, but he accepted the explanation readily, as he was likely to do.

But Witz became silent. A strange doubt stirred in his mind. He looked across at his recent captor with suspicious eyes. If spies were about, who could tell in what guise they would be? He remembered that puzzling exclamation of surprise when the Zeus plane had appeared, and his doubt grew.

And with this doubt there came a fear as to how far he might be involved, either if he spoke, or kept quiet. It was clear that he could say nothing without exposing his own breach of discipline. It was almost equally certain that, should the spy, if such he were, be ultimately discovered by other means, the question of how he had established himself in the aerodrome would arise, and perhaps in a way that would be even worse for himself.

On the whole, duty and personal safety seemed to point the same way. If a spy he were, Airman Witz was the only one by whom he should be denounced. But a false accusation, which would have no result but to draw attention to his own fault, would be a folly he would not risk.

While he pondered thus, the man who had spoken before said: "I was at Retzbach last summer. I met your cousin then. He was with Wilhelm Reichert, the miller's son. You will know him?"

"I'm afraid not. I have not been in Retzbach for many years. It is my native place, but I have lived long in Berlin."

The reply seemed evasive to Witz, and increased his doubt. But if Gumpert had no better knowledge of Berlin than of Retzbach, he saw that his exposure could be easily made, for he himself had been born in a Berlin street. He said: "I suppose Barnim Street is not one you happen to know?"

Private Gumpert was ready in his reply: "Oh, but I think I do. Is it not off Neue König Street, on the right side going north?" He went on more freely than he had spoken before: "I live less than two miles from there; or, at least, I did for some years before I was called up."

He mentioned street and house with particularity, and the names of shopkeepers and others prominent in the district, till he found some who were known to Witz, and they could exchange memories concerning them. Witz could not doubt that he knew Berlin, nor that he had lived there in recent years. His doubt lessened, but did not die.

In the meantime, talk turned to speculations of what might be the cause of the sudden secret activities in the subterranean aerodromes. The Germany of that day was not ruled by the press, nor did its Government listen to popular clamour, nor think it necessary to make its decisions known before they should be demonstrated by the event. The present stir might be no more than a practice drill, or precaution in a time of political tension: a mere insurance against some cloud which was expected to rise, but which might yet drift across the horizon, leaving the skies of peace as serene as they had seemed but a week ago.

There had been similar activity before the day on which the annexation of Austria had been announced; and after that, for one dreadful week, the clouds of war had blackened the central heavens.

Men had looked up, waiting only for the moment when the lightning would cross the sky.

At that time, there had been few of the great cities of Europe where the gas-masks had not been served out, the skies live with patrolling squadrons of fighting planes.

But that shadow had moved away, when it had become known that it was an issue on which England refused to fight. There had been reasons for that, besides the obvious one that it would have been foolish to make cause of war of what had been true in all but name for some months before it had become fact in a formal way. Of all the clauses of the Versailles Treaty which had been potent to vex the world, there may have been none of a more futile stupidity than that which stipulated that men of kindred blood and adjoining lands should be held apart except by their own resolves.

But it was not that consideration alone which made England resolute that she should not be drawn into such a war. There had been another fact, as obvious at the time, which she had been less willing to see. Forgetting that nature abhors a vacuum, she had half-abandoned India, and then expressed a naive surprise and indignation when the Russian Communists showed an active disposition to pick up the reins she loosed. There had been a moment when she had been on the verge of war with the spreading ulcer of Bolshevism, which was then threatening the foundations of human freedom almost as acutely as chemical discoveries threatened the material structures of civilisation.

In such a strife, her natural allies would have been Germany, Poland, Japan. With this quarrel acutely upon her hands, could she make alliance with France and Russia, for a war which would have had no further purpose than to keep Germans nominally apart who were already joined in all but the outward bond?

So the moment of tension had passed; and England, lightly forgetful of how France had been fooled and robbed less than three years before, had bargained with Russia that the propaganda should cease, on her receiving a loan of fifty million pounds, which condition was honourably observed until the money had passed securely to Moscow's control. And if it had afterwards been resumed with a double zeal, was it not a most natural result, when it had proved so profitable and so safe?

The German Air Force of 1938 did not expect to be told the reasons for what it did. It was its part to obey. Now the great aerodromes at Staaken and Nürnberg, at Frankfort and the Baltic coast, were inactive and understaffed, but orders had been given that the hidden fleet should be made ready for instant use. That was all they knew: all they expected to be told.

Even in the meal-time gossip among themselves, Private Gumpert observed signs of nervousness, of reserve, of the dying-down of half-spoken words. The men knew that a loose tongue was a road to trouble, certain and short; an accusation of communism, of disloyalty to the Third Reich might acquaint them with a firing-squad and a shallow grave.

But there were no indications of such a spirit latent among these men who might at any hour be the living dice that would be cast in the deadly hazard of war. They were cheerful, self-assured, confident alike in Germany and themselves.

Private Gumpert left the table. He sat down on a bench. He pulled a letter from his pocket, which he commenced to read. He appeared to become absorbed in its pages letting the envelope lie carelessly at his side. Airman Witz, loitering past, was able to read the address, and his suspicions further declined. He watched while the letter was returned to the pocket from which it came, and its owner folded his greatcoat to rest his head and stretched himself on the bench. He looked down on a man who slept. He heard the whirr of the electric bell which called him to his own task. He went out, but, as he worked, his mind went over the night's events, and his doubts returned with a new strength. He made excuse to return to the place where he had left Private Gumpert sleeping, with the intention of asking him a few questions to which it might not have been easy, even to his ingenuity, to give satisfactory answers; but he found that the bench was bare.

CHAPTER XVIII.

HIS Excellency Sir Geoffrey Cullender, British Envoy Extraordinary and Minister Plenipotentiary to the Republic of Czechoslovakia, had held his present office for about eighteen months, which he would have described as the dullest with which he had been cursed in the course of a wide and varied experience in his country's service.

He had commenced his diplomatic career with minor posts at Athens and Moscow, and then, after a short experience of the gaieties of the French capital, he had held positions of greater responsibility as head of the legations of two of the more turbulent of the South American republics.

Accustomed, during those periods, to the frequent rattle of machine-gun fire under his windows, and to the precaution of telephoning for the President's name before addressing him by any written communication, he had now been transported to an atmosphere in which the months drifted uneventfully by, amid a constant apprehension of trouble that never came.

He listened to Lawrence Norton's account of his night's adventure with an inward envy of one whose less responsible office might in some measure condone a latitude of conduct impossible to himself; and even the fact that No. 973 had last been seen dodging the unwelcome attentions of a German searchlight produced no more than an expression of cheerful certainty that Steele could be relied on to wriggle out of any hole he was in.

With equal cheerfulness, he heard the account of Herr Schmit's illicit use of Perdita's suitcase, and even of the abruptness of his probable end, though his official rectitude, which was a trained instinct, quite separate from the levity of his personal disposition, caused him to approve Lawrence's attitude in declining to handle the documents, in so decided a manner that it seemed to his secretary a discreet reticence to avoid mention of that final sheet which his pocket held.

But when Lawrence went on to speak of his wish to persuade the ladies to return to England while the journey could be safely made, he roused Sir Geoffrey to indignant protest: "Send them home!" he exclaimed. "Just because Hitler's blowing off steam? And when we haven't had an English girl here worth a look since Lady Clipperton left last August! Langton wants her back? Well, so he may. But that's no reason for us to sing the same tune. Yes, bring them here to dinner, of course. And you'd better round up a few more guests of the right kind. Get Janda to come, with that pert little Hungarian, and But it's sleep that you ought to be having now. I'll tell Harvey to see to that."

Lawrence admitted that a few hours' sleep would be welcome, but deferred that indulgence until he had found the Legation archivist, and had handed him the cryptographic sheet, in a well-founded confidence that its cipher must be of unusual ingenuity if it were to defy his elucidation.

CHAPTER XIX.

IVAN SCHOTT, Minister of Justice to the Republic of Czecho-slovakia, was a worried man.

He did not object in itself to the method of Herr Schmit's removal, or doubt its necessity, but he had been a man of substantial business interests and important connections. His disappearance would require somewhat more explanation than was usually considered necessary when a secret service agent met with sudden death on the too-numerous frontiers of Eastern Europe.

It would have been far more satisfactory if he had been arrested with incriminating documents bulging his pockets, or even if there were any such regarding which his complicity could be plausibly alleged. That argument alone would have been sufficient for the continuation of active enquiry; but Ivan Schott sought with another and more urgent impulse.

A week earlier, he had captured a German agent, Fritz Hansel, and this man had postponed his fate for two days by the betrayal of his associates, including Johann Schmit, who had previously avoided suspicion. He had stated that Schmit would be the channel for conveyance of instructions of particular importance and secrecy during the following week, and the Minister of Justice had aimed not merely at the elimination of a dangerous agent of Nazi conspiracy, but at the capture of documents for which the German Government might be prepared to do much, rather than that they should be published to the surrounding world.

With the information he had, and having had advice that Schmit was upon the train which was then crossing the Czechoslovak frontier, he had actually boasted in advance to his fellow-ministers of the haul he expected to make, though he knew this to be an unlucky thing to do. For every reason, those papers, of the existence of which he had little doubt, must be traced and seized.

Considering every possible channel of secret communication, he did not overlook the two English ladies who had been the travelling companions of the German spy. It was no more than the routine of his department which brought their descriptions to his office within half an hour of their arrival at the Ambassador Hotel. These did not suggest them as probable accomplices of a Nazi agent, though even that possibility was not dismissed abruptly, the fact that Caresse was the wife of a prominent official of the British Foreign Office being carefully pondered.

When the next morning brought report of an armed attempt to burgle the hotel during the night, obviously by the organisation which those papers were meant to reach, a much less intelligent man than Ivan Schott would have seen the incident in its true significance. But that same intelligence warned him not to overleap the logical implications of the event.

The Nazis might have acted on a blind guess; they might have conducted a fruitless search. Or, whether by force or consent, the papers might have already passed into their hands. He saw that, in either event, they had been first, and he was likely to do no more than poke in an empty hole. He was acute enough to see, also, that the manner of the night attempt was inconsistent with the idea of the English girls being the willing agents of Nazi intrigue.

It was rather in the spirit of efficient routine, than with expectation of any harvest to reap, that he determined to call himself upon the English visitors.

It was only a few minutes after Lawrence Norton's departure that Caresse's telephone rang again. Perdita, having been the more expeditious to gain the bathroom, had now yielded it to her more leisurely friend, and was better situated to take the call.

She found herself listening to the voice of the hotel manager himself. He said that Herr Schott was here. Should he come up, or would the ladies come down to him?

Perdita, feeling that she had had enough of bedroom invasions for one morning, and conscious of very scanty attire, was somewhat curt in reply. Caresse heard: "No, he certainly can't. No, we can't. I don't know who he is, but if he wants to see us, he'll have to wait. You can say half an hour. You say he's *what*? Well" (in a somewhat altered voice), "whoever he is, he'll have to wait."

She put the receiver down to silence the expostulating voice that came from below.

"Caresse," she called, to the half-opened bathroom door, "it's the Chief of Police now. He wants to come up at once."

"Is the door locked?"

"Yes. I suppose so. It locks itself, doesn't it?"

"And what happens if they stick keys in from the outside? You'd better put ours in, and make sure."

Perdita frowned for one puzzled moment, and then saw the value of the suggestion. Secure from the disconcerting possibility of a suddenly-opening door, they discussed the problematical purpose of this unexpected visit.

"It's probably nothing at all," Caresse said cheerfully. He's come to ask whether we had a good night."

"I don't suppose you're far wrong about that."

"If that's it, you'd better see him. You'd only have to tell him you didn't wake."

"I don't mind doing that. Don't you think we'd better ring up Lawrence again?"

"Not till we know what the trouble is. It's ten to one it's nothing at all."

"I wouldn't mind betting on that, and at worse odds. I think this is the liveliest place I was ever in. Shall I answer, or let them ring?"

"Tell them, if we can't get any peace, we shall expect it to be taken off the bill."

Perdita went back to the telephone. "Would you please—?" she began, and then: "Oh, Lawrence, I didn't guess it was you. Yes, thanks for letting us know. And, oh, I say, we've got the Head Policeman waiting downstairs. Yes, that's the name. What do you want us to say to him?"

There was a pause before the reply came: "Tell him you're not sure how long you'll be likely to stay."

"Is that what you think he'll be wanting to know?"

"What else can there be that concerns him?"

Perdita's mind was alert to understand the significance of the deliberate words, and of that which he was too discreet to say without knowing to whose ears it would go.

She answered, "Thanks. I expect that's about my limit. I never was much good at languages." She rang off promptly.

"Lawrence says there'll be some guests to meet us at the Legation tonight. He thought we might like to know. He thinks the less we say to the gentleman downstairs, the sooner he'll be likely to clear. I'll go down now, if you like."

"Well, he won't have so long to wait."

"If he carts me away to jail, you'll be able to let Lawrence know."

With the comforting knowledge that she had good friends at her rear, and a sense of peril too slight to give her more than a pleasant thrill, Perdita went down to interview the Chief of the Czech Police.

The manager, bowing guest and visitor into a private room, heard her say: "Mrs. Langton isn't up yet, so I thought—" as the door closed. He reflected that the lady who was not up had already received a member of the British Legation, and the head of the secret Nazi organisation, in the room which the Minister of Justice was not permitted to enter.

He had not mentioned these earlier visits to the latest caller, nor would he have admitted knowledge of the identity either of Herr Müller or Lawrence Norton. He knew that silence, and an apparent blindness, are the first qualifications for the successful management of an hotel in Eastern Europe, and he might have known less than he did, if he had said more. The Minister of Justice explained that he had called to assure himself of the comfort of the so-distinguished English ladies whose visit was an honour to Prague. Might he hope that they had not been alarmed by the most lamentable disturbance which had broken out in the street during the night?

He spoke in fluent French, his English not being equal to a prolonged conversational strain. Words and manner might suggest that it was his habit to visit the Prague hotels to convince himself of the comfort of foreign patrons.

"I didn't know much about it," Perdita answered; "I think it was nearly over before I waked."

There is no greater error than to suppose that those who are practised in falsehood are most competent to deceive. It might rather be said that the capacity for successful lying decreases with every time that its use is tried. Herr Schott had given Perdita no more than one comprehensive glance before deciding that she was no conscious instrument of Nazi intrigue. He listened to the misleading verity of her first reply, and he acquitted her, experienced in duplicity as he was, of all knowledge of the missing documents.

After a ten-minutes' talk, in the course of which he touched discreetly upon the events in the train as well as the disturbance during the night, he returned to the office of his administration foiled by Perdita's apparent frankness, and convinced that he must look in other directions if he were to succeed in a search the importance of which even he was very far from correctly estimating.

Perdita lingered for a few minutes at the hotel bookstall, purchasing English newspapers, and acquiring information as to the attractions of Prague, and then returned to inform Caresse of her easy victory.

She found her busily superintending the activities of a chambermaid whose services she had secured for the unpacking of one of her major trunks. Display of evening dresses made a gay litter on bed and couch. The minor irritations of life, and absurd suggestions of leaving a city which she had experienced some discomforts to reach, were forgotten in the more serious question of what she should wear at the Legation dinner.

"Gone, has he?" she said easily. "I thought you'd be able to settle him."

"They say," Perdita went on, "there's a Jewish cemetery here that's a thousand years old, and a cathedral with somebody's silver tomb, and a castle that—"

"There always is," Caresse answered carelessly. "There'll be time for them after we've finished the shops."

CHAPTER XX.

LAWRENCE lay down with a resolve that he must not allow himself more than five hours' rest, even though it might be necessary to be out again during the next night.

He could have done with fifteen hours, rather than five, and it may have been either the fear that he might sleep too long, or the excitements through which he had passed, that caused him to wake half an hour before it was time to rise.

He lay pondering the question of how he could attempt the rescue of No. 973, if he should have escaped the first pursuit, and the subsequent dangers of night and day, between speculations of whether the sudden crisis of quarrel between German and Czech, the acuteness of which only those who were on the spot seemed able to understand, would die down, as a dozen others had done before, leaving scars that were surface-healed, but without removal of the deep-rooted inflammation from which they sprang; or whether it would break on this occasion into the swift horror of such a war as would not be matched even in the blood-guilty records of men. And then his mind wandered backward among memories of his old tenderness for Caresse. He had thought that to be buried and cold until the moment when he had heard her voice—the old gay, imperious, plaintive, petulant voice—and the former tyranny had resumed its power.

Was there a time when he could have tempted her to a deeper folly than had been theirs? Or to join her own lot to his then more precarious future, rather than to Gerald Langton's established reputation and assured position?

They were both questions to which he found no certain reply. That was the baffling quality of Caresse. She was passionate, and yet cold. Seemingly impulsive in all she did, and yet wary of its results. Simply religious in her conscious beliefs, and subtly pagan in her unconscious codes.

It was her enigmatic attraction that you could be sure of nothing in act or mood. He could believe that she had faced the intruder coolly during the night, as easily as that she might fall to panic with lighter cause.

Did he regret that he had not been bolder, or less scrupulous, five years ago? Perhaps it would have been to the same end—to find that the last weak barrier had an impregnable strength.

He put resolutely aside a question which had passed the time of any useful reply, but it was pleasant to know that she was in Prague, and obviously willing to stay. He was inclined to admire his unselfishness in having urged her, for her own safety, to leave.

He thought less of Perdita. She had been a mere child when he had met her before. Yet he saw her as one who was little changed. She was the same, then as now, in her cool, fresh, confident youth. It seemed natural that she should be serenely equal to all that came. He was not self-conscious enough to give a thought to what she might think of him. Of the plans that those of an older generation might make, he was indifferent, or unaware.

Ought he to urge them again to go, in spite of what Sir Geoffrey had said? He was uncertain again, inclination and judgment falling in different scales. He wished that Perdita had not retained that last cryptic sheet. It seemed to put them both in a special jeopardy, apart from the general danger that lay in the threat of war. Perhaps he could judge better how to advise them when he had discovered the secret its cipher hid.

Rising with these thoughts, he went down to meet Sir Geoffrey, who burst out with: "Norton, I've just rung those girls up, and told them to come here to stay while they're in Prague."

"Thank you, sir. Did they say they would?"

"I spoke to Mrs. Langton first, and she didn't seem able to make up her mind. Said she'd just unpacked, or some rubbish, and then the other one, Miss—yes, Wyatt—came on, and she said they'd be glad to. Pleasant voice that girl's got. If she's all *en suite*—"

Lawrence assured him that there would be no disappointment to fear, and Sir Geoffrey went on: "I've ordered dinner in my own room, as it's a small informal affair. We'll do better for them before they leave. You'll dine with us, of course. And I've asked the Jandas. And I was going to ask—but Monsieur Flambert rang up, and I thought he wanted a talk, so I've told him to come, and bring Madame along. If I have to take him away after dinner—well, they're your guests rather than mine. I think Flambert's worrying over this last incident more than he need. France doesn't want any complications in Europe now, with Algeria giving her the trouble it is. He thinks it's a case where the Czechs ought to toe the line. But it's time for you to be getting off. I told Williams to have the Bentley ready for you to fetch them up. They'll like a good car better than that old ruin of yours."

Lawrence thanked him, and hurried off to have a word with Richard Cunningham, the Legation archivist, before leaving.

He found him seated at a desk in his own room, with the cipher sheet before him, and a litter of papers covered with diagrams and calculations.

"I've had five hours," he said, "at this damned conundrum you brought me."

"And no progress?"

"That's how I feel. But, of course, it's not quite correct. I've eliminated whole classes of ciphers that it can't possibly be, and that narrows the field. You know, it's said that there's no cipher that can't be read if it be attacked in a patient systematic way."

"So I've heard. It isn't a truth I'm ever likely to prove. But I hope you won't fail; for I've got a feeling that it may be something rather urgent to know."

"Yes? They mostly turn out the other way. You'll be in luck if it's worth half the trouble it's cost already. But I don't like to drop it, having taken it on."

"No, I don't suppose you'll do that," Lawrence said comfortably. He went out to the waiting car.

CHAPTER XXI.

PRIVATE GUMPERT had risen as soon as he could be sure that he was no longer observed. He left the room in which the airmen's meal had been served for the main cavern in which the bombers were ranged, and here he strolled idly about, among men who were too busy to give much notice to him, explaining his presence at times in an easy, casual way, but otherwise content to keep his eyes alert and his tongue still.

When he had seen all that he would, he climbed into the cockpit of an aeroplane where he was likely to be left undisturbed, and thinking that, if he were found, he might not be blamed for having chosen it as a place of rest.

It was so placed that he could settle himself in a position to see when the great doors should be open again, which he supposed might be when dawn should come to the outer world, for he considered that, when that should occur, he could not be too quick to depart.

For the night, he thought that his worst dangers were passed; and if he were once clear of those sliding doors, he had some confidence in himself that he would not be easy to catch.

He felt that he had discovered most, if not all, that was to be learned either from observation of that subterranean cavern, or conversation with those it held. His first duty now was to find his way safely back, to convey the knowledge that he had so perilously obtained.

He had seen that the cavern contained a vast central chamber in which two hundred of the Zeus night-bombers were ranged; those which had arrived during the night completing the number, and being the only ones that lay, like gigantic moths, with extended wings. The wings of the others were folded in such a way that the space they occupied was largely reduced.

He saw that the aerodrome was designed to enable the bombers to be sent out in a rapid orderly way, overcoming, as far as possible, the disadvantage that such hidden caverns could not wholly avoid— that a large fleet could not take the air in an instant flight.

The exit here was sufficiently broad for two of the bombers to pass out, side by side, with extended wings, and was so designed that they would have gained some speed before they would emerge to the outer platform. The great steel sliding doors were too deeply recessed in the hillside to be bombed from above. When they opened, quick-firing artillery within the cavern converged upon the entrance Doubtless, there were concealed anti-aircraft batteries without, to resist attack from the upper air.

Within, men swarmed round the planes like attendant ants, filling their tanks, loading them with their hellish cargoes of bombs, overhauling them in every detail, that they might be ready, on instant order, to take the skies.

In the deep cavern, crouching with indrawn wings, like rows of fantastic beetles under the arc-lamps' glare, it might be thought that they still lay in the infernal matrix of the demons who had devised them for the undoing of men—of men whose folly must be the constant laughter of hell.

No. 973 did not consider them thus, having more urgent thoughts at this time. Yet a similar metaphor came to his mind, as he recalled how he had once destroyed a nest of wasps when he had choked its hole with a burning rag. Wasp by wasp, it would have been futile to chase them down. If there were to be hope for the human race (or for its present civilisation, which may be a much smaller thing), it might lie in the possibility of destroying these evil nests before the stinging insects could rise. Thinking thus, and considering the possible significance of the activity which prevailed around him, he saw the weight of responsibility which was his, that he should not fail in ingenuity to escape, and to bear the tale.

If he could be successful in that, it would still be true that he could tell only of one, it might be out of a score of such dens of death: true also that the information might lead to no action which would prevent the issue of those two hundred bombers to their merciless goal. But such questions troubled his mind the less because they were beyond his responsibility and control. It was his part to discover, and to report, and it was in that that he must not fail. He became aware that the steel doors were moving apart, and that the cavern was invaded by the colder, more penetrating light of the winter day.

He made his way briskly to the entrance, as it would be natural for Private Gumpert to do. He anticipated no difficulty in leaving the aerodrome, or, at the most, none that he could not overcome by reference to the officer to whom he had reported when he came in. He supposed that his difficulty would be in escaping over the frozen hills, and through the sentries whom he knew to make a circle round the reputed mine.

His confidence was not lessened when he saw that the same officer was on duty about the doors, but when he would have passed him with a silent salute, he was stopped by a sharp command.

"You are Eugene Gumpert? You must not go yet. You are required to give an account of what you saw during the night. Report to Room 23."

Room 23 was one of a row of small chambers hewn out of the wall along the side of the main cavern. Still not greatly concerned with what might be no more than a routine of enquiry as to the alarm of spies during the night, he entered the narrow door to face the cold eyes of a colonel of military police, and to become aware that he was in the midst of an armed guard, which closed upon him from either side, with a significance which was very easy to guess.

"Disarm him."

He submitted quietly, for it would have been folly to resist. He did not even protest, preferring silence till he should know more of the peril in which he stood.

"Search him."

That, at least, was an ordeal he had no reason to fear. Eugene Gumpert's meagre possessions were laid out on the deal table which separated him from the seated officer, and he was content to see that they gave their silent support to the identity of the German infantryman he professed to be.

Colonel Wieck looked at him with a slight puzzled frown, but with no diminution of the hostility of very sceptical eyes.

He asked curtly: "Who do you say you are?"

"Eugene Gumpert, sir."

"Anyone else?"

The sarcastic question did not wait for a reply. The colonel went on: "Eugene Gumpert's body was found two hours ago."

The eyes of the two men met, but those of No. 973 did not flinch, nor did he appear disconcerted by the implication the statement bore. He said simply: "I suppose he was dead?"

The Colonel stared at an effrontery he had not expected to meet. He asked: "Having been killed by you?"

"It was a necessity which I much regret."

"You will have cause for that in the next hour. Will you say how you came here?"

"I would prefer not."

"Listen, spy. You will be shot when this order is signed." He looked down on a paper beneath his hand. "It is a fate which you will not hope to avoid. But, if you will, you may communicate with your friends. You may have any priest that you will. You may have an hour to compose your soul. Or you may be shot within three minutes from now.

"If you prefer some delay, you will tell me of what nation you are, and what purpose has brought you here."

"It is what I am anxious to do."

Colonel Wieck regarded his prisoner with a more puzzled look than before. He had a keen, hard face, of somewhat Jewish cast, which suggested that he must have had exceptional influence or good fortune to have held his post when the most of that unfortunate race were exiled five years before.

He was a man who dealt straightly, though it might be in a merciless way. It seemed to him that the captured spy was less perturbed than it was natural for him to be. If he thought that he could buy his life by any confession he would be likely to make, he must be disillusioned thereon. There must be many who would know that spies had been in their midst, and who would know or guess that Eugene Gumpert had died by their hands. It must not be supposed that there could be mercy for such as he. They must be assembled to see him die.

"You make," he said, "a wise choice. You are a man who has almost done with this world, and you must buy what you yet can with the only coin that is current here. But it must be clear that you will have nothing further to hope, either of favour or of delay."

"It will be for you to decide."

Colonel Wieck picked up a pen. He drew a sheet of paper from a drawer of the table. He asked curtly: "Your name?"

"Adolph Zweiss."

"Nationality?"

"German."

Colonel Wieck looked up sharply. "It will be useless to lie. From where did you come here?"

"Prague."

"Where you are known by that name?"

"No. When I am in Prague, I am an Englishman—Richard Steele."

"Is that where you live?"

"I have lived there for some months."

"Before that?"

"For several years in Berlin."

"As Adolph Zweiss?"

"No. It is nineteen years since I used that name. It was too well known "

The Colonel raised his eyes again from the paper on which he wrote. He stared harder than before. Recollections stirred in his mind. After the Great War—he had been a young subaltern in its last year—the name of Adolph Zweiss had become famous throughout Germany as a secret service agent whose exploits in Italy and France had been almost miraculous in their successful audacities, and momentous in their results. But it was an absurd thought. Contempt came back to his voice as he asked: "Do you ask me to believe that you are a German spy?"

"I would tell you more, if there were fewer to hear."

"I am not one to be fooled. You can give me a straight tale, or I send you out to an instant death."

"What I have told you is true. I will tell you more if you will. It is for you to decide."

Colonel Wieck looked at his prisoner. He thought it likely that the man had some wild idea that he might escape if the guard retired. He did not believe what he had heard, but he was anxious to learn who the spy might be, and from whom he came. He was not a coward, and he was the larger and probably the stronger man.

He said: "Bind his hands."

When this had been done, he laid a pistol upon the table before him. He said: "Stand back to the wall." When the man in Eugene Gumpert's uniform was three yards away, he ordered the guard to withdraw to the other side of the door.

When they had gone, he said: "You can talk now. You will do well for yourself to avoid lies. I am hard to cheat. You must also be brief, for I have larger matters with which to deal."

"I have told you the fact. I was a German spy in the last war. As to what I did then, I suppose the record remains. After that, I was made the subject of public talk. I became known. It was needful to lose myself, if I were to be of aid to Germany in the next war. That is what I think I have done."

"As the spy of a foreign Power?"

"What could be better than that? When the next war comes, I shall be an officer in the secret service of England. I may say that there are few whom they trust more. It is as their agent that I have lived secretly in Berlin during recent years. You will see how I can serve Germany thus."

"What of the man you have killed?"

"There is an English proverb that those who would make omelettes must not scruple at the breaking of eggs."

"But to kill one of your own blood?"

"I was ordered to come here. I had to do that, or to lose all the work of the last nineteen years. I should have told them little they could not have known in another way. What is the death of one man? There may be millions dead at the year's end. I have learnt to be thorough in all I do. It is the one way to success."

"I do not believe a word."

"Yet it is true. It may not be beyond easy proof."

"There we agree."

Colonel Wieck called the guard. He said: "Keep this man. It is your lives against his. If he escapes, I will have no mercy, nor heed excuse. He is to be shot at midday."

He telephoned to Berlin, and was told that he would be answered within an hour.

In less time than that, he received a telegram:

ADOLPH ZWEISS DISAPPEARED MAY 1919 IF SLIGHTEST DOUBT DO NOT EXECUTE BUT SEND THE MAN HERE FOR IDENTIFICATION.

Colonel Wieck read it somewhat sourly. "For this hour," he thought, "it seems he has saved his skin."

But it was no more than a few minutes later that a second telegram came:

ADOLPH ZWEISS BIRTHMARK ON RIGHT LOIN SMALL SCAR UNDER CHIN BLACK MOLE ON LEFT SHOULDER-BLADE THESE MARKS CERTAIN IDENTIFICATION ON WHICH RELEASE OR EXECUTE.

He smiled grimly as he ordered that the prisoner should be brought before him again.

CHAPTER XXII.

COLONEL WIECK had the two telegrams under his hand, and he surveyed his prisoner with sardonic eyes. Having obtained that which would prove the truth beyond further doubt, and having already dismissed that doubt from his own mind, he was disposed to make sport of one whom he supposed to have played with him.

"I have referred your case," he said, "to Berlin. They have wired me that you are to be sent for identification there."

He had thought to see the relief of fate postponed on his victim's face as he said this, which he would destroy with his next word. But he saw no change, or rather it seemed to the keenness with which he watched that there was a trace of annoyance, as though the news were less good than the impersonator of Adolph Zweiss had been hoping to hear. If it puzzled him, it no less confirmed his assurance that it was imposture with which he dealt.

He went on slowly, lifting the second telegram from his desk: "But I have further instructions, by which the enquiry is left to me."

He rose, and crossed the room to where the prisoner stood, with his hands still bound, between watchful guards.

"Adolph Zweiss," he said sharply, with a sarcastic inflection upon the name, "lift your chin."

The prisoner raised his head so that his throat showed. Close under the jawbone, Colonel Wieck saw that there was a small scar.

It was not much, and scars are common among those who make a business of war. Yet it was something he had not expected to see. He asked, touching the spot with a stretched finger: "How long have you had that?"

No. 973 looked slightly surprised. He answered: "It was while I was still in the army, before Verdun. It was no more than a bruise from a pebble that leapt where a bullet struck. I did not know that it showed. I was transferred to the secret service a few weeks later."

Colonel Wieck was shaken by this, but he reminded himself that there is nothing singular in a scarred chin; also, a man may make his own scars. He said: "Loose his hands. I would have him strip."

A minute later his manner changed. He had seen a black mole where he had been told that it ought to be. There was no doubt that it was a genuine mole. He had tested that with a rough thumb. His imagination was unequal to guess the truth, that a mole may be grafted on by the device of one who is farseeing, and very thorough in all he does. And his instructions were clear.

"Comrade," he said, "I have been instructed to sign an order for your release, which it will be much pleasure to do. You will forgive the usage of war. In sign of which, will you dine with me before you go?"

Adolph Zweiss (as he had become for the present hour) did not refuse, but he was not gracious in his reply.

"If I accept, we shall dine alone? You have put me already in more peril than I prefer."

Colonel Wieck looked the offence he felt. He considered the most famous of spies to be of less rank than his own. He had done no more than his duty was, and it might even be said that he had saved a forfeited life when he had referred to Berlin, which some officers in his place might have been less active to do. At the worst, the invitation he now gave was a condescension, making ample amends. It should have been received in a different way.

Adolph Zweiss saw that his reply was not understood. He added: "I did not mean you had put me in peril here. But if a British agent had overseen—. We do not know where they may be. It would not only be to risk my life when I return. It would be the work of nineteen years lost in an hour. If we dine together, I would not have it a tale that a score could tell. As it is, I may have to make a false tale of how I contrive escape, which it is a danger to do."

The Colonel took these words in a better way, seeing reason upon their side. With a doubtful logic, they served also to turn his mind from a suspicion that he might still have perceived. For who could say that Adolph Zweiss had not become a British agent in truth? It might be a treason to his own race which would be hard to believe, but such desertions are not unknown, and the circumstances under which he had been caught required some hardihood of explanation to bear them through.

CHAPTER XXIII.

THE city of Prague (as its ruins show) lay on both sides of the Moldau river, the larger half on the more level ground of the eastern bank. On this side was the city's central life, its railway station, its theatres, its hotels, its commercial quarters. It was a most ancient city, its origin going back beyond the written records of men. It had some broad and beautiful streets, and others, in its older wards, which were narrow and highly built, and so tortuous that it had become a common device to connect them by foot-passages through or under the houses, making it a difficult city for the unguided stranger to traverse, except with much crookedness and delay, and a most convenient one for those who were more concerned to avoid than obey the law.

The river's western bank rose steeply in two hills, one of which was crowned by an ancient cathedral and palace, and by the government buildings which had been newly planned to accord with the dignity of a sovereign state.

There were many old buildings upon these hills, of ancient beauty and size and strength, among which the palace of the Counts of Thun, which the British Government had purchased for its Legation, was not least, either in dignity or extent.

It lay immediately under the wall of the ancient castle, its first-floor windows opening to a wide stretch of park-like garden, and to a noble terrace looking across the river and over the city of Prague. The ground fell so sharply away that there was a steep upward approach to the main entrance, the heavy gates of which were of the solid strength that a fortress needs, and themselves at a level fifteen feet below that of the terrace and garden grounds.

The evening was fine, and the streets had been cleared of snow, as Lawrence drove his guests rapidly through the city and over the Charles Bridge. The sky was brilliant with stars: the streets sparkled with frost. There was exhilaration in the cold still air.

In the atmosphere of Caresse's gay, inconsequent chatter, and the quieter happiness of the younger girl, it was easy to forget that the nations of Eastern Europe, restless as kennelled hounds, were perpetually alert either for a chance to fix their fangs in a neighbour's throat, or lest those of another should close on their own loins. The sinister shadow of war faded to the unreality of a dream. Had not the skies of Europe been black for the past three years with tempests that never broke?

The perilous experiences of the last night, and the question of what might be attempted for the rescue of No. 973 during that which was now coming, had the atmosphere of adventure, the excitement of which obscured the gravity of the issues through which they came. He had even put the responsibility of what he could attempt for his friend's rescue out of his mind since he had known that the Czechoslovak Air Minister would be at the dinner that night.

He knew that, if there were anyone who had Steele's confidence, it was Janda to whom it was given. Janda, also, would be best able to appreciate the nature of the peril in which he lay, and the possibility of attempting his rescue by air; and he was the only one who could supply the means for such an attempt. Lawrence found it easy to put the whole matter aside until he should have the opportunity of discussion which the evening would be likely to bring.

He had been delayed for some time at the hotel, his guests having been unready when he arrived, for which the blame lay with Caresse, who had objected to the acceptance of the invitation that Sir Geoffrey had given.

A confusion of impulses, unanalysed in her own mind, had disinclined her to accept an invitation which she erroneously supposed to have originated with Lawrence Norton, and to have been addressed primarily to herself. To Perdita she seemed perverse, as she often would. She knew that Caresse had no habit of giving logical reasons for the preferences on which she acted. But she knew also that, though they might often have the appearance of being no more than petulant whims, the reasons, cool and solid by Caresse's standards of life and conduct, would still be there.

Usually, Perdita would give way with no more than a smile, or a comprehending word; but, in this instance, she had opposed the perversity of her friend's decision with an equal obstinacy.

She had faced the events of the last twenty-four hours without allowing them to disturb her outward serenity, or stir her pulses above the pace of excitement which is pleasant to the spirit of youth. But she was not therefore blind to their implications, nor anxious to face again either Herr Müller or the Minister of Justice, with the knowledge of that cipher sheet which she had given to Lawrence's charge, and which she correctly guessed that both of them would be pleased to have.

She felt disposed for a quiet night, and was sound in judgment that it was most likely to be found within the Legation walls.

Caresse said: "When we've just unpacked everything!"

"I'm quite willing to pack, if you want to rest."

"There wouldn't be time before you ought to begin dressing."

"I'll have it done in an hour."

"I've told the manager that we'll be here for at least a week."

"Well, I'll tell him we won't. I daresay he'll stand the shock."

"We ought to know our own minds."

"Lawrence doesn't want us to stay at all."

"Do you think we're going to listen to that nonsense?"

"If we were at the Legation, he might be more willing for us to stay."

"We'd better say we'll come back tonight, and talk it over tomorrow."

"It would be more sense to say we'll stay there tonight, and talk over what we'll do after."

"But there's no time to pack now. Can't you see that?"

"We needn't take much for one night."

So they compromised at the last, after loss of time which left less than enough for the limited preparations that were required for a single night, and so it happened that the other guests of the evening—the French Envoy, Monsieur Flambert, and his wife, and Janda, with "that pert little Hungarian" he had married three months before—arrived earlier, and Sir Geoffrey withdrew Flambert aside from the drawing-room to his adjoining study, for the talk he had asked to have.

Monsieur Flambert was a short man, faintly rotund, with a small white beard trimmed to a point, and eyebrows that were still black over shrewd, lively eyes of the same colour. There was mutual confidence and respect between Sir Geoffrey and himself, as may often be with men of contrary dispositions, and they had done much, working together during the past year, to maintain peace in this troubled centre of European intrigue.

"My dear Sir Geoffrey," he said, drawing his chair close, which was a habit he had, and speaking in a voice so modulated as to give an impression of confidence, though there could have been no one to overhear, "I thought it well to take counsel with you, for I had a talk this morning with the President, and with some of his Ministers who were there, and I heard the words of some foolish men."

Sir Geoffrey was not impressed. "Why," he asked, "what did you expect? They will boast and grumble among themselves, and in the end they will give way, as the weaker must, if they get no backing from you."

"They will get none. I told them that in a blunt way. France will have no danger of war at this time—not to save the lives of all the plotters in Prague. I was plain on that, but I am not sure that they will give way."

"They cannot believe that France will fail in support, if Germany press them too hard?"

"They are difficult to convince. Nor will they admit the strength of the case she has."

"You think her case good?"

"I think she has much cause to complain, and particularly so in regard to the recent plot."

"So I agree; but I have seen the boot at times on the other leg."

Monsieur Flambert hesitated for a second over a metaphor which he had not met with before, storing it in an orderly mind, as he replied: "So have I. But it is not the hour to remember now."

"What do you ask me to do?"

"I ask you to urge on the German Envoy here, as I know that your Ambassador does at Berlin, that they shall make the path of satisfaction easy to tread."

"That was what I already meant. England desires peace, as you know. I will ask that; and you, on your side, will urge that satisfaction be not denied. But, my dear Flambert, which of us should you say will talk to the deafer ears?"

The French Envoy lifted his shoulders slightly as he replied: "What would you have? It is not the disease, it is but the symptoms with which we deal. It is not that Prague has a love for Communists which is of uncontrollable strength. And to be a foe to Nazis is not to be friend to her. But we must allow that it may have a very similar sound. Berlin may ask no more than a friend should be quick to do, but does she ask with a friend's voice?"

Sir Geoffrey said heartily that he would do all that he could. He had little doubt that the trouble could be composed, as had been a dozen before, but Monsieur Flambert was right when he said that they dealt with symptoms alone, leaving the disease to go on in its own way.

He saw also that the fact that France was anxious for peace, having her hands full in Syria and Algiers, was not an argument to hold Germany back.

They were interrupted by an announcement that dinner was served.

CHAPTER XXIV.

THEY were seated at a small round table, suited to the number of guests. Sir Geoffrey had Madame Flambert on his right hand and Caresse on his other side. Beyond Caresse were Monsieur Flambert and the Hungarian bride. Lawrence Norton, Perdita, and Janda completed the circle.

The table was not so large that conversation must be confined to immediate neighbours on either side, and Perdita, content to listen and observe and leave the talking to other tongues, was not resentful that Lawrence's head was turned most often away from herself in conversation with Mme. Janda, or farther away to where Caresse was dividing attention between himself and in chatter with the French Envoy in the fluent French that was the tongue of her mother's land.

Perdita knew Caresse to be Lawrence's friend, as she was hers also. She was married to Gerald Langton, whom there was reason to think she loved. It was natural that she and Lawrence should find topics for ready talk.

Perdita was content to observe and learn. Lawrence had been a girlhood's hero to her four years before. She did not see him now as less than her dreams. She still thought him one whom it might be easy to love, but that was surely too strong a word for any emotion that stirred her now. She looked at him with cool, quiet, friendly eyes, seeking to read what he had become through the changes of the last four years.

So far, she had found him to be one who made appointments he did not keep, and spent his nights in a sleepless way which he did not explain. Yet she felt instinctively that he was one she could trust at any critical need. It was of other qualities she was less sure. Of the difficult loyalties of routine: of the affinities that....

A clerk had entered the room, and was handing a slip of paper to Sir Geoffrey, which he read with an expressionless face. He looked round the table to say: "Will you excuse me a moment?" and then: "Lawrence, will you come with me?"

They went out together, and a moment later the Air Minister was summoned in the same way, so that M. Flambert found himself left alone to the task of entertaining the four ladies, which he was quite equal to do.

In Sir Geoffrey's room, the three men debated a decoded telegram, handed in at the post-office of an obscure Bavarian village:

DO NOT COME RETURNING SAFELY.

The Air Minister regarded it with satisfaction, but without surprise. "I knew," he said, "that Steele would fall on his feet."

Lawrence said: "We don't feel equally satisfied."

"You think it queer that he should be wiring at all? So do I. But I suppose that he wanted to save you from going back and getting into a mess."

"It isn't that," Sir Geoffrey explained. "The telegram was in a code that we gave up using six months ago because the German Secret Service had found it out."

CHAPTER XXV.

M. FLAMBERT glanced round at the four ladies who were his remaining table companions. His mind was sharply intrigued as to the nature of the incident which could have required immediate consultation between Sir Geoffrey Cullender, his secretary, and the Czechoslovak Air Minister, to his own exclusion.

He knew that Sir Geoffrey was not one to fuss over matters of small account, and that he would be likely to be more concerned over any appearance of discourtesy to his guests than the continued existence of Eastern Europe. M. Flambert would have been better pleased to make a fourth at the consultation which must be going on at the other end of the suite of rooms, but there was no sign of such thoughts in the smiling satisfaction with which he said: "I have the good fortune to be allowed to remain."

He spoke in English, the language in which the general conversation had been maintained, both in courtesy to Sir Geoffrey's guests, and to the table at which they sat. It was one which he could speak with entire ease. Mme. Flambert followed it with occasional difficulty, and lacked confidence in its use. Mme. Janda was bolder, if not more proficient; but the general effect of the withdrawals which had occurred was that the conversation must be sustained by the French Envoy and the English visitors.

Caresse, at his right hand, gave him provocative eyes. She would be discreet, except in her lighter moods, with those of her own age; but she would always flirt with elderly men, if they were of a manner which she approved.

"But that," she said, "is just what we are told that we must not do. Do you also wish us to leave Prague?"

"Surely no," he replied. "It would be cruel beyond belief to do that, when you have scarcely arrived."

His words were as light as hers, but his brain, behind smiling eyes, was cool and alert to the implications of what he heard. It gave him an added sense of the gravity with which the position must be viewed from the English side. But his instructions were that peace must be preserved at whatever cost, and he must therefore deprecate any word or act which would encourage alarm.

Perdita was blunt in explanation: "They seem to think that there's a war hanging about, and we should get in the way."

M. Flambert lifted his eyebrows in amused expostulation: "My dear young lady! There is always a war here that will come in the next week. That has been the safeguard of peace for the last three years. They are the expected wars that do not arrive."

Mme. Flambert, a plump, elderly lady, with a reputation for good-humoured dullness of which she was well aware, and may have actually cultivated, was quick to see that her husband did not wish them to go, and supported him, as her habit was, without concern to understand the reasons of what he did.

"There is the Red Cross Ball," she said, "at the Castle tomorrow night, which you must not miss. It is the event of the year."

As she spoke, the three men returned to the room. Sir Geoffrey apologised, but did not explain, beyond saying: "It was a small matter of a rather puzzling kind, but it was not one in which anything could be done."

In fact, they had decided that the telegram must be genuine, in spite of its obsolete code. For, had it been of another kind, would it not have been so worded as to decoy No. 973's friends to a waiting trap? To tell them that there could be no need to come to his aid—. No, there could be no duplicity there. And, as Janda had pointed out, to fly a rescuing plane into the Bavarian hills so secretly that it would not be observed by its watchful foes, and yet so that Steele would have come to it, or been found in the short hours of the night, was not an enterprise that could have held much hope of success.

Caresse paused for no second more than courtesy to her host required. Here was something of real importance, of which she might not have heard had there been no woman present who could assess values in a sane way. As Sir Geoffrey's brief words of explanatory apology ceased, she asked: "A Red Cross Ball? We had not heard about that. Of course, we are not going to leave. Is it a public affair?"

"It is charity. No, it is by invitation. But you will be asked, of course. Mme. Janda—will you not, Zita?—will care of that. It is held each year in the Great Hall of the Castle. It is still unfurnished, but has been restored. It is too vast for any but a most public affair."

Zita Janda said: "Oh, but yes! It is I—I am glad to do." She gave Caresse a quick smile, showing white teeth between lips vivid with natural colour.

Their words strove against a cross-current of talk of another kind, for Perdita had said to Lawrence, as he resumed his seat at her side: "Monsieur Flambert does not agree with your anxiety to send us away."

Lawrence said: "No?" in the voice of one whose mind was on other things. He thought that the Frenchman might alter his opinion if he knew what their experiences had been since they had crossed the frontier, little more than twenty-four hours before; and then wondered whether he might not have been told already. What indiscretions of speech might there not have been during the few minutes that they had been out of the room? He recovered himself to say: "Of course, I don't want you to go. But it isn't my advice on which you have to depend. There's Mr. Langton's telegram."

"I don't think Caresse means to go, even for that."

"She won't take it seriously?"

"Not very. She's more interested in other things."

"And you?"

"I don't understand. You can't say you've been very fluent in explanation. But I'd much rather stay, if you mean that."

Sir Geoffrey caught the last words, more clearly spoken than the halting accents of Zita Janda's reply. He said: "Stay? Of course you'll stay, now that you're here. Langton always was fussy. It's no good worrying over what's going to happen. You always find that it never does."

He tried to turn the conversation with an anecdote of a man (he said) he had known, who consulted two doctors regularly, lest one or other should be ill at a time of his own need. He said he had made the man quite miserable by pointing out how rash he was to have only two. Suppose an epidemic of influenza— Probably he had three now.

But the shadow of the thought of war seemed to be over the table in a manner that would not lift, although at least five of the eight who were seated there were only anxious to let it die. It was Zita Janda who gave it new life now, by a question she asked Caresse, which might have led to a full disclosure of the adventures of the last hours, such as would have been indiscreet, even in that circle of seeming friendliness, had not M. Flambert been adroit to turn it aside, without knowing how much he did.

He helped Mme. Janda over some difficulty of English idiom, and went on to a pauseless talk in which he became absorbed in his own philosophy of the causes of war.

The modern objection to war, he propounded, was not that it was immoral, but that it was uncomfortable. Comfort was the most potent of the new gods that were leading men—surely not one that would lead to glory, nor—it might be hoped—to the grave. Having abandoned Liberty for Comfort, was it not an even more reasonable proposition to abandon War?

He might have said more, having intrigued himself in his own speculations, but he looked round his audience, and was aware that (unless Perdita, of whom he was unsure) there was no one there who gave him more attention than the obligations of politeness required.

If he had succeeded, it was by making war a dull subject on which to talk.

As his voice paused, Mme. Flambert came to his aid in a surer way. She addressed Caresse, to give an account of the dance of a year ago.

CHAPTER XXVI.

No. 973, or Adolph Zweiss as he now was, sat with Colonel Wieck at the meal which he had been asked to share. They were alone, except only when the dishes were changed by the Colonel's servant, who would then discreetly withdraw.

The Colonel was not an officer of the Regular Army, but of the Military Police, in which capacity he had control of the arrangements by which the secrecy of the subterranean aerodrome was maintained, both in its immediate surroundings and in the valley below.

Adolph Zweiss did not suppose him to be in the inner counsels of the German Government, but he might have knowledge from which important inferences could be drawn.

His doubt was whether he could be induced to talk freely to one whom he had regarded before as a foreign spy, and now knew to be in the employment of the British Intelligence Department, even though it might be agreed that he was a traitor to them.

On his side, Colonel Wieck had given the invitation with more reason than to make amends for the rough usage of the earlier day. He supposed that one who was German at heart would give him all the information he could, including the means by which he had arrived, and how he would have left, if suspicion had not fallen upon him.

Foreseeing the ordeal which must be met, No. 973 decided to let the Colonel dispose of whatever might be in his own mind, before attempting to obtain what he hoped might be more important information from him.

He answered the expected questions with apparent candour, and an actual disclosure of more than he would have yielded to bribe or threat under the accusation of being an English spy, justifying this to himself by no more than a logical application of the argument he had used to defend his previous actions on the assumption that he was a German agent. The illusion must be maintained, even at the cost of some minor betrayals.

He therefore described his arrival, and how he had been left behind, with little deviation from fact, at which Colonel Wieck was quick to ask: "And they will return to fetch you away?"

"It is possible they may attempt that."

There was a gleam of grim anticipation in the Colonel's eyes as he said: "Then we shall catch those whom we cannot mistake."

Adolph Zweiss did not dispute that. For a moment, his face reflected his companion's satisfaction at the idea, but then it gloomed to a doubt.

"Yes," he said, "so you may, if you do not think you will buy them too dear. You may catch an air-pilot, or perhaps two, but you will make it unsafe for me to return. It is what I told you before. We may wreck the pretence I have been building for nineteen years, if we are not careful what we do now."

"But, my dear Zweiss! Would you have them look round, and fly safely off?"

"Not at all. They might see too much. I must get a message through which I will warn them to keep away."

Colonel Wieck accepted this, though with a sour look. He asked: "How shall you tell them that you escaped?"

"I shall tell little but truth, for to do that is the hardest lesson that those of our trade must learn. A lie may look like a new shoe as you draw it on, but it soon pinches the feet. The truth may be leaky, and somewhat patched, but it is more comfort to wear. I shall tell them that I used my recent residence in Berlin, and other knowledge I have, to persuade you that I am an officer in your own service.

"I shall say I do not think you were quite convinced, and I found that, while you tried to keep me at ease you had referred to Berlin for proofs; but before they had arrived, I had slipped away."

The Colonel approved the wisdom of this, and No. 973 went on: "I shall have to tell them some things I have learnt from you, and I shall not wish either to make such a report as will draw suspicion upon myself, or to tell anything which would do Germany harm. You should be careful to tell me nothing you do not wish England to know, so that I cannot make a mistake. Yet I should like something, at least, to be true, such as would seem of value, and have a genuine sound."

His auditor thought this to be reasonable also. He considered what information of the kind he could give. He said: "Last Tuesday night, a large force of night-bombers and fighting planes—you may say more than five hundred—were secretly flown southward from the Baltic coast to the Sakrow aerodrome, near Berlin."

"That is true, and it will do our country no harm for it to be told?"

"None at all, for it was known to the French Embassy at Berlin on the following day, through a foreign spy."

"Whose activities have now ceased?"

"It is a safe guess."

"That will be fact enough. What else should you like me to say?"

"You can say that you have learnt that it was no more than a practice movement, to discover how swiftly and secretly it could be done. You can say also, regarding this aerodrome, that you have learnt that it was an experiment of last year, but that the idea was not further developed, as the difficulties of entrance and exit were considered to outweigh any advantages it might otherwise have. That is why it is used only for bombers of an obsolete type, and these are not flown, so that they fall out of condition. But when it is felt that the peace of Europe is so assured that men can be spared from the active aerodromes for a time, they are transferred here, to refurbish the planes."

Adolph said that that was enough to add to that which he had seen with his own eyes, and which he would use in a discreet way.

He rose to go.

He said: "If you will give me a start of not less than half a mile, I will ask no further favour than that. I will find my own way back, as a man who had so escaped would have no choice but to do. Indeed, if you will order your men to send a few bullets upon my track, I shall be obliged."

"So I will; but you will prefer that I tell them not to take too careful an aim?"

"Not at all. At that distance you can tell them to aim at me with special care. For it is that at which they aim that they will be most certain to miss."

So it was done, even to the spatter of harmless bullets as a trudging man showed for a moment, a dark speck on the snow of a distant ridge.

Eugene Gumpert (as he had become again till Bavaria should be left behind) walked on till he came to a little village among the hills. Here he stopped to send the telegram of which we have heard before. He used the old code, so that, if it were examined, the German police could read it, and observe that it was in accordance with what he had expressed his intention of saying, and also that he might deny knowledge of the newer code, if he should be detained and questioned again.

"They will be puzzled," he thought, "in Prague, but what matter for that? They will decide at last that there is nothing that they can do, which is how I wish it to be."

CHAPTER XXVII.

CARESSE stood with Lawrence on the Legation terrace that overlooked the river and the city of Prague.

The sky was clear, the moon high and cold, the air still; the scene sparkled with frost.

Behind them rose the long-deserted castle, now stirred to reviving life with the new freedom that Prague had won, and the yet older cathedral, pointing its incongruous towers to the frosty stars.

She said: "How beautiful! But how cold." She drew the white furs more closely around her throat. She was not insensitive to the beauty of what she saw, but she was more aware and content with that which her presence gave. She had not asked to be shown the moonlit terrace that she might admire the midnight beauties of Prague. She had a request to make to which she had been leading for the last hour, while Perdita had been occupied at the bridge-table with the Jandas and Mme. Flambert, and Sir Geoffrey had made excuse to draw the French Envoy aside to another room.

Gerald was pressing her to return to England again, and she was resolved that she would not go. But it was not a simple matter to be ignored, if Lawrence should throw his weight in the same scale, as he was showing a disposition to do.

Suppose that Gerald should write to Perdita's mother, asking her to summon her back? Caresse saw that she might be caught in a net that she could not break, if she should meet the event with no more than a passive front. And all for a scare that both Sir Geoffrey and M. Flambert said was too silly for words!

She was resolved that Gerald should have a reassuring telegram, which, coming from those on the spot, must outweigh whatever rumours of trouble had reached his ears. But not from Lawrence. She recalled her thought that personal jealousy might have prompted Gerald's first desire that she should not start.

She saw now that it must have had some other basis than that, yet the doubt was not wholly dead. The telegram must not appear to spring from Lawrence's desire that she should not leave. It must be from Sir Geoffrey himself.

And she felt assured that it was a request that he would not refuse, if it were made through Lawrence, and it were clear that it was her own wish.

Subtly, also, she regarded the idea as a means of re-establishing her relations with Lawrence on the old intimate personal footing. It was a matter requiring that she should draw him apart, as she had now done. It would be a favour to her, easy to grant, and pleasant to confer. A man (she believed) will always choose that a woman be in his debt, rather than that he be under obligation to her.

"How beautiful! But how cold." She was aware as she spoke, with a pleasant thrill, that her nearer beauty held his regard to the exclusion of outer things.

She did not love him. So she told herself, in a cool mind. She loved Gerald Langton, whom she did not intend to lose for a foolish whim. But it was pleasant to play on the slippery edge of that she would never do.

Pleasant to play with life, mingling imagination and fact in a fantasy she would not endeavour to hold apart. But for any deeper folly than that, for the entanglements in which it is so easy to catch the feet, so difficult to break free, she supposed that she was too sure in her self-control; that she was too cold at the core.

And then his voice answered her spoken words, but as though they had held the meaning of all these secret separate thoughts.

"Cold? I should say it is like to like. You are as beautiful as before. And you will say that you are unaltered in other ways?"

His voice lowered to the repetition of lines that they had discussed on another night, which had not been unlike to this:

> "*The autumn winds thy garth shall grieve,*
> *The scentless roses fall:*
> *The lustres of thy siege shall leave*
> *An unadventured wall.*"

Vividly, they brought the old attraction, the old intimacy back to her unreluctant mind. How did they go on?

"Slow fall the night's unchanging snows
Where the red roses fell—"

Slowly, flake by flake, too thinly to drive them in, the snow was falling around them now.

She shivered, in spite of the heavy wraps that she wore. She drew closer to him, as though she shrank from an outer fear. Unimaginative as she was, or rather impervious to all but herself and the dreams she wove, she felt a cold foreboding of what had been no more than an interfering annoyance an hour before.

She seemed unaware that she was closer against his side; unaware that he kissed her throat. She did not protest at that, nor did she respond, nor withdraw. But her voice had become vibrant with anxious doubt as she asked: *"Lawrence, will there really be war?"*

Behind them, in the lighted drawing-room, the card-party had been disturbed by the entrance of Richard Cunningham. He looked for Lawrence, or Sir Geoffrey, and saw only the four guests whom he did not know.

"Excuse me," he said, "can you tell me if Mr. Norton has left?"

Perdita looked up. It seemed natural that she should be the one to answer an English voice.

"I don't think he's far off. Do you want him now?"

As she spoke, she saw in his hand the paper which had been left with her when Herr Müller had taken the rest.

She asked: "Have you found out what it means? Was it worth all the fuss there was?"

He was surprised, not knowing that it had come from her, and cautious in his reply.

"Yes. It's rather urgent. I should like to find Mr. Norton as soon as possible."

"Wait a moment."

She went out through the window that opened to the terrace to call him in.

Unconscious that they were seen, unaware of any except themselves, she saw the two that she sought embraced in each other's arms.

She stood for a silent minute, oblivious of the midnight cold, though she had come out with a bare neck. Then she turned back. She said: "I'm sure Mr. Norton's somewhere outside. If you would call him from here?"

CHAPTER XXVIII.

LAWRENCE answered at once. He came back to the lighted window, Caresse following closely behind. The terrace had been swept clear of snow during the afternoon, as the custom was, and her eyes fell on Perdita's footmarks, clearly outlined on the thin fall of the last hour, where the reflection of lighted window slanted across the pavement.

She gave no sign that she saw either this or the confirming whiteness of Perdita's shoes, as she said: "Why didn't you come out? It's a lovely night. But the cold! We had to walk briskly to keep alive."

It was clear, at least, that her vitality had not suffered, by whatever means it had been sustained. As she threw off the heavy furs she had worn, and brushed a white flake from her hair, her cheeks were vivid with life, her eyes bright as the frosty stars.

Perdita said: "I should have loved to come out, but I couldn't break up the game."

As she turned back to the card-table, her eyes met those of her friend with a quiet serenity which left Caresse puzzled and foiled. How much, if anything, had she seen or guessed?

Lawrence had already gone, a hand under Cunningham's arm drawing him to the door, when he saw the paper he held.

"Not here, Richard," he said, "even Sir Geoffrey doesn't know about that—yet. You didn't mention it in the room?"

"I didn't mean to. The young lady at the card-table—Miss Wyatt?—seemed to know all about it. I turned it off, asking for you."

"Did the others notice anything?"

"I don't think the men did. Mme. Janda was wide awake."

Lawrence didn't look pleased. He said: "There isn't much that little cat doesn't see. But it can't be helped, and it doesn't seem to amount to much. Anyway, she's Janda's wife. There shouldn't be any trouble from her. The real question is, how does it read? I suppose you wouldn't have come, if you hadn't discovered that."

"Only partly yet." He went on to explain: "It's in two distinct ciphers, if not more. I've made out almost alternate lines. This is how it reads now:

> "But these preparations must be
> 3z replica azooz xbat pli
> bg ommo v bg ayffo qar
> leaving the entrance of the
> qdsssbb dorx fgi ap
> destroyed at any moment after
> o' t bg xinnx v bg
> signals already mentioned in
> hhgpyyb v ecaii w
> ägyptische Helena (Strauss)
> tt ap balwzee sup nuwub bg
> announcement from the Nürnberg
> ripo."

Lawrence studied it in a puzzled silence. Then he asked: "You think you can get the rest?"

"Yes. It's only a question of time. The hardest part ought to be done now."

"What do you make of it?"

"Not much. But I should think it would be important to some-one."

"So do I." He went on to explain how it had come to his hands. He added: "When Herr Müller found that he hadn't got the end of his instructions, or whatever they are, he must have felt rather annoyed."

"I should say it won't be long before he tries to see Miss Wyatt again."

"That's how it looks. But I don't intend her to run any more risks. The papers are really nothing to us. It's not our business to interfere between Germany and her agents here. I propose to return it to him. I shall make it clear that I don't understand what it means, and if it should be something he won't expect me to hand over,— well, he'll be all the more sure that its secret is still his. But you'll keep a copy, of course. It's just as well to know what's likely to happen, whether or not we should feel we could interfere."

"I think Sir Geoffrey should know."

"Well, so he shall. I'll tell him tonight. But you know he'll agree. He always wants us to keep clear of both sides of these Nazi intrigues. And the less he knows about them himself, the more pleased he's likely to be."

CHAPTER XXIX.

PERDITA undressed quickly, scarcely conscious of what she did. She had to adjust her world to a new fact which she did not like, and one the significance of which was hard to resolve.

She believed herself to be able to put emotion aside, and to judge with a cool blood, being the boast that her generation would make; but human nature does not change, though its customs may.

She might face the world with gravely confident eyes, having youth and courage to aid, and turning romance aside with an armour of denial or hard reserve, but it was the instinct of self-protection that put it on, she having been wounded at times before, when she had lowered a careless guard.

She was already in bed when Caresse knocked at the door.

"May I come in?"

"Yes, of course."

Caresse entered, switching on the light. Had they been in an English bedroom, Perdita might have risen, and they would have drawn chairs to the fire for the talk that Caresse plainly purposed to have.

Here, where there was no fire in the heated room, Caresse pulled a low chair to the side of her friend's bed.

"You didn't see Lawrence after he came in?"

"No."

"Neither did I. After he came back from that Mr. Cunningham, he went to Sir Geoffrey's room. I didn't think I'd wait up when I saw you'd gone. It's late enough now."

As Perdita made no answer to this, Caresse added: "You weren't far wrong when you said we should be in the way."

She laughed slightly, as at a proposition too absurd for annoyance to be allowed.

Perdita, puzzled for a moment, remembered her remark at the dinner-table. She saw that Caresse resented that Lawrence should have appeared to forget her, since they had come in together, for what should have been an obviously less important concern. Had she come to talk only of that? Anything was possible with Caresse.

But the next question showed that the same thought was in both their minds, and that it was one that Caresse did not intend to shirk.

She asked: "You came out on to the terrace while we were there?"

"Yes. Mr. Cunningham said he must speak to Lawrence at once."

"And why didn't you tell him?"

"I didn't think you wanted to be disturbed."

"Of course I didn't. I should have come in if I'd finished what I went out to do."

"What was that?"

"I wanted him to get Sir Geoffrey to wire that there's no reason for us to go home when we've just come. Of course, I had to coax him a bit."

"So I saw…. Did he promise that?"

"He would have done if Mr. Cunningham hadn't called."

"I don't know that I want to stay if it isn't safe."

"Don't be absurd. As though you'd really care about that! If a war did come, I don't suppose it would make much difference to us. It's just these old people who've been through one before. They've got wars on the brain. You don't think I should interfere, if you really want him?"

"I don't want him at all."

"It's no use saying that, when you know you do."

"Not that way. I mean, he'd have to want me first a great deal more than he ever would."

"That's silly. You haven't tried."

"I shouldn't ever do that."

"That's sillier still. It's the way to get what the others leave."

Perdita said: "Yes?" in a voice that implied indifference, if not doubt. Her mind admitted that the statement had a sensible sound, though she suspected a flaw.

"Well," Caresse concluded, "don't be a goose. I didn't mean anything. I never do. Lawrence knows that."

She kissed her friend, and returned to her own room, her mind satisfied with her own wisdom and generosity, and divided between a pleasant conviction that she could carry the flirtation she had commenced to any length that she would, and a quite honest desire to advance Perdita's interests on a more permanent basis.

Perdita lay awake for a time, adjusting her world to the new focus the events of the night required.

As to Lawrence, the distance that had lain between them since their casual association of four years before, and which had been no more than "the space that makes attraction felt," appeared to have widened to an uncrossable gulf.

As to Caresse, she had done that of which she herself would have been ashamed—which, had she been married, as Caresse was, she felt that she would have regarded as an impossible thing. But it was different with Caresse. She could see that. She had always known her friend to be capable of a levity of conduct alien from her own moods. And it had been a gesture of generosity to come as she had done, and to say what she had.

No, there was to be no quarrel with her. In fact, you couldn't quarrel long with Caresse. You had to take her for what she was, and just say nothing when you didn't agree. There were ways in which you could always rely that she would be no less than a loyal friend.

She turned her mind resolutely from such thoughts to wonder what would be the outcome of the strange atmosphere of intrigue and tension to which they had come.

It was the atmosphere of Eastern Europe, no doubt natural to those who had been born to its plots and hates, but what concern could it be to England, aloof in that Western Island,

"Where, higher than all, she stands"?

What difference could it make to her?

CHAPTER XXX.

THE dawn of Friday, February 4th, 1938, moved over Europe, as more than seven hundred thousand days had dawned since Christ gave His message of peace to men.

It was cold and clear, a day of clean, bright, windless skies from the Ural heights to the storm-scarred cliffs of Connaught, as though Nature paused to watch an arena where fierce base passions drove mankind to ghastlier wreck than her own blind-striking tempests would ever work.

It was a day that would go down in unbroken peace, but with the forces of hell already loosed, to an end that no man could tell.

Yet it may be doubted whether, of all the millions whose fate was weighed in the trembling scale, there was one man, even of those who ruled, who had clear foresight or settled will for that which the midnight brought.

Even among the Council who met during the afternoon in Berlin, by whom the Ultimatum was worded, and, at last, unanimously approved, there was none who could more than guess what its reception would be, and it is certain that Herr Seifert, who supplied its most minatory phrase, did it in the belief that, the more emphatic its language, the more certain it would be that the Czechoslovak Government would give the satisfaction that it required.

In Germany, the control of news and of public opinion was too absolute for any general premonition to be aroused. Its people had been trained to learn what its Government did on the next day, rather than to debate its intentions the day before.

In France, the desire that the peace of Europe should not be disturbed, while her Colonial army was occupied in the suppression of the Algerian insurrection and with the disorders in Syria, was so strong that it had the effect of a determination in the minds of those in whose hands her destinies lay.

They had told their Czechoslovak friends that they must handle matters, for this time at least, in such a way as to avoid the crisis of war, and, having said that, they did not contemplate that there would be sufficient courage, or perhaps folly, in Prague to put their advice aside.

In England, where the British Cabinet met nominally at the same time as the Berlin Council, though actually at a later hour, the public interest was so slight that the loitering crowd of those who find satisfaction in watching Ministers cross the road was of little more than its customary size, and its excitement was mainly centred in a rumour of difference between the Ministers of Agriculture and Transport regarding a proposal for the further widening of the third-grade roads.

Italy, normally armed and alert, may have gauged the acuteness of the crisis with greater accuracy, but she, like Germany, was not ruled by popular clamour, nor encouraged to debate aloud.

She had been like an armed camp, urging peace, but with her Alpine bulwarks showing a front of war, since the day when Austria had become a part of the German State. She was watchful, but gave no sign.

CHAPTER XXXI.

HERR Müller had a permanent suite in one of the more palatial of the new hotels which surrounded the Wilson station.

He was a man of German birth, of known wealth, and evident leisure.

His extensive landed properties in Czechoslovakia were sufficient explanation of his presence in Prague.

The Minister of Justice might have an assured belief that he was the head of the Nazi organisation there, but it was a conviction which lacked proof for its support.

It was not a crime that other Nazis should call upon him at times, and have long conferences which the ingenuity of the police had been unable to overhear.

It was no breach of the law that the hotel residence of a wealthy man should have its doors strongly barred against the intrusion of those who might attempt entry with burglarious aims, nor that he should be served exclusively by men of German birth, whom he chose and paid.

When he had entered the bedroom of the Ambassador Hotel, it may have been the first time that he had taken an overt part in the activities he controlled, and it was then only after his agents had failed in the night, and with the knowledge that the last chance of averting the ruin which threatened himself, his followers, and the cause for which they plotted and lived, was to reach that room before the police should be on the scene.

Lawrence sent up his name, and was promptly invited to enter a lift private to Herr Müller's suite, which was the entire fourth floor of the hotel.

He was guided by an armed servant of semi-military appearance to the door of a room where Herr Müller received him alone, and with more affability than he had experienced when he had been the caller himself. Lawrence came to the point at once, and Herr Müller accepted the missing sheet without surprise, as though it were an expected thing.

"I felt sure," he said, "that you would bring it along."

He laid it down, as though being of no great account. He offered wine and cigars. He was plainly ready to talk, and Lawrence thought that he would do well to show a similar mood.

His host said: "You have been friendly in this. It has been so for the last three years. England has been the one Power which has not been our open or secret foe."

Lawrence was measured in his reply: "You must not thank me too much. I have done no more than restore a paper I cannot read to one to whom I have cause to think it belongs. England desires peace, and to be friendly to all."

"And that," Herr Müller replied, "is all we have ever asked. It was enough when the nations of Europe chafed that we should draw closer the bonds with our Austrian kin."

"The League of Nations," Lawrence began, "at that time—"

Herr Müller's gesture showed his contempt. "The League of Nations!" he exclaimed. "The impotent bleating fools! Why, it was dead before then. It had been no more than a walking ghost since the first day it had shirked to impose the sanctions itself devised. Paraguay, Italy, Greece—I do not recall which was the first to contemn its rule. And the mandated islands—dared it to demand them back from Japan?"

He checked the high note of his voice, as he resumed with a smile: "Does it matter now? It was doomed from birth but it might have gone to death in a more dignified way."

Lawrence did not reply, having no desire to deny evident fact. He supposed that Herr Müller had more purpose in what he said than to make Geneva his jest.

Seeing him silent, the Nazi leader went on: "You desire peace? So do I. This is my land, though I have no love for the people who rule it now. I dislike the wastage of war. Mr. Norton, your people plead at Berlin. I tell you, they knock at the wrong door. If they would have peace, *let them join the urgence of France.* Let them tell the Government here to agree to whatever terms they are asked—to whatever terms.

"You have done that which is friendly to me, and I give you a friend's counsel for those whom I suppose you would seek to save."

Lawrence asked bluntly: "It is to be Austria over again?"

The question seemed to check Herr Müller to silence, as though it were not easy to answer, or warned him that he might already have said more than was wise.

"Austria?" he said at last. "There is no parallel there. For this is less than a German land."

He turned the conversation to lighter things, and Lawrence soon rose to go, seeing that there would be nothing more said that it would be worth waiting to hear.

Clearly, Herr Müller thought that there was a grave danger of war, which he would avert if he could, and it was equally clear that he was convinced that the German Government would not yield. If the crisis of the week were not to burst into the unmeasured horror of war, it could only be through Czechoslovakia accepting whatever demands might be made by the stronger Power.

CHAPTER XXXII.

IT was nearly noon when Lawrence returned to the Legation. At the breakfast-table that morning, the two girls had been induced, it had seemed, by Sir Geoffrey's bluff insistence rather than his own persuasions, to agree to leave the hotel and take up their residence at the Legation, so long as they should remain in Prague.

As to how long that should be, the decision was still delayed. Caresse had received a letter from her husband that morning, over which she had frowned at times, but had been uncommunicative as to its contents.

It was shortly afterwards that she had made a direct request to Sir Geoffrey to telegraph to Gerald Langton that there could be no cause for anxiety as to their safety in Prague, and had been disconcerted by receiving no more than a politely noncommittal reply.

"I've told you," he said, "Gerald's too fussy. Perhaps I'll write him a line. Anyway, you'll stay over the Ball tonight. It's the event of the year."

He might not think there was sufficient cause for English women to scuttle out of Czechoslovakia, but he did not forget the position which Gerald Langton held. Such a telegram as that for which Caresse asked, and addressed to him, might be taken as implying much of which he was becoming more doubtful with every hour.

He had been stationed in South American republics where an outbreak of revolution or war was no more than the weekly routine, and his experiences there had made him sceptical of these talks of a war which all men feared, but which never came.

But those same experiences had taught him to scent the atmosphere which precedes the storm. Now he was beginning to say to himself, for the first time since Bolivia had been left behind, that there was war in the air.

Lawrence had received a promise from his guests that they would remain within the Legation walls until he should be able to tell them that the cryptographic sheet had been returned, and that there would be no further fear of molestation on that account.

After that, and, if possible, before lunch, he was to accompany them to the Ambassador Hotel, to remove the major part of their luggage, which was still there.

Now he hurried back, with a consciousness that his talk with Herr Müller had left little time for this promise to be redeemed, but he stopped abruptly on observing the shabby figure of one who talked with a servant beside the gate.

"Hullo, Steele," he said casually, "been away, haven't you?"

"Yes, sir. I've been a bit rheumatic, and the weather being so bad, I— But I thought you might find me a job tonight, being that it's the big dance—"

"I expect we can. You'd better come in, and have a word with His Excellency."

"Beg pardon, sir," the other man interposed. "His Excellency's not in. Novák's just driven him to the French Legation. He said he shouldn't need to be fetched back until after lunch."

"Very well. Steele, I'll have a word with you all the same. You'd better come up with me."

When they were alone together, and a stout locked door divided them from the outer world, Lawrence pulled up an easy chair for a weary man, and No. 973 told of his adventures since they had parted less than two days before.

After narrating how he had escaped from the close shadow of death in the secret aerodrome, he said that he had subsequently experienced little difficulty in finding his way back.

"There's no trouble," he said, "for anyone wearing a German uniform, or who can speak with a German voice. They can cross the frontier almost anywhere that they like, so long as they keep off the trains and the main roads. They're all Germans—or at least five out of six—on both sides of the frontier along the west, and some of them will cross two or three times a day."

"You look worn out."

"I'm a bit tired. But there's no need for much talking now. I've written everything here." (He laid several closely-written sheets on the table.) "Everything that I've seen or heard that's worth noting down, including all that Colonel Wieck told me to say. But you must take most of that the contrary way, because it's not what's true, it's what he wants you to believe. But I'd be glad if you'd let that part be shown to someone who'll be likely to betray it all back to Berlin. It might be my one chance, if they catch me again."

"You're not going back there?"

"That's just what I am. I'm going back in a few hours. It was while I was wandering about, getting home by a crooked way, that I came on something else that I can't leave.

"It won't be easy. It's an isolated village, with a three-metre wall closing it in, and it's floodlighted at night on all sides, with every tree and bush grubbed up for a distance round that you'd find it hard to believe, so that there's no way to hide as you get near. I don't know for sure, but from something I heard said when I took some lunch at an inn near, I believe I've found the place where they manufacture the bacillus-bombs, that we've always suspected, but not located before.

"Anyway, I've decided that another look wouldn't do any harm. I don't want to call on Herr Janda myself. I have to be careful now of every step that I take. I'll just go home and rest, as I said. But I shall be glad to have a light scouting plane at 9.30 tonight, in the field where he always leaves them for me. I don't say he'll ever see it again, but he'll be well paid for that, if you let him know half that I've written here."

No. 973, having talked more than his habit was, went without further words. He was worn with fatigue, and it was easy for him to move with the gait of a sick man, but he was resolved that the seven hours' rest that he planned to have must suffice to fit him for the strain of the long night-flight, and what he supposed to be the most desperate adventure his life had faced.

CHAPTER XXXIII.

No. 973, returning to the room he rented over his cousin's shop, paused on his way out for a sufficient chat with the Legation porter to explain the length of his privacy in Mr. Norton's room.

He had been taken suddenly faint, and the Secretary had been most kind; but it had been agreed that he was too ill to drive one of the cars that night, as he had been hoping to do. He would go home to bed. The porter readily accepted a tale which his looks confirmed.

Lawrence, meanwhile, had gone in search of his neglected guests. Before Sir Geoffrey had found that it would be necessary for him to visit the French Legation, he had invited the ladies to lunch with himself. His suite consisted of four rooms overlooking the terrace, opening out from one another, in which he had entertained them the night before.

Here he was accustomed to take his meals alone, or with occasional guests, the Legation staff dining apart.

Finding himself obliged to leave, he had said that Lawrence, on his return, must take his place as their natural host.

Now they sat in the lounge, conscious of a solitary and wasted morning, and that the hour for lunch had already come.

"I'm fearfully sorry," he said, "but Herr Müller kept me longer than I expected. It's all settled now, and if you don't mention the incident to anyone, as of course you won't—and particularly not in connection with him— I don't suppose you'll ever hear of it again."

"We were getting quite anxious," Perdita said, "when you didn't return."

"But not," Caresse added, "since we've known that you've been talking to one of the servants for the last hour."

"I'm sorry—there was an urgent reason—you see—"

"You needn't try to explain. We've noticed you never do."

"Well, anyway, I'm here now. You must try to forgive. You can reckon my time's yours now till you...."

Caresse laughed. "I shouldn't be too quick to say that. There's Mr. Cunningham running round for you now like a—"

The metaphor, whatever it might have been, was unspoken, for Lawrence had disappeared.

"Perhaps," she concluded, "it would be better if we go home after all."

Lawrence made his way quickly to the archivist's room.

"I suppose," he asked, "you can tell me what it is now?"

Cunningham looked up from the diagrams upon which he worked.

"I can tell you what the words are. I won't go beyond that. I should say it's the last page of a silly hoax, or a wild Communist plot."

"I don't think it will be either of those."

"Well, here it is. You must judge for yourself."

He handed over the script.

CHAPTER XXXIV.

IT was nearly half an hour later when Lawrence returned to the lounge. He apologised for his second absence with an evident sincerity, but with an equally evident preoccupation of mind, and with the failure of adequate explanation which Caresse had remarked and resented before.

As he followed the girls through the curtained archway that opened into the adjoining room, where the belated lunch was to be served, they heard him say to the man who had announced its readiness: "Paul, I want you to ask Mr. Harvey to let me know at once when His Excellency returns," and the order was given in such a tone that the man went on his errand at once, leaving them for the next three minutes to gaze at their empty plates.

Caresse looked speculatively at her old-time lover.

"I hope," she said, "if he does, that they won't stop serving the lunch." And then, as Lawrence only looked at her with exasperatingly vacant eyes: "I only mean that we don't mind being left alone, but we've both got an objection to being starved."

Lawrence put the contents of that startling cryptographic sheet resolutely from his mind.

"No," he said, laughing, "I'll undertake, if I disappear again, that the lunch shall go on. I'm sorry I've seemed so rude, but...."

"But you're ready to disappear again, the moment that Sir Geoffrey comes in?"

"I'm afraid I may have to for a time."

"Is it that paper again?" Perdita asked. "I felt sure it would turn out to be something exciting."

"Yes. But, you see, it was only the last sheet. We've got it deciphered now, but it isn't easy to tell what it implies."

He changed the subject rather obviously as he asked: "Have you the invitations yet for tonight?"

Caresse answered: "Oh, yes, we've had them, but we're not likely to go."

"Not likely to go? Why not? If you mean that I—"

"I don't mean anything, except that all the things we should wear are at the hotel, and it's two o'clock now."

"I've said how sorry I am. But there's lots of time. I can get you there before three."

"That is, if Sir Geoffrey returns, and if he doesn't keep you till six?"

The question disconcerted him with the realisation that he would not be prepared to go out before he had seen Sir Geoffrey, and that his time might not subsequently be under his own control.

While his reply hesitated, Perdita spoke.

"We shouldn't be such a bother if you hadn't got us to promise that we wouldn't go without you."

So he had stipulated in the morning, but he reflected that that was before he had seen Herr Müller, and before the return of the final sheet. There was less reason to think that anyone would molest them now.

Prague was not a lawless city; certainly not one in which it was unsafe for two ladies to be driven through the streets in the daylight hours. If he should give them his own car, and a driver whom he could trust. But his car was not large.

"How many trunks," he asked, "did you leave behind?"

"You mean you don't want to break the back axle?" Perdita asked. "Well, why shouldn't I go alone? I should be back inside an hour."

She had had enough of sitting idly indoors, and she knew that Caresse spent most afternoons stretched on bed or couch with a book that she would most often be too lazy to read.

"Good idea, if you don't mind," Caresse said. "There's no sense in more going than one."

"I don't mind. I could find the way in the dark. It's too easy to miss."

"You don't mean that you're proposing to drive?" Lawrence asked.

"Yes, she does," Caresse answered. "Why not? There aren't many cars that she can't. It would be better than the back seat, with two trunks over her lap."

"Can't I send for the luggage for you?"

"No, you can't. It isn't all packed; and there's the bill to be paid; and—anyway, those are reasons enough."

So it was settled, after some further debate. It did seem the most sensible plan. Lawrence added, when he had ordered the car and Perdita rose to go: "You'll keep to the left, like in England, here; so you'll have no difficulty about that. Pedestrians do the same, except over bridges, where they reverse. Weird, but true."

Perdita said that if she had occasion to walk over a bridge, she would remember the etiquette that the occasion required. She listened to Caresse's anxious admonitions regarding the care of her unpacked possessions, and went cheerfully out.

It was two hours later that a police message came through on the telephone to say that a car which was the registered property of Mr. Lawrence Norton was standing in a side street, near Wenceslaus Place, unattended, and loaded with luggage. The police asked, with the politeness due to a member of the staff of a foreign embassy, that Mr. Norton should arrange for its removal at his early convenience.

CHAPTER XXXV.

IT will be remembered that, after the reconstruction of the Cabinet which took place in December 1937, Mr. Lloyd-Davids undertook the office of the Air Ministry, while Mr. Ganston was transferred to that of Foreign Affairs.

The changes which occurred at that time, and the inclusion of Mr. Lloyd-Davids, while of some temporary advantage in strengthening the Government's precarious majority, were probably undertaken with the larger object of uniting the anti-socialist forces for a fresh appeal to the country, which was generally regarded as being inevitable at an early date, and likely to be decisive in its results upon the fortunes of the British Empire—so little do men foresee that future for which they scheme.

Mr. Marmaduke Bewdley retained the Premiership. He was discreet, urbane, moderate in his own views, and tolerant towards those with whom he did not agree. Intellectual, without arrogance. Of comprehending rather than originating genius. Of an integrity universally recognised: an ideality to which the more generous of the community responded readily.

He had never, throughout his political career, been an object of popular idolatry, perhaps because he lacked the more seductive qualities of platform eloquence, the faculty by which Mr. Lloyd-Davids would send all inconvenient truths whirling helplessly down the stream of his impetuous verbosity.

Yet he was probably the only man who had prestige, sagacity, and discretion sufficient to hold together the jealous and unruly forces of those who were now united by no better bond than a common fear of that Communistic menace which some of themselves, in earlier days, had been active to nurse to its existing vigour.

Mr. Bewdley's mental attitude, as he took his seat on the plum-coloured chair which had been sacred to British premiers for more than a century past, and glanced round amicably at his somewhat heterogeneous colleagues, ranged along the narrow table which stretched right and left from his central seat, was rather that of the chairman of a potentially quarrelsome meeting which he must calm and accord, than that of its ruling head.

He had a hand on the steering-wheel, and a firm foot on the brake. It might be said that it was he who drove, and that he could drive well. But it was those who wrangled on the back seat of the car who chose the road on which he must prove his skill.

He had been at the Foreign Office during the past half-hour, and had walked over with Mr. Ganston, endeavouring with friendly insistence both to moderate and delay the proposal of his forceful colleague.

"I would not urge such a course," Mr. Ganston had said finally, as they had paused on the lower step, "if I were not convinced that it is the only means of averting war."

"Or of involving ourselves?"

"Yes. We must risk that. It is a case in which safety lies in the bolder course."

The Premier hesitated a moment. He had a high opinion of Mr. Ganston's ability, and though he was pacific in temperament he was not lacking in the moral courage which will challenge fate with sufficient cause. And he was not sure that Ganston was wrong! But the ultimate responsibility must be his. To England. To his own conscience. To God.

Through his mind passed the prayer of the Victorian poet—an aspiration, whether noble or base, to which none of the younger poets of his own day would be likely to give the cunning music of words:

> *"Pray God our greatness do not fail*
> *Through craven fear of being great."*

These were the thoughts of a moment during which he was saying aloud: "Ganston, you don't think you're letting Gerald influence you too much?—and he worried about his wife?"

Mr. Ganston perceived an implication which he did not like, though he could not resent it.

Was it possibly true? Of the permanent officials in the Central Division of the Foreign Office—that which dealt both with German and Czechoslovak affairs—he regarded Gerald Langton as having the soundest judgment, and it was true that he was largely relying upon the opinion he had given, and the reasons with which he had supported it. At least, he had relied on him for the facts. The proposed remedy was his own.

He knew that Langton was anxious about his wife; that he had wired her to come home by a southern route. Was it possible that his judgment was somewhat warped by that anxiety? That he had communicated a degree of apprehension that he would not otherwise have felt?

Was it even absurdly possible that he might himself be advocating what was almost an ultimatum to Berlin, with no better cause than that Caresse Langton had gone to Prague? (And he had told Langton an hour ago that the little devil could take care of herself in a worse place. He had met Caresse.)

He put the thought aside. No; his fear was better founded than that. He heard Mr. Bewdley say: "Well, we'll see what the others think. You shall put it your own way. I wish I were sure you're wrong."

Now he was availing himself of that opportunity. He was speaking with a slow impressive urgency, different from either his House of Commons or platform manner, conscious that there were four men only who counted there—four men, of whom two at least would be instinctively critical of any proposal that came from him—

whom he must convert if his words were to be more than a mere wasting of breath.

"I am convinced," he said, "that if there be one influence that can restrain the German Government to a further patience, and to such ultimate moderation as will ensure a peaceful solution of the present difficulty, it will be the emphatic knowledge that the friendship of this country is explicitly dependent upon it.

"With that object, I propose to cable instantly to our Ambassador at Berlin to make immediate representations to the Government there that any act that may lead to a breach of peace will be regarded as unfriendly to us."

"Why," Mr. Lloyd-Davids asked sharply, "should you assume Germany to be wrong?"

"I don't suggest that we should. Frankly, I am not sure that she is. Not unless you think it sufficient answer for Czechoslovakia to say that she's being paid back in her own coin. We know that Germans have committed political murders in Prague and slipped back to Berlin, where the Government winks and lets them go free.

"But you can't expect that Germany will think that's reason enough for allowing plotters in Prague who aim at nothing less than her President's life."

"You think that's true?" The question came from the Home Secretary, a man of cautious, judicious mind, who disliked any conclusion which appeared to be supported by less than a legal proof.

"Yes. Our own agents confirm that. It's no more than right to recognise that Berlin hasn't complained without cause."

"Then why," Mr. Lloyd-Davids asked irritably, "should we interfere?" The time was passing, and he had his own furrow to plough. He was to address a mass meeting of his own supporters in Manchester next Tuesday night, and he had still to obtain the authority of the Cabinet for some rather startling pronouncements which he had in mind for that occasion.

"Because, if you don't, you'll have Armageddon over again. Twenty-four years ago, did it matter whether, or how far, Serbia was wrong? Could not England have saved Europe then, if she had had the courage to say that whoever might break the peace would find her their instant foe?"

(Mr. Bewdley, silent, mentally alert, listening to all sides with an open mind, and a heavy consciousness that the final responsibility must be his, thought: "For how long would that peace have endured?" But it was a question to which no answer will ever be.)

Through Mr. Lloyd-Davids' vivid imagination there came a memory of those distant fatal July days; a vision of such another time, when England, desiring peace, had blundered forward into the vortex of war.

"If I believed that," he thought, "I should be inclined to run over myself, and see what I could do." It was an impulse that, had it been translated to action, and time allowed, might have changed the future of Europe, for there have been few men in the world's history possessed of his faculty of persuasion, eloquent, subtle, sincere, and unhindered by the restraints of logic, or the prosaic fetters of fact.

But he remembered his Manchester meeting. He might not be back in time! He had enough to think of before Tuesday, without this, having among other trifles, to persuade Lancashire that it was an actual advantage to her to lose the last remnants of her Indian trade. Though he was not overmuch concerned about that. He knew that when he had been on his legs for half an hour he could make the most stubborn fact in the world retire with a drooping tail, feeling bewildered and very sick.

Besides, why not use the occasion to warn Germany in a public way? It was a mission for which he considered himself peculiarly adapted, and the fact of it being entrusted to him would demonstrate his importance in the Government which he had so lately joined.

"Can't you leave this till Tuesday?" he asked. "I might say something at Manchester which would clear the air."

There were some murmurs of approval at this suggestion, as one that seemed good in itself, and might have the happy consequence of making way for more important matters which their sponsors waited to urge.

But Mr. Ganston said, rather curtly: "I'm afraid it may be too urgent for that. I heard from Ragge this morning, and from Cullender this afternoon—"

"I shouldn't take too much notice of him," Mr. Lloyd-Davids interrupted impatiently. "I shouldn't wonder if he isn't making the trouble worse." He had been moved to this excess of negatives, which his colleagues had no difficulty in understanding, by remembering that Sir Geoffrey came of an old Tory family, and drawing the reasonable conclusion therefrom that he was a man who would make a mess of whatever he undertook.

Mr. Denver, the Minister for Transport, being one of those whose own business was impeded by the unexpected discussion, said rather brusquely: "I think there's too much fuss about war. If it's got to come, it mightn't turn out to be half as bad as we're scared to think. It might be over within a week, and the air cleared. What's the worst we might have to fear? I suppose you think London'd get bombed?"

"Yes. That's more likely than not. And with a loss of life that might reach appalling figures."

"Meaning how much?"

"There might easily be a million casualties."

Mr. Denver considered this, but was not impressed.

"Why," he said, "that's no more than we polish off on the roads every five years—used to do it in four till I took it in hand last year. Down to 200,000 a year now, and everyone thinks it's a satisfactory total. No, we needn't lose any sleep over that."

Mr. Bewdley's eyebrows lifted slightly. He interposed for the first time, to say with a restrained sarcasm, which the Transport Minister did not perceive: "But you know, Denver, there would be loss of property and dislocation of business, in addition to the surrender of human life."

Mr. Denver looked serious. He was too shrewd not to perceive that people who had been bombed into a multiplicity of unsightly fragments would be unlikely to continue instalments upon their cars.

"Sorry," he said, "that I butted in. I expect we're all wise to keep to our own jobs." He became silent, reserving himself for the real struggle of the afternoon, when they should reach the question of the proposed widening of the third-grade roads.

Mr. Bewdley, watching the discussion, was aware that the Foreign Secretary had obtained little support. Nothing but an emphatic declaration from himself would convert the meeting to an inclination to interfere decisively in Mid-European affairs, and even that declaration might have no practical effect beyond exasperating antipathies among themselves, which it was his anxiety to reduce.

His mind strayed a moment to wonder, was Denver possibly right in thinking that modern war might seem more terrible in imagination than in fact it would prove to be?

Was it worse for a child to be blown apart by a bomb than to be crushed under a lorry's wheels? Might it not even be a better death for a man to die? What was Meleager's lament?

> *"But I would that in splendour of battle mine hands*
> *had laid hold upon death."*

The contemned Victorian poets again!

After all, we had kept the German tiger unfed, while we had stood by, letting his claws grow, and pretending to each other that they were not there, because he had kept them sheathed. That was up to three years ago, when Mr. Bewdley had been a member of a Government which had made public protestations that Germany was unarmed, and had then blandly eaten their own words, as though having no occasion for shame, when the German Government had made a boast of the armaments which they possessed. Did we think the tiger would never feed? *Ex ungue leonem.*

He was careful not to quote the Latin proverb aloud, being too courteous to show a knowledge of tongues which the most of his colleagues did not possess. What he said was: "I think, Ganston, you might send Ragge a wire, asking him to see the Chancellor himself, if possible, and urge him not to take a decisive step till we've had another chance of seeing what we can do. Tell him to put it as strongly as possible, so that it's clear that it doesn't go beyond the limit of friendly request."

Mr. Ganston saw that it was the most that he would be likely to get. Further discussion might whittle down even that. Was it to be Gallipoli over again? The curse of seeing, and being unable to give the vision to denser minds!

But even that might be enough. And the priceless minutes went by.

He went hurriedly out, leaving the meeting to quarrel over the expediency of sterilising the surface of countless thousands of English acres to increase the width of the third-grade roads.

* * * * * * *

In Berlin, Sir James Ragge lost no time. His representations were promptly made, and he was informed, with a courtesy equal to his own, that the German Government was profoundly anxious to give the fullest consideration to the views of the Government of His Britannic Majesty, but a message had already been sent to Prague requiring that the satisfaction demanded seven days ago should not be longer delayed. Doubtless the Czechoslovak Government would see the wisdom of compliance, and the skies of Europe would clear again.

CHAPTER XXXVI.

IT was ten minutes to four on the afternoon of the day which was to end the twenty years of Europe's uneasy peace in a deluge of blood and fire, when Sir Geoffrey Cullender returned from lunching with the French Envoy, where he had found that the Italian Minister was a fellow-guest. After that, the three ministers had called together upon the Czechoslovakian Chancellor.

At that hour the German ultimatum had not arrived, and their joint representations had been received with a courtesy beneath which was impatience hardly concealed.

It had shown itself in an exclamation of protest, when Signor Rinaldo had spoken with almost sombre gravity of "the edge of peril on which you stand," to which the Chancellor had replied:

"It is an edge of peril indeed! But it is one over which we are not likely to slip unless we are pushed by our own friends, as you are united to push me now.

"Do you think your coming here is a secret thing? That Germany does not know the words that you are instructed to speak? If you would but show her the common front which was pledged at Venice two years ago, it would be arranged in an hour."

Sir Geoffrey came back to his own Legation feeling that, whatever the issue might be, he had done all that he could. He had already dispatched a wire to London advising the Foreign Office there of the critical nature of the position—as he judged it to be—and of the fact that he had been unable to get in touch with the German Envoy in Prague, who had pleaded indisposition, and remained within his own doors during the last two days, which Sir Geoffrey's South American experiences caused him to regard as a very ominous incident.

He was considering whether anything could be gained by getting in touch with London again as he entered his own rooms, where the prolonged delay in his return, and Perdita's absence, had left Caresse and Lawrence together in a privacy unlikely to be disturbed by other intruders.

Piqued that he should have neglected her during the earlier day for Prague's tiresome affairs, Caresse had been resolute to use the occasion in vindication of the potency of her own attractions, and she had reached a feeling of satisfaction in the uses she had been able to make of the regrets of past recollection and the pleasures of present lure, when they were disturbed by Sir Geoffrey's entrance at the farther end of the suite.

Lawrence rose hastily, leaving her to the pleasant consciousness that she had not wasted the afternoon, and to a sudden realisation that Perdita had been nearly two hours away.

He went quickly through to Sir Geoffrey: "I've been waiting to show you this, sir. I thought you'd wish to see it at once."

Sir Geoffrey read the solution of the cryptographic sheet, now fully disclosed:

> "but these preparations must be
> so far advanced that, in
> the event of the German Envoy
> leaving, the entrances of the
> bomb-proof shelters can be
> destroyed at any moment after
> sunset, after the reception of the
> signals already mentioned, in
> confirmation of which Die
> ägyptische Helena (Strauss)
> will be played without previous
> announcement from the Nürnberg
> station.

"It's a pity," he said, "that we haven't got the earlier sheets, but it seems clear that the playing of this music from the Nürnberg broadcasting station is to be the signal for the destruction of the bomb-proof shelters in Prague, presumably as an overture to an attack from the air."

"Yes, sir. That's what Cunningham and I thought."

"And it reads as though it's a very imminent possibility."

"Have I your permission to let Herr Janda know about this?"

Sir Geoffrey's reply paused. On the one hand, he remembered that it was no part of his duty to interfere in the intrigues or quarrels of two friendly States, and he knew that he had the approval of his Government in the attitude of aloofness which he maintained.

On the other, he considered that the sheet had been found in the luggage of an English subject, who had been no party to its transit across the frontier.

Beyond that, it was not pleasant to think of the helpless crowds, trained already to rush to their subterranean shelters at the first sound of the warning gongs, or of the sirens after the darkness fell, finding the entrances of their refuge blocked, while death-fumes rained from the sky. And in how many hours, or how few?

"Yes," he said, "you can let him know. We can rely on him not to disclose that he has had the information from us."

As he spoke, the telephone rang.

Lawrence, picking up the receiver, heard the call of his own name, and took the police message regarding his deserted car.

"I'm afraid," he said, "there's something wrong. Miss Wyatt—"

And then the telephone rang again.

He heard a voice which spoke good English enough, but with an obviously German accent.

"That Mr. Norton is? It is for the gentleman you met this morning I speak. He has heard that the young lady of yours has most dangerously her way lost. He could recover her without hurt if he should make a great haste.

"He will do this, having much friendship for you, if a pledge you give that the secret of his you hold you will not reveal."

"The low hound! How—"

"It is your pledge he will gladly take."

"I wasn't going to ask that. Is Miss Wyatt safe now?"

"For a minute, yes."

"Wait a moment."

"It is the all that I can."

Lawrence put his hand over the receiver, as he turned to Sir Geoffrey to say: "The Nazis have got Perdita. She's to be returned if we undertake not to—"

Sir Geoffrey interrupted impatiently: "Yes, I can see that." He had already rung for a servant, who entered as he spoke.

He said quickly to him: "Get the police on the other line; tell them to listen in, and to find out who is speaking to us."

He had already pushed the solution of the cryptographic sheet into an envelope which he closed, and on which he scrawled the name of the Minister of Police.

He came over to the telephone, taking the receiver from Lawrence's hand. He said: "I'll deal with this, Norton."

At such moments, he became his natural self; dropping the patient urbanity which is the technique that the diplomatic service requires.

"That Müller's man?" he began. "Of course you are! Do you think me a fool? Now you just listen to me. The game's up. As to that document that one of you put into a place where it had no business to be, there's a copy directed already to the police, who are the proper people to deal with it.

"Tell your friends that they can't leave Prague too soon for their own health, but if I hear within five minutes that the lady is safe and free, they'll have half an hour after that.

"But if Miss Wyatt should be further annoyed—"

He was interrupted by a voice of protest: "But it is not we who would think of that! She is not with us. It is to recover her we propose, if you will but—"

"Don't waste that chatter on me. You can tell Müller I don't care a damn for your dirty plots, but it's an English lady you've got, and if harm should happen to her, there'll be no corner of Europe where he can hide without feeling his collar-button's a bit too tight."

"But," the voice protested again, "I tell it is not that we—"

"And I tell you you're wasting words, and wasting time that you haven't got. If I don't hear Miss Wyatt's voice within five minutes to tell me she's safe and free—well, I needn't warn you again."

He slammed the receiver down, as he said: "There's only one way to deal with that kind of blackmail. I should have been quicker to cut him off, but I wanted to give the police time."

He laid his watch on his desk. "It's four-fifteen now. We'll give them five minutes, and then call up the police."

"You think they'll release her?"

"Heaven knows! But I've tried the best chance. I've seen those games played in Bolivia more than once before, and if you show yellow you're done."

"You think she's in real danger? I don't like sitting here—"

"It's only four minutes now. You can send someone to fetch your car."

Glad of the relief of action, Lawrence went out. As he closed the door, Caresse entered through the archway that opened to the further rooms of the suite.

She said: "I thought Lawrence was here. I'm getting rather worried about Perdita. She's been nearly three hours away."

"I'm afraid she's let herself get caught in a Nazi trap." In a few words Sir Geoffrey explained what the trouble was, and, as he concluded, Lawrence returned to the room.

"I thought," Caresse said, "they'd had the paper back, and everything been arranged."

"They must have found out that we kept a copy," Lawrence explained, "and know or guess that we've found out what it means."

"But how could they have done that? Oh, I know. It's Mr. Cunningham's fault. It's that Janda woman, of course."

"Mme. Janda?" Sir Geoffrey's voice was sceptical. It seemed a wild suggestion to suspect the Air Minister's wife.

But Lawrence echoed the suspicion: "I thought of Zita Janda at once. I don't see who else it could be. She's been Janda's wife for three months, but she's been Hungarian a lot longer than that. And who knows why she married him? She's about the coolest liar I ever met."

Sir Geoffrey said that the Air Minister ought to be warned. And yet what proof had they to show?

They might know more when (or must they say, if?) Perdita returned. But the five minutes had passed, and the telephone gave no sound.

Caresse said: "I don't see what the trouble is. You've only got to let them know that we shan't tell."

"Which I am certainly not going to do," Sir Geoffrey said, with decision. "It is a matter on which thousands of lives may depend."

"It would be no worse than if we hadn't seen it at all."

"We've no time to discuss that. I shall give them half a minute more, and then ring up the police."

"You don't think she's in real danger?"

"My dear lady, I can't tell. We'll hope not. There was a time when even a Chinese brigand wouldn't have kidnapped an English girl without finding that there would be hell to pay. It isn't like that now. We're living in smaller times. But it isn't the kind of thing that the German Government would approve, and if any harm comes to her, they won't thank their agents for what they've done.

"They'll either repudiate them, or else set up that Miss Wyatt knew more than she did. They might try to make out that she first offered to help them to get the documents through, and then betrayed them to the police here.

"It wouldn't be a very credible tale, but the fact that they've kidnapped her at all shows what a desperate fix they're in. I suppose they feel that, if the police once get their hands on this sheet, nothing else matters much, whether bad or good.

"But we're wasting time with this talk."

He took up the telephone again, and asked to be put through to the Minister of Police.

CHAPTER XXXVII.

GERALD LANGTON took the Foreign Secretary's instructions without comment. He had no doubt that Mr. Ganston had endeavoured to persuade the Cabinet to a more virile decision. In any case, he had said all that he could, and the final responsibility was not his.

When he had drafted and dispatched the wire to the British Ambassador at Berlin, he said: "Can I have leave of absence for three days?"

Mr. Ganston looked his surprise. "I'm afraid not. I can't spare you just now. On your own advice—"

"Then I am afraid that I must resign."

"It is a resignation that I could not accept. Why do you want leave?"

"I have had a letter from Mrs. Langton this afternoon declining to take my advice. I am proposing to fetch her back."

"Three days?"

"I shall go by air."

"I thought you had never flown—that you disliked the idea."

"It is a case of the quickest way."

"You think it is so urgent as that?"

"You know what I think. Germany has never accepted the Czechoslovakian frontiers, except under compulsion. Now that she has a real grievance to urge, and that France is preoccupied with her colonial troubles—. It is an occasion too good to miss."

"You feel sure it is war?"

"I don't go that far. Prague may lie flat to be kicked. But I think, after the wire we have just sent, my wife will be safer in Lon—" he corrected himself to say "in England than Prague."

Mr. Ganston paced the room restlessly as he replied: "Langton, you know I'd have dealt with this in a different way. I've done all that I could. But I'm not going to give you leave of absence now, and resignation's absurd."

His voice changed, and a smile came to his lips as he added: "What I want you to do is to run over to Prague, and get Cullender's opinion at first hand.

"And see Benes yourself. There's no one living who understands this ghastly chaos of Eastern Europe better than you. You mayn't be too late even now to find a peaceful solution—"

"It's unusual for one of us—"

"So's hell."

Gerald Langton wasted no time in considering the theological implications of this dictum. His hand reached for the telephone. He asked to be put through to Imperial Airways at once. He said: "I want to book that passage to Prague. In an hour's time? Rather less? Well, I can do that. But it is a matter of official urgency. If necessary, you must delay the plane."

CHAPTER XXXVIII.

WHEN Caresse had said that Perdita was an expert driver, it had been no more than the truth. Like many of her generation, she was more at ease with her hands on the steering-wheel than with her feet on the pavement. But she was conscious that she drove a strange car in a strange city, and mind and eyes were intent upon traffic and signs, and the uniformed police at the crossings.

Her glance did not wander to see that she was observed by Zita Janda, coming out of a shop in the Vaclavske Boulevard, nor was she aware that the Hungarian girl got into her own car, which had been drawn up at the pavement, and followed at a discreet distance.

When Perdita arrived at the Ambassador Hotel, Mme. Janda stopped her car a short distance away and entered a telephone kiosk, where she rang up Herr Müller. She gave a name which would not have been recognised by her friends, and had a short conversation of a quite innocent nature, ending with a formula of adieu which was an understood signal that the real point was to come. She added casually: "I've just seen her. She's come alone in the car. The one who had it, I mean."

There was no answering voice. The information she had given was either sufficient or not required. She went quickly back to her car, waving a gay greeting to the daughter of the Hungarian Envoy as she drove off to her own house. She had been shopping all afternoon, and it was time to dress now for the Castle Ball. And she had also some private packing to do, difficult to explain if it should come to her husband's knowledge—but that would be an unlikely trouble.

Half an hour later, Perdita, driving back to the Legation, was held up as she turned out of Wenceslaus Place by a traffic block in a narrower street, where a car which had pulled out from the pavement seemed to have some mechanical difficulty in restarting.

As she waited, a child came to the side of her car. She spoke in a careful school-English, not easy to understand.

"It is Miss Langton say you her friend. She try dress. She say will you to come?"

"You mean Mrs. Langton is in one of the shops?"

"Yes. She is so near. It is this way you shall come."

The girl pointed to the entrance of a covered foot-passage between the shops, such as were frequent in Prague.

Perdita alighted without hesitation. It was so like Caresse to have come out to the shops, after deciding to stay indoors: so like her to send that message instead of coming herself, if she had seen the car stop from a shop-window above.

She followed the child a dozen yards along the passage, and through the door of a busy prosperous shop of the better class. Assistants moved briskly about. Several customers were being served. Had she been more alert than she was, she might have entered the lift to which she was guided without suspicion being aroused.

It ran up to the top of the building, and when it stopped she stepped out automatically, to find herself in an attic-room lumbered with packing-cases, obsolete dummies, and the miscellaneous discarded litter of the business below

She turned round to say: "I think this must be the wrong floor," suspecting no more than that she was the victim of such an error as those who move among people of foreign speech must expect to meet.

But she was faced by the blank sheet of metal which was the door of the lift, as it was closed upon her. She heard the moan of its swift descent.

She looked round for a lift-bell which was not there, and then in bewilderment, now roused to a faint alarm. There must be a door— or stairs?

A door there was. It opened at the farther end of the room. A man stood in the entrance, clothed in blue-grey uniform, bright with polished buttons, giving it a military aspect, which might not be that of any recognised force, either of Prague or elsewhere.

She was too ignorant to judge of that, but she realised the menace of the heavy leather-sheathed pistol that his belt showed, and of the abrupt gesture which interpreted words less easy to understand.

He spoke in German, and then in a guttural French almost as unmeaning to her, standing aside for her to enter the further room.

"I think," she said, "there is a mistake. Is Mrs. Langton here?" But she could not tell whether he understood.

She went forward, and would have been glad to know how little she betrayed her increasing fear.

The further room was very differently furnished. It had comfort in a solid style, as for the ease of a man of wealth and affairs.

There was a man of such aspect seated at a broad flat desk, whose eyes met hers, in a cold critical stare.

He was old, as was shown by the whiteness of the close-cropped head, and the deep lines of the rugged face, which yet gave no sign of slackening either in mental or physical vigour.

Had he risen, his height would have made him appear thin, but it was a gesture of courtesy which did not enter his mind. He motioned to a couch opposite to his desk, and said curtly: "Sit down."

Perdita ignored an invitation which was too like a command. She said only: "I was told that Mrs. Langton was here. I think I have come to the wrong floor."

"You have come where you were brought."

He spoke her language with ease. It seemed natural that he should be efficient in all he did.

Perdita could not know that she faced the man who, since the day when the independence of Czechoslovakia had been declared, had been its most bitter foe. Of Czechoslovakian birth, but of German blood, he had been known as the head of the Nazi organisation in Prague until two years ago, when he had been accused of complicity in a theft of State documents, and was supposed to have fled the country.

In his absence, he had been sentenced to five years' imprisonment, and from that day he had remained concealed on this upper floor, his presence in Prague unguessed even by its vigilant police.

From this room he still exercised the authority of the executive head of the Nazi organisation for which Herr Müller supplied the plans, the instructions, and the ample funds from which it derived its power.

Perdita controlled the sense of peril that chilled her heart, to reply: "You had no right to do that. I cannot stay now. I have left my car in the street."

"The police will be sufficient to deal with that."

The reply came with a sneer. Two days ago, he would not have permitted the kidnapping to take place in such a way that the car would have been left standing almost at the door of his unsuspected refuge; but now, with the instructions which Herr Schmit had smuggled through at his life's cost under his hand, he felt that the end had come.

There was still the doubt—the possibility—that the signal for which he waited would not be given; that the cloud would clear, and no tempest would rend the skies. But, even so (which Odin forbid!), he knew that it would only be on such terms that Prague would be at Germany's feet on the next day.

There would be amnesty for himself: probably a position of political power. Otherwise, he would be clear of the doomed city before the next dawn should rise. In either event, his two years' hiding was over now.

Perdita asked: "Why have you tricked me to come here?"

"What did you do with the last sheet of the script which had been left in your charge?"

The question lifted the shadow of fear from her mind. If he did not know, and had taken this method of getting it back—

"Oh, that!" she said. "You might have taken a more decent way, if you wanted to get it. Mr. Norton returned it to Herr Müller this morning. If it's yours, you'd better ask him. And now perhaps you'll tell me how to ring for the lift."

But he took no notice of this request, nor was there any increase of cordiality in his manner as he replied.

"So I know. But it was not that which I asked. What was done with it before it was returned?"

"You had better ask Mr. Norton that."

"I am asking you."

"It ought not to have been in my luggage at all."

"It is sufficient that you evade reply. I have something to say to which you should listen well, if you value life, as most women do.

"The page which you kept was a secret thing, and I am assured that it has become known to some of your friends at the British Legation, whom we are unable to reach.

"But there is nothing there that they are not welcome to know or guess, if they make no dangerous mischief by disclosing it to the police here. It is that which we cannot risk.

"What I require you to do is to speak to Mr. Norton from here. You will obtain his promise that its secret will be preserved, and you will make it clear that your life is dependent upon that pledge being given, which you must understand is no less than true."

Perdita looked at the door through which she had come, which was blocked by the man who had summoned her to enter. There was no other visible exit from the room. The window was high and small. Through it she could see only a trail of cloud, moving across a background of winter blue. It was strongly barred.

She saw that she was caught beyond hope of escape. She said: "I will speak to Mr. Norton."

"You will tell him just what I have said?"

"Oh, yes! I will tell him that."

The tone was less satisfactory than the words. He looked at her with suspicious, merciless eyes. He said: "You will be wise if you do."

He took up a desk telephone to give the order: "I want Mr. Lawrence Norton, at the British Legation."

She recognised the name, but not the low rapidly-spoken instructions that followed, given in the Czech tongue, and ending with: "Yes, at first; on the second line."

A moment later, he passed the receiver to her. She stood by his side to speak, as he did not rise.

"Is that you, Lawrence?"

The answering "Yes" came faintly over the wire.

"I can't hear you very well. Can you hear me?"

The reply came faintly again: "Yes. Quite clearly."

"Well, I'm glad you can. I've been rather a fool and got caught by those German gentlemen the papers belonged to. They want you to promise that you won't let anyone know what they are about. I'm detained on the top floor, lingerie shop, inside passage, near 58, Wenceslaus Place. Of course you won't promise anything."

She spoke the concluding sentences very hurriedly, expecting every moment to have the instrument seized, and prepared to struggle if necessary for its retention until she could conclude what she had determined to say.

But there was no motion from the man at her side, and she paused only on the realisation that there was no answering voice.

"Are you there, Lawrence?" she asked, and the Nazi leader replied.

"There is no one there. You have been talking on what I think you would call a dead line. It was to test what you would say.

"You have lost your chance of speaking to your friends now; and you will be a very fortunate woman if you have the sense to listen to me."

She saw the trick he had played, and, for the moment, anger overcame fear.

"I have done nothing to you, and you have no right to detain me here. You will find that you cannot do what you like to an English girl, and get away from the police. You will be very much wiser to let me go."

"I think differently. And it is a matter for me to judge."

"You will end in jail, if you keep me here. The British Envoy will see to that."

She spoke with confidence, thinking of her friends at the Legation and the prestige of Britain, which should be her sufficient shield.

He was outwardly unmoved by her boast, looking at her with coldly speculative eyes.

"So you think?" he replied. "Will it console you when you are dead? You should hope that your friends will—how do you say that?—play to the different tune."

In the privacy of his own mind, he did not like what he had been instructed to do. He was not sure she was wrong. But he recognised that the preservation of the secrecy of that errant sheet was a consideration before which all else must give way.

And the very gravity of that which he had already done increased the peril in which she stood, for he saw clearly that he could not release her except on such terms of peace as would not be easy to make.

But it was useless to look ahead. He must take confidence from the knowledge that it was Herr Müller upon whom suspicion would most naturally fall, if she should not return.

And Herr Müller, whose telephone was said to be regularly tapped by the police, and who was being particularly careful to remain all afternoon where his movements would be observed, would be in a position to disprove any accusation which could be formulated against him.

And who knew that the next day might not find England and Germany divided by such an outbreak of the forces of hell as would make the death of a single woman, of whatever nation, a triviality to which no government would have leisure or inclination to listen?

The one thing certain was that, unless he could make the terms with the British Legation at which he aimed, he could not afford to let her go free, to disclose his refuge to the Prague police, or (if that should soon cease to matter) to make possible trouble between the British and German Governments, in which his part could not be concealed, and in which he might find himself repudiated and sacrificed for the sake of more important considerations.

He called to his servant, who held the door: "Fritz" (speaking in Czech), "take her back to the next room. What time does the shop shut tonight? Six? At six-fifteen, if you have no further orders from me, you will tell her that she is free to go. You will let her down by the quick stair."

The man said "Ja" to that, in a stolid way. He knew the order to mean that, at six-fifteen, he must tell the English woman that he would summon the lift for her use. She would see him press a concealed bell. She would approach the door of the lift, in a natural haste to be gone. After a time, it would slide open to let her through. As she moved forward to enter, he would give her the needed push. The lift would be in the roof over her head and she would fall down the empty shaft, to a certain death.

It was astonishing how slight a push would be sufficient to overbalance anyone advancing to the opening which they would suppose to give access to a waiting lift.

He had a practised knowledge of this, for it was so that he had twice sent men to death who had been suspected of disloyalty to the Nazi cause. And a mere girl—it could be done with one hand. There would be no need for the lifted foot with which he had sent Jan Kopec spinning forward into the void.

CHAPTER XXXIX.

IT was 4:25 when the Minister of Police received Sir Geoffrey Cullender's urgent call, and it was still less than 4:40 when his car drove under the heavy castle archway which was the approach to the British Legation in Prague.

His department had received the warning call in time to tap the last words of Sir Geoffrey's conversation with the Nazi agent, but had failed to capture the speaker, who had been using a telephone kiosk in the neighbourhood of Wenceslaus Place.

He expressed his regret for this, but added the disconcerting information that Herr Müller could not have been directly concerned, either in the abduction or in the attempted negotiation that had followed. His movements were too closely and constantly watched, in the vain effort to prove his complicity in the plots which he was believed to plan and direct. No, they must look in other directions, if Perdita were to be found.

He expressed regret also for the inconvenience (he would not call it by a stronger word) to the English lady, and gave assurances that his officers would be vigorous in their efforts for her release; but it may be excused that it was the occasion rather than the fact of her abduction which primarily engaged his mind.

"I have to thank Your Excellency," he said, rising hastily within ten minutes of his arrival, "for the disclosure of a most infamous plot. You may be assured that we shall be equal to the discomfiture of those who would wreck the peace of the city in which they dwell."

He drove away with his mind in a turmoil of conflicting thoughts. He was chagrined that Herr Schmit had foiled him, even at the moment of his own death; angered that his officers should have been outwitted, and have allowed the luggage of the English ladies to pass without adequate inspection, and most wroth of all that he had now obtained no more than the last sheet of documents that he rightly thought might be of momentous consequence, if they could have been communicated to the more friendly chancelleries of Europe four or five days before.

Even now—? But might it not be the last hour? Might it not be of the most urgent and vital consequence that the plot should be frustrated without a moment's delay? And how was that to be done? By what method could it be intended that the entrances to the bomb-proof shelters should be destroyed?

Was the evidence he now had of a nature and quality sufficient to justify the wholesale arrest of all Nazis within the city who were suspected of hostile activities? What effect would such a step have upon the political crisis which was already causing his Government sufficient concern?

He saw that the President ought to be informed instantly of the discovery which had come to his hands, and that it was his duty to consult his colleagues before taking any decisive action; while it was equally clear that such action was of insistent urgency.

With his mind so filled, what thought would it be likely to give to the comparatively trivial fact that an English girl was in Nazi hands?

Lawrence gave words to his perception of this condition when he said: "We shan't get much help from him."

He paced the room impatiently as he exclaimed: "If I only knew where to look!" And then: "You won't want me, sir, for the next hour?"

Sir Geoffrey was drafting a wire to the Foreign Office in London; he looked up sharply from his desk to ask: "What are you meaning to do?"

"He's going to find Perdita, of course," Caresse answered for him. "We can't leave her like that."

Sir Geoffrey was not indifferent to the girl's fate, but he felt that everything practical had already been done, and, as with Herr Schott, his mind was on larger issues. "It is a matter," he said, "with which the police should be able to deal."

He looked at Lawrence to add: "What do you propose to do? Herr Müller won't admit anything. You'll find you'll get nothing from him. Even the police can't put any salt on his tail."

"I'm not sure about that. There might be some bargain that we could make. They won't gain anything by keeping her, now that their threat's failed. But I wasn't going to him. I reckon Steele's our best chance. There isn't much of these plotters' haunts that he doesn't know."

"Sorry, Norton, but I can't allow that. It isn't only that, on what you've told me yourself, Steele has something more important to do, and needs all the rest he can get. I can't have you going to call on him, when every step you take may be watched. It wouldn't be a natural thing for you to do. Even the Czech police haven't guessed that he's anything but a hanger-on here. There's only Janda who knows. It would make them wonder at once if you go there now."

"I can't sit here doing nothing, without knowing what danger she may be in."

"It's probably less than you think. But, for the moment, we've done all that we can. I shall want this telegram coded and sent off at once."

"Can't Harvey do that, sir? You don't mind me sending Steele a note? There'd be nothing queer about that."

"If it's done discreetly. Yes, you can do that. Send Harvey to me."

Lawrence's note was brief:

> "Miss Wyatt has been kidnapped by Nazis here. Where would they be likely to hold her?
>
> "I have told Paul that I am writing to know whether you will be well enough to give us some help tonight."

He sent the letter by the hand of the servant he mentioned, telling him that he was to refuse to return without a reply, even if he were met by the difficulty that the man was in bed, and had given orders that he should not be disturbed.

It was 5:45 P.M. when the reply came to his hand:

> "Passage from Wenceslaus Place, cycle depot right, ladies' outfitters left.
>
> "Top floor outfitters' premises. Highly dangerous. Secure lift. Other exit by roof. Shoot to kill. Good luck. S."

Lawrence showed it to Sir Geoffrey at once. "What ought I to do about this? Is it a thing we can manage best by ourselves, or shall I get Herr Schott to help?"

Sir Geoffrey was decided in his reply. "You'd better go there yourself. You've got something to bargain with now, which you wouldn't have if you'd told the police.

"The Nazis can't want to have any trouble with us, and they'll have nothing to gain by detaining Miss Wyatt longer, if they have our promise that we won't disclose where she's been kept.

"It's ten to six now, and if I don't see you back, or hear from you by six-thirty, I shall put the police on the right track. But I shouldn't be too quick to think about shooting, if I were you. If you talk sense, it ought to do the trick better than that."

The advice was sound, on the information they had, and came from one who had watched such events before, with the detachment of those who are not directly concerned. But there was another motive that weighed heavily on his mind.

He preferred that the curiosity of the Czech police should not be directed upon the source of the information that No. 973 had supplied. He neither wished it to be observed that he had better means of information than their own, nor suspected that Steele was anything other than the shiftless odd-job man that he appeared. And

these reasons were sufficient to give him a strong preference for securing Perdita's freedom, if possible, without the assistance of the
police.

Lawrence accepted the advice with alacrity. He asked: "Do you
mean that it would be better for me to go unarmed?"

"No. I don't say that. If there's any shooting, you should be able
to do your share. But don't be too ready to begin."

Lawrence said he would bear that advice in mind, and went
quickly out.

By this time his car had been brought back and unloaded. As he
reached it in the yard below, he found Caresse at his side.

She said: "You'll have to hurry. We've no time to lose now."

He did not follow the special cause for haste which was dominant in her mind, but he saw that she was intending to get into the
car, and stopped with his hand on the door.

"I'm afraid it won't do for you to come. We don't know what
sort—"

"Of course I can, if Perdita's there. I may be more use than
you."

"You don't understand. It isn't exactly a woman's job. There's
some reason to think—"

"Of course I do. I heard all that was said. It's the one chance
you've got, to take me along."

As she spoke, she got in at the other door of the car. He restrained himself to say patiently: "If you could make me see that—"

"So I can. Didn't Sir Geoffrey say that we'd better do this in a
quiet way?

"Well, you walk into the baby-linen shop, or whatever it is, and
you look round like—anything silly, and in about half a second they
see that you're someone who hasn't got any business there. There'll
be a shop-walker, or someone worse, asking you what you want, and
leading you back to the door, before you've even had time to see
where the lift is.

"But if they think I've brought you in to pay for all the things
that I'm meaning to buy—they'll just ask you to take a chair, and
you can look round, and then stroll up to the lift, and—well, I suppose you know what you mean to do after that."

"I don't want you to get into needless danger. There's trouble
enough over that with Perdita now."

"Neither do I. When you go upstairs, I shall just go back, and sit
in the car. It'll be far better than leaving it with nobody there."

He wavered, seeing some reason in this, and objected weakly: "But you don't want to buy anything."

"Don't I? You'll find I shan't make any difficulty about that. It'll be a queer shop, if I don't find something I can bring out.

"But if you only wouldn't waste time in this maddening way! Can't you see that it's almost six now, and the dance at eight, and Perdita and I have both got to dress after we get back?"

"Well," he said doubtfully, "I suppose there's no real harm, if you stay below."

"Of course there isn't. It's no use looking sulky, when you know I've made up my mind to come. If you waste any more time you'll find the shop's shut, more likely than not."

Lawrence recognised defeat. He got into the car, and turned it swiftly downhill on the road to the river bridge.

CHAPTER XL.

PERDITA became increasingly bored as the hours passed, but she was not greatly afraid.

She had a well-founded confidence that her captors would lose no time in approaching those with whom they must bargain for her release; and she knew that, if they should fail to do so, her disappearance could not be overlooked.

She remembered that Caresse's possessions, as well as her own, were in the car that she had left in the street below; and that alone would ensure a speedy enquiry into the reason for her delay. Why, it must be almost time to be dressing now!

She strolled for a time round the lumbered room, idly examining its contents, while her gaoler seated himself on a packing-case, and became absorbed in the contents of a dull-covered book on some technical subject, obviously indifferent to anything she could do for her own escape from that attic room.

Her instinctive realisation of the ruthless character of the men into whose power she had fallen might have roused her to sharper fear had she been less confident in her own position, and that her friends would have the power, and would be active, to secure her release.

She was still only vaguely aware of the existence, and incredulous of the strength, of the sinister world-forces which were already commencing to move beneath her, like the first faint tremors of earthquake shock, and to which she was of no more weight than is a feather upon the air at the tempest's height.

She was informed, as the quarters passed, by the chimes of the clock of the nearby church, which were echoed, a second later, by another a short distance away; but even when the slow booming strokes of six o'clock sounded, her thought was less of any peril threatening herself than of how wild Caresse would be if her luggage had not arrived.

But as the further minutes passed she became aware that the man was regarding her with a livelier interest. He observed that the time had come at which the shop would be closed, and the striking of the next quarter would be the signal for the execution which he had been instructed to undertake.

It was a method of obvious convenience, by which the victim's body delivered itself to the ground floor from which it must finally be disposed; and having the further advantages that it entailed no evidence of bloodshed or violence on the scene of the crime, and that, in the event of discovery, it must be difficult, if not impossible, to prove that it was not a case of accidental death.

On the two previous occasions, that which was sound in theory had proved to be equally satisfactory in practice. The victims had both been standing by the lift in anticipation of stepping into it as the door slid open.

There might even have been waste of energy in the hearty kick with which Jan Kopec had been sent over the edge, and a one-handed push had proved to be all that the second occasion required.

But as the man considered the present case, he observed a difference in the fact that the idea of departure had to be conveyed to his victim's mind, which his own linguistic resources might be unequal to do.

He even considered the expediency of a blow on the head from a pistol-butt as a preliminary to the major operation, and it is probable that Perdita would have found it extremely difficult to avoid this unpleasant experience, had he not had good reason to remember that his superior officer required that his instructions should be literally obeyed.

He rose, therefore, while the four strokes of the quarter were still reverberating upon the air, and gathered his slender resources of foreign tongues as he advanced toward the lift-door, to say: "Voulez-vous—to go—ja."

She understood the gesture better than the gruff command of the halting words, and though she had less expectation of freedom than that he was merely proposing to guide her to some other place—perhaps for food, perhaps to a room more suited for prolonged confinement—there was nothing in her present situation to render her unwilling for such a change.

As she saw him pass his hand along the upper cornice of the lift-door, and press upon studs which she had not previously observed, she advanced willingly toward it, but standing somewhat back in anticipation that he would be the first to enter.

She heard the long whine of the ropes as the lift made its ascent, and then the sheet-metal door began to slide slowly open.

CHAPTER XLI.

As the quarter of six-fifteen which brought Perdita to the threshold of violent death chimed from the tower of Loretto Church, the German Envoy waited upon the Czechoslovakian President in the same room where they had confronted one another a week before.

His instructions did not require that he should exercise courtesy or restraint in the execution of the errand on which he came, and his temper had not been improved by the fact that he had been kept waiting for fifteen minutes, since he had arrived for an appointment that he had made by telephone half an hour earlier.

The room in which he sat had stout walls and a thick door, but they had been insufficient to prevent a discord of angry voices coming to his ears at times, from which he rightly concluded that a Council of Ministers was being held, among whom a united decision was hard to reach.

Even so, it was an insufficient reason for the rudeness of this delay, and his indignant surprise was not placated when the door opened at last to admit, not the President alone, but the Ministers also of Police and War. As he saw them, a doubt entered his mind. Could their Secret Service have informed them already of the errand on which he came?

"I am here," he said, rising stiffly, "to hear your answer to my request of a week ago."

"And we regret that a more serious matter has come to our knowledge within the last hour, to which we must ask you to listen first."

"There can be nothing more urgent than this, as you will understand if you will hear the message which I am instructed to give, and which should have been delivered nearly half an hour ago."

"Can you judge the urgency of that of which you have not heard? But perhaps you already know that a certain paper has come into our hands?"

"You must be plainer before I reply."

"Is it the act of a friendly State, with whom we are still at peace (as I hope we may ever be) that they should require us to listen by night and day lest *Die ägyptische Helena* should be played from the Nürnberg station?"

"I do not know what you mean."

The President recognised a note of sincerity in the impatience of this reply. He said: "Then will you read this?"

The German Envoy took the proffered sheet. He read it with an expressionless face.

"I neither know," he said, "what it is, nor to what it alludes. It is unsigned, and"—he turned it over with a contemptuous hand—"it is on paper made in your own land, and in an ink that is scarcely dry."

"It is a copy of the last sheet of instructions sent to Herr Müller a few days ago."

"Herr Müller? We have no accredited agent of that name. And an alleged copy of what? If you will furnish proof of whatever you think may give you cause to complain, it shall be fairly considered at a more opportune time. But my mission now—"

"If we will furnish proofs! Were they not my very words to you last week, and how did you answer then?

"We desire peace, knowing well that we are less powerful than you. But it must be a better peace than that in which you plot and watch for a moment of sudden war.

"Excellency," his voice sank from its indignation to a note of urgent, anxious appeal, "I ask you to show the justice—the generosity that your strength allows. Let us meet each other with the friendly frankness the position requires, and if we are assured that your own purpose is pacific towards ourselves, there will be no reasonable satisfaction denied. But if you demand that against which reason and justice rebel, and in a voice that is not that of a friend—if you refuse us the satisfaction of proofs which yourselves require in a like case—then we can but say that you ask more than our own honour will allow us to give; and if you call that an unfriendly act, we must appeal against you to the conscience of all mankind."

"I have explicit instructions to require the undertakings for which I asked seven days ago."

"And I must reply that you cannot ask us to expel those against whom we have no complaint, and against whom no evidence is produced, beyond the fact that they are on a list of names which you furnish to us."

"I cannot argue on that. If you decline, my instructions require that I leave Prague without further delay."

The three men to whom he spoke looked at one another in a silence which would have been quickly broken had they not been in the presence of one who, by that word, had become little less than their open foe.

The feeling dominant in the mind of the Minister of Police was one of anger that the gravity of the discovery he had made should be so contemptuously denied.

In that of the Minister of Defence there was the relief of feeling that the hour of crisis, long regarded as inevitable, had come at last, and of confidence in the spirit of the army which he had prepared for the forecasted moment.

He knew that the Air Minister was of a less confident mind; but that was the reason that he had not been with them when they entered the room.

Only the President, still half-incredulous that Berlin would push the issue to the extremity of a war of which no one could see the end, made a final appeal:

"Excellency," he said, "you will recall that your country was charged with the guilt of the last war—I do not say whether justly or not—and that it was a stigma that she was at much pains to refute. Have you thought that, if she should again disturb the peace of Europe, she will earn the execrations of all mankind?"

"As to that," the Envoy replied, "Germany is her own judge. But you may be assured that she will so act that the peace of Europe will be more securely arranged."

He went without further words, and within ten minutes a wireless message informed Berlin that his ultimatum had been rejected even before it had been presented in a formal manner. Five minutes later, he left the city by his private plane, and his suite followed in the next hour.

It was a little later that a telegram reached the Hungarian Legation, ending with the expected words: *The price of flour will go up.*" Within an hour, the Legation was deserted. Without the formalities of leave-taking, the Hungarian Minister's car left the doomed city to make its rapid way toward the safety of the Bavarian frontier.

Almost without intention, without the certain knowledge of those whose words and actions had brought it to be, the War of 1938 had commenced.

Even among the Ministers of Czechoslovakia, there were still those who thought it no more than a baseless scare which the next morning would clear away.

The War Minister himself, in the midst of a hundred urgencies of command, expressed a doubt of the same kind.

"They have," he said, "no intention of war. They have not mobilised a single division. They are less ready than we ourselves. We shall be glad tomorrow that we have stood firm, when we are met with overtures of a different tone."

The President himself, his telephone reaching out to the ends of Europe in appeals for support or intercession, was still anxiously hopeful that the difference could be bridged in a peaceful way.

Only the Minister of the Air, already busy before the German Envoy had gone with the instructions which it was his duty to issue, prepared with a single mind for what he knew could be no more than a futile strife; while, from a score of her hidden aerodromes, the German bombers rose like clusters of swarming bees to range themselves in the moonlit night.

CHAPTER XLII.

THE man saw himself to be confronted by the difficulty he had feared. Perdita showed neither fear nor unwillingness, but she stood back as though for him to go first, and the door was already sliding apart.

He saw that he would have to throw her down in the end, and if she should remain in the rear and then start back at sight of the vacant space, in the next moment he might be under the necessity of pursuing her round the room.

If his purpose were guessed, he might be engaged in a struggle with a desperate frightened girl which he would prefer to avoid.

He did not doubt its result, but he knew that he would earn the more praise if his work were quickly and quietly done. His hand came firmly under Perdita's arm, drawing her forward to the opening gap.

She was unused to be handled in such a manner, and repulsion, reinforced by a swift instinct of fear, caused her to wrench sharply away, in an effort which only tightened the rough grasp of the stronger arm.

And, at the same moment, the sliding door revealed, not a vacant well, but the level floor of the lift, and Lawrence Norton stepping into the room.

It was in a second's space that the man's hand went to his belt, and the two reports had the sound of a single shot but Perdita's struggle, and the fact that he was completely surprised, while Lawrence had been alert to whatever might be revealed by the opening door, had made that half-second's difference on which life and death may, at such moments, depend.

The man fell forward, a twitching heap, at Perdita's feet.

She said: "Well, you do know how to come at the right time!" She was conscious that her heart beat at something more than its usual pace, and that she had some difficulty in controlling her voice, but she recovered herself from the moment's shock as she asked: "But you're not hurt, are you?"

He looked down at a shoe the leather of which was torn on the inner side.

"No," he said, "I think not. He must have let off as I got him, before he had finished raising his gun."

His words ended abruptly, as he fired twice at the gap of an opening door at the farther end of the room and saw it hastily closed.

He crossed over to it, and was glad to see a bolt on his own side, that he could drive in.

He asked: "How many more friends have you got here?"

"Only one that I've met," she answered. "But there may be more. I said before that Prague's the liveliest place I was ever in."

"The sooner you're somewhere else than you are now, the more likely you are to die of senile decay. Did you see how they work this lift?"

They had entered it together now, and he was vainly pressing the studs.

She got out again, as she answered "Yes. See here. There are some buttons or something. But they are too high for me to reach."

The man had ceased moving now. He had lain with his head fallen forward into the lift, and as they entered, Lawrence had put a foot under his shoulder to push him further away.

There was a little blood on the floor where he had lain. Nothing more dreadful than that. Perdita looked down with no conscious repugnance at what she saw. He was not one whom she had any cause to regret.

She would see worse things than that before the rise of another sun.

Lawrence was now pressing the studs in the cornice over the lift. He said: "Be quick to jump in if it starts to move. I don't want to risk one of us being left behind."

She stood alert, as he sought the method of control, anxious neither to be left, nor to descend alone, but the lift did not move though the door did, closing them out.

After a time, he abandoned a hopeless effort. "I think," he said, making a correct guess, "the power must be cut off."

"How long are we likely to be shut up here?"

"Oh, we'll find a way out. I believe there's one over the roof."

He crossed the room to the bolted door. He listened, but heard no sound. Probably whoever had been there had fled in haste, thinking that the police were upon the scene.

Had he been alone, he might have withdrawn the bolt, but it was a risk that he paused to take with Perdita upon his hands; and the thought of the police reminded him that they were to be informed at six-thirty if Sir Geoffrey had heard nothing from him by then. It must be nearly that now.

He said: "I reckon we shall have the police here within half an hour, though I'm not quite clear as to how they are to get up when they arrive. But that's their trouble, not ours."

They sat down side by side to await the expected rescue, on the packing-case which the dead man had used for the same purpose.

"How on earth," she asked, "did you find me here?"

He told her briefly, omitting mention of the source from which the address had been obtained.

When he described how he had come, she interrupted to ask: "Caresse came? You don't mean that she's here now?"

"Unless she's got tired of waiting, she'll be outside in the car."

"Oh, she'll be there. She wouldn't leave us like this. But she'll be wild at the waste of time."

"I didn't know that time counted at all with her."

"It does when she's got something worth while that she wants to do."

"I shouldn't have thought she'd have had the pluck to come as she did."

He spoke with an appreciation from which Perdita observed that his admiration of Caresse was evidently not a declining quantity. She said: "You don't know her at all, if you thought that. She'd be too restless to keep out of a thing like this."

She felt the word to be less than adequate, and capable of ungenerous interpretation. She added: "Besides, if she thought I'd got in a mess, she'd want to see what she could do."

He replied by describing how Caresse had piloted him into the shop below, and how adroitly she had contrived that he should have an opportunity of passing unobserved into the rear of the premises where the lifts were placed.

He had hidden behind a long rack of gowns, over which a dust-sheet had been thrown for the night; and from that position, he had watched the porter send the lift which he regarded as most likely to be the one he sought, up into the roof, as was, no doubt, its customary position during the night.

He had fetched it down as soon as the man withdrew, and had had it under control and set for the top floor, at the time when Perdita's captor had attempted to manœuvre it in another way.

"I had no difficulty," he said, "in controlling it then, and can only suppose that the power can be cut off from this floor, and that the gentlemen in the next room did it before they bolted."

So it was; but it had, in fact, been no more than the routine of the night. The Nazis had been too shrewd to make more than occasional use of the shop, even in daylight hours, and in the night they had only sought security against being surprised themselves from below.

He described how he had seen Caresse withdraw from the shop, after an exhibition of inability to describe her needs in a foreign tongue, which had concentrated the attention of several assistants upon herself; and from that they wandered into discussion of the courage and resource of those who make a profession of timidity, treating it rather as boast than shame.

They were not uncritical in praise of what she had done, but Caresse, had she been able to hear, would have been content with the significance of the fact that the thoughts of both were upon her rather than on themselves.

It was little after seven when the whine of the sinking lift told them that the police had entered below, and had switched on the power.

Three minutes later they were in the street, where Caresse still sat in the waiting car.

"Here you are at last!" she exclaimed, in a tone of casual impatience. "I thought you would never come. What a place it is! I'm nearly frozen to death waiting like this."

There had been a crowd round the entrance to the passage, which the police now guarded, and they had some difficulty in pushing their way through. But the attention of the onlookers had not been directed upon themselves, but upon a plane which could be dimly seen as it circled over the city and disappeared northward into the night.

"I believe," Lawrence said, as he took the wheel, "that was the German Minister's plane."

Caresse, impatient though she might be, had no cause to complain of the pace at which he drove through the frozen streets.

CHAPTER XLIII.

CARESSE, having been sitting with Lawrence in the front of the car, and having kept her place while she had been waiting for him to bring Perdita out, it naturally followed that Perdita found herself alone on the rear seat, with the benefit of a few minutes' quietude in which to adjust her mind, from the experience through which she had passed, to the environment which it had abruptly disturbed.

While she remained happily unaware of the extremity of peril from which she had been rescued, she realised clearly enough the jeopardy, even to life itself, in which she had been placed at the hands of ruthless and desperate men.

Though she did not know the sinister purpose for which she had been dragged to the opening door of the lift, yet the pain of a brutal grasp, the memory of those instant shots, and of the body that became so easily quiet, a thing to be kicked slackly about at another's will, were sufficient to emphasise the gratitude which her rescue owed, and that no less because it had been effected in so casual a manner.

She looked at her two friends with grave eyes, under slightly frowning brows. The rapid pace at which Lawrence twisted his way through the crowded streets did not prevent an animated conversation proceeding between them. The words were not always easy to catch, but the substance, light, intimate, shallow in itself, and yet profound in its rejection of the atmosphere of the fevered streets, was easy for one who knew them to understand.

Perdita did not resent that she was alone on the rear seat, recognising that it had occurred in a natural way. She did not resent that the conversation seemed oblivious of her own existence.

She saw the quick characteristic gesture of casual intimacy in which Caresse laid her hand on the driver's arm, and heard the word of laughing protest with which it was shaken off: "Not when I'm at the wheel, if you don't mind."

She saw her friends' eyes meet in a way which brought sharply back to her mind how she had seen them together on the terrace the night before. "I didn't mean anything," Caresse had said, turning the evidence of that close embrace lightly aside. "I never do."

Perdita recognised the genuine quality of the excuse: she felt no resentment, no jealousy of Caresse.

But would she be willing to join her life to that of one who would kiss any woman who "meant nothing; who never did"?

Perhaps, she told herself, "any" woman was less than fair. Perhaps, if he were married, he might act in a different way.

And she had some confidence in herself, some assurance that she would not be less than equal to holding that which she should make sufficient effort to win.

Her real trouble was that she was disturbed by a standard of conduct alien from, and lower than, that which she had been taught, and which her own nature required.

Her mind went back to the serene atmosphere, the implicit ideals, the gracious security of her own Warwickshire home.

She knew, with a sound instinct, that such intimacies of act and speech should not mean nothing, but much; even though the immaturity of a generation boasting, with naive arrogance, of the modernity of the perpetual present which never ends, may deride the wisdom of all the ages that are behind.

The healthy carnality of youth had reached out sensitive tentacles of emotion, seeking untried experience, and had shrunk back, baffled and chilled by the revelation of an incontinent triviality which was neither serious nor ashamed.

He certainly had the gift of coming at most opportune times! She was duly grateful for that. She recognised him as one who would be adequate for the protection of those who might be under his care.

And though Caresse might act with the bewildering levity which often made it an insoluble problem to decide what she thought or was, Perdita was acute enough to admit the casual quality of the flirtation that she observed. Probably it was really nothing to her! But to Lawrence? Nothing to him? She was less sure.

She became aware that her arm ached where it had been grasped so rudely a few minutes before by a man who now lay dead on the floor of that upper room. What would he have done to her in the next moment, if Lawrence had not arrived? She would not go to the dance. She did not think that she would be greatly missed.

On his return, Lawrence was summoned at once to Sir Geoffrey's room.

"Norton," the British Minister said, "this is private now, though it's the sort of thing that everyone knows in an hour's time.

"The German Minister's left, and if it isn't the threshold of war, it's the best imitation I ever met. But the Government doesn't want any panic, or anything to get about till they announce it themselves.

"The latest move is that they're trying to get Poland to intercede.

"Anyway, nothing's to be allowed to interfere with the Red Cross Ball, and most of the Ministers will be there.

"I can't come myself, but I want you and Harvey to go, and, of course, you'll take the ladies, as you've arranged."

"Very well, sir. Of course, I'll say nothing. But I should say the panic, or at least the flight, has begun. The streets were crowded with cars, and by one or two Nazis that I recognised in them, I should say that the schedule of names that was in Miss Wyatt's case was a list of those that the German Government wished to have warned, so that they could leave if they saw their Minister go."

He added: "We ought to get the girls away in the morning somehow. We don't know what this place may be like in a week's time."

"There is a telegram waiting for Mrs. Langton," Sir Geoffrey replied. "No doubt her husband's insisting that they leave without further delay."

But when Caresse came down, in a smiling satisfaction that had forgotten more trivial things in the knowledge that her own beauty was adequately arrayed, her news was of an opposite kind.

"I'm afraid," she said, "we shall have to go back to the hotel I've got a wire that Gerald's coming tomorrow."

She expected that Sir Geoffrey's reply would be to say that his hospitality was as free to her husband as to herself; but, instead of that, he paused a moment, as though the news were of a puzzling, if not an unwelcome kind.

"How is he coming?" he asked.

"He says he's coming by air."

He made no answer to that. His thought (which was best unspoken) was that commercial planes might have difficulty in getting through. She wondered vaguely whether Gerald could have had some difference with Sir Geoffrey of which she was not aware, and put it out of her mind.

It would be quite easy to go back tomorrow to the hotel.

CHAPTER XLIV.

IT was 8:30 P.M. when No. 973 rose and dressed himself in Private Gumpert's uniform, taking a special care that there should be nothing in his appearance or possessions incongruous with the character which he assumed.

Jarmila, his reputed cousin, a small, bustling, elderly woman, having prepared a meal for him of the kind which his English instincts preferred, sat down on the other side of the table to her own repast of cold fat bacon, and supplied him with the exciting gossip which she had collected from the crowded streets as she had been out shopping half an hour before.

Government proclamations, following one another at intervals of a few minutes, were being posted throughout the city.

One of these, perhaps intended for a wider public than that which jostled to read it in the uncertain light of the street lamps, declared that Czechoslovakia, although the German Envoy had left, was still striving and hoping for peace, and enjoined that there should be no outrages against people of German birth.

Another, of a different significance, summoned two classes of reserves to report at once to their various depots, and warned all citizens of military age to hold themselves in readiness to be called up on the following day.

A third, more urgently worded, summoned all reserve airmen, and those on leave, to report instantly to the military aerodrome five miles away.

A fourth, scattered through the city while still wet from the printers' hands, was a drastic warning against profiteering in food. Shopkeepers detected in such practices would have their stock confiscated and their premises closed.

Jarmila said that panic buying was rapidly emptying the shops. She was contemptuous of the greed and stupidity that her neighbours showed in this foolish scramble, and regretted, in the next breath, that she had not gone out with a basket of larger size. As it was, she seemed to have brought home an incredible quantity of provisions of sundry kinds; and there were the two gammons of bacon that Otto Popper had promised to deliver in the next hour. Woe betide the old gutter-bred Hebrew if his whining promise should not be kept!

She told also of wild rumours (lies, as she supposed them to be) concerning the safety of the great air-raid shelter opposite the Wilson Station, which had been recently finished, after being commenced more than two years before, and was said to be, in some ways, the best that Europe could boast.

It was not of the extent of the catacombs which Paris had converted to the same use, nor had it the advantage of the hundred entrances which London had obtained by adapting her underground railway system; but it was well-lighted, well-ventilated, furnished with a water-supply which could not be cut off from above, and contained great stores of food, and well-appointed hospitals.

It was designed for the accommodation of 50,000 people, and adapted to maintain them in health, if not in comfort, for a sufficient period to ensure that the most persistent of low-lying gases could be cleared away.

Now its entrances were guarded by a regiment of soldiers, who blocked its approaches on every side. They had invaded the surrounding buildings, and searched them from roof to cellar, arresting many indignantly protesting citizens, on the principle that it was better to detain a score of innocent persons rather than that they should overlook the malefactors for whom they sought.

She reported that the general tone of the street talk was anxious, but not despondent. If war should be at the gate, they were confident that Czechoslovakia would be equal to do her part. She would not be without strong allies!

Was it not better to have it over, even though at a heavy cost, than to live in a constant state of tension, terror, and gas-mask drill? Perhaps, when the hated German was truly crushed, Europe would be blessed with a real peace.

No. 973 listened, and ate well. There was little unexpected in what he heard, and he was in some doubt of what or where his next meal would be likely to be.

When he had finished, he rose, saying: "I do not know when I shall return. You may not see me again. Keep my room locked. If I am absent too long, let the British Minister have the key."

He gave the old woman's shoulder a friendly pat as he went out, to which she responded: "Ah, but I shall soon see you again!"

She was sure of his ability to come through any danger he might encounter. Her thought was not of herself. She was old, but tough. She did not doubt that she would be there on his return, to cook him the queer dishes that he preferred.

Was she likely to think that she might be sent to death before the next dawn would come, or that her danger was greater than his would be when he should rise into the perilous skies?

He got into the driver's seat of the ancient, shabby saloon car that it was his reputed living to drive for hire, throwing his soldier's cap into the back seat, and drawing a cloak over his German uniform, which it might be injudicious to show that night in the streets of Prague.

He drove slowly through the crowded traffic, observing that he had become part of an exodus that left the city mainly to east and north, amid some insults and jeers, but no attempt to obstruct their flight.

He heard: "Let the cowards run"; and "There'll be fewer traitors in Prague." He saw a car swerve as a cabbage was flung with too good an aim at a driver's face.

He saw all faces raised, and a murmur of excitement rise to a cheer that spread from street to street till it seemed that the whole city shouted its joy, as four-score of fighting planes, slender, deadly, and swift, came down the river-valley, and circled over the city as though in demonstration of its defence, their signal-lights flashing yellow and red as they ranged themselves in battle-squadrons and disappeared northward into the night.

Their passage had given confidence to the cheering crowds. Prague was awake, reliant upon herself, and defiant of hostile power. The zone of danger was far ahead, away beyond the darkness into which her brave airmen flew. Their advance seemed to push forward the deadly frontiers of war.

Only Janda, whose order had sent them out, had no hope in his heart. Courage he had, but it was the courage which does not delude itself with a false count.

He had less than six hundred planes of all types which were in condition to take the air.

The Germans admitted to three thousand. He had been ridiculed a week ago when he had called it five—without counting commercial planes which were of easily convertible designs. Even without those, he might have said ten thousand rather than five, and would not have exceeded his own belief.

And the information he had received this morning through the daring of the English agent would have destroyed hope had he deluded himself before!

But if there were no hope in his heart, he was no worse fitted by that for the post he held.

He counted his six hundred planes, disposing them where they could be used to the deadliest ends, whether in attack or defence.

He felt as the rat that twists to bite at the crushing heel. Prague might fall, but it was his part to raise the price of his country's death.

His orders involved that every plane would be in the air before midnight came.

"In six hours," he thought, "be the war over or not, I know that my part will be done. In half that time they may have bombed every aerodrome that I have. But, if they do, their bombs shall fall on no more than the empty sheds."

CHAPTER XLV.

No. 973 drove clear of the city, and came to the hilltop where he had turned off once before through the little wood, to the field, open and high, where he would find a plane for his secret use.

Again the watchful sentinel stepped out to hail him.

"That you, Karel?"

"Yes, sir. You'll find all ready in the field."

He drove on relieved, for it had been easy to think that his request might have been overlooked or refused in the crisis that had developed during the day.

But he was not prepared for the sight of the heavy bomber which darkened the farther end of the moonlit field, nor for the voice that introduced itself as he approached.

"I am Wing-Commander Klíma. I have orders to take you whither you may desire upon German soil."

"There appears to be a mistake. It was a single-seat scouter for which I asked. I need silence and speed."

"There may have been none such that could be spared on this night."

"Talk sense. I must know what is meant, or I do not go."

"I have my orders. I know nothing beyond them."

No. 973 made no reply. He walked up to inspect the ancient bomber more closely.

He asked: "What speed can you make?"

"About ninety miles per hour, with a full load."

"And you are loaded now?"

"Yes."

"Is that to help you to set me down?"

"I must obey the orders I have."

No. 973 saw that he was reluctant to speak, but was there anything that could not be seen with a half-closed eye?

He had asked for the loan—or rather the gift—of a scouting plane which would convey him swiftly and secretly to the isolated munitions village which he had found, and into which he was resolved to penetrate.

The Air Minister had not refused his request, but he had sent a slow heavy night-bomber of semi-obsolete type in which he was to be passenger, and therefore guide to the munitions village, which was to be bombed after they had set him down.

Should he accept a passage under such conditions?

He had, strictly, nothing to do with the coming war, on whichever side his sympathies might lie. But it was his duty to his own country to discover what he could of Germany's secret armaments, and for that purpose he should not cavil at the conditions on which he could get the assistance which he had asked.

But were they likely to be able to do him the service which he required?

"What," he queried, "shall you do if you fall in with their fighting planes?"

Commander Klíma was frank: "We should be their sport. We have no chance but that we shall not be observed."

"Having neither silence nor speed?"

"It can be tried. It is for such use, or else none. We defeat ourselves if we do not attempt."

No. 973 saw that he had met a comrade with whom it would be pleasant to be, whether for success, or to mere death in the air.

He considered the jeopardy of his own life (which it was his duty to guard) if he should take flight in a plane which was so ill-fitted either to fight or fly, and was engaged in a hostile act in a war which was not that of his own land.

But he considered also that, while his peril might be more in the air, it might be much less at a later stage, if he should agree to be carried in this way.

For he did not doubt that the plane was loaded with bombs that were to be dropped on the munitions village, immediately after they had set him down, and his prospect of entering it undetected might be far better when it was paralysed by, or recovering from, such an attack, than it would be at a quieter time.

"I will come," he said, "if you will be plain with me as to what you are ordered to do. You are to bomb the place near to which you will set me down?"

"You ask more than I know. It must depend upon my observation of acts of war, or upon the wireless instructions that I receive."

"That is good enough. You know Merseburg? No? It is twenty miles west of Leipzig."

"You want me to set you down there?"

Commander Klíma's voice had a note of wonder, if not of active dissent.

"Not precisely. It is a place called Leuna I seek. But if you make a compass to leave Leipzig twenty miles to the east, you will come near to pass over the spot."

The Commander was slow to reply, being a puzzled man. He said at last: "I was told that we should make flight to the Franconian hills."

No. 973 saw that the Air Minister had made a natural deduction, though it was not true.

"That," he said, "is because I do not say more than the moment needs. I did not return by a straight route, acting, at one time, as one who would reach Berlin, where I had said that my home lay."

"Well, I was told to set you down at your own place. Is there safe landing there in the night?"

His thought was on the different nature of the country to which he must now go. His mind had been on desolate flat-topped mountains, where he supposed that No. 973 had observed a practicable and lonely landing-place. But now he was to fly to a flat, thickly populated, industrial district.

No. 973 understood his thoughts, and answered more than he asked.

"It is more isolated than you suppose. I had observed a place where I could have alighted with little risk while the moon shone, but I had not thought of so large and loaded a plane."

Commander Klíma's shoulders lifted slightly, but he said no more than: "We waste time. Let us go."

It was at least true that the route was likely to be safer than that which he had expected to take. He thought he knew the directions from which the German air fleets might be converging upon the Czechoslovakian capital, and he thought it likely that his present course might steer safely between them. But every moment's delay must narrow the intervals between those converging fleets.

No. 973 was briefly introduced to the three airmen who completed the bomber's crew. He climbed into the cockpit.

With the buzz of a giant hornet, and taking the full length of the field, slowly, heavily, as though reluctant to face its fate, the loaded bomber rose into the air.

CHAPTER XLVI.

THE distance, in the straight flight that the air allows, was less than 150 miles, and, loaded though they were and facing a wind that blew from the northwest with increasing strength, it should be somewhat less than two hours before their destination would be reached. A night-bomber of any of the newer types would have done it in a third of the time—rather less than more.

It was now 10:00 P.M.

They struck almost due northwest with a rising flight, having the high range of the Erzgebirge Mountains lying across their way. The night clouded as they advanced, and they rose higher again, seeking clearer air.

At a height of 8,000 feet, they skated a carpet of cloud that the moonlight pearled, looking, in the clear frozen air, as though they might have stepped out to a solid ground.

It seemed as empty of life as though they skimmed the snow of an arctic night, until, breaking the carpet of cloud as flying fishes might leap from the sea, they saw a squadron of rising planes coming almost directly upon them, and not half a mile away.

It was no more than a second's sight, for Commander Klíma sank through the mist as a frightened rabbit dives into its hole.

He swerved westward, and flew blind through the clouds, seeking only to hide from those who could outpace him, three yards to one.

Fore and aft, his two gun-turrets rose, and their gunners listened and peered through the flying mist.

But the minutes passed, and there was no sign of pursuit. The plane came round on to her course, and, after a time, ventured to rise again to the clearer air.

If it had been seen at all, it had been ignored by those who had orders too urgent to be delayed for a casual prey.

But Commander Klíma was no longer in doubt of what he would have to do. In the moment before he dived, he had seen enough. He had not recognised the pattern of the planes, but he had seen the formation of the three-fold wedge, the three sevens, one in front, and three trending backward on either side, which was general throughout the German Air Force at this date, and he saw the direction to which they flew.

Already they had crossed the frontier. In how few minutes might the Plzen munitions works be under their hail of bombs!

They went, twenty-one strong (if there were no others in their support), as one of a score of details which the great Air Force of Germany could afford to spare from her main objectives. They went, twenty-one strong, to do precisely that which he must attempt with one old, lumbering, obsolete plane—the "dustbin" pattern which had been superseded in the British Air Force nearly three years before.

He scribbled on his note-pad: "*C'est la guerre,*" and passed it to Steele, to whom he had given the seat at his side, and received a nod in response.

An hour later they were flying low under a heavily clouded sky through which the moonlight had little power.

The lights of Leipzig and of a dozen smaller towns, shining with their usual brilliance, had been a gesture of German contempt for the neighbour it had resolved to chastise.

It was a war which she would fight beyond the frontiers of her own land, as she had done several times before.

Czechoslovakia, struggling, gasping for life, would have neither thought nor power to invade the land of her stronger foe.

Even the sound of the single bomber flying under the clouds did not produce any obvious excitement. No gunfire burst from the batteries over which, at times, they must surely have passed: no plane rose in pursuit.

Only once, a searchlight lifted to inspect the strange plane that made its single way through the German skies, but before it could focus upon them they had gained the cloak of a friendly cloud. So they came to the Leunawerke.

It lay, as No. 973 had seen it before, in a sea of light and a surrounding circle of steel. For four years—from a time before that on which Germany had become open in her contempt for those who had bound her by treaty to remain unarmed, but had lacked courage—or what?—to enforce that which they had required her to undertake—the Leunawerke had specialised in all the devilry of chemical inventions intended for the wholesale murder of men.

As though self-conscious of the moral leprosy of the occupation by which they lived, the inhabitants of Leuna isolated themselves, by the conditions of their employment, from intercourse with their own kind.

The three-metre metal wall which surrounded the works and the eighty houses of which the village consisted was surmounted by a frieze of barbed wire, charged with a high-voltage current which would be as fatal to any who would leave their self-chosen hell as to an intruding spy.

It was dominated by seven towers, of which the highest bore a reflector so powerful that the surrounding country was flooded with light during the hours of darkness.

Far out from the walls, the ground had been levelled and cleared. In that brilliant light, a worm could hardly have crawled unseen.

Those who dwelt in its walls knew no more of the outside world than the Government thought good for men engaged in that fantastic degradation of science which turns it deliberately to the destruction of their own kind. Even their newspaper, the *Leuna-Zeitung,* was

Government-controlled and private to the isolated community among whom it circulated.

The range of factories which it contained, advertised as being engaged in the production of dyes and other chemicals in commercial demand, were divided into sections, of which some were actually occupied in that manner, some were engaged in the search for high explosives of a more deadly kind than those with which their scientists had already cursed the world, and one, the F section, a complex of buildings most secret and segregated of all, was utilised for the culture of bacilli for the poisoning of water, and the distribution of many deadly diseases for man and beast.

From the height at which Commander Klíma flew, he observed this lighted village while still several miles distant. He was at no great height, for the clouds were now driving heavy and low before the rising force of a northwest gale, making it necessary for him to descend beneath them to observe the country to which he came.

The moon was hidden, and the light from the Leuna Works, blinding them as they approached, made a denser blackness of the surrounding landscape.

The Commander scribbled a note on his pad:

"I cannot venture to put you down, now that the moonlight has failed.

"Will you jump or stay?"

He pointed to the parachute which was hanging at the back of the cockpit.

No. 973 considered alternatives which he did not like. He looked down into the blackness beneath, and thought of the meagre length of the field on to which he had planned to alight, and of the weight and size of the loaded bomber, and he could not say that the Commander's refusal was without excuse.

Now that the moon had failed, he was not even sure that he could direct him to the field that he had in mind.

He saw also that the plane was increasing its own peril by every moment that it delayed.

He leaned over to write: "I will jump, but give me more height." The airman nodded. The plane rose steeply into the clouds.

No. 973 adjusted the parachute. The two men grasped hands in silence. No. 973 dropped out.

CHAPTER XLVII.

HE fell fast. He could not see the parachute overhead, and there was a moment during which he thought that it had failed to expand, and that he rushed down to a certain death.

But after that he became aware that his fall slackened, and that his weight was sustained by the spreading canopy that he could not see.

He became aware also that he was buffeted by a freezing wind, and his face stung with a driving sleet.

A moment later he was clear of the cloud, and the dark fields were rising slowly towards him.

He struck water at last, and came down in a little brook, where he lost his footing and was dragged along, half immersed, for a moment, before he could get the parachute loose.

He gained the bank, and stumbled hurriedly up a rising slope to watch the drama which was to come.

It was a drama of which the first act was already done.

He had been scarcely conscious, as he had sunk through the darkness and fallen into the stream, of the sound of a bursting bomb, and then of three others that came almost as one, but now he looked up to see the bomber clearly visible in the white light that spread beyond the bounds of the circling wall, and although he could hear the sound of its engines, which were running to the limit of their capacity, it seemed to be stationary in the air, as a kestrel lies on the wind.

It had circled round, descending and gathering speed, while he had sunk through the air, and it had rushed forward, straight and low, looking down on the roofs of the works that it was its mission to destroy.

It had released one aimed, deliberate bomb, even at the moment that it had been checked, abruptly, as though met by an invisible wall.

It found itself being forced backward, as though by some invincible magnetic control, against which the power of its engines contended vainly. It had dropped three instantaneous bombs as it had seen the wall recede from beneath it.

Now, as No. 973 watched the duel he could not aid, there came a burst of gunfire from the roof of the nearest tower.

For two seconds the doomed plane replied with her futile guns. For three seconds more she was the target of bursting shells, of which there was not one that avoided its mark; for the same power which had forced her back ensured that she would draw their muzzles magnetically upon herself.

At the fifth second, the guns ceased.

The bomber, its engines shattered and stilled, remained suspended, as though by miracle in the air, an impotent flaming wreck. Then the mysterious power which held it must have been cut off, and it crashed suddenly to the ground.

The wreck blazed redly for a moment in the cold white light that flooded the outer plain, and then an explosion shattered the air and was repeated again—and again—from its cargo of loaded bombs.

No. 973 ran forward, indifferent to whether the whole of the bombs had burst and the danger were over now, for he saw that his chance had come.

When he gained the scene of the wreck, it was already being inspected by an officer and a dozen men, who paused to look at him as he ran over the lighted ground.

He saw a rifle raised, but he kept on, confident in the uniform that he wore.

He was met by the officer's curt order as he approached: "Stand back there. Who are you?"

"I'm on leave, sir. I came to see if I could help."

He was conscious of the draggled appearance that he presented. He added: "I had to wade through a stream."

He saw that he was believed, for the officer's voice changed as he replied: "That's the right spirit to show. But you must clear off, all the same. You're not wanted here."

But Steele stood his ground.

"It wasn't this, sir," he said.

The officer's eyes followed his own. He looked back to see a high column of blue flame that rose from the building on which the first bomb had dropped.

"*Gott in Himmel!*" he swore, forgetting, in the extremity of his emotion, the army order which forbade recognition of any gods but those which Germany had made for herself and which were therefore of the high standard her civilisation required.

He went back at a run, followed by his men, whom Steele did not hesitate to join.

It had been a spirit of foolhardiness that Leuna had clothed itself in a blaze of light, though being on the eve, and so near to the frontier of war. Its controlling scientists had a complete confidence in the efficiency of the invention by which they could repulse and direct the movements of any approaching plane, so that it would be no better than a fixed target for their converging guns.

Indeed, they would have cast their light to the sky had they thought it to be thickly strewn with invading planes, regarding it as the lighthouse beams which are a lure of death to migrating birds.

But they had not expected attack.

All the more, perhaps, because they would have welcomed it, and were so fully prepared, they had dismissed the thought, for this night at least, as beyond their enemy's purpose, if not her power.

Either Prague would submit, or Germany would attack with annihilating strength. They had no thought that a Czechoslovak plane would fly in the German skies.

And so, there had been the instant of indecision, the doubt of what it might be, as the obsolescent bomber, nondescript in pattern and nationality, had appeared out of the clouds; an instant sufficient only for it to cross the boundary wall, and to have dropped its first bomb, before the protecting power had gripped it, and forced it back.

For the instant, the human factor had failed in control of the demon its arts had raised; and now the long blue flame rose spectrally through the whiter light. It did not bend in the wind, for, as Steele ran on, he became aware that the Leunawerke lay in an oasis of windless air. It seemed that there had been discovery of some power, or mixture of gas, which, as oil will flatten the roughest waves, would control the surrounding air from commotion too violent for the comfort or safety of those who experimented with strange forces within its walls.

He entered with the rest through an open, unguarded gate. They ran on till they came to a street down which half a score of workmen came running with a panic outcry that "the transit corridor is alight."

The officer shouted: "Back, you swine!" He ordered his men to fall into line across the width of the street. He pulled out an automatic and ruthlessly shot down the foremost of the running group. Till his pistol was empty, he continued to pour the bullets into the prostrate form.

The workmen stopped, hesitating between two fears.

As they stood thus, the light went out in the central tower. There was darkness around them now, except that an unearthly light from the burning building fell upon the faces that looked up from the narrow street, giving them a chalk-blue colour, as of men who were already dead.

The officer moved forward menacingly. He shouted: "Cowards! Can you not see that the power is cut off and the danger gone?"

The workmen showed no sign of accepting the assurance he gave. They retreated before his advance, but reluctantly, and their looks were those of men shaken with a great fear.

No. 973 fell somewhat behind. He saw a crowd round the farther side of the burning building. They were directing hose-pipes upon the fire. They toiled as men in a frantic haste, and there was sweat and terror on every face.

He thought: "It would be folly to toil for that which it is not my business to save, or to perish if it explode."

He drew farther away, avoiding another military advance which would have driven him forward to the flames, by dodging down a side street.

By this means he came clear of the works and entered among the houses at the farther end of the village.

Here it was too dark for there to be much risk that he would be seen, nor could he see the faces of those who ran distractedly in the streets. There were no lights in the houses, for these had been derived from the single source which had now been cut off; yet some power there must still have been, for the slow thud of a heavy engine could now be heard, of such strength that the steel-walled houses vibrated to every stroke.

He drew back within the arch of a closed door, his mind debating what he should do. If the fire should be put out, and he should not have been seen among those who had been active in its suppression, his position might not be easy to explain. Almost certainly, he would be expelled, even if he were not subjected to an inquisition it would not be easy to meet.

He was inclined to blame himself for the caution which had withdrawn from what had looked too like a place of unprofitable danger.

As he stood thus, he heard the voices of those who ran past, some as with a settled purpose, and others, women and men, as though distracted by panic fear.

More than once, "number forty-two" caught his ears. "It is forty-two that it must not reach." "Yes, but how will forty-two stand the heat?" And once a more sober voice made reply: "But the F section would be a worse danger than that."

There was complaint from some, who must have attempted flight, that the gates were guarded and closed.

From the inside of the door against which he leaned he heard the voice of a woman soothing a wakeful child. He heard—strange sound in the Germany of that day, and in such an outpost of hell—the low notes of a Christian hymn. Apart from that, the street became still.

As he stood thus, the light of the fire lessened, and this decided him that it would be best to go back and make himself conspicuous among those who appeared to be successful in overcoming it.

He stepped out from his retreat, and, as he did so, a siren sounded—two short blasts, two long, and a short again.

He guessed it to be a warning signal, for it was followed by a confused murmur, as though the whole place was roused thereby to a new impulse of active fear.

He turned to go down the street, thinking it best to avoid the place of the fire, till he should better understand what had occurred. He saw that his ignorance placed him in a more deadly peril than were any of those around him, who had doubtless been taught what such signals meant, and drilled in what they should do.

Almost at once, he was aware that water was swirling around his feet. It was being flooded into the street. Was he about to be drowned? It was hot—hotter than his feet could endure with comfort. Was he to be boiled alive? He was aware also that the strange stillness had gone, and that a wind blew on his back.

As he quickened his pace, a man ran past him. He called: "Not that way, you infernal fool!"

Another, close behind, added, gasping with haste: "This way, man—the north gate—it's the freezing gas."

He turned and ran back, splashing behind them through the hot flood, and as he came to the door against which he had stood, a woman's voice, which he recognised as that which he had heard singing before, called in a tone of urgent despair.

The two men in front of him must have heard it, but they ran on.

Her voice guided him, through darkness and blinding steam.

"There is a child," she said, "with a broken leg. There are the babies as well."

He answered: "Quickly. I can see nothing. Show me the way."

She took his hand, guiding him in.

Soon they were in the street again, he carrying the lame child, and she with two younger ones in her arms.

Her pace was not great, and they were soon left alone in streets in which he would have been lost in the blinding steam. But she knew what she had to do, if only time would allow.

"It will be the north gate," she said. "We must face the wind." And then: "Thank God that you heard me call! How I prayed there would be someone to come!"

As they went on, the steam cleared. The water was cooler around their feet. The moon was struggling dimly against the clouds, and they could see the house-shadows on either side.

The fire had died down to a dull glow which flickered into occasional flame, as though content with the evil that it had done.

When they came to the gate, they found two sentries there, stolidly checking the names of those who passed out.

"Hullo, Martha!" one of them said, "glad to see you got help. I reckon you're about the last we shall see."

"I suppose," she asked, "everyone else has got out more quickly than we?"

"Yes, about all on this side. There'll be two or three hundred that were down the wind when it began to escape. We don't expect to see them."

The other sentry meanwhile had challenged Steele, as a man whom he did not know. But his uniform, and the explanation he gave, proved sufficient to pass him out; suspicion, perhaps, being additionally put to sleep by the rescued child that he bore.

The man said: "You'd better hurry on. We might be dead in three minutes now, if the wind dropped. It's a lucky thing that this gas doesn't last many hours."

He added: "There'll be lorries coming up to the crossroads. They might be there now."

There were lanterns hanging over the heads of the sentries, by which the woman must have seen his face for the first time, for she said in a voice of wonder, as they hurried on at the best pace she could make: "You are not one of us. I have not seen you before."

"No," he said. "I was passing by."

He became silent, seeing danger in her curiosity, if it should be answered at all.

His disguise had served him well, but it would be an added peril if it should be reported to the Intelligence Office at Berlin, that "Private Gumpert," or Adolph Zweiss, as he claimed to be, had penetrated the Leunawerke (and at such a time!). It might easily develop a sharper curiosity to enquire on which side his loyalty really lay.

With these thoughts in his mind, they came to the crossroads, where the lorries of which they had been told had already arrived, and were loading up the refugees in a rapid, orderly manner.

He lifted the lame child into one of these, and helped the burdened woman up. He was turning away, when she caught his hand.

"You are not going?" she asked. "You have not told me your name? Where you live? I would thank you again at a better time."

"My name?" he said in awkward evasion. "There is no matter for that. You must say I am he for whose help you prayed."

"So I do," she replied. "I will thank God for you to my last hour. But I would thank you also again."

"No," he said, "I am overthanked. You would see that, if you knew more than you do."

He pulled his hand free. He recognised the indiscretion of his last words.

He withdrew quickly, while she looked after him with wondering eyes. It was an amazing thing for a stranger to appear in the Leunawerke, where the years passed and few entered or left. Certainly, he had been sent by God.

Through her simple mind there passed a doubt of whether he were not a visitation from the angelic world in which she believed.

He walked away, pondering a different doubt that her words had stirred.

It was through him that this catastrophe had occurred: that part of the Leunawerke was a blazing ruin; that more than two hundred (as he had heard) had died in some dreadful way, through the escape of a freezing gas.

Did he regret that? He could not say that he did.

Yet he had risked his own life, fleeing at a slow and burdened pace, that he might save four people of German blood.

He was reminded of a line in the Greek Testament that his hip-pocket would usually hold, both because it contained good reading for every mood, and that it was a book which could be carried in any country (except Germany) without either indicating its owner's origin or bringing him under political suspicion of any kind. "*The things that we would not, those we do.*"

He was not clear how far, or to which of his own actions it would apply; but he saw that to judge justly of human motives and deeds must require a wisdom beyond the reach of the minds of men.

He was roused from wandering thoughts by the challenge of a sentry's voice: "Not this way. You can't go this way."

A bayoneted rifle was pushed forward to cross his path, but the hand that held it was unsteady from cold or fright, and the voice shook.

He was disposed to talk to a man whom he felt that he had little reason to fear.

"Why," he asked, "what's the trouble along here?"

"It's the freezing gas. It's down there, following the wind. Can't you feel the cold?"

The man shivered visibly as he spoke. Certainly, it was a very cold night. Perhaps abnormally so. But Steele had used himself to the severities of Bohemian winters, and Private Gumpert's uniform had been made of a good cloth. Anyhow, he was quite willing to walk the opposite way.

What should he do now? It might be peculiarly dangerous to remain in a district where everything was likely to be subject to minute enquiry. He knew that whatever havoc the night had made would be cleared up in the thorough, plodding, systematic German manner.

But he was unwilling to leave till he had learned something more of the freezing gas, the malignity of which he had been told would be gone "in a few hours."

He would hang about, at least, till the dawn came.

And then, as he thought this, he became aware that Leunawerke had broken into a wider blaze.

CHAPTER XLVIII.

THE aeroplane on which Gerald Langton had taken passage was known as the Tokyo Local. It was a large airliner of luxurious pattern, but seldom used for the longer journeys, on account of its frequent halts and moderate speed in the air.

It was, however, the best available for his purpose, being the only liner which made a direct passage between England and Prague.

It called regularly at Brussels and Frankfort, and was liable to make other halts, if there were passengers alighting, or to be picked up.

It was scheduled to leave England at 6:00 P.M., and to reach Prague at 1:45 A.M. (Mittel-Europa time).

Knowing from Caresse's letters that she was staying at the British Legation, Gerald concluded that it would be impossible to do anything before the next morning, either for his wife's safety, or in attempting to pacify the political maelstrom to which he came.

He resolved to go to an hotel for the night, and to call on the British Envoy at an early hour the following day, when he would insist that his wife and Perdita should leave by the best route available, whether land or air, unless he should find the political skies to be much clearer than they had appeared from a distant view.

The liner left the Croydon airport with about two-thirds of its full complement of sixty passengers; and, after it had set down at Brussels, about half of its seats were empty.

Alert for signs of that which he feared and yet expected to meet, he asked a steward whether it were usual to have so light a passenger list at that time of year.

The man answered indifferently: "No, sir. We're full up, more often than not. It's just how it happens to be. We might take in a lot at the next stop."

He felt rebuked by the man's tone, rather than the wording of his reply. Was he becoming obsessed by a baseless fear, so that he must see portents even in simple, innocent things?

As they left Brussels, dinner was served. It was an excellent meal, and he found his appetite unimpaired. The liner's flight was steady and smooth. He had always had a foolish dread of the air, which he now ventured for the first time, and found it to have been no more than a needless fear.

Was he getting timorous as his years advanced? Was it the fussiness of middle age that had brought him here, when he should have been in the comfort of his Sussex home?

But he was not old. Forty-six. That was youth, in these days. He knew over-caution to be a fault of which he was sometimes accused. Caresse had mentioned it more than once in her more petulant mood, or when he had tried to restrain her from some impetuosity that his judgment did not approve.

Well, he would call it a short holiday. He would be glad to join Caresse, and he did not doubt that (probably after some first quarrelsome words) she would be glad he had come. And if he found that his fears exceeded the facts—well, of course, she could stay, and no one would be more pleased than himself.

And he would be glad to see Geoffrey again—Sir Geoffrey Cullender, for whose appointment he had been largely responsible. Not quite the ordinary type of Minister for such a post, but one who had justified his selection, as he had been confident that he would.

If Sir Geoffrey said that the storm would blow over, he would be ready to put his own doubt away.

The German gentleman at his side, who had joined the liner at Brussels, apologised for some trivial omission of the courtesies of the meal. Being answered in his own tongue, he went on to say how marvellously steady these liners were.

Conversation developed. He proved to be a business man of the better sort. Intelligent, genial, well-informed. He talked freely of the latest eccentricities of American literature; of the political crisis there; of the disconcerting world-discovery that declining population and increased prosperity were not synonymous terms; of the sinister crudities of a recent exhibition of Russian art; and then of the music of Strauss—a subject brought to his mind by the playing of *Die ägyptische Helena* on the radio which the airliner carried for the entertainment of its dining guests.

His destination, he said, was Frankfort. Had Mr. Langton seen it? Well, it was home to him. But he would admit that Germany had more beautiful cities.

It was only when Gerald said that he was going on to Prague that the talk halted and died.

He saw the look of surprise that came to his companion's face, with the exclamation: "But we are not—"

He checked himself obviously to say: "I did not know we were calling there."

Gerald replied that it was on the regular schedule. Though fully assured of this, he called the steward for its verification.

The man asserted cheerfully. Prague? Yes, of course. They always called there. Ten minutes' stop.

The German apologised for the folly of his mistake. He became silent, as though fearing lest he might already have said more than he should.

He had heard a refusal at the Brussels booking-office to issue tickets to Prague, with the explanation that "owing to atmospheric conditions" the liner might prefer the Vienna route.

He had wondered then whether the true explanation might not be of another sort, but had put it out of his mind, both as an improbability in itself, and because the German of that day had learned that thought (which may lead to the inadvertence of speech) is a dangerous habit.

Now he saw a new significance in the fact that, if the liner were to be diverted from Prague, the change of route was not yet known to its own crew. And the explanation of adverse weather conditions clearly would not suffice. There was nothing abnormal in them. But if his country had resolved to chastise Prague, and would have the secret kept till the last possible hour, it was not his business to let it out with a loose tongue.

Yet, in fact, he could have told less than was known or guessed by the officers of the liner, who were now occupied in an examination of tickets, which was unusual at this stage of the journey.

The official who inspected that of Gerald Langton said, in as casual a manner as though he remarked that the liner would be five minutes late: "I should be ready to get out at Frankfort, sir, if I were you. We've just had instructions to enquire there what route we shall take."

"I thought you stopped at Prague every day?"

"So we do, sir, mostly. We've got special orders come through."

"How's that?"

The man seemed to be disconcerted by the directness of the question.

"I don't know more, sir. It's just the order we've got."

Gerald was sure that he could say more, if he would, but at that moment his superior officer came out of the pilot's cabin, and approached them directly.

"Passenger for Prague?" he said. "The only one, is he? No, sir. I'm afraid you can't. We're not taking that way. We're going down at Wien. You can go on to there, if you like, and by rail to Prague. Of course, you'll get a refund."

He checked further enquiry with an abrupt: "Can't say, sir. Very sorry, but it's the order we've got."

He moved off as he spoke, as though resolved to avoid further discussion.

To Gerald's mind, the meaning of this order was plain. Germany and Czechoslovakia must be on the verge of hostilities, if they had not commenced already, and the air-routes were being closed to commercial traffic.

The fact that they were to be diverted south to Vienna was in itself of a decisive significance, for, Warsaw being their next port of call after Prague, it would have been a less divergence to go north by Berlin. Things must be happening in northern Germany as well as in Czechoslovakia which were not for the world to know.

But why should there be this secrecy about the cause of that which turned them aside? If it were war, it could not be kept for more than a few hours from the watchful ears of the world. Was there not a suggestion here that what Germany had in mind she willed to complete with an instant speed, and before interference could raise its head?

He became more resolute than before that he would get through, by whatever means.

He had noticed that the chief officer spoke with a German accent. His assistant was clearly English, and he thought him to be the more likely source from which further information might be obtained.

He watched for an opportunity of speaking to him alone, which came when the chief officer passed into the pilot's cabin again.

He left his seat, and drew the man as far aside as the narrow confines of the saloon allowed. He took a fifty-mark note from his wallet.

"I am a representative of the British Foreign Office. I am on official business of urgency. How can I get to Prague in the quickest way?"

"I don't know what you can do, sir, beyond Frankfort. We're not calling at Prague."

"What does it mean?"

"I don't know, sir. There's some queer rumour about."

"War?"

"Not that I know, sir. I shouldn't like to say that."

He seemed afraid to speak freely, but he took the note that Gerald held out. He said: "If you'll take my advice, sir, you'll wait at Frankfort till you know a bit more. You may find it's the safer way."

"Never mind that. What I'm asking you is, how can I get to Prague?"

"There'll be the train from Vienna, sir, if you like to go on from there."

"Or from Frankfort, I suppose? But they're no good to me."

The man was silent for a moment. Then he said: "You might get off at Frankfort, and ask for Jack Bromley to fly you back."

"I don't want to go back."

"Jack Bromley'd go anywhere for a ten-pound note. He'd go to hell for a lark." His eyes said more than his words as he repeated: "Ask for Jack Bromley, *to fly you back*."

Gerald Langton returned to his seat, with the feeling that five pounds had rarely been better spent.

CHAPTER XLIX.

IT was about 9:30 P.M. when the Minister of Police entered the Air Minister's office.

He was in a condition of nervous irritation hardly controlled, and as he sat down at the side of Herr Janda's desk he tapped its surface with restless hands.

"Any news?" he asked. "Vacek tells me to go to bed."

"None as yet. You know that it is a point on which the Minister of Defence and I do not agree."

"The President says the same, in another way. He says we are to do nothing to suggest that we are expecting attack. Not even to darken the town."

"That is," Herr Janda corrected, "so long as violation of the frontier does not occur. I have told you that you shall have instant warning of that. It is a mission on which our scouts will not be likely to fail."

"It would be short warning by then."

"So it will. It is not a plan I approve. Yet it may suffice, if no moment be lost. It will be to give you the time you need that our own airmen will die."

"You have a depressing mind."

"I see facts which are no occasion for jest."

"You said that they would be over the frontier half an hour before this."

"So I did. I suppose they take time to assemble in greater force. If we have no news in the next hour you shall go to bed, and we will agree that I have made a bad guess."

"Vacek says that air attack cannot succeed, unless it be supported by land invasion. He is sure that the German Army is not prepared, either in numbers or position, for such a movement. He says that he could himself be over their frontier with 100,000 men before they could meet him with equal force. For tonight, at least, he is sure that we have nothing to fear."

"It is a point, as I have said, on which Herr Vacek and I do not agree. Do you know that my wife left more than an hour ago?"

"You mean you thought it prudent to send her away?"

"It was a matter on which my advice was not sought. She found a seat in the Hungarian Envoy's car. It has occurred to him, as you are likely to know, to take a late drive on the Munich road."

"But you knew she was intending to go?"

"Yes."

He did not add that it was a discovery that his wife did not know he had made. For the past twelve hours he had known that Zita was false, both to him and to the country which, by her marriage, had become hers.

He had considered what he should do, and resolved to remain silent, and let her go if she would.

Afterward—if he were alive in a week's time—in triumph or ruin, in peace or war, he would decide what he would do.

But to have denounced her now—to have procured her arrest—would have served no useful end, beyond a revenge that he did not seek.

He changed the subject quickly to ask: "You are assured that the shelters are safe?"

"We have taken all the precautions we can. We have occupied the buildings near to the entrances, which are surrounded by such a cordon of troops that it would puzzle a rat to get through."

"I suppose your trouble will be when the people are crowding in?"

"Yes. If it come to that. But I hope we've got the whole gang laid by the heels, except those who bolted before we could pick them up. I suppose you've heard that Herr Müller's gone. What I should do if—"

He was interrupted by the entrance of an officer who saluted, and laid two forms silently on the Air Minister's desk.

Herr Janda read them, and passed the first over to his colleague.

It was from Air-Marshal Doubek, who was in command of the eighty fighting planes which had been seen over the city three hours before.

"Estimate 300 German fighting aeroplanes approaching frontier following Elbe Valley and flying low.

Am attacking now from direction Warnsdorf according to Plan 2. Doubek."

Herr Schott looked up to ask: "He will delay them? How long?"

"I cannot say. Perhaps not at all. They are four to one. But if there were no others behind, I should say that you will not be troubled by them."

"Doubek has a good plan?"

"So I think. It is one which could not have been used on a clear night, nor against foes who were flying high.

"But they must be flying under the clouds, following the river's course. They will not be seeking surprise, but to find our planes, relying on numbers for their success.

"They will aim to destroy our own fighting planes, so that their night-bombers may work their will without interference from us."

"And Doubek has a plan to prevent that?"

"No. How could he? But he will aim at delay, and to do them the most damage he can. His plan is to dodge their scouts, and to approach them behind from a greater height. He will descend through the clouds, and attack them upon their rear."

"Could you not have given him more than eighty planes?"

"No. For how many have I in all? But there is an even better reason than that. Such an attack could only be made by planes which are at least as swift as those they pursue, of which pattern we have one hundred, or scarcely that.

"But there is another squadron which will attack the Germans upon the left flank at Leitmeritz, where the river bends to the east."

"And how many are they?"

"There should be four or five score assembled for that purpose by now, but I have a mind to divert forty of them to another point, as you may understand when you read this."

He handed over the second dispatch, and Herr Schott read:

"German scout crossed frontier 9:03 P.M. chased and shot down over Kronow 9:14 P.M. Aeroplanes approaching from direction Glatz heavy night-bomber type pattern unknown very swift number over four hundred. Chvojka."

The Police Minister read it, and jumped up sharply, with the air of a man whose nerves were hardly controlled.

"How long have I?" he asked.

"I can promise you half an hour. You can hope for more. I can encounter these with more than two hundred planes. But I suppose that the main attack will come from the Bavarian side."

"The main attack! What do you call these?"

"You can call them what best pleases yourself. Do you not see that we push the ocean back with a broom?"

Herr Schott moved restlessly to the door, but he did not go. He said: "The President must be told. Half an hour! What can I do in that time?"

"More than you do while you stand here. I will inform the President—and Vacek also. Can you not see that the seconds count?"

He spoke impatiently to a man whom he saw to be less than adequate to the emergency that was thrust upon him. And he himself had urgent orders to issue, requiring control of emotion and concentration of mind, though he might be cooler and better prepared, having no more to face than that which he had foretold and expected to be.

But, as Herr Schott bustled out, the telephone rang, and he must summon him back.

"It's your office," he said. "They want you to know that the Nürnberg station is playing Strauss. Yes, I'll tell them that they must prepare for aeroplane attack and that you're on the way now."

CHAPTER L.

CARESSE said: "Aren't you ready yet? I wondered whether there were anything I could do."

She entered the door of Perdita's room, a shining vision in crimson and opal-white, having finished her own dressing; and with a mingled purpose of commencing to collect the tribute of admiration which was (as she did not doubt) to be her occupation till midnight came, of hurrying Perdita if she were not ready, of telling her of the telegram she had received, and of hearing more of what had happened during the afternoon than she had yet done.

She looked round in an irritated surprise, observing that the dress which should have been on Perdita's back (or rather across her shoulders and hips, a distinction which will be clear to those who remember the evening fashions of 1938) was still lying upon the bed.

She asked: "Whatever's been hindering you? You're not often as long as I."

"I don't think I shall come," Perdita replied. She added doubtfully: "Unless, perhaps, I wore the kingfisher-blue."

"Don't be absurd. It's got arms. You'd make everyone stare. They're not savages here. To judge by some of the shops—"

"Yes, but look here—"

Perdita turned as she spoke. Caresse's protest changed to an exclamation of: "How on earth have you done that?"

The smooth white skin of her friend's right arm showed, slightly above the elbow, the black mark of the Nazi's thumb, and four longer bruises, distinct in themselves and yet blending into one livid blue-black patch, recorded where his fingers had gripped on the under side.

"It was when the man was dragging me to the lift, before Lawrence came."

"Then it was time he did! I told him not to dally talking to me."

She saw an implication in that which she had not meant, and added: "I mean he would go on arguing about not wanting me to come too. I suppose you've tried powdering it?"

"Yes, I'm afraid it's beyond that. I don't think I shall come. I don't really mind."

"It's rotten luck if you don't. I suppose it really is this? There's not anything else?"

"No, of course not. But it isn't as though I could tell people how it happened. Lawrence asked me not to say anything about how they got me this afternoon."

"But he hadn't seen that. Of course, you'd have to explain."

Perdita did not argue on that, being aware that what was "of course" to Caresse might not be equally obvious to masculine minds.

She said: "Well, I don't think I shall come. I don't really mind. I've got a feeling that—well, I wish we could get away!"

Caresse looked her surprise. It was not like Perdita to be swayed by unstable moods, nor to refuse a welcome, whether eager or quiet, to the adventure that came her way.

Caresse's own feelings had changed from the mood which had disturbed her with sudden fear as she had talked with Lawrence on the terrace on the previous night.

If she had not cast it aside at an earlier hour, it would have fallen from her as the frock slipped to her feet which she had discarded for that which she now wore.

In any case, her mind would have been free from alarm after reading the telegram that she had received since her return.

She did not know that she was glad that Gerald was coming—that he would be here in a few hours.

She would probably be cross with him when he arrived (it was a point requiring more consideration than it had yet had), and it might be necessary to coax him to let her stay, if their wills should clash (and coaxing Gerald would be a bore, and was not always easy to do); but, under all, there was the comforting sense that he would be equal to deal with whatever trouble there might be around them here.

She seldom allowed herself to be worried about matters which were Gerald's affairs, as her security and comfort certainly were.

She said: "You must have been shaken up more than you know, or you wouldn't have such feelings as that. I think Sir Geoffrey showed the most sense when he said that the things we expect are those that never happen at all. I've just had a wire from Gerald. He's flying here during the night."

"Coming by air? Then he must think—"

"Oh, I don't know! He's always so cautious. Everyone says that. But he never likes me to go off anywhere for more than three days."

Caresse, having gravitated to the mirror as the conversation proceeded, looked at her reflection, and decided that her husband's feelings were of a most natural kind. There was sufficient explanation here without concluding that Europe was slipping over the verge of war.

Perdita took the news differently. She became aware of decision already made.

"I shan't come," she said. "I don't think I shall go down again."

Caresse repeated: "It's rotten luck. But I daresay you'll be more comfy here than downstairs. You can have dinner sent up."

She kissed her friend and went down, feeling that all was well in a friendly world, in which her comfort was well secured.

Left to herself, Perdita got into bed. She rang for some dinner to be sent up, which she ate with the appetite of her vigorous youth.

She got a book, which she read at times, between intervals of far-wandering thoughts.

She did not notice the passing of time, until the blast of a siren disturbed the night. There were three short blasts, and a long following wail. After a minute's interval, the signal was repeated again.

She was in a strange land, and it was not easy to guess what the significance of such a signal might be. Possibly—even probably—nothing to her.

It was about a quarter of an hour after the last wail had died into silence that the lights of the room went out.

She reached to the bedside switches, but found that they moved without any result.. It must be late. Perhaps the lights in the house were always cut off at this hour? But that was absurd. She wished she could see her watch, to know what the time was. It might not be long before Caresse would be back. She would be sure to look in, and have much to tell. On such an occasion she would be likely to sit on the bed talking, perhaps for hours.

But not in the dark. Doubtless the light would be restored before then.

At the back of Perdita's mind, entertained rather as errant fancy than probable fact, was the thought that the siren-signal and the failing light might be related to a coming attack from the air.

It was an idea which a native of almost any other country of Europe would have accepted at once. But Britain was held separately from them by something more than its narrow dividing sea.

It was the one country in which some remnants of liberty still remained. Discredited and ashamed, its boundaries narrowing further from year to year as science and bureaucracy combined to fix their restrictions upon mankind, liberty was yet not wholly forgotten there, nor was it absolutely subdued.

Britain was the one country of Europe in which conscription was not imposed, the one country which had not instituted a universal compulsory gas-mask drill, the one country which regarded with impatient resentment the degradations with which military science was active to scourge mankind.

To those who surveyed the continent of Europe as a chessboard on which they would move the nations in deadly hazard of war, Britain, whether doubted, feared, or contemned, remained the one unassessable factor, both in purpose and power; the one piece that might remain unmoved, or prove at last to be queen of all, or no more than a taken pawn; and it was this doubt which may have been most potent of all to delay their game.

Perdita lay in the dark, and became aware of silence rather than sound. But it was a silence which had an undercurrent of continuous murmur. There was an immediate silence, but below, across the river, the city stirred.

She got out of bed, feeling her way to the nearer window. She drew back the curtain, and looked out at a night of clouds, through which the moon had diminished power.

Houses and streets were in an absolute interior darkness, only faintly relieved by their outer mantle of snow. Far off, far down, a single light twinkled a moment, and was cut off. Dimly, through all, she could discern the dark line of the twisting river.

And then, beyond the river, from the city's midst, there came a great sheet of flame. For a second, the whole city was plainly shown in that lightning glare; the room behind her was lit to its farthest end.

The light failed next second, and was followed by a rumble of dreadful sound. There was a rattle of breaking glass; something slid noisily over the floor.

She had felt herself struck as though by the force of a sudden wind, so that she would have been thrown back, had she not been holding the side of the open window with a firm hand.

There was no silence now, but the air was filled with a wailing of men, as though a great ship went down with its living freight.

She was unaware that she asked the night: "*Oh, God, what is it?*" with a sob that there was no one to heed or hear.

She felt her way back to the bed, her eyes still blinded by the sudden glare they had faced; and then, with a mind cool and clear above the emotion that shook her soul, she began to dress in the dark.

CHAPTER LI.

BACK in his own office, and surrounded by subordinates of more courage than his own, Herr Schott regained some of the dignity and self-control which had faltered before the imperturbable pessimism of the Air Minister's attitude.

The intelligent energy of his subordinates had already resulted in the issuing of instructions that the bomb-proof shelters should be opened and prepared for the reception of the inhabitants of the lower and central city, all of whom they were sufficient to accommodate. Those who lived on higher ground, or farther away, would be expected to fly with equal speed to the open hills.

It only remained for him to give the final order to sound the siren which would be signal for the population of Prague to adjust the gas-masks over their own and their children's faces, and proceed to shelter or flight as their regulations required.

He did this at once, and having Herr Janda's assurance that it must be half an hour, if not more, before hostile aeroplanes could appear, he directed that there should be an interval of twenty minutes before the moving crowds should be retarded by the difficulty of darkened streets.

It was before the siren had ceased to sound that a police-sergeant reported the capture of Friedrich Neidelmann, the Nazi leader whose ruthless sentence would have thrown Perdita to death a few hours before.

He had been recognised by the captain of a military patrol, as the car in which he was flying from the city was stopped in a traffic-jam, and had been arrested after a desperate resistance, in which a companion had been killed, and he himself had been felled by the rifle-butt of a soldier who remembered that there was a reward for taking him alive, which his dead body would not secure.

He now came before the Police Chief, with a bandaged head, as a criminal against whom there was an outstanding conviction, for which the penalty had not been paid, and further charged with resisting arrest, and causing the death of one of the soldiers who had endeavoured to effect his capture.

At such a time, Herr Schott might have been content to dismiss him to custody with a curt word, as one with whom the magistrates would deal on the next day, but that he had a quality of sleuth-like persistence which had been mainly instrumental in raising him to the position which he now held.

He remembered at once that it was to the hands of this man, if not to Herr Müller himself, that the documents which Johann Schmit had smuggled over the frontier had almost certainly gone.

He would at least know what they had contained, where they now were, and, in all probability, how they could be recovered, to the enhancing of his own reputation, and the probable advantage of Czechoslovakia in her quarrel with Germany, before the eyes of the world.

The Minister of Police may have been additionally influenced by the fact that the tune which was to be the signal for the destruction of the entrances to the bomb-proof vaults, had the plot gone unhindered, had been played within the last hour from the Nürnberg station.

So far, the designed catastrophe had not occurred. He concluded, reasonably and rightly, that this was the result of his own vigilant energy, either in the protection of the entrances themselves, or in the wholesale arrests with which his subordinates had been occupied during the latter hours of the day.

He might have given fuller recognition to the importance of the information that he had received from the British Legation, which had enabled him to raid the rooms where Neidelmann had successfully hidden until that day, but for the fact that it had resulted in the discovery of little more than an empty shell.

The alarm of Lawrence's previous entrance had given time for flight over the roofs to another Nazi hiding-place, from which escape had been made to the street, and it appeared that that flight had not been too hurried to allow of the removal of whatever written evidence the rooms may have contained.

"Neidelmann," he now said sternly, "you have eluded justice too long, but you have to learn that its pursuit does not relax, and its end is sure. I understand that you have now added murder to the crime of which you are already convicted."

The man to whom he spoke looked down on him with a contempt which showed that neither the wound he had received, nor the fetters that held his wrists, could subdue his confidence in himself or the German cause.

He did not affect not to understand the language in which he was addressed, but it was in German that he replied.

"I am no more criminal," he said, "than yourself, or perhaps less. Had they left me alone, the man would not have died; but I was violently set about, and I fought for freedom and life, as a German should.

"But you are, I suppose, an ape too foolish to know that you chatter in your last hour.

"Even now, the doom of your country is written, and the vengeance of those you have flouted is near to fall."

"By which you mean that German aeroplanes are on their way here, with the purpose of bombing Prague?"

"If they are so, it is your business to know."

The Minister of Police was stirred by his prisoner's tone to a mood of higher manhood than he had shown when he talked to one who had the voice of a friend. He would have liked to reply that the coming of the German Air Fleet was not only known, but that it was already obstructed by those who had lain in wait to descend upon it out of the clouds.

He would have liked to boast of the batteries which surrounded Prague, with searchlights ready, and uplifted muzzles await, the value of which might yet prove to be more than their foes assumed. But he restrained himself, having an object before his mind for which such boasting would not avail.

He said: "You think, as I suppose, that your friends will be here in time to save you from the fate which all murderers must expect to meet. But, if I order you to be shot tonight, will that be consolation to you?"

The contempt in Herr Neidelmann's eyes did not change, nor his confidence lessen, as he replied: "It is that which you would not dare, having too much regard for your own neck, which might be stretched at a later day."

"It remains to be seen what I shall think proper to do, at a time when martial law is already proclaimed, and you having the record of which we know. But you will allow that, if you are put in the common jail, which is a very prominent place, and you are hit by a bomb which your friends drop, they will not blame me that your limbs may be scattered abroad.

"But I have the power," he leaned forward, tapping the desk with an upright pencil, as he concluded, with slowly-spoken impressive words, "to order that you be safely confined in the bomb-proof shelters till the danger be past; and I will do that, if you will give me help in another way."

He watched his prisoner keenly as he said this, having a double purpose in mind.

It was a genuine suggestion of a bargain that he was more ready to offer than (he supposed) Herr Neidelmann would be to accept, but, beyond that, he had a more subtle object in view. For he supposed that, if the plot to destroy the entrances to those shelters were still an existing menace, the offer would be unattractive to one who must know the peril of the place to which he would be consigned.

But the prisoner showed neither eagerness nor reluctance to accept the offer. He said coldly: "Can I discuss terms which I have not heard?"

"There are certain documents," the Police Minister replied, "which reached your hands a few days ago. If I tell you that the last sheet was somewhat delayed, we shall both know, beyond cavil, what we discuss.

"If you will give me such information as will lead to those papers being seized, I will both give you the promised shelter tonight and undertake that you shall not be tried, except by the civil power, and by full process of law."

The German's face flushed with anger, as the infamy of this proposal entered his mind. "Do you take me," he asked, "for the kind of dog who will buy safety in such traitorous ways?"

But, even as he spoke, his face changed, and the indignation faded away.

"Yet," he went on, "what harm could it do? Or what use will they be to you at the next dawn? Even if I think of my country alone, my safety is of more worth than the price you ask."

"I can see," Herr Schott replied, "that you are a wise man. If you will tell me—"

"I will do better than that. I will guide you myself to the place where they are hidden away."

A long experience of the wiles and tricks of those over whose necks the noose is likely to fall caused the Police Minister to reject this proposal in curt and definite words.

"You will do what I ask, and no more. You will tell me where they are hid, and when they are on this desk I will keep my promise to you."

"I cannot do that, for it is a place they would never reach."

"You must be plainer than that, and in few words, if at all. I have given you too much time as it is."

"The papers are in a hiding-place that you would not find, in a house you do not suspect. They are so placed that, if they be approached by those who lack right, they will be destroyed, and he who would have tampered with them will also come to a quick end."

"Then you can tell me how the danger can be set aside, as you clearly know."

"I am not sure that I could, but, be that as it may, I tell you, in the brief words you require, that it is something I will not do."

Herr Schott glared at his prisoner for a moment in angry silence. He was reluctant to withdraw from the position he had assumed, but he was still more so to abandon the hope of obtaining the documents that he sought, and he was sufficiently intelligent to perceive that he might be faced with an obstinacy to match his own. Was there a trick here by which the Nazi leader would make escape, or befool him in some way that he could not guess?

As though perceiving his thoughts, Herr Neidelmann spoke again: "You can send me with the strongest guard that you will. Can I fool you except to my own loss? Or could I destroy the papers by use of the protecting device, without involving myself in the same fate, which I should be unlikely to do?

"If you think, you will see that the trust is entirely mine, I having your word alone for a reward which you will not give, unless you agree that my part is performed."

The Minister of Police observed that there was one flaw in this reasoning.

If the Nazi leader spoke truth when he said that the papers were hidden in such a way that he who attempted to pilfer them would destroy himself, then it was possible to suppose that he might be tempted to work that device in such a manner that it might involve him in a destruction which his captors would share, regarding his own life as already forfeited to the law, and thinking it to be a more seemly end.

Considering the character and record of the man, it could not be dismissed as an idea too fantastic to entertain; but he also considered that (1) it was a risk which must be allowed, since the papers could be obtained in no other way, (2) that it was unlikely that a plan so desperate would be entertained by one who looked, with some substance of reason, for likely rescue by the event of war, and (3) that the lives which would be risked would not include his own, as he was now at a post he could not leave, and the recovery of the papers must be entrusted to subordinate hands.

He lost no time in further debate, but gave instructions that the Nazi leader should be taken where he would, within the city limits, under a strong guard; and being, in his own profession, a very competent man, he was careful to order that he should not be allowed to enter any premises such as might contain an ambush of friends, until they had first been inspected by other eyes.

CHAPTER LII.

HERR NEIDELMANN found himself in a taxi with his left wrist manacled to the right wrist of a police officer who may have been a head shorter than himself, but there was no comfort in that, in view of the weapon which was in his further hand (he being a left-handed man) and the two other policemen, equally armed, who filled the opposite seat.

Two other taxis, bearing armed servants of law, were before and behind, in evidence of the value which the Police Minister set upon the missing documents, and his determination that he should not be overreached by Nazi cunning or force.

But the prisoner showed no sign of discomfiture, regarding his escort with indifferent eyes.

He appeared to be more interested in the congested streets, in which the lights would not be extinguished for some minutes more, and the pavements of which were now occupied by a hurrying, jostling crowd, all moving the same way, and all wearing grotesque masks, showing the large round discs of a lynx's eyes, and the protruding snout of a hog.

One who looked on with a detached mind might have marvelled that the submissive folly of men, and their sharp hatreds and fears should have led them to submit to such degradation, while those who contrived their discomforts, tortures and deaths, should live in comfort and honour for their reward.

But Herr Neidelmann had different, and (he would have said) more practical thoughts. He concluded rightly that this rush of gas-masked men and women, and of the stumbling children around their skirts, was sufficient proof that the German war-fleet was in the skies, and war no longer a blackening cloud, but a tempest already burst.

He had a well-founded doubt of the efficacy of those unsightly masks (one of which he saw a hurrying woman vainly striving to fix to the face of a baby of a few months, who strove with small impotent hands, and cries which the traffic drowned, to thrust it away), but it was not only because he doubted their utility that his lips curved in a cynical smile.

He doubted whether his country would think it needful to use her newest gases, unless in an open field, or against a more potent foe. There were secrets which it would be wiser to keep against the war of—never, or the next week? It would be for Europe to say…

The three taxis followed the direction he gave, and, as the street lights went out, they drew to the pavement before a house in a side street, at no great distance from the destination of the hurrying crowd.

Herr Neidelmann, observing with alert and curious eyes all that opportunity would allow, looked up as he left the vehicle, curious to know if there were yet the noise or vision of strife in the upper air.

The darkening of the city lights had given clearer sight of the cloudy skies, which were as yet bare of hostile attack, but a squadron of aeroplanes, of old and miscellaneous types, moved slowly and very noisily overhead.

He recognised them (it having been his business to know, and to keep his own Government informed) as the dregs of the Czechoslovakian air-fleet: planes too weak to avail, too slow to manœuvre in serried strife, but now brought out to wait where their foes must come, and to do such harm, if any, as valour might contrive and good luck allow, before they should be shot down to their certain end.

As a cow that would pursue hares, as a rabbit that would bare its teeth in the fox's face, so, Herr Neidelmann thought, would they appear before the great fleet that was now converging upon them from every side. And there were greater countries than Czechoslovakia that would send their airmen aloft to such hopeless strife, if they should be misguided enough to challenge the German power.

The house before which they stopped was, in fact, one of those which had been emptied by the police a few hours before, and its inhabitants placed under restraint, on no better pretext than that they bore a German name, and that a half-burnt envelope with a Munich postmark had been found among raked-out ashes.

Herr Neidelmann, still manacled to his companion's arm, led the way, by no better light than a pocket-torch would supply, to a basement room, the floor of which was spread with a dusty carpet.

This was lifted at his request, or perhaps order would be a more accurate word, for he had a habit of short command which he was not careful to check for no better cause than that the police of a race he scorned had their handcuff upon his wrist.

When the carpet was raised, he counted the floor-boards, and said: "You must leave this to me and stand back."

He waved his free hand towards the wall on the left. "There will be a shot," he said, "when I raise the board, but it will not touch any of you, if you are obedient in where you stand. I shall need a tool."

A claw-headed hammer was found for his use, and while this was being done, he addressed the officer who was so closely attached to himself.

"I could do better with two hands, but I may find one enough. There will be a shot when I raise the board (if not more), which it will need care for both of us to avoid; but I will advise you as to your position as best I can. You must please yourself."

By this time, the wooden shutters of the window had been closed, and a lantern lighted the room.

There were half a dozen armed men crowding around and others were on the stairs and guarding the outer door. The officer decided that it could be of no avail to his prisoner, but might make a material difference to himself, if he should loose the handcuff till the board had been raised, so that he would be able to stand farther away.

Herr Neidelmann knelt by the fifth board, which was not in a single piece for the full length of the room, but was joined and nailed down where there must have been a beam crossing below.

At the point of junction, he commenced to prise up one of the boards, being careful not to lean over, as would be natural for anyone engaged in such work to do.

As it lifted, there came a shot from the gap beneath. It was followed by others in quick succession. They came from an automatic pistol, which had been mounted in such a way that it moved as its bullets were discharged.

As it ceased, the wood of the unplastered ceiling showed, by a wide circle of holes, what the courses of the upward bullets had been.

Disregarding these, and content that the policemen showed no haste to advance to the inspection of a gap from which such greetings had issued, Herr Neidelmann, bending forward with no occasion for further caution, ran his hand beneath the crossing beam to which the board had been nailed.

He was not feeling for documents which, as he well knew, had never been nearer that spot than when they had been carried out of the Wilson Station in Perdita's suitcase, but for a concealed stud, which he pressed with a steady thumb.

He looked up as he did this, to observe where the lantern stood, and to say: "I'm afraid we're too late. The papers...."

The sentence ceased as a bright light flashed through the shutter-chinks, and the crash of the near explosion deafened their ears.

Herr Neidelmann was the only one whose senses were not stunned by the sudden sound, nor directed upon its cause, it being to him an expected thing. Before their eyes had recovered from the flash of the dazzling light, or their ears from the bursting din, he had leapt to his feet and dashed the lantern against the ground.

In a moment, he was through the door, and on the stairs, in the rear of those who were already running up to see what the explosion might mean.

He called out: "Run! Run!" in the Czech tongue. He came out, among men who did not regard him at all, to a street in which the light of the clouded moon was vanquished by falling dust.

He walked on blindly for a short space, seeking to discover the extent of the devastation that had been caused by a pressed stud, and guided by a murmur, confused and dreadful, from which single cries of agony or terror would break at times, rising single and distinct from the sea of surrounding sound.

He could see nothing at all. He breathed smoke, and a choking dust. He thought: "There is nothing that I can see. It will be better to go."

He turned, and stumbled over some fallen bricks, and then into a shallow hole, the nature of which was not easy to understand.

He got clear of that, and went on with direction lost, finding himself entangled next moment in the boughs of a fallen tree.

He concluded that the explosion had scattered ruin over the whole of the surrounding area, and guessed, with partial accuracy, that he must have come to the edge of the open square.

If so, he must be going in the opposite direction to that in which safety lay.

He turned back, and stumbled next on a shattered corpse. He came to the ground slipping in a mess of blood.

As he would have risen, the darkness was faintly pierced by the street lamps, which had been ignited again, to discover the horror which he had wrought.

The mine had been the work of the last two years, the tunnelling having been commenced almost as soon as the site of the shelters themselves had been chosen. It had caused an explosion of such magnitude that several thousands had perished as its direct result, as they had pressed forward, congesting the square and the surrounding streets; besides those who, with little hope of rescue or life, were now buried beneath.

For those who had been too slow for their own deaths, the hope of shelter was gone. They must find their way back to what cover their own cellars could give, or commence a flight for which they were unprepared to the frozen country around.

Herr Neidelmann, struggling to rise, received the benefit of those relighted lamps. He looked down to see his hand pressed among the entrails of a man that the explosion had torn apart. He saw a short-cropped head, absurdly bent at the neck, its face grotesque in the hog-like mask.

He withdrew his hand quickly. An expression of repulsion lifted his lip, for he was of cleanly, fastidious tastes.

As he rose, he looked up. Above him was the dark shadow of a wall that the explosion had damaged, but which still stood.

There was a second during which he was puzzled by the strange way in which the dim shadow seemed to be descending towards him...another second during which he had time to know what his end would be.

After that, there was no more than the noise of another building that fell; another cloud of dust to hinder the feeble light of the lamps and the struggling moon.

CHAPTER LIII.

THE Great Hall of the ancient Castle which overlooked the more ancient city of Prague, was gay with motion and music, bright with colour, and brilliant with flooding light.

Restored and modernised from the neglect to which it had fallen during the period of Austrian domination, the hall was too vast for the holding of any but public functions, to which the whole of the wealth and aristocracy of the city could be trusted to give support.

The Annual Red Cross Dance was such an event—was, indeed, the event of the year, in which the pursuit of pleasure and the excuse of charity combined to bring together all of intellect and beauty, of power and wealth, that the city held.

Its attraction on this occasion had been equal to prove its power against a harder test than it had been likely to meet, flaunting itself in the terrible face of war, and if the numbers of those who crowded its shining floor were somewhat less, and though there may have been few women there, and still fewer men, into whose hearts there did not come at times a thought of fear which they would not speak, the movements of the dance were no slower therefore, the music was not less gay.

There may even have been some who found relief in the rhythmic concord of light and colour and sound, as a gesture rejecting belief in the woes which men contrive for each other, and for themselves; as making the outbreak of sudden war a more remote, a more incredible dread; as though the advancing shadow might be defied or ignored away.

As to Caresse, she put it out of her mind as lightly as she would have thrown aside a glove of the wrong shade for the coat she wore.

Perdita was not coming tonight: tomorrow Gerald would arrive. The narrow moment was hers.

So she felt it to be, as the first hours passed, and she found that Lawrence kept to her side.

It would be understatement to say that she was indifferent to the inferences of those who, looking on without full knowledge, or judging by the broad normalities of conduct and character which must always be inexact when individually applied, might suppose themselves to be witnesses of an intrigue of infidelity to an absent husband.

Rather, she might have felt the greater satisfaction in what she did: a thrill of triumph, as of one who has won the arena's crown while having escaped the certain dirt and likely peril its strife required.

"No sleep till morn when youth and pleasure meet." So she meant it to be. So far, she had missed no dance, but the night had scarcely begun.

The dance programme was varied to please the choice of all who would be gathered at such a function. Dances of East and West, old and new, even to the obsolescent fox-trot, must all have turn. Caresse stood out for the first time when the band struck up the music of the Congo Flap-jack, the new American dance which was said to be the rage of London and Paris.

It was one of those ugly, sensual dances which were introduced from time to time from the Western World on the spurious pretext that they were outstanding examples of genuine Negro art.

It had not yet been received in Prague with more than a doubtful welcome, and the floor was less crowded than before as the low, languid music with which its movements commenced quickened tempo toward the delirium of the whirling end.

Caresse said "I don't want to dance this. Tell me who all the people are."

She spoke in casual assumption that he would remain at her side, and with a pleasant undercurrent of consciousness that there must be others there who would have expectation or hope of more notice from him than her monopoly would allow.

He showed no unwillingness to comply, but as he did so he became more sharply aware of how many were absent whom he would have expected to see, particularly among the more prominent politicians and Government officials, and the staffs of foreign embassies to whom attendance at such a gathering is a pleasure which can be undertaken in duty's name.

"I haven't seen Mme. Janda yet," Caresse said, and with the words he became aware that not only was the Air Minister's wife absent, which she was unlikely to be without a compelling cause, but that none of her friends of the Hungarian Embassy could be seen.

He thought: "They expect war." And as the anticipation became definite in his own mind, he wondered, did this gay, seemingly carefree crowd understand how quickly such a storm could approach their doors? In theory, they must have been taught and drilled to consciousness of the peril under which the cities of Europe lay—the price of having let its scientists live, and even paid them for each new torture that they devised. But there is so wide a gulf between that which is only theoretically allowed and that to which experience adds its warning call.

"I don't believe," Caresse said petulantly, "you're listening to a word I—"

She spoke more loudly than she was aware, her voice contending against the music's crescendo sound, and checked herself sharply as she became conscious that it had abruptly stopped.

The dancers, arrested grotesquely in the midst of a movement the nature of which was not adapted for registration in such a way, looked up in protest to the musicians' gallery, and their faces changed as they saw the figure of their President, standing with one hand on the rail, and waiting for the silence which he required.

He spoke with simple directness, having had no time for the preparation of words, but they were of a substance for which no embroidery was required.

"I have to tell you," he said, "that we are at war with Germany. Through no wish or act of ours, we are attacked by a stronger Power.

"Even as I speak, our air-fleet may be engaged.

"It is an outrage against which we protest to the whole world that we have done no deed, that we have spoken no word, to commence or provoke war.

"We have strong allies. We have a good conscience, and a good cause.

"I am already assured by our Minister of Defence that our army is well prepared against a threat that has been too often and too openly made.

"You will not forget that we shall fight for the freedom so lately won, and which we will not surrender again while our lives endure; nor that we shall take the sword in defence of that Sacred Faith which our foes deny.

"Being so inspired, I am confident that you will not fail.

"At this moment I must say no more. I ask you to disperse quickly and quietly. There is no occasion for haste, but the siren may be expected to sound, and the lights may be extinguished at any moment, according to the routines for such occasions, in which you have been instructed.

"In such events you will act as the regulations require."

He looked down, as his words ceased, on a sea of upturned faces in which varied emotions showed. There had been some confusion, even from when he began, caused by those who had turned at once to withdraw, and would pull others away.

But there were many in whom his words waked a response as resolute as his own, and whose voices joined in the cheer which filled the hall, as he stepped back to instruct the band. The next moment, they burst into the Czech National Anthem, which was taken up by a hundred voices below.

Caresse had forgotten herself for the moment in the dramatic interest of a scene in which she did not seem to be nearly concerned.

She felt Lawrence's hand on her arm. He said: "We needn't wait to hear this. You'd better come. There'll be a crowd at the dressing-room now."

What was the Czech Anthem to them? It was his duty to get her home; acting, of course, with the dignity that his position required.

Caresse, feeling the increasing pressure of his hand on a bare arm, which she did not mind, was perverse that she would not go.

"What a ruffian you are!" she said. "If you don't take care I shall have a bruise like—why, I believe it was your doing really, and she'd promised she wouldn't tell! She almost said that, now I come to think."

The memory recalled the graver side of the experiences through which they had passed in the last two days, and she was moving toward the door as she changed her tone to conclude: "But it isn't really our matter at all!"

As she spoke, the siren opened its warning blasts, and the sound was like a physical impulse, urging the assembly toward the doors.

Lawrence might be thankful for every yard the previous minute had gained, as he used height and strength to protect Caresse from a pressure that became hard to endure.

"No," he answered her last question, half literally, half in the jesting mood that such moments bring, "we're not in it, but we've got to get out."

His thought was that it would be hard enough, even if the lights should continue, to get her wraps among some hundred women all congesting the corridor with the same aim, but, if they should be thrown into sudden darkness, what chance would there be?

What, outside, might be the chaos among the cars?

It was little more than a five-minute walk to the Legation; but could he take her out as she was, half bare, to the freezing night?

For the next fifteen minutes, however, the lights remained. He had the satisfaction of seeing her wrapped in the furs that the night required, and of getting out at last, somewhat breathless, and without having delayed to attempt recovery of his own coat.

Before then, she had come closer to the reality of the horror which she had been disposed to put carelessly or fretfully aside; for some of the more prudent of the guests, who had come prepared for that of which many had talked but few believed, adjusted the gas-masks which they had brought, before going out to the road.

To her eyes, they were an abomination beside which death was a trivial risk.

She saw a woman who had been radiant in beauty before adding herself to a group whose gas-masks gave them the aspect of Circe's swine, and Lawrence felt her tremble upon his arm.

"I wonder," she said, "that women haven't stopped it before now."

He made no answer to that, his attention being fixed upon the problem of the car, which he had driven himself, and tipped one of the door-porters to park till he should require it again.

As he looked round for the man, the street-lights went out, and the surrounding buildings sank into darkness.

It might be no more than precaution, or it might mean that German bombers had already entered the skies. From what he knew, he supposed the latter to be the more probable fact.

Anyway, it was not a place in which to remain.

There was some light from a clouded moon, and the crowding cars were easy to see as they moved darkly over the courtyard of fallen snow. It was not lack of light so much as panic haste to be gone that caused a collision that blocked the gate.

It was no use to stand at the pavement edge, now that the light had failed which had been thrown out from the open doors. He had not seen the man on whom he relied. Doubtless, a score of others had equal claim to his help. He might have bolted, ignoring all but that which his own safety required.

Lawrence did not know where his own car might be, nor could he drag Caresse about through the pushing, clamouring crowd, and the vehicles that hooted, started, and backed in a chaos from which the relief of exit was now denied till the gate should clear.

He said: "We can get out by a side gate. It will be better to walk."

She made no demur, and only laughed when the way he took plunged her almost knee-deep in the frozen snow.

But, as she struggled to firmer ground, there came a light, sudden and broad, which showed the surrounding scene in an instant's flash, and then left her with blinded eyes and aware that she had been thrown roughly back on to a soft cushion of snow, and that the night was rent with appalling sound.

Next moment, Lawrence was helping her to her feet.

"You're all snow yourself," she said. "What was it? Did we both fall?"

"It was the explosion that threw us back. We were fortunate to have such a soft bed."

"Explosion?" She was quicker than he would have supposed with the right guess. "You mean they've blown up the shelters as they said they would?"

"Yes. I'm afraid our warning wasn't much use."

As he spoke, he was drawing her toward the gate; but, unexpectedly, Caresse jibbed.

"We can't go like this," she said. "You brought the Bentley. Isn't that Sir Geoffrey's own car?"

"Yes. He said I was to have it for you. What of that?"

"Couldn't we find it, and telephone him to be ready for when we get back?"

"Ready for what?"

"He's sure to want it to get away."

"I don't know about that. I don't suppose he'd leave the Legation without orders from home. Not unless the Government here withdraws to a safer place."

"It sounds a silly thing to stay here."

"We won't argue that. But if you want me to find the car, the quickest thing you can do is to come on now. There's a way down here that won't take five minutes, and after that I can come back and look."

She said no more, concealing her resolution that he should not venture out again, when they were once within the shelter of solid walls, in which, like millions of others, she still felt the instinctive confidence that had been taught by millenniums of past experience. If they went out again, it should be together, to put the car to the use for which the occasion so plainly called.

They came to the head of a broad, paved pathway that curved downward under the castle wall. It was a declivity so steep that it became at times a row of descending steps.

At first, as they hurried down, they had a wide view over the river and the lower city, the farther centre of which was now the scene of a score of blazing or smouldering fires.

After that, the view was obscured by the buildings that intervened.

The street lights came on again, and there was an increasing noise of people who fled up from the lower town, but they did not encounter any of these fugitives on the way by which they descended, it being too steep for choice, until they came out on the more level street.

Here there were a few yards to traverse where they must push their way against the upward rush of a frightened, hurrying crowd, from which a woman's voice, calling a lost child, rose frantically over the rest. But it had no meaning for Caresse, being in a language she did not know; and in the next minute they had turned into the solitude of the cul-de-sac which led to the Legation entrance, and they could move freely once more.

They rang the bell, and passed through the gate which the porter cautiously opened, to enter such security as could be found that night under the English flag, and within the strong walls that Count Thun had built to shut out the dangers of other days.

CHAPTER LIV.

THEY found the Legation staff gathered in Sir Geoffrey's room. He looked up from the telephone, at which he was engaged in conversation with the French Envoy, to say: "Hello, Norton! Glad you're back. And Mrs. Langton none the worse?"

He spoke with the spontaneous cheerfulness of one who might thank his fate for whatever circumstance disturbed the dull monotony of routine, and resumed the sentence that their entrance had interrupted.

Perdita was there, pale and quiet, but inwardly wondering at herself that her emotions declined to react, after the first shock they had received, in what she supposed to be a natural way.

She had experienced the same spiritual dilemma before, as a small child, when an aunt had died, and the feeling of grief which she understood that the occasion required had declined to come, leaving her in childish wonder of what defect there might be in her own soul, and with the difficult choice of hypocrisy, or being judged of a heartless indifference to the emotions of those around her.

She saw Caresse enter, her hand still under Lawrence's arm, to whom she clung as though unable to walk alone.

But there was no look of exhaustion, and little of the aspect of fear in the face she showed, as she threw back the furred hood from her head in the heated room.

It seemed to Perdita that her friend had used the occasion, as she had done that of the terrace before, to advance that intimacy which "meant nothing; which never did," but that also was in a mood of dispassionate observation, as of one who looked on from another sphere.

Caresse said: "I can't stand this here, it's too hot." She slipped off the fur coat she wore, showing the gay bare-waisted dress, crimson and opal-white, which had flaunted itself, in its shameless conventionality, on the ballroom floor less than an hour before.

Now it was draggled with dirt and snow, and the supporting lace, the slender cordage of which had united the upper and lower portions, had broken on one side, where it had been strained by her fall, so that it sagged over the hip.

Perdita checked an exclamation, and stepped forward with an instinctive impulse to help her to resume the cast-off coat; and then stopped, seeing that Caresse showed no consciousness of the exposure which came from that broken lace.

She looked down, and her eyes fell on a bleeding foot.

"Why," she asked, "what have you done? You have lost a shoe."

Caresse laughed. She stretched out a small wet shoeless foot, which showed blood where the silk stocking was torn away.

"I left the shoe in the snow. I didn't notice till it was too late to turn back."

Perdita saw that there had been different cause for the support of Lawrence's arm from that her first judgment supposed.

Contrition and sympathy joined to break through the stunned mood of which she had been conscious before. She no longer felt as one who looks on at a play in which he will have no part. She was her natural self as she said: "You had better come to my room," it being the nearer to where they were.

As she was bathing the injured foot, which proved to have no more injury than some scraped-off skin, Caresse said cheerfully: "I suppose the trouble's about over now, as the light's come back."

Perdita, having spent the last quarter of an hour in Sir Geoffrey's company, was better informed.

"I'm afraid it doesn't mean that. They tell me the regulation is that the light is cut off completely for a sufficient time for people to close the shutters and curtains of rooms in which they are allowed to have lights afterward on condition that nothing shows through.

"They've been drilled in all this, and the cutting-off of the light is only intended to be a temporary thing. It's a warning, beside, that no one can overlook or misunderstand.

"Sir Geoffrey says that, anyway, it can't be much good on a night like this, because the river and bridges can be seen from above when there's anything like half a moon, and they're a guide to the whole place that a child couldn't mistake.

"If there's a real raid coming, as he supposes there is now, the darkening is to make it as difficult as possible for the bombs to be aimed correctly at the water-works and public buildings, and other places they particularly want to get at."

"So that," Caresse interposed sharply, "if they aim at the Foreign Ministry, or the Castle, they'll be more likely to get us? I don't think much of that!"

"I suppose they think that we matter less. But now that there's been this terrible explosion, Sir Geoffrey says he expects they want all the light they can get to help the people, and see what the damage is; and to attempt concealment isn't much use either, with great fires in the town."

"I shouldn't think they'll bomb them any more now. They ought to see that they've got trouble enough."

Perdita agreed to the principle of conduct that this suggestion implied, without expressing any confidence that the German airmen would see matters in the same light.

"Well, I'm glad Gerald's coming," Caresse concluded. "He oughtn't to have let us get into such a mess."

Meanwhile, in the room below, Sir Geoffrey had concluded his conversation with the French Envoy.

It appeared that M. Flambert, like himself, had decided to hold his ground, unless he had explicit instructions from his own Government to withdraw, or notification that the Czechoslovak authorities were removing to another centre.

It was true that Signor Rinaldo had left, but that was neither blame to him nor example to them, he having obeyed an explicit instruction from Rome which had reached him two hours before.

It was improbable that the decision of the representatives of England and France would be simplified in the same way, for during the last hour both telephonic and telegraphic communications between Prague and the outer world had been completely cut off.

Only the wireless station was still striving to force the cry of a city's anguish through to the outer world, and even this was without evidence of success, for the surrounding stations had spread confusion upon the air.

Sir Geoffrey asked if Mme. Flambert were also staying in Prague, and, receiving an affirmative answer, proposed that she should come to the shelter of the British Legation, which offered some slender margin of greater security than that which was protected by France's flag. But the offer was gratefully declined. It was an occasion on which Mme. Flambert preferred to remain at her husband's side.

Laying down the receiver, Sir Geoffrey turned to Lawrence to ask if he had observed any sign of attack from the skies, such as might not be known in that shuttered room.

He said no. There had been some noise of planes that passed overhead, but he took those to be no more than defending patrols.

There had been no dropping of bombs, no outbreak from the batteries which would have been loud in protest, if not in protection of Prague. Only in the central city there had been that dark fire-lit horror indicating ruin and death, the extent of which could only be dreadfully guessed by those who looked down from a height that was perhaps two miles away.

"I suppose," Cunningham said, "the fact that they've blown up the bomb-proof shelters means that they'll use gas, if they attack from the air. I don't think I should mind anything overmuch, except that it must be a beastly death—and in a quarrel that isn't ours!"

"If that's your worst worry, Cunningham," Sir Geoffrey said cheerfully, "you can put it out of your mind. I'd bet a tenner, if there were anyone here whose money I'd like to have, that they won't use gas at all, or, at any rate, not for the first attack.

"They may have had it in mind when they first planned to put the shelters out of use, but even that doesn't follow."

He went on to argue that high explosive, used on a sufficiently large scale, would always be more effectual than gas, and more certain in its results.

Beyond that, the withholding of gas would be regarded as a demonstration of humanitarianism, which might be little consolation to those whose homes were wrecked, or bodies scattered abroad, but might be very useful when Germany came to talk to the world, as she must do on the next day.

Also, he observed (not being the only one to whom this had occurred) that, if Germany aimed at no more than a sudden coup which would leave Czechoslovakia at her feet, she might not wish to disclose all her latest and most secret discoveries in the art of human destruction. She would conceal them for the surprise of those who might enter the field as her later and stronger foes.

He said further that Prague was not, by its position, well adapted for successful gas attack. Their own location, on the steep side of the hill, and with the northwest wind which was blowing now, was such that they would have little to fear from most of the known gases, unless they were directly hit by a bomb which would penetrate before it should burst.

"We'll call up the Air Ministry again," he said, "or the Police, and if they haven't had news of any coming attack, I think most of you can go to bed, as the ladies seem to have had the sense to do already."

William Harvey, who held the position of second secretary to the Legation, a quiet competent man, somewhat older than Lawrence, and with a mildness of manner suggesting that his most probable position at a time of danger would be under the bed, said: "Then, if you won't want us, sir, before morning, may I go down into the town?"

Sir Geoffrey looked dubious. "Why," he asked, "do you want to do that?"

"I thought they might be glad of all the help they could get."

"If you mean that there must be rescue work in which you might be able to help— Yes, I can spare you for that. But you won't forget that we're neutrals, in time of war. You'd better try to get through to the Air Ministry now. Don't trouble Janda. He'll have more important matters on hand than answering idle questions from us. I'll speak to one of his staff."

But there was no answer from the Air Ministry. The local exchange, the staff of which had remained steadily at their posts during the alarums of the last hours, replied that they were unable to make the connection, and would, or could, say nothing further in explanation.

Sir Geoffrey, knowing already that the trunk service was cut off, and suspecting that the Nazi exodus from the city might not have been so complete that none remained to do further damage, supposed that the local service also had been dislocated. But a call to the office of the Police Minister was put through without difficulty.

Herr Schott answered himself. He showed a more confident mood than had been his at an earlier hour.

The explosion that had occurred was, he admitted, of an appalling magnitude. It was, as yet, impossible even to estimate the numbers of those who had been buried under the falling debris. Probably thousands had perished. Thousands more were known to be imprisoned in the underground refuges, and their fate was uncertain. But some of the ventilation fans were still working. There was reason to hope. The work of rescue, both for those above and below, was proceeding, though under great difficulties.

But, apart from that catastrophe, he spoke with the tone of one whose news was unexpectedly good.

There had been a glorious victory in the air. On the northern frontier, near Warnsdorf, a German air-fleet had been attacked at its rear, and from a higher altitude, by Air-Marshal Doubek, with the elite of the Czechoslovak Air Force. It had lost heavily. Continuing on its course, in a position which confused flight and advance, it had been attacked in flank at Leitmeritz by a second detachment of fighting planes, and in the resulting conflict it had lost its formation, and become no more than a scattered rout.

There was also, it appeared, news of heavy air-fighting toward Glatz, and though that was of a less decisive character, and the Czechoslovak losses were not light, it also had been successful in holding off the attack.

Sir Geoffrey asked if Herr Janda were satisfied that the danger was over.

Herr Schott would not say that. Herr Janda had always foretold that Germany would prevail in the air, and it was hard for a man to change an opinion so publicly and strongly expressed.

But Herr Vacek, who might be expected to take a broader view, had always held that an attack from the air only must be of an indecisive character. After the German air-fleets had been repulsed in two directions, without reaching their objectives, was it likely that they would persist in that form of attack before their land forces were ready?

So far, the Prague batteries lifted silent muzzles, searching the sky for foes who did not arrive.

As to the lack of response from Herr Janda's office, that was simply explained. He had said that he would be too occupied during the next hour to do more than communicate events as they occurred in the element which was his concern. He had asked that his office should not be disturbed. He would communicate all of moment that occurred in the air, which as yet was the sole front of war.

Sir Geoffrey looked up to say: "It appears that the German air-fleet is checked. There may be no further news for this night. You can go to bed, if you will. But you should be very ready to rise."

There was no conviction in his tone, but he had seen enough of war to know that the unexpected is a very frequent event.

"Lawrence," he added, "you won't omit to have the phone switched through to wherever you are."

He went to his own room, passing that of Caresse, the door of which was too solid and well set to show any ribbon of light, or for the sound of voices to come through, even had she been there.

He paused a moment, hesitating as to whether any word of reassurance or advice would be wise. Had they really had the sense to get quietly to bed?

"I wonder," he thought, "when that girl had her last meal? She must have left too early—" When he had closed his own door, he took up the house-telephone, and called down to Paul, telling him to ring up Mrs. Langton, and ask whether she would like anything sent up to her room.

He knew from past experience that emotional balance at such times is maintained by insistence on the routines of life being scrupulously observed.

He had not yet switched on the lights in a room he knew, and which was faintly lighted by the uncertain moon. He went on to the window, which looked outward to east and north, for any signs that the sky might give.

Had he done well to tell them to go quietly to bed, with no further precautions against the various deaths that might rain down before morning came?

He thought he had. He disliked the idea of skulking in cellars to avoid bombs that might never come. And there seemed an added ignominy in such an attitude in regard to a war in which you were not directly concerned.

Besides, there was the dignity of England to be maintained. It was hard enough, Heaven knew, while her politicians betrayed her honour at home in ways of which men who had left their youth and become rather full-blooded should avoid thought. There might be no attack, and he should not wish the servants to be able to chatter of the basement-huddling in which the staff of the British Legation had spent the night.

He stood at the window, looking up to a clouded sky which seemed peaceful enough, and out on to a city the streets of which were now lighted again, and from which there arose a continual murmur, like the sound of a distant sea.

It had patches of smouldering redness in the neighbourhood of the railway terminus, and in one place there was the glow of a mounting fire. He wondered how successful those new fire-extinguishing devices had proved to be.

He gave little thought or imagination to the appalling misery which must be hidden by the semi-darkness of the city, dimly-lit and glimmering faintly under its pale mantle of snow. His mind was on larger things.

He had been present at other scenes of violence and blood, and his duty had always been to look on, taking no part, but thinking ever of what it meant, and to forecast the event of the further day.

Now he wondered, was this a flicker which would die down with a city's death, or was it a mere episode which would be forgotten tomorrow in more momentous events, or remembered after as no more than prelude of war?

He looked up again to the northern skies, and his attention reverted sharply to present things. The city batteries were silent still, but was there not a flash of light—and again—through the drifting clouds? Was there not a sound of quick-firing guns coming over the murmur of the wounded city?

As he looked, the street lights went out. He stepped to his own switch, to ascertain that the lights had not been completely cut off again. The light came at the touch.

He switched it off quickly, though he saw how futile it was, on such a night, for Prague to trust to the darkness to foil her foes. But before he did so, he had looked at his watch. It was scarcely an hour since the explosion.

CHAPTER LV.

IT was at the same time that Sir Geoffrey Cullender lifted his gaze to the skies that Herr Vacek entered his car to leave the city by the southeast road.

He felt some exaltation of mind, having come to the moment for which he had lived and worked for the last fifteen years, with a single-hearted devotion to the cause of the land he loved, and with a conviction that the hour of conflict would come, in which he was being justified by the event.

Now he could feel that, thanks mainly to his own efforts and plans, the hour did not find his country unready to meet the storm.

He had been somewhat disconcerted at the first moment of learning that the telegraphic and telephonic systems had been so completely severed, doubtless by the hands of the Nazi traitors who, by his own advice, would have been hanged or expelled at a much earlier day, but he could congratulate himself on the promptitude which had issued the most vital orders half an hour earlier, and on the fact that his preparations for such a moment were so complete that brief orders were sufficient now. Besides, the day was past when communications could be stopped by any cutting of wires.

He had just had some angry exchanges with the Air Minister, such as would have ruffled his temper more at a quieter time, he having been refused the support and cooperation which he felt that he had a right to expect, and which the moment surely required.

But it might be that Janda would yet see things in a better light, or be persuaded by colleagues with less prejudiced minds.

He put that annoyance aside to dwell on the secret plan of which even his own Generals had not been made fully aware till the last hour, and which would demonstrate that Czechoslovakia was sufficient to vex her foes, even before her allies had time to come to her aid, as he did not doubt that they would be active to do.

A German army invading Bohemia would naturally advance by the Elbe Valley, that being both the easiest approach and the direct road to the capital city. It would be equally natural that it should come by the broad track of the road that ran by the river's side.

It was no more than a routine of military precaution that he had had this road most elaborately mined. The Germans would have been wary of that; but he had prepared their minds by allowing the plans and contacts of those mines to fall into the hands of a spy, by whom he was pleased to know that they had been sold to Berlin.

Doubtless, an advance patrol would disconnect the contacts, and the army would advance securely over innocuous mines. That was how he meant it to be.

It was a closer secret that there was a second system by which they would be automatically fired, at a time when caution would have been put aside, and the road be congested with guns and lorries and thronging with human life. Yes, let the Germans come, if they would. He felt that he was well prepared.

He did not suppose that he could dictate their strategy to the German Staff, but he saw that the line of their advance would not be rendered less certain by the fact that it would be held by no more than a weak delaying force till within twenty kilometres of Prague.

His own strategy was to move instantly on Vienna, now a German city, with the whole available strength of his first-line troops. Let the reserves defend Prague, which, for a week at least, they should be able to do. They would fight best behind trenches, and in the city's defence.

Vienna taken—as he thought it would surely be—would not Italy's action be well-assured? Would she not come to his aid before it could be recaptured by the powerful neighbour whom she was so loath to see encroached on her northern boundaries?

For this plan, he had sacrificed every minor consideration. Even the dangerous Hungarian frontier would be denuded of all but second-line troops, by the orders that he had issued two hours ago.

Let Hungary move if she would! In his own way, he saw far; and he knew that it is the last laughter that does not die.

It was a pity that they had not quarrelled at a time when troops were more easily moved. But that again showed the foolish casual way in which Germany must have blundered into hostilities!

The conditions of roads and adverse weather might delay his own contemplated march into the Danube Valley, but they would be equally detrimental to a swift advance upon Prague, which the German General Staff would be more likely to have in mind.

These reflections increased his confidence in himself, as the one man who knew both his own mind and the factors with which he dealt. But it did not prevent a feeling of irritation at the slow pace of the car, which had left Prague more than half an hour before, and was not yet twenty miles on the way.

"Musil"—he picked up the speaking-tube to address the driver—"we're not making the pace we ought. Can't you do better than this?"

"Not on this road, sir. Not if you want to get through. It'll get worse as we go on, more likely than not."

One of his companions, General Benda, a man of outward stolidity, who had won the peace-time reputation of being a very sound and capable officer, but now showed signs of the nervous strain of the hour, remarked that it wouldn't make them any quicker if they should skid into the ditch; and then interrupted himself to ask: "But what's that over there?"

It was a question to which the other occupants of the car were less able than himself to give a reply, not having the advantage of his position at the near-side window.

He had seen a light which looked like the red streak of a falling star, and he answered his own question with the next breath: "It looked like an aeroplane crash."

Herr Vacek leaned over to look through the window of the moving car. There was nothing that he could see. He remarked: "It isn't likely that there'd be fighting here."

He felt some irritation at what he supposed to be the imagination of a nerve-strained man. But his senses being now on the alert, he thought he heard a sound of firing, heavy and far away.

It came, if he were not wrong, from behind—from the direction of Prague. Was it really being attacked? It might be no more than that a few planes had escaped from a losing fight, and were now being shot down by the batteries that surrounded Prague.

Or it might be that, like General Benda, he was in a condition to imagine that which he did not hear. Prague must be twenty miles behind now. But it was from that quarter that the wind came, and he knew that his hearing was good.

Was there not also a sound of firing ahead? Less heavy, but nearer? Was there not—different, unmistakable—a sound of exploding bombs?

He remained silent. The facts—whatever they might be—would be known sufficiently soon, and it would be worse than useless to disturb his companions with idle guesses. Major-General Belsky, sitting opposite, did not appear to hear anything. Indeed, he showed symptoms of coming sleep.

He himself had always said that there was not overmuch to be feared from the air: little but noise, and the foolish panics that terror breeds. At the last, it must be the army that will decide.

But half a mile farther on there was a slight rise in the road-level, and as they came to the crest of the ridge, the driver, his eyes searching ahead, as they had good reason to do on that dark, snow-cumbered road, pressed his foot on the brake, and put the speaking-tube to his mouth to ask: "Shall I go on, sir? I think it's the wireless station being attacked."

The road by which Herr Vacek was now seeking to reach the headquarters of an army already assembling for the Austrian inva-sion he had in mind (which he intended to stimulate with his own presence, even though the obligations of the office he held might not allow him to lead it over the frontier, or to command it on the field of battle) ran by the side of the government-owned transmitting-station, which was situated twenty-five miles to the southeast of Prague.

There were stations farther away, at Brno and Bratislava, from which news could be sent out, if it should reach them, and if they should still be intact, but, for that night at least, the destruction of the Liblice station would mean that Prague was cut off from the world.

"No," he answered. "Go on."

"Very well, sir."

"You can go slowly, and switch off the lights."

Two miles farther on, the car came to another hill, on the crest of which it stopped, under a shadow of pines.

The occupants got out. They stood in the cold wind, careless of whether the thick garments they wore were sufficient to resist the iron cold of the night.

Half an hour later, they got back into the car. There was nothing further to watch, nor any further danger to fear.

They had seen a score of German night-bombers raining de-struction upon the station and silencing its defending batteries. They had seen the two great masts that supported the aerial totter and fall.

If there had been any effort to defend the station from the air (as in fact there had), it had been defeated before they came.

PRELUDE IN PRAGUE, BY S. FOWLER WRIGHT * 195

Now the German bombers had gone, forming like a flight of geese, and rising into the night. They flew south, having done their work, from which direction they may have come.

Herr Vacek spoke no word as he got back into the car. He remained silent for a long time, having thoughts which he did not like. He would not admit fear, but in his heart he knew that he was less confident than before.

If Janda had been able to repulse the German attacks, both to north and east, at an earlier hour, how was it that he had failed to make adequate defence at so vital a point? He was no less wroth because he knew well what Janda's answer would be.

CHAPTER LVI.

IT was no less than true that a German air-fleet had been defeated on the frontier over the Elbe Valley—had, in fact, been destroyed as a fighting unit, by numerically inferior forces, in a battle which had continued down the wind for a distance of forty miles, before the German formation was finally broken at Leitmeritz, by the attack which had been planned to take them in flank where the river bends.

The action, which since has become known, somewhat inaccurately, as the battle of Warnsdorf, has acquired historical prominence from the fact that it was the first time that air-fleets had met in anything more serious than the mock-battles of aerial manœuvre, which, for very obvious reasons, could make little approach to the conditions of actual conflict.

It is true that there had been air-fighting, both sanguinary and heroic, during the war of twenty years earlier, but it had been Homeric in character, a matter of flight and chase and single duels among the clouds. The unit had been no more than the single plane.

Now fleet met fleet from strategic positions forethought and planned, and with theories of combined manœuvre which must be tried by the hard issues of life and death.

The conflict demonstrated several principles of aerial tactics which have since been accepted as fundamental, and which are closely similar, in several aspects, to the experiences of naval warfare.

It brought an undying fame to Marshal Doubek, whose own life was lost at a time when the victory was complete, and he was ordering the airworthy remnant of his own fleet in such a way as to inflict the utmost of further loss on a routed foe.

It is no detraction of what he did to observe that the strategy from which victory came was of Herr Janda's design, nor that the German commander, who also perished, may be accounted unfortunate, both in having been ill-served by his own scouts and afterward in encountering additional foes, where he had had good reason to expect a reinforcement of German planes.

His orders had been to approach Prague by the straightest route, and without disguise. His mission was to bring the Czechoslovak air-fleets to battle whenever and wherever they might be found, and to destroy them so that the night-bombers, which were to arrive in overwhelming force during the next hour, should be unimpeded in their subsequent operations.

He knew his own fleet to be stronger than any that he was likely to meet, and that other battle-fleets, of more or less similar strength, were converging upon their outnumbered foes.

One of these, by the bewildering cross-chances of war, was to have effected a junction with his own over Leitmeritz, being the same place at which Herr Janda had planned that a fleet of his slower fighting-planes should be assembled for Marshal Doubek's support, or to be used in a last effort to delay the passage of the German fleet, if it should have defeated the first attack.

The actual course of the battle was that the German fleet, which consisted of 210 fighting-planes, and was flying at its highest speed, in a formation of ten wedge-shaped squadrons, each of twenty-one planes, extended in column of route, found itself suddenly attacked by eighty planes, which descended upon its rear from the upper clouds, and were of equal, or slightly superior, speed.

The later stages of the battle have been the subject of acute controversy, the discussion of which would be outside the scope of this narrative, but the complexities of the dispute will be readily understood by those who may be familiar with the difficulty which experts commonly find in agreeing the details of military or naval operations, although such conflicts must be confined to a single level, whether of land or sea, which is not the case when men make war in the upper air.

But it is agreed that the Czechoslovak fleet attacked the two rearmost of the German squadrons, closing from both sides, upon flanks and rear, and pouring into them a concentrated fire from the slightly higher altitude which it maintained; and it is clear that these two squadrons suffered heavy losses, and that their formation broke.

Within three minutes—so rapid may be the event when battle-fleets clash suddenly in the air—these two squadrons, as units of manœuvre, had ceased to exist.

It is clear also that the German commander attempted to retrieve the position by a general order which, in non-technical language, required that the whole fleet should wheel to the right, rising as it did so, and executing this movement in such a manner that it would have retained its formation in column, as it curved backward to face its foes.

But this order was not properly executed. Some of the airmen, perhaps too anxious to meet their foes, swung too abruptly round, instead of following the line their commander led, acting as though they had been ordered to convert their right flank to a line of front, and the German fleet fell into an immediate confusion from which it never entirely recovered.

Marshal Doubek must have had some expectation of this development, for not only did he take instant advantage of it in so directing his own fleet that it cut completely through the confused mob of its foes, but it appears that he had issued orders before the battle began, in anticipation of this event, and calculated to inflict the maximum of loss before the position could be reformed.

It was at this stage of the battle that the German Commander himself was shot down, but not until he had sent out a general order that the whole fleet should resume its course toward Leitmeritz, which, in a straggling way, it proceeded to do.

It is evident that this order had an aspect of flight, and did, indeed, resume the position from which the fleet had suffered already, with Marshal Doubek upon the windward side, and pursuing upon its rear.

But it can be plausibly argued that an order for flight would not have continued the previous course, that being directly into the enemy's country. It may be accepted that the more probable intention was to draw Marshal Doubek toward the spot where he would be likely to encounter a second fleet of his foes; and this result must actually have followed, but that the second fleet was thirteen minutes behind the scheduled time at which it should have arrived.

For thirty miles there was a running fight, following more or less closely the twisting course of the Elbe Valley, as was proved by the trail of the fallen planes, during which, in spite of a preponderance of German losses, their fleet appears to have drawn together again, and to have resumed something of the coherence that it had lost.

It still possessed a numerical advantage over its pursuers, and, up to this point, it cannot be asserted beyond denial that the battle was lost or won.

But here, where it expected friends, it encountered foes, and did not recognise them for what they were until the second Czechoslovak fleet, consisting of a type of fighting-plane somewhat slower but otherwise as formidable as those they met, had ranged itself on their flank, and actually opened fire upon them at so close a range that more than one of their battle-planes was shot down before it had even got its own guns into position to make reply.

From that moment the fight was done. The German fleet broke apart. It became no more than a scattering rout that soared, or dived, or dodged, or trusted to simple speed, to escape the chase of its eager foes.

Some score of planes that kept together, and still endeavoured to make a combined resistance, were pursued beyond Habstein, where they appear to have made an attempt to dive and double back under their foes, with a result so disastrous to themselves that seven lay wrecked in the space of a single mile.

Ten minutes after the battle broke over Leitmeritz, the second German air-fleet, consisting also of 210 fighting-planes, passed the same spot, knowing nothing of what had been, and flew on toward Prague, being no more than one fleet among ten that searched through the dark skies for foes too few for most of them to obtain a prey.

Within three hours of that time, so rapid is the course of aerial warfare, so decisive are its results when there is an overwhelming disparity in the strength of the forces engaged, the German air-fleets had gained complete dominion in Czechoslovakian skies.

Its enemies' fleets were scattered; their hangars bombed; their petrol stations fired.

If any Czechoslovakian aeroplanes still held the skies, they flew like homeless birds with no safe place on which to alight: they lurked furtive among the clouds, seeking only the opportunity to inflict some further damage upon their foes before they should meet their end; or they fled through the night to find, it might be, a rest upon neutral soil.

But from all the welter of strife that made confusion in the skies of that tortured night, the battle of Warnsdorf stands out, separate and distinct. It was first, by some minutes, in point of time; it was fought with some approach to equality in the numbers and capacity of the forces engaged; it had a clear tactical plan, dividing it from encounters that were mere scrambles of flight and chase, or blind death-grapples among the clouds; and it was the one victory that Czechoslovakia, in its short history, would be able to boast, for which even its constant foes need not grudge to give the honour that is its due.

CHAPTER LVII.

SIR GEOFFREY stood for some time at the window of his unlighted room, watching a sky which had been troubled to northward with sudden flashes of fire, but had sunk to darkness again.

Perhaps that was all there would be. Perhaps the air-fleets which Germany had been able to use for her swift surprise had not been more than Czechoslovakia had been equal to meet. For this night, at least, she might have underestimated the strength and watchfulness of her weaker foe.

He concluded that Herr Schott's report, that the first air-battle had resulted in German defeat, might be no more than the truth. He began to hope that it might have done all that the moment required, though he saw it to be no more than an improbable guess.

He considered his own position. He was cut off from all communication with his own Government. He must rely on himself alone. He could not tell whether Prague would be left to its own defence, or whether half Europe might not be already astir.

He was clear that, until he should receive further instructions, or unless the Czechoslovak Government should withdraw from the city, it was his duty to remain—and, of course, to retain his staff.

He had been approached by several British residents during the day, and, in all cases, he had advised, and, if necessary, assisted them to leave the city.

As to these ladies who were his guests, he should have made their position secure by bringing them within the Legation walls, and under the sign of the English flag. Yet he was not easy on that. The indiscriminate savagery of modern warfare may well slay stranger and friend in its blind assaults.

He was glad to think that Gerald Langton would be here tomorrow. Yet would he? How would he get through? Knowing what he did, and no more, he could only doubt.

But he supposed that he ought to get them out of the city tomorrow, if Langton did not arrive, though it was not simple to decide where, or by what route they should go.

Tomorrow, half Europe might be at war, and it would be hard to say where safety might best be found. It would be easy to make a mistake, so that his guests would be interned in a hostile land. What was that to the northward again? Flash after flash scattered along the sky. The sound of gunfire, continuous but not loud.

It did not seem that it could be more than an affair of some outpost planes. Or, of course, it might be that there were but few there to resist a wide-fronted attack.

And next moment he saw that that must have been a sound guess, for Prague's searchlights rose, and her anti-aircraft guns waked to a clamour that did not cease.

With a constant crackling thunder of sound, a hundred flashes struck upward into the night; and over the noise of a hundred guns, there came the steady, dominant sound of the engines of many planes.

It was clear that the guns were not futile to vex their foes, for the first aircraft that Sir Geoffrey was able to see were those that fell in flames from the sky, and these were not one or two, but they fell frequent and fast, like a procession of falling stars.

To one who could not see the darker, more numerous forms of those that the barrage missed, it might have seemed that Prague's virginity was secured by that outer girdle of guns.

But it was no more than seconds before the whir of the engines was overhead; and then that sound, with all others, was drowned in the detonation of bursting bombs.

The sound in itself was not new to Sir Geoffrey's ears. He had heard the bursting of bombs in London twenty-two years before. But that experience was sufficient only to warn him of the difference of that which was round him now.

He had heard them then as grim, single, sullen thunders of sound. They had been sufficient to show what Germans would be willing to do, if they had the power; that they would destroy any civilian population that they could reach with as little compunction as an army about their gates.

But though they had the will then, they had lacked the power; and what they had been able to do had been of little further result than to harden the temper of English people, who had been growing somewhat weary of war.

But now the sounds were not single, nor far apart. They were a constant tumult, separate in themselves, and yet so many that it would have been hard to give hearing to any one. They came as fast as the rattle of hail on a tin roof. And under them the city buildings fell down in ruin, or rose in fire.

Sir Geoffrey turned from the window. He decided that it was not a night to be spent in sleep, or on which sleep would be likely to come.

He would have been surprised to know how cheerful he really felt as he went downstairs, though he was consciously aware that it was his duty to show courage and confidence to the household in which he was the official representative of his race.

"I said it would be high explosives at first," he said to himself, with the natural satisfaction of one who observes his own prediction to be fulfilled.

He found some members of his staff, and two of the men-servants, were assembled in the room where he had left them, or they may have remained discussing the position after he had withdrawn, more freely than his presence had admitted before.

He looked round on faces pale with anxiety or terror, quiet, excited, or self-consciously unsure of what the occasion required. He said: "Gentlemen, it seems that it will be a warm night."

He directed Paul to go round the house, to make sure that there were no lights, except in well-shuttered rooms.

"Not," he said, "that there will be any difference in that. I should say they're dropping bombs like a man sows corn in a field. What we really want is a luminous flag. Where's Harvey?"

Lawrence answered: "He's gone down into the town. You said he could, if he liked."

"So I did. I hope he'll be all right. He's too good to lose. I daresay he'll be as safe there as here."

"I think I ought to go out after the car," Lawrence went on. "We left it somewhere up by the Castle."

"And you think it may be still there?"

"It was left locked. We might need it before morning. It's hard to say what may be happening now."

"Well, it may still be there. It isn't likely, if anyone found it useful to give them a lift. And I don't know that we shall. I don't want you to run into any danger for that. But I'm not sure that the streets aren't as safe as anywhere else. It used to be supposed not, but I never quite understood why."

Lawrence rose at once.

Sir Geoffrey looked round to say: "I don't think there's anything much to be done. It appears that the Germans have decided to destroy Prague in what I should say will be a thorough manner. I believe they pride themselves on being thorough in all they do, so there's no need to be surprised about that. We've got to stay, and it's not our business to interfere. If we're alive and well when the bombing stops, we may find something to do to help.

"For the present, you can go up to the roof, or down to the basement, or stay here, whichever seems the most sensible thing to do.

"I believe these bombs can penetrate several ceilings before they burst. If you're on the roof, you'll have farther to fall, and if you're down below there'll be more to fall upon you."

With these cheerful alternatives, and to the sound of shattering glass, and a falling wall, as a bomb burst in the street below, Sir Geoffrey sat down to draft a report to his Government on the events of the last few hours, and looked up, as he reached for his pen, to observe that the two girls had entered the room.

CHAPTER LVIII.

CARESSE had discarded the damaged dress for one of sea-shell pink, the new colour that had been introduced in Paris a few weeks before.

She had removed all traces of the flight through the snow, and was as carefully dressed as though she were going back to the interrupted dance. She controlled the nervousness in her voice to all but Perdita's ears, as she said lightly: "We couldn't sleep in this noise, so we thought we might just as well come down." She looked round to ask sharply: "Where's Lawrence? Isn't he here?"

Sir Geoffrey explained where he had gone, and was answered shortly: "It can't be safe. I didn't think you'd have let him go."

He didn't trouble to discuss that. He thought that Caresse was taking it very well. His experience was that, at such moments, people's tempers are often inclined to give way.

He looked at Perdita with more concern. Her eyes were quiet and grave, but he saw that her hand shook as it touched a paper-knife in an idle way upon the table beside her.

She asked, as their glances met: "There are a lot of people outside. Don't you think you ought to let some of them in?"

"No," he answered, without explanation. "I don't know that we should. But I don't know either that it would do them any good. I might consider it if I did. They ought to get to the open fields, and scatter about."

His mind went back to an occasion when he had been in charge of the Legation in Oruro, and had closed his doors firmly against the demands of two rival Bolivian factions who were exchanging revolver shots in the street below and who were alike in thinking that they could pick off their opponents more comfortably from the windows of the English Minister's residence.

He remembered that they had been alike also in promising him very rich rewards when, as was their equal anticipation, they should be occupying the seats of office on the following day.

But it was his place to remain aloof, alike from civil disorders or international warfare. Yet was this war? Was it not promiscuous murder, equalling the worst massacres that the black records of history held?

Yet he could not consider it as a new thing, to which precedents would not apply. It had been tried in the last war, though in no more than a trivial, experimental way; but sufficiently for men to understand what it was, and what it could be developed to be.

And then there had been a long pause. For twenty years men had considered it, discussed it, and finally and deliberately adopted it as a method of war.

They would not now be able to plead at the bar of God that they had blundered into it in a blind way, or been betrayed by rulers of evil minds. They had faced it for twenty years—and, at the end of that time, Europe had become a hellish arsenal of night-bombers, and of laboratories for the manufacture of poison-gas.

Sir Geoffrey, concerning himself with such questions only so far as they might direct him on the narrower issue of diplomatic propriety, decided that war is war, in whatever manner it may be waged, and the duty of neutrality must remain. He might even have gone too far when he had let Harvey go as he did.

In any case, what could he do to alleviate the thousand miseries of those who crouched await for the falling bombs, or whose bodies already bled? Potentially, even probably, he and those around him were destined for the same fate in the next hour. For, over the city, from end to end, the bombs were falling like steady hail. Would they never cease, till the whole city was down?

Lawrence, meanwhile, had gone out to the sight of that which could only be guessed by those who remained within shuttered windows and walls.

He had scarcely left the Legation gates before he must move with caution, in the gloom of the cul-de-sac, to avoid the bricks of a fallen wall, where one of the side-houses had been struck in such a manner that its interior, dark and vacant now, had been exposed to the street. But after that, when he reached the turn, he looked up and down without observing that any damage was done, and, for that first moment, he had a hope that the havoc worked was less than the noise implied.

But the sky was still filled with the swiftly-passing bombers, though there was none directly over his head, and the bursting bombs, near and far, made a continuous volley of sound.

The narrowest street was empty to the first glance, and then an open car, of ancient pattern, came up the hill. It was crowded with people, even to some who held on at the sides, with their feet on a broken step; and as it jibbed, with such a load, at the steeper hill, there was a loud quarrel as to who should get off and walk, and a man was thrown roughly backward on to the stones.

Lawrence saw the lightened vehicle resume progress at last, and the fallen man get unsteadily to his feet, and then commence a lumbering run, as he screamed wildly, in a Moravian dialect, that they should not leave him behind.

He left the street for the steeper way of the steps which climbed up to the level of the castle courtyard, and so came to where he could look out on a wide panorama of river, city, and sky.

He stood in a freezing wind, and looked up to a veiled moon, and a heaven of driven clouds, across which there came the black, swiftly-gliding shadows of the night-bombers, squadron by squadron, following in what seemed to be an unending procession, and dropping their seeds of death, invisible as they fell through the dark air, but each causing an upward flicker of light as it struck upon roof or street, so that the whole of the lower city was covered with dancing twinkles that flashed and failed, but of which one, here and there, would remain to burn redly into a broadening glow.

The northern batteries had been silenced, but there were still occasional gun-flashes from south and east when the bombers came sufficiently near to those sides of the city for their batteries to avail. Except for that, Prague had ceased to resist. She lay prostrate, dying, under the rain of the ceaseless bombs.

Of her population, which at this time may have been somewhat over 200,000, it has been calculated that about a third had fled by various means before the attack commenced, although the larger number of these had got no farther than the surrounding villages.

Of the remainder (apart from those—estimated at 6,000—who had been destroyed in the first explosion, as they had been crowding into the entrances to the bomb-proof shelters, and about 13,000 who were imprisoned beneath the ground, of whom none survived), it appears probable that less than half made belated attempts to flee for safety through the dangers of the bomb-strewn streets.

There were, of course, a considerable number who remained loyal to the public services in which they were engaged, and in the hospitals (already hopelessly overcrowded during the previous hour), and in vain efforts to fight the fires, of which ten would break out for one that was brought under control.

There must have been many physically unfit for the ordeal of flight on the winter roads, and these—all of age, illness, and childhood the city held—must be left to their lonely deaths, or the strong also must stay.

There may have been others of more material greeds who had possessions too dear to leave, too heavy to bear away.

When the bombs rained, there were thousands who went to earth in their lowest cellars, where they lay in darkness, as though there were protection in that, and they would be unobserved by the searching bombs. They crouched and trembled; they cursed or prayed, as their habit was.

Others came out. As a rat dashes from hole to hole, they scuttered from place to place, thinking that they could dodge the descending death.

A huge crater that a bomb made in the street was crowded with those who thought that two would not fall on the same spot. But they found no safety in that, for, as Sir Geoffrey had said, the Germans are thorough in all they do.

Lawrence, coming out on the higher level, had a first wonder of whether the German airmen might not have had orders to leave this part of the city uninjured.

The great extent of the castle, now silent and dark, showed no evidence of having been struck, nor did the new Government buildings, which might have seemed an attractive, as they were certainly a conspicuous, mark. St. Veit's Cathedral still lifted its incongruous towers.

But farther away, where the hill that had once been the site of castle and palace, the reservation of prelate and prince, had been recently covered with huge blocks of flats (emphatic symbols of a civilisation which, as it neared its fall, had become indifferent to the earth that bred it, and to the young that it was its own duty to breed), there was the glow of a rising fire; and in the open space he must now cross there were craters in the pavement which it was not difficult to avoid, as their black gashes interrupted the snow.

He thought: "Here, at least, the bombs have done little harm," and had a moment of wonder as to where all the life of the Government buildings had fled. Had they left the city, while those whose duties were less evident and direct had resolved to stay? He might be making a wrong guess. From the farther side of the square, through the confused thunder of ceaseless sound, there came voices loud in excited dispute, and a woman's scream.

Then his attention was drawn to a nearer thing. The overcrowded car which he had seen in the street below, and which had now come to the same point as himself by a longer way, had been less successful in avoiding the gap which a bomb had made in the middle road.

Now it stood, tipped half over, and derelict with a broken wheel.

Most of its occupants had left it, to continue their flight on foot. But Lawrence saw that there were still some who stood round, and the impulse to help, foolish and futile as it must be among the conditions that faced him now, caused him to go nearer, and then withdraw from that which must solve itself.

A woman stood by the door of the car, and there was a small child in her arms.

On the floor of the car, and now dragged out, half over the running-board, was an old man, who appeared to be in a dying state. Blood ran freely from a wound that an effort to get him out may have opened again.

A younger man bent as though endeavouring to raise him into his arms.

The woman screamed in reproach: "Josef, are you a fool? You could not bear him for twenty yards."

"But, Zuleika, I think I can. Shall I leave my father to die?"

"Will you keep us here, where the bombs fall? Have you no thought for me? For the child?"

"You can go on. I will follow. I cannot leave him to die."

He raised the old man in his arms as he spoke. He may not have been of a great weight. But as he was lifted, the life went. The head hung loose at the neck.

The younger man stood hesitating for a moment, the burden still in his arms. Then he laid it down, and ran after his wife.

Lawrence went on, seeking the car. It should be securely locked, if the attendant had done his part. He had trusted the man with the keys, but there was no trouble in that, Sir Geoffrey having handed him a duplicate set.

He found it easily, now that the parking-space had been cleared, standing behind two others that haste had wrecked.

There had been an attempt to use it, for one of the near doors had been forced open, and must then have been left to swing loose, and have been struck by another car, so that it now hung on one hinge.

But it had successfully resisted whatever efforts to start it may have been made, the switch lock having justified its makers' warrant.

Lawrence found no difficulty in driving it now, but as he turned it toward the courtyard entrance, a doubt came to his mind, stirred by the sound of approaching voices along the road.

Should he be able to drive it down to the Legation gates without efforts being made to wrest it from his control by fugitives desperate with fright? It was a longer way by the twisting road than by that he had come, and he would make but a poor pace on the steep frozen surface, with the risk of a bomb-crater at every yard.

He did not like the idea of fighting for the possession of the car with these poor wretches frantic for life; perhaps of having to choose between being thrown out himself, and using the pistol his pocket held. And if he should get it safely back to the Legation, the road might be blocked by fallen ruins before they should decide to use it again for their own flight.

He was not even sure that there would be saving of time, when he thought of how few minutes would be required to come up by the shorter way, which would be impossible to the car.

On these reflections, he ran it back under the shadow of the wall, locked it again, and returned on foot, as he had come.

As he emerged to the road, he was aware that a flight of bombers came more directly overhead than had any that he had observed previously. With the instinct of a bird that darts back to the hedge when the hawk's shadow crosses the field, he withdrew to the shelter of the gateway arch through which he had come.

Right and left now, as it seemed at no distance at all, the deafening explosions came, the crash of the falling walls, the cries that told of life that had lurked silently within them, hoping that death in the darkness would pass it by.

Reason told him that there was no safety in where he stood, and though instinct clamoured a different tale, it gave way to the thought that it was clear duty to return with no avoidable delay.

As he stepped out again, a motorcycle came up the hill. In the opposite direction, fifty yards away, a bomb burst.

The explosion did not reach them to any hurt, but he saw the cyclist's face in the sudden flash, and that he had slackened his speed for an instant, as it had seemed that he would have run into the explosion itself. He called: "Herr Janda, you are not hurt?"

The Air Minister stopped at the sound of a voice he knew.

"No," he answered; "but you should have been gone from here before now. Is Sir Geoffrey stubborn to stay? You can tell him from me that there is no further use for Legations here. He has the choice to go, or to be dead in the next hour. As I suppose, they have only begun."

"He will believe that there are few left when I tell him that you are gone."

"He should have better reason than that. My work here is finished, as I suppose. I have issued the last order my fleets will hear. But I do not go for that cause. I have a call to make of a special kind."

He put on speed as he spoke, as though reminded by his own words of that which must not delay, and Lawrence, conscious of his own urgency, hurried in the opposite direction, his pace hastened by the dark shadows that were swooping low overhead, and by the bursting bombs that were frequent around him now.

He came to the lower street, which he must descend for a short distance before turning left-hand into the cul-de-sac which ended in the Legation gates, and as he approached it he heard a noise of voices and many feet that ascended toward him.

He saw that a score of men, and some women, pursued two who fled. They hunted them in a spirit of savage hate that made them blind to their own dangers, and all beside.

As he looked, they caught one. He was struck down, and became the kicked plaything of many feet. Over the struggling form a woman bent with a knife, striking downward blows.

The fall of the one man was his companion's gain. He was pursued by fewer, and those were they who had been farthest behind. His first thought was not to avail himself of that relief; but he turned, seeing his companion fall, and raised a pistol as though to fire. Finding it empty, he appeared to realise that rescue was out of his power, and resumed his flight.

Lawrence had turned into the Legation opening, having no mind for further delays on matters beyond interference or understanding by him. Herr Janda's advice and warning should be reported to Sir Geoffrey at once. Even now, there might be time to fly in safety from the inferno in which they were. There might still be hope that their lives would survive the night.

As he pressed the bell, he became aware that the fugitive had turned into the cul-de-sac. It was a natural error, it being as wide as the street, and less steep, but, being done, the man was in the case of a cornered rat.

He ran with a dozen men at his heels, who howled with an evil joy, seeing the blunder that he had made.

The porter opened the smaller door, and Lawrence stepped through. He looked back, and saw the running man, not three yards away. He wore the uniform of an officer of the German Air Force.

Lawrence had no time even to guess what he might have done, or for what cause he was hunted, with such savage lust for his death. He had but a second in which to resolve. He pushed the porter back, holding the door wide.

There was barely time to close it, and drive the first bolt into place, before the great doors shook to the rush. The baffled rage of the pursuers rose through the dins of the night, like a scream from the depths of hell.

Lawrence looked at the German uniform with no kindliness in his eyes. He said: "You had better come in. I don't know what His Excellency will say."

He saw a man who was young and tall, and handsome in the blonde German style. His left cheek was black from a recent bruise, but, beyond that, he showed little sign of the experiences through which he must have come during the night.

Lawrence had spoken in German, but he was answered in his own tongue: "I am sorry if I intrude. As yet, I do not know where I am. But you are English, as I suppose. If you would be so kind as to let me have some water to drink, I should be better able to talk."

The porter having provided this modest need, Lawrence led his guest or prisoner up to Sir Geoffrey's room.

It seemed to him, as he entered, that there had been no change since he left, he would have been surprised to learn how few minutes before.

Sir Geoffrey was still writing at his desk, and the other occupants of the room were grouped about it, as though waiting for a guest who did not arrive. Outside, the noise of bursting bombs, and of falling walls, had become louder, nearer, as though the messengers of death were giving closer attention to a part of the city which had been neglected before.

As the British Minister looked up at his entrance, Lawrence reported: "I've found the car, sir. It's all right, except for a damaged door. I thought it better to leave it up there than to try to get it down through the streets as they now are."

Sir Geoffrey said: "I've no doubt you did the best thing." He spoke as one whose mind follows another track, his eyes on the German uniform of the man standing behind. He asked sharply "Who is this?"

Lawrence explained what he knew, which was not much.

The officer stood silent, as though waiting invitation to speak. Sir Geoffrey looked at him without favour. He said: "So you rescued him from the mob?"

"Scarcely that, sir. I shut the door when he came in."

Sir Geoffrey approved the diplomatic adroitness of the reply: "If you can dodge the bombs for this night as well as you dodged that, you should go far." But his smile was for Lawrence alone. He said to the stranger: "I will hear who you are, and what you are doing here."

"I am Squadron-Captain Karl Dürer, of the Sakrow air-fleet. My plane was damaged as we came over the barrage, and I made a forced landing. I escaped with a companion who was killed by the mob. I have to thank you for a refuge which saved my life."

"It is a refuge I do not refuse, but it carries conditions that there was no opportunity to conclude, and which, as a man of honour, you will observe." He changed his tone to ask: "You are hurt?"

"Not seriously, I believe."

"Well, there is no occasion to stand. And a drink should do you no harm."

"I thank your kindness, but I have had a glass of water already, which was all that I required."

"Water?" Sir Geoffrey was genuinely shocked. "Did you think we could offer nothing better than that?"

He forgot the severity of his previous demeanour, and the gravity of the position in which they stood as he considered the parody of hospitable reception which Captain Dürer's reply disclosed. To Sir Geoffrey, water was a fluid in which you washed, or which was useful for floating ships.

But it appeared that Captain Dürer was a drinker of that beverage only, and when conviction had entered the British Envoy's indignant mind, it promptly reverted to the more serious question of the status of this uninvited guest.

"You will understand," he said, "and I am well assured that your honour will observe, that when you took refuge within these walls you abandoned the right to engage in further operations of war, this being the official territory of a neutral State."

The young German looked curiously at the British Envoy, not as though he would dispute so elementary a principle of international law, but as though it were mentioned without apposition to the circumstances in which they stood.

He said: "I will be advised by Your Excellency. But do you propose to remain here?"

"This," Sir Geoffrey replied, with some stiffness of tone, "is the British Legation in Prague. Will you tell me why I should leave?"

"Our orders are that Prague is to be destroyed during this night. It would be a cause of regret that any who are neutral, as you have said, and as we hope that those of your country will ever be, should be involved in a danger which is not theirs."

Sir Geoffrey heard this, and appeared to be neither grateful, nor to show disposition to accept the offered advice.

"Then," he asked, "why do you not respect the flag of a friendly Power? Do you call this a legitimate operation of war? I should incline to the use of a different word."

Captain Dürer gave an answer which had been given to him in the general orders issued to the German air-fleets.

"We do no more than to put out a fire which would have spread had it been left longer alone; and Europe should not be blind to perceive that the shortest war is the most humane."

"You may miscount on a short war. I should say that you have stirred that which you will be less able to stop."

"It is a war that should be over at dawn; and it is our aim to give Europe a lasting peace."

The conversation was punctuated at this point by an explosion so near and loud that it was evident that an adjoining building, if not a part of the Legation itself, had been directly struck.

Lawrence felt that it justified interrupting an argument which he had separate evidence to support. He said: "I met Herr Janda, sir, a few minutes ago. He was leaving the town. He said there could be no occasion for us to remain longer here."

Sir Geoffrey asked sharply: "Leaving? Where to?"

"He said he had a call of special importance to make. It was not clear what he meant."

"So I expect he had. It is a place which all men should leave whose business allows. If Herr Janda goes, he has a mission elsewhere of more importance than that which would hold him here. And you are about to leave with an equal cause."

He closed and sealed the letter which he had been writing, and went on: "You will take this letter to London at the best speed that you can, but choosing the safest route, on which your own discretion will be your guide. It is written in plain words, for there is nothing there that the whole world is not welcome to hear.

"As to Captain Dürer, I have added a few lines, to explain how he has come here. He can go with you, or remain, at his own choice, acting thereafter as circumstances and his honour dictate. But I should suppose that, with the uniform which he now wears, he may be safer here than outside, however active his friends may be from above."

But it appeared that Captain Dürer did not agree: "There is one chance of life," he said; "to leave Prague; and the time is short, if it have not gone, as I should think it easy to hear."

Lawrence hesitated; he was not less ready than the German airman to go, but he was urgent that Sir Geoffrey and others should not remain, to meet what looked to be little less than a certain death.

To this point, Sir Geoffrey's leisurely coolness had given tone to the demeanour of those around him, who might otherwise have reacted in different ways. It was consonant to the quiet dignity of the ancient room, which rejected the evidences of outer sound, as discords which left its harmony undisturbed.

But now he raised his voice for the first time in the irritation which opposition would always be liable to stir at more trivial issues.

"Am I in charge here, or who is? Am I the judge of what my own or England's honour requires? Or shall I ask directions from you? Has your training been to argue the orders which you receive? I suppose you would have Harvey come back, if he ever should, to find that I have scuttled away?

"You will take the letter with speed, or I will add a few words which you will not like."

Caresse heard Sir Geoffrey's decision with less satisfaction than she would have expected an hour before.

She had said little up to this time, her silence being the measure of a stress of emotion which she could not fully trust her ability to control, nor feel content that it would be a correct attitude to disclose.

Sensitive to atmosphere as she was, and disposed to the deliberate cultivation of emotion, or its simulation, as the dramatic interest of the moment required, it seemed hard to believe that there was less of peril without than in the peace of that stately room. She thought vaguely of discomforts to be faced, such as she had always been adroit to avoid; perhaps privation, ugliness, dirt, and pain.

She had never failed in ingenuity of excuse, and she felt now that Gerald had come to her rescue even before he arrived, as she said: "I don't think we can do that. I can't go before Gerald gets here. It might be any time now. Of course, Perdita can, if she likes."

She was conscious, in the next breath, of unwillingness that she should be taken at her own word, that Lawrence and Perdita should go together, and she remain. She looked at him, and felt an impulse to go.

Perdita had remained quiet until now. She was silent and self-controlled, though her more natural colour showed a pallor suggesting that which Caresse did not allow to appear. Now she said: "I shan't go without you," and Caresse's mind swayed again. It would be best—safest—to stay in the sheltered luxury of this ordered house, resolutely indifferent to the discords beyond its walls. Were they not to be most sanely regarded as warnings of what must be faced when its gates were left? Hardships—unseemly things. She shrank from thoughts of cold and darkness, of dirt and blood.

And in the moment these thoughts required Sir Geoffrey put her excuse aside: "Nonsense. Langton won't come now. He wouldn't get through, even if he'd be foolish enough to try. And if he did, he'd be glad to find that you weren't here. But of course he won't. You don't think traffic aircraft will come through this?"

Caresse looked at Lawrence to ask: "Had we better—?" Her mind swayed uncertainly. If Lawrence should go—and Gerald should not arrive—? What would tomorrow be likely to be, in this hateful place where the earth and the heavens shook?

Their eyes met, and she inclined to that which she had feared before. In the car, they would soon be distant from here. She would feel safety with him.

She said to Perdita: "You shan't stay for me. I'm a coward, as I always am. We'll both do as we're told. We'd better go up and pack."

She laughed, calling herself coward, and giving (she felt) a show of courage for those around to admire.

A nearby building—perhaps the one that had been struck a few minutes before—crashed down with a rumble of thunderous sound

Sir Geoffrey said: "You won't pack, you'll go."

He had taken a handful of paper money from a locked drawer of his desk. He divided it into three portions. "If you should happen to get separated—," he said in explanation.

Caresse said: "Go in these?" She pushed forward a thin slipper, little more than silk-trimmed sandal in shape, showing a bandaged foot. "I think not."

Perdita added, in a graver voice: "We won't be long really. We'll just bring what we can."

Sir Geoffrey must observe that there were limits to the authority which he could exercise in his own Legation. But who could say what difference the delay would make? They might be killed here, through this trivial, needless delay. Or they might have escaped a death into which more haste would have blindly run.

CHAPTER LIX.

HERR JANDA pursued a cautious way toward the field to which No. 973 had gone before to a waiting plane. There was no reason for haste, there being long hours of darkness ahead, and he had a purpose in which he did not intend to fail.

So he rode slowly over the broken cumbered surface of the hard-frozen road, having bitter thoughts the while in a very resolute mind.

Behind him, the city burnt. There were still parts that had escaped the bombardment, or resisted its worst effects: there were streets that were quiet and still. But as the moments passed, it could be seen that the fires were higher, that they were more numerous in one part of the city, and that, in another, they were blending into one general glare.

It could be plainly seen from the high road that Herr Janda took; for the wind, which was inclined to rise as the night passed, drove the smoke away to the southeast. So also might he have seen the dark shadows of the swiftly-gliding bombers which passed in unending procession under the clouds.

But he had no care to look back. There was nothing there which he had not foreseen or foretold to unheeding ears. Europe might, or might not, avenge the ruin the night had brought, but there would be nothing for her to save.

War should have been commenced, if at all, at their own time, with the skies already filled with the war-fleets of strong allies. Otherwise, or until that position could be contrived, it was useless to talk of war, which must be mere destruction to them.

But Herr Vacek would not agree. Well, he would be learning it now in the school of his country's death.

The Air Minister had stayed at his post till he surely knew that his work was done. He had kept the German air-fleets back for an hour: he had inflicted more loss upon them than it had seemed reason to hope.

There might still be some Czech war craft that held the skies, but as an organised force, as instruments either of offensive or defensive war, her air-fleets had ceased to be.

He had issued a last order, which, if it should reach those for whom it was meant, gave them the choice to surrender, or flee, or fight on to a fruitless death. They would each do as his nature led. For himself, he had a purpose which had been resolved at a quieter time.

He must go slowly for the broken litter and the constant risk that a bomb-crater might break the road, but the straggling fugitives that he passed were few; for the main tides of flight were to south and east, and the exodus of most who would ever leave was already done. He heard the government, of whom he had been one, cursed to as deep a hell as the German murderers overhead, and was of a disposition to say amen.

He found the sentry still holding his place, though he had the voice of a frightened man.

He reported that Mr. Steele had been there about four hours before, and had flown away in the bomber which had been left for him in the field.

Since then, another aeroplane had settled down, and the airman who brought it had gone.

But, beyond that, he had an unlikely tale. A squadron of German bombers had passed overhead, flying low, and one had dropped a bomb into the field. Whether by chance or design, it had exploded close to the waiting plane. He could not say what damage had been done, having remained at his own post by the gate.

Herr Janda was not of a superstitious mind, but he had a moment of wondering doubt. It was impossible that the plane, waiting in the shadow of the little pine-wood, could have been observed from above, nor was there anything in that solitary place which would tempt the lightning to fall.

It was a chance incalculably remote that the lonely spot would be struck by a random bomb, and that at a time when it was clear that the attacking fleets were concentrating upon the destruction of the city.

Had the secret thought of his heart become known to some divine or demoniac power? Some heathen devil potent to guard his own, such as were the official deities of the Germans now? Some angel, shocked at the blasphemy of that which his heart conceived?

But when he reached the plane, it appeared that chance, or supernatural power, had failed, though by a margin of yards alone.

A bomb had fallen indeed, and within the very edge of the wood. It had driven into the ground, and burst with a shattering force among the roots of the crowding trees.

To approach the place where the plane lay, they had to clamber over the trunk of one that had fallen far out into the field. When they had done this, they looked up to another that leaned overhead, as though waiting to fall and crush them when they arrived.

But, as though to add a second miracle to the first, the plane itself was unhurt, or, if damaged at all, it was something the darkness hid.

"Shall you be coming back, sir, tonight?" the man asked, as Herr Janda mounted into the cockpit.

"No. You can go to your own home. There may come a day when you can fight for freedom again, but it is not at this dawn, nor is it one I shall be likely to see."

The man watched the plane glide along the slope of the field. Dimly he saw it, a dark shadow, rising into the air.

After that, he thought that he could still detect the sound of its receding engine among the noises that vexed the night.

When it had utterly gone, he turned also, to go to he knew not what. He knew that Prague burned. He had heard the confused cries, the lamentations of bereaved women and ruined men, the wild rumours that came from the lips of those who had fled along a road that now fell to quietness again. But what rumours might not fall short of tomorrow's fact?

He remembered a scripture he had heard read the Sunday before, foretelling, as it was not hard to believe, the terror that now fell from the kindly skies: *There shall two be in the field: the one shall be taken and the other left.*

It seemed that he was one to be left, for this night at least. He crossed himself, muttering prayer. He went off to his mother's cottage among the hills, avoiding the road, and going by narrow paths through forest and snow-strewn fields, as a rat slinks through the shadows in fear of the silent owl.

But Herr Janda rose through the night. He flew, he supposed, to a certain death, and there was peace in his heart, as there had not been since he had entered the office which he had left but an hour ago.

He had had joy enough when he had married Zita three months before, though it had proved a flickering and uncertain flame, but it was not the immortal joy of those who pursue death to a capture they will not miss, and learn that its terrors are only for those who flee; who may yet live while the cares and burdens of life are burst and forgotten bonds. He rose through the night, clear in purpose, and doubtless of his success.

Tomorrow, the world would hear of two things. It would hear of the destruction of Prague, with, it might be, threescore thousand of innocent, random deaths at the hands of their brother-men. But it would hear also of a loss of a different kind. Would it move the imaginations of men, so that they might turn, as the last hour struck, from the brink of the chaos to which they came?

He rose through the night. He faced the gale, and the freezing sleet. He rose higher to clearer skies.

There were eight thousand in all of the night-flying angels of death that Germany had let loose on a weaker land. They did not only crowd to the destruction of Prague. There was not an aerodrome, not a munitions factory, not a railway centre, not a military depot, that did not go up in fire before morning came. There were bombers so swift that they had returned to bear a second cargo of death, and would have loaded a third before the late winter dawn would have shown the horror of what they did, had they not had orders to waste no more. For their work would be done by then, and Germany would conserve her bombs for tomorrow's foe.

There were fighting-planes that flew swiftly about the skies, now in squadrons of seven only, like flocks of vultures, hunting for any Czech plane that might not yet have gone to earth, either for refuge while life remained, or shot down to a headlong fall.

There were scouting planes that made wide circles over Mid-Europe in the heights of the stormy air, watchful lest there should be air-fleets of other lands rushing to interpose before the work of destruction were wholly done. At such a sign, they would have sent their wireless messages back to where four great fleets of Germany's fighting-planes were held in reserve, and await to rise and fly toward any point from which threat of invasion came.

But, for this night at least, the advantage of surprise was in German hands. The dark hours passed, and in the Chancelleries of Europe there was only a confused fear, the receipt of rumours they could not prove, and the urgent seeking for facts that were slow to come.

For the hours were short, and Germany had seized the voice of the air.

There were many war-planes aloft that night, but the realms of air are both wide and high, and Herr Janda, soaring over the clouds, and making a wide circuit to west and north, flew for an hour in the silence of empty skies.

Far below, through the broken clouds, the snow-piled heights of the Erzgebirge rose, and were left behind for the long ranges of lower hills.

Coming round to an eastward course, he descended at last, when Grossenhain was a few miles ahead, to see the black line of the Elbe dividing the snow-white fields; and here he turned a farther point to the south, following the river's curves, and approaching Dresden from the side on which it would be least likely to watch for foes.

If there had been strategy in the indirectness of his approach, he had abandoned it now, relying solely on clearness of purpose and such speed as he could command.

From this point, he was resolved that he would neither turn back nor aside for any opposition that he might meet. He would fly straight for the goal that he had pondered since he had first imagined the issue of such a war as had come, and—unless he should be shot down before he could reach it now—he would do that which his heart had planned.

As he approached Meissen, now flying low, and at the utmost speed he could raise, he came on the first sign that his foes were watchful for danger out of the skies.

It might have been different had he come at an earlier hour, but the Leunawerke disaster had caused orders to be hurriedly issued that all the country should be darkened from Berlin to the frontier, and the first indication that he was approaching Meissen was in the searchlights that swept the skies.

He had some confidence in the bomber in which he flew, that it would serve to confuse his foes, as, like that which he had provided for Wing-Commander Klíma, it was not one of any of the designs which the Czech Air Force recognised on its active list. He had not attempted to disguise it as a German machine, which would have been obviously futile, but, as there were some of the same design still in use in the Hungarian air-fleet, he had had it painted with the device which that country used.

He had calculated that that would, at least, cause the momentary confusion of doubt which would enable a battery to be safely crossed; but here, again, he was defeated by the earlier Leunawerke disaster.

Seeing the restless searchlights ahead, he rose and swerved widely westward to avoid the inquisition that they proposed. He thought that, except for one doubtful moment, he had succeeded in this, but next minute he was aware of a scouting plane, which could do five miles to his two, diving toward him out of the clouds.

A light flashed in his direction, and was darkened again. For a moment, the small, swift plane flew beside him, the next it had disappeared. It had not used the single machine-gun which was mounted at its pilot's side, being intent only on observation, and to retire with safety. He was unable to use the gun that his own plane carried, it being operated from a turret, forward of the cockpit, so that he could not reach it without losing control.

He knew that nothing but speed would avail him now, and took the straightest course to where Dresden lay up the river-valley, nine miles to the southeast.

His engines were running smoothly and well, and it would be a matter of no more than six minutes, even to the obsolescent bomber in which he flew, before he would be over his goal. But would that six minutes be his?

Ahead, Dresden's searchlights had become active among the clouds. They moved hurriedly, in a nervous way, as though aware of a coming foe that they must be instant to find.

He decided that it would be vain to attempt to pass them unseen, unless at a great height, and he must fly low, to be certain in what he did. He would lose no time in soaring, or subterfuge of approach. He would use the seconds that still were his.

So he flew low, with the river beneath him for guide and warrant that there would be nothing higher than a crossing bridge which would bar his way; and as he did so he knew that he had been wise to stake all on speed and a straight course, for there were two aeroplanes on his rear.

They were of the smaller and older of Germany's fighting planes, such as would have been her boast three years before, but would now have been nuisance rather than source of strength in her battle-fleets; and they were therefore used to be scattered about at a time of war, to assist the defence of towns, and patrol the air.

He knew at once that they would be swifter than he, but while he could keep them behind he had little fear of the fire which they were already directing upon him, for he was least vulnerable from the rear, and the goal was close. It was but a minute he needed now.

He had a doubt whether the race would be theirs or his, but they seemed reluctant to make full use of the speed they had, and the cause was plain when the batteries opened upon him, from both of the river-banks.

For five seconds, he flew through a barrage of bursting shells. His sight was blinded for a moment by one that burst so closely before his face that it seemed that he cut the explosion through.

The plane swayed and heeled, so that he thought that it had been struck, and that he must fall to death in the near river below. But the fixity of his purpose held. Stubbornly, while his sight returned, he strove to regain control, and to fly on, whatever damage he had sustained.

The next moment, flying low as he was, he passed out of the range of the guns. He was aware that one of his engines had ceased to run, and, in the same instant, that his pursuers were close behind, and had opened fire again on his crippled plane.

Almost too late, he knew also that he was passing the goal he sought.

The Zwinger Palace, with its priceless treasures of art and literature, was almost directly beneath him now. He skimmed the Crown Gateway with no more than fifty feet of dividing air. It was not this palace he sought, but his foot moved on the bomb-lever. Once—twice—the bombs dropped, as he swept on to the great Picture Gallery of the Stallebäude building, which was the ultimate objective at which he aimed.

Behind him, the bombs burst. One fell in the Zwinger Courtyard, with no more result than to fling a hundred tons of its pavement into the air, and leave a crater at which men would curse and wonder when morning came. The other fell upon the Natural History Museum, and penetrated to the upper floor, where it burst with devastating effect.

One of the pursuing planes had been so close and low on Herr Janda's rear that the instant during which the second bomb fell and burst had been sufficient to bring it over the spot. It rose to the explosion, as might a shuttle-cock struck from below, and spun downward, a flaming wreck, into the midst of the shattered building, to which it acted like an igniting match.

At the same moment, Herr Janda's plane flew over the gallery which contained, with a score beside of the greatest pictures the world has known, the Madonna which Raphael painted for St. Sisto's nuns.

Checking to his lowest speed, he loosed the bombs as rapidly as the lever would move.

The second of the pursuing planes, having narrowly escaped the fate of the first, was now close on his rear, its machine-guns pouring their streams of bullets into a crippled prey, and he knew that there could be no hope, either of victory or escape.

He glanced, for one irresolute second, at the parachute which might have taken him to precarious safety had he been flying a thousand feet higher, and put the idea by. He swung round too suddenly for the pursuer to avoid the shock. The two planes met head-on, and fell in a common wreck.

In a high and narrow room, the supreme treasure of art that the world contained had been mounted on an altar apart, that it might bring no confusion to smaller things.

Even in these latter days, when the diseased vanity of the German rulers had absurdly flouted the Christian faith for the worship of Odin and lesser gods, there had still been a steady pilgrimage here of those who would come to gaze on a dream of diviner things. Here the lovers of perfect art had worshipped the beauty which is more than righteousness: the pure in heart had seen God.

Now the long-quietened room leaned somewhat sideways. A wall sagged. It sank farther, with a rumble of falling stone.

Slowly, deliberate in its approach. a little flame crept up to the picture's base. The paint blistered and cracked...

Outside, over the smoke of burning palace and gallery, the last fleet of the German bombers detailed for the destruction of Prague flew southward among the clouds. Two hundred and ten in all, in ten wedge-shaped squadrons of twenty-one, they passed like migrating geese, and the noise of their engines died.

CHAPTER LX.

"YOU don't mean me to take the Bentley, sir?" Lawrence asked, when the girls had gone back to their own rooms, to make such preparations as time allowed. "We shall be only four, and my car's large enough."

When he had gone to investigate the condition of the one that Sir Geoffrey kept for his own use, it had been on the assumption that he was intending to leave himself, with the whole of the Legation staff, and his reluctance to go now, with the ladies only, was increased by the feeling that he would be taking the largest and fastest car.

Sir Geoffrey was short in reply. "When I send dispatches to London, I use the best means of transit I have. You can take any of the servants who care to go."

A brief enquiry disclosed that Novák had already bolted. Williams would stay, either from loyalty to his master or because he preferred the apparent security of solid walls to the fears of the open street. But Paul would be glad to go.

"Then, Paul," Sir Geoffrey said, "you'd better go up at once, and fetch any hand-luggage the ladies have ready. But tell them to come at once. It isn't getting any better outside, to judge by the row."

The man came back a moment later, Perdita following. He bore the two suitcases which had attracted Herr Schmit's attention a few days before on the luggage-rack of the Berlin train.

She said: "I've thrown in what I could. I suppose we shall just have to leave the rest. But now Caresse says that she won't go. She says that she's too frightened to move. She's hoping Mr. Langton will come. It's what you can see from the window upstairs. It looks as though the whole city's on fire, and the bombs are dropping all round."

She was pale, and her hands shook slightly as she drew on the fur gloves that the night required, but she had been helped to forget herself by the argument with Caresse, in which she had endeavoured to bring decision to her friend's fluctuant moods.

"Norton," Sir Geoffrey said, "you'd better go up. Don't stand any nonsense, but fetch her down."

Lawrence left the room with no reluctance, and returned a minute later with Caresse, who showed little sign of emotional disturbance, as she said: "Of course, if you're all sure it's the safer way!" throwing the responsibility upon those around, as her instinct was.

"It's common sense," Sir Geoffrey said shortly. "You won't want to be here when tomorrow comes." He bustled them to the door as he added: "I don't suppose I shall stay myself many hours. There'll be communications established again. I daresay I shall see you in London within the week."

He had more doubts than his words expressed, seeing, among other things, that Germany might have lit a fire which she could not quench, but he had greater dread of hysterical parting than of death from the falling bombs. He went on hurriedly: "Passports not forgotten? Yes, I could trust Lawrence not to overlook them. You ought to get through easily with the papers you've got, unless all Europe's gone mad. And you, Paul?"

It appeared that Paul's passport had not been overlooked. Indeed, that careful man had not only had it, and his more portable property, packed in anticipation of the moment when he might have permission to leave; he had a hamper of food ready, that those who journeyed might not be delayed or inconvenienced upon the way. They found themselves bustled down the stairs to the courtyard below, Sir Geoffrey's voice following them with a cheerful: "Don't forget, Mrs. Langton, to say the right things to your husband for me. I shouldn't wonder if I see him almost as soon as yourself."

They went out of the gate to face a city that rose in fire, and a sky from which ruin fell. They turned to go up by the shorter way, and found it blocked when they were halfway up, by a fallen wall and a shatter of broken steps.

Lawrence was in advance with Caresse, leading a way that he knew. She made slow progress, taking full toll of the arm he gave. When they must clamber upward over the stones, she stopped entirely.

She said: "I don't think I can do this. It's my foot. I'm not being a fool."

He heard the note of sincerity in her voice, and he knew that, at the best, she was ill adapted for such a climb up the broken stones, and in the heavy furs that she wore, with no better guidance of light than came from the burning city below.

He said: "I might get you up," and she felt herself lifted in arms of a pleasant strength; but it was an effort which took them no farther than a few yards where they came to a barrier of fallen masonry to surmount which would have needed both hands and knees.

He put her down, and said, after a moment of doubt: "We must go back. It will be quicker to go by the longer way."

Perdita and Captain Dürer were close behind. She had felt compelled to take her own suitcase from the overburdened Paul, and this had passed, by a natural sequence, to the hand of the German officer.

They had walked in silence until they saw Caresse lifted into Lawrence's arms, and Captain Dürer looked down on his companion to ask: "You will need such help?"

She answered shortly: "I should say not!" She was of more athletic habits than Caresse, and more independent of mood. And her feet were sound. She was conscious of some ungraciousness in her tone, and looked up with a smile to add: "And you with the suitcase too!"

She had a puzzled consciousness that there had been nothing repugnant in the idea, that she felt an instinctive attraction to this alien stranger. It was queer that the nations warred with such savage hate, and that individuals could be so friendly, even in the same hour.

With this thought inarticulately in her mind, they turned at Lawrence's word to retrace their steps, and looked back over the burning city.

The wind, being from the northwest, and now blowing a halfgale in the upper air, drove the smoke up the way of the river valley, or there would have been little that they could have seen, even of their own surroundings. The night-bombers had been crossing the city by the wind's way, in an almost continuous stream, but with short intervals between the passage of different fleets, and there was one of these pauses of quietness now.

At this hour, there may have been nine buildings in ten that still stood, and eight of ten that had not yet been reached by the spreading fires, but it was already clear that there could be but one end.

There were dark patches where the fires had not taken hold; there were whole streets that were glowing flame under a cloud of smoke that the wind drifted away; there was a great red disc where the mine had burst, as though the city had broken out in a central sore, which spread outward on every side.

Perdita, a stunned wonder filling her mind, said: "And you have helped to do this!"

He answered, not her words only, but the discordant emotions from which she spoke: "It was not my will. We must do as our orders are. It is the way of all war. But it is not against your country, or you. I would be friends, if I may."

They were going down, and the wider view of the city was hidden again, as she answered, with less inconsequence than appeared: "You speak English well."

"Do I? It is kindly said. I was at Oxford for two years."

"You liked it?"

"It was the happiest time I have known."

"Then you will come to England again?"

For a moment they had forgotten even the imminent perils through which they walked, in consciousness of the space that held them apart, and of the attraction that drew them on; but again the noise of the German engines was in the sky.

He put his free hand under her arm. "Can you walk faster? The bombers are coming over again."

"I could. But we can't leave them behind. I shouldn't know which way to go."

But the others were hurrying also now, and were close behind. They were in the street by this time, going upward again.

Here, between the houses, where the bitter wind had less power, they found that the heat from the burning city had softened the frozen snow. They splashed through pools of water; they waded in slush.

Caresse jibbed. She said: "It will just ruin my shoes."

Lawrence thought, not unkindly, nor without cause, that she might interrupt the Last Judgment on the impulse of some petulant whim. But, for this time, he was less than fair, she having more reason behind her words, as she often had, than her excuses would show.

Now, at every step, the shoe rubbed the place from which the skin had been scraped, and extended a bleeding sore. But she could endure pain with a braver mind than the thought of how she would look when the daylight came. (And, of course, Perdita would have failed to pack the things that she would most need!)

Lawrence took her into his arms again. Even with the heavy clothes that she wore, he had strength enough to bear her for the short distance they had to go.

So far, they had traversed an empty street, between houses that still stood, and in the darkness of which any life that remained cowered silently in basement and cellar, awaiting an end which would not delay.

Only one house had been wrecked as yet, and that had not broken into fire. Over its ruins a man worked in a frantic haste, tearing at stone and beam with his naked hands, and throwing them backward into the road. They did not pause to enquire whether he toiled to uncover those who would be unlikely to live, or some treasure without which he refused to flee.

But the sight brought back to Perdita's mind a doubt she had felt before, at the thought of how William Harvey had gone so quietly to offer help when the first explosion had come. Was it a coward's part to slip away in a car, when there must be so many in desperate need of the help that the hale could give?

Yet reason told her that the more who stayed, the greater the loss of life, and the longer the tale of the maimed would be. They were not immune because they looked on at a war which they did not share.

So they hurried on, and as they did so it seemed that the war-planes had filled the sky, though they flew higher than the first-comers had done, to avoid the heat and smoke of the burning town, and the oscillations of shaken air as the bombs burst, which they were now doing on every side.

They hurried on, surrounded by deafening noises of bursting shells and of buildings that crumbled down. And as they gained the higher level there was the sound before them of a man's voice, loud in expostulation and vibrant with urgent fear.

He spoke in Czech, so that it was to Lawrence only that there was meaning in what he said. Terror had not made him insensible to the kindly bondage of love, for he urged a woman along whom it was clear that he would not leave, though her steps were stumbling and slow. But in her arms was a weight that he importuned her vainly to cast aside, that they might make better haste from that place of death.

"Can you not see," he protested, "the child is dead?"

"I can see nothing," she said. "It is mist and blood. But Aninka is still warm. She cannot be dead. Her heart beats. She may be healed if we can get her away."

As she said this, following the man's dragging arm with uncertain steps, a child of six years or more was heavy and limp in her own.

Lawrence came level with them, their pace being much slower than his, and the man turned to him in appeal. "If she would leave the child, I might get her away. Will you tell her that it is dead?"

Lawrence looked at an evil sight, though it was no more than must have been repeated a thousand times in that city that was beaten down by a blind violence out of the clouds. In the uncertain light, he could see that the man himself was not whole. His clothing was fouled and torn. His shoulder was bound about with a bloody rag. But the woman had been so hurt that her forehead, for three fingers' breadth, had been stripped of skin. The blood dripped over her eyes.

Her weak arms strained the weight of a child who might not be dead, but the man was right when he said that to save her was past their power. Regarding the injuries that she had, it might seem mercy that the woman was unable to see.

Lawrence put Caresse down. He said: "I shouldn't look. Go on till I catch you up."

He said to the woman in her own tongue: "The child is not alive. You must believe those who can see. You must go on to a safer place, where you can get help for your own hurt."

He took it gently from her arms, to which she submitted dumbly at the sound of quiet authority in his voice, and the man hurried her on at a better pace than before.

He laid the dying child down in the snow, which was still frozen hard on this more open and higher ground. The cold roused it to a convulsive movement, and a weak cry for the mother who had left it forever now. He looked up to see Caresse at his side.

She said: "You must do something. What are you going to do? You can't leave her there. Can't you see she's alive? Can't you— can't you *put it back*? I didn't know it would be like this."

They were all standing round now in a silent group.

"I told you to go," he replied, in a simulated anger, which strove to subdue both his own emotion and the hysteria in her voice. "There is nothing that we can do. She will not live in the cold."

But Caresse knelt in the snow by the dying child. "You can go on if you like," she said. "I can't leave her like this. It's a wicked thing."

"I think, sir," Paul said, with respectful but hardly restrained impatience, "we'd do better to go."

He looked round in an apprehension not without cause. It seemed that the air-fleet which was now crossing the sky must have had orders to concentrate its attack on the Schlossberg Hill, and the great buildings—palace, castle, cathedral—which still stood thereon, overlooking the burning city.

Captain Dürer stood silent. He felt Perdita tremble upon his arm. She loosed it to bend over Caresse. "We must think of others," she said. "It's not fair to stay. We can do no good."

Her last words were drowned in an explosion that came so near that they looked at each other in doubt that they had been struck by something more than the dirt and flying snow that had filled the air.

But they were uninjured, as though protected by invisible power where so many died.

Perdita asked, perceiving the acrid scent of the fouled air, in a voice that she found hard to control: "It's gas, isn't it? What harm will it do?"

Captain Dürer replied: "No. We're not using gas. It's the picric acid. It won't harm you at all."

Lawrence stooped to take Caresse up, raising her without further protest. He felt her sob in his arms. She said again, as though to herself rather than him: "I didn't know it would be like this. Why do people have wars?"

His own thought was: "It would have been kinder to kill it. But we don't kill a child. We let it die in the cold."

So they passed under the archway entrance of the courtyard within which he had left the car, and saw it standing, as it had been left, in the shadow of the wall. There was little shadow now, but a great light, for the castle burned.

Lawrence said: "There it is. In three minutes from now, if we can get the engine to start, we ought to be clear away."

He hastened his pace a little, to cross the sixty yards that divided them from what would so quickly make safety sure, and was half-way across when the bomb fell.

It did not fall upon them, but upon the gallery of the castle, which ran over the stone archway beneath which they had just passed. It struck the top of the wall, and burst without penetrating far, as its downward course would have been through the solid stone. The explosion seemed to pass over their heads, and to three of them it was a less alarm than that through which they had passed safely before; but Lawrence fell, loosing Caresse, so that she was thrown somewhat forward of him, and face downward upon the snow.

She looked up to see Perdita bending over her, and to say: "I think he slipped." And then in a sharper voice: "He isn't hurt, is he? Help me up. I seemed to get a knock in the back."

But Captain Dürer had pushed Perdita aside. He said: "He'll be all right. Never mind about him. I think you've been hurt. Let me look."

A pocket torch shone in his hand. Behind her left shoulder he saw that the fur coat had a ragged downward tear. Through it he saw blood, and a fragment of splintered stone.

She made a motion to rise, which his hand moved to prevent, but it had ceased of itself, with a sharp cry. There was a convulsive movement of sudden pain, which checked, as by an instinctive fear, but it had been enough to loosen the stone which had been driven in between broken ribs, and the blood pulsed from a pierced lung.

There was an incredulous terror in her voice, as she asked: "I'm not really hurt? Not to matter? I'm not likely to die? You wouldn't let me till Gerald comes! He always knows what to do."

Captain Dürer made, and abandoned, an effort to stanch the wound. It was so plainly useless to try. His eyes met Perdita's as she bent over the dying girl, and she read the verdict she could not doubt.

She answered: "I expect he'll be here soon." She bent down, kissing her friend through her blinding tears.

Caresse's voice was as that of one who speaks in a dream: "You're not crying for me? I shall be all right. It's only till Gerald comes." She repeated, as one convincing herself on the edge of sleep: "I shall be all right. I'm so young. God wouldn't do that to me."

A shell burst, near and loud. A part of the castle wall collapsed, with great fragments bounding outward, almost to where they were. The air became dim with dust.

The crash roused a moment of consciousness in the dying mind, bringing with it, it seemed, the knowledge of coming death.

She said clearly: "Tell Gerald I love him best. I've loved no one but him. It's my silly fault to have kept you here."

But the energy in her voice had died quickly away. The last words had been hard to catch.

Perdita, bending to listen, knew that her mind had wandered backward to other days. She heard Gerald's name mingled with intimate playful words, so that she drew back, as from something not meant for her to hear.

She heard Paul answering Captain Dürer: "Yes, sir. He's quite dead. Hit his head it did, and must have glanced off to the lady's back, unless there was more than one."

With a quiet rapidity he had already possessed himself of the keys of the car, and the diplomatic papers his master carried. In fact, he had cleared his pockets of all contents.

He rose as he said: "We'd better go, sir, while we're alive. This wouldn't have happened if we hadn't waited before."

He picked up the luncheon hamper, and began to move toward the car as he added: "That is, if you're coming with me."

It was clear that he thought first of escape from that place of death, but it would be hard to say he was wrong. His duty was not to them, but to carry on the dispatch which had been in his master's charge.

Captain Dürer drew Perdita to her feet. He said: "The man is right. She is dead now. There is nothing more you can do. We will go back, if you prefer."

She saw that he would stay with her, if she should be obstinate to remain, in this place where the fires still rose, and the bombs and the buildings fell. And the thought came to her distracted mind that, with the uniform he wore, it was a double peril for him.

She stooped again to leave a kiss on the dead face of a friend to whom life had been very dear, and got up to go.

CHAPTER LXI.

WHEN the airliner in which he had embarked arrived at Frankfort, Gerald Langton received definite confirmation of the fact that it was not calling at Prague, and no objection was made when he required to be set down, with the reasonable argument that he had no desire to be taken to places to which he had not booked.

"I'm told," he said, "that there's a man named Bromley on the staff here who could be trusted to fly me back."

He was assured in reply that there was no occasion to look for other assistance than the Air Line itself would provide. There would be a liner due for London in about four hours.

But he replied that he would prefer to leave without that delay, and being offered the services of other pilots, he replied with truth that he was not accustomed to flying, and he would prefer to trust himself to one to whom he had been recommended previously.

In the end, Jack Bromley appeared. He was a small, somewhat jockey-like, spare-limbed man, with impudent lively eyes. He had nothing Teutonic in his appearance, but his German accent belied his name.

There was simple explanation of that in the fact that he had been born of an English mother in a German concentration camp twenty-three years before. He had been reared in Hanover after the war, where his father had business interests to protect, and, being legally a German citizen, he had obtained employment with the Lufthansa when he had become old enough to choose a career.

Now he belonged to a class which had become numerous during the last two years: pilots who owned their own planes and were ready to hire themselves for any destination their patrons would— the taxi-drivers of the air.

Would he fly to London forthwith? Yes. Or anywhere else. In half an hour? Yes; or less, if required. Did he undertake longer journeys? He should think he did. He owned a Duplex two-seater monoplane, not so comfortable as a liner, of course, but half as fast again, and with a range of 2,000 miles, if the passenger's luggage were not more than 180 lb.

"Your prices vary," Gerald asked, "according to the length of journey, and any risks that may be involved?"

"According to distance, of course. There's no risk in a Duplex, go where you will, land or sea—not in such weather as this."

Gerald said, in a casual voice, but not loudly enough to be overheard: "You'd have a price, for instance, to Prague?"

"We're not booking that way tonight."

"But suppose?"

"It couldn't be done. For one thing, the office wouldn't issue a permit. And, besides that—" He checked himself to say abruptly: "It couldn't be done. Not tonight."

"I don't see how anyone could be stopped by not having a permit. It must be easy to turn in the air."

"And how about when you come down? A nice mess you'd be in then."

"So there's no price at all? Not even one that you name yourself?"

There was a moment of thoughtful silence, during which the spirit of adventure showed in the twinkling eyes, and plans formed in a quick brain.

"I suppose you know what you're doing?"

"Yes. I think I do."

"Well, I don't. There'll be no price for this."

Gerald was uncertain whether it were refusal that he had heard, and was debating in mind with what measure of confidence it might be judicious to urge his plea, but Jack Bromley went on: "You can pay me when we get through. We shan't differ for that. And you'll have to see me through any mess that you get me in. Do you mind saying why you're so anxious to go tonight?"

"Among other things, my wife's there."

"Ten minutes do?"

"Yes. Or less."

The man was as good as his word. There was a brief formality for him to go through at the office, where he booked out to London, with a record of the passenger he would be carrying, about whom it was improbable that any difficulty would be raised.

There could be no objection to Mr. Langton returning to his own land. It was satisfactory that he was prepared to do it with so little protest. The undercurrent of excitement which existed among the airport officials, who whispered and wondered concerning that which it might be unwise to debate aloud, was busy with other and more important issues. In less than fifteen minutes the small, swift Duplex left the airport, rising high on the outward London route.

It held, for some minutes, a western course, until Gerald had some excuse for doubting whether he might not have been deceived, like a foolish child, by a lie designed to get him quietly into the plane that would take him home. But the fact was that the traffic lines at that time were too full, the number of alighting and leaving planes was too great, for Jack Bromley to risk transgression of the settled traffic-rules of the air.

The gauges under his eyes enabled him to direct his flight as exactly as though he drove on the narrow width of a paved road, and it was not till he was twenty miles on the London route that he ventured to change his course, and swept round to south and east on a rising curve that was soon headed direct for their distant and doubtful goal.

It was true of the air at this time, as it had been of the ocean during the previous century, that though there were lanes of traffic which were constantly thronged, there were wide spaces between which were seldom entered except by such craft as the tempests might drive aside, and Jack Bromley, seeking these solitudes of the air, and taking a somewhat southerly course, flew unmolested and unobserved, until he approached the bleak Bavarian heights which divide the Danube Valley from that in which the Moldau begins its long journey towards the Elbe and the Baltic Sea.

Gerald Langton was strange to the air. But he was one who from childhood had loved the sea. He felt no air-sickness at all. The experience, which he had avoided until that time, from a habit of caution which may be consistent with high courage and cool judgment when danger comes, would have been pleasure had his mind been free from that urgent fear which had received ominous confirmation in the fact that the liner had been diverted from its accustomed route.

But as they made their flight through the empty skies, and the pilot used his speaking-tube from time to time to inform him of the country which, swiftly and dimly, glided away below, his fear lost its edge with the anticipation that he would be in Prague in so short a time; that his meeting with Caresse was so nearly due.

When he would be there, with the credentials he carried, the prestige his position gave, he did not doubt that he could make dispositions adequate for his wife's safety, nor that, after a first petulant outburst, she would be glad and happy that he had come. If there were cause for fear, he would make it plain, and if there were none he would not bring her away.

He was naturally self-reliant, and experience had taught him to trust his own ability to bring that which he took in hand to a good end. This was different from when he had been in London, feeling that he could do nothing but watch the sinister course of events which were beyond his power to control. He was acting now, and his success in coming on where most men would have been turned back or delayed, was a good omen of what he would be able to do on the next day. Flying swiftly through quiet and empty skies, it was easy to think that he had been alarmed beyond instant cause. For this night at least there might be no more than the threat of a nearing storm. Suppose Germany thought to put fear into the heart of her weaker neighbour by blockading her from the air?

It would be an unprecedented form of warfare, but which was certain to come with the development of military operations in the new element.

This sanguine theory was not wholly negatived when, as the white summits of the Mittagsberg were passing beneath them in moonlit glimpses through uncertain clouds, he became aware of that which Jack Bromley had seen at an earlier minute, for he had already dived with a sharp swerve to the retreat of a covering cloud, when a scouting plane, showing the German eagle upon its wings, drove swiftly across their way.

Its signal lights flashed an order which the pilot could not mistake, and when it was not obeyed with the promptitude that it required, its machine-gun opened a rapid fire.

Gerald Langton may be forgiven if his heart missed a beat as he heard the rattle of its discharge, and knew that they were fired upon in that height of air with no means of resistance, nor speed of flight from so swift a foe. But the bullets were not aimed directly at them, but across their way, as a warning they could not ignore.

Jack Bromley turned his plane, and for five miles they flew back with the scout watchful and suspicious upon their rear.

It left them with the discharge of a dozen bullets, as final warning, and they continued a backward course until it became certain that the pursuer had left their track. Then the pilot raised his speaking-tube to enquire: "Shall we try again, or go back?"

He grinned cheerfully as he got the answer: "Try again, if you don't mind." He switched off his own lights, which was, of itself, an offence for which his pilot's licence might have been lost by the International Code of the day, as he turned north-eastward again.

Flying at a great height, and buffeted now by a rising north-western gale, they crossed the bleak range that divides Bavaria from the Bohemian land, meeting with no opposition, nor threat of greater danger ahead, until they blundered into one of those dramas of flight and chase that drove so often that night across the height of the stormy skies.

They had encountered a tempest of sleet in the freezing cold of the upper air, and Jack Bromley had chosen to fly in that hiding cloud, trusting for direction and altitude to the instruments he carried, and when they came suddenly out to where the wind's caprice had made a clear channel of moonlit air, for an instant they were in the midst of a flying strife, which, in thirty seconds, was gone.

There were two Czech planes that fled through the night, seeking the asylum of neutral skies, and it seemed—there was no time for more than a doubtful glance—that a dozen German aircraft were on their track.

The night was loud with machine-gun fire, and for a second they were crossing the very path of the deadly hail, between pursuers and those who fled.

The next moment, Jack Bromley had taken a downward glide, and a different course, and the flying strife had passed, leaving them unregarded and unpursued.

Gerald Langton, looking upward and back, saw one of the Czech planes collapse and fall through the night like a ruddy star.

His attention was held by this sight, and by the certainty it brought that war had already commenced. He gave no thought to the pilot on his right hand, and might not have observed cause for alarm had he had a less occupied mind.

But Jack Bromley had felt a sharp knock on his ribs as he had planed down from the path that the bullets took. He knew he was badly hurt, but he was not one to forget that in which a pilot's honour is fixed. He strove with a stubborn will to maintain control of himself, and of the machine which he must bring safely to land. For the moment, he would continue that downward slant through a lower stratum of cloud, until he could judge better how long he could rule his wavering mind, and what prospect of landing the night would show.

Gerald thought: "There is war waged in the air. I was right to come. But, for this night, Prague may not be attacked, or may hold its own. And, within half an hour, we may be there. Even if it have been attacked, Caresse may have got away. There would have been time enough, and she would be prepared, having had so much warning from me. And, at least, I shall soon know."

There was anxiety in his heart, but the more dominant feeling was joy that he had come so near to see her again; satisfaction that he would be on the spot to advise, to insist on that which discretion urged.

And then, suddenly, his mood changed. He had a feeling that Caresse was in present peril or pain; that she was needing him now. Clearly, her voice came to his ears. She called to him to come, in an urgent way.

He heard her as though they were divided by no more than an open door. *Tell Gerald I love him best. I've loved no one but him.*

But why should he imagine that she said that? It was what he knew well—would never have had the folly to doubt. There was no need for her to protest. It showed what tricks imagination would play at such moments. He told himself that he had been thinking so intently of her that her voice became a fantasy to his outward ear.

But the feeling did not go. It became acute, to the point of pain. He felt that Caresse cried to him through the night, making distance and darkness naught.

Well, every second was making that distance less. If she needed him, she would believe that he would be there. They flew fast.

He renewed consciousness of the flying plane that slanted slightly downward on a steady and rapid course. He looked at the pilot, who was rather huddled upon his seat, as one who shrank from the cold. The plane crashed head-on to the mountain-side. He did not know of the coming of death. It was too instant for that.

CHAPTER LXII.

THE car ran rapidly over the frozen road. On its left, faint and cold, there was the coming of dawn.

Paul sat silently at the wheel. Behind him was the German officer, and by him Perdita, exhausted, slept, unaware that his shoulder gave her support.

They were near the Bavarian frontier now. Around them were neat upland Bohemian farms in their winter white. There was silence, and peace, and snow.

Perdita stirred: she sat up. She looked at Karl Dürer with surprised and bewildered eyes, to which memory came, bringing fear, and a great grief.

She had a hope that she still slept through an incredible dream, which she fought to break with a frightened will; but the dream endured.

She asked, as though begging to be denied: "Was it all true?" She was too stunned for the facile outlet of tears.

Captain Dürer, who had watched her sleep for the last hour in the growing light, said: "It is over now. You must try to forget."

"Forget?" she asked, in a voice of wonder. "I never shall. No one could. Will there be wars everywhere now?"

He answered that in a confident way, as he had been taught to believe: "No. It is almost over now, if not quite. There will be consternation, not war."

Perhaps to draw her from the memory that was a distress in her eyes, perhaps to justify what had been, to his own conscience or her, he went on to explain much which had been secret whispering till that day, even among those of his nation whose trade was war, but which was no secret now, for the world must know before the next sunset came.

For one day Germany had shown much of her strength, though not all, and when men looked back they would see that it had been done in a most merciful way, and that only after the Czechs had obstinately declined to accept the will of their natural lords. Would there have been mercy in the length of exhausting war?

There need not have been a life lost, or, at most, few. There had been time for all men to flee. All that Germany had required was the destruction of the material city of Prague, as a demonstration that she had become fit to enforce her will, as her great destiny required that she should be able to do.

Why, they had actually had orders that they were not to drop bombs on the flying crowds, outside the limits of the city itself!

Nor had they been permitted to use the new gases that Germany's skilful chemists had prepared for the day of war. As to them, there were things that he could not tell, that even the army was not allowed to know. But there was no secret about the gases that would make men imbecile; that would make them blind; that would freeze them to solid ice. There were elaborate plans for sowing disease among man and beast, for poisoning water in wholesale quantities, in ways that no filter would catch, and so tasteless and slow in its deadly work that whole nations might be labelled for death before they should observe occasion for fear. These, which were common talk, were no more than the first line of attack. He supposed that weapons of more and more deadly kinds would be brought up against a foe that might harden its heart, or that might show that mercy was a mistake by reprisals of similar kinds.

Even the mining of the bomb-proof shelters, of which he had not known before, could be defended as having no worse purpose than to drive the people of Prague out of the city bounds, and away from what might have proved a most deadly trap when the city burned. Perhaps it should have been done at an earlier hour, before they had crowded in. Perhaps something had gone amiss, as it will often in time of war, be the plans laid with the utmost skill.

But all this was no more than to survey the weapons with which science has armed those who serve its altars with single zeal. This was a war to avert war; which he did not doubt it would be equal to do.

And it was not a quarrel in which England had any part. Germany would be friends with her. Perdita had stumbled upon a dreadful, fated event, which even Germany could not wholly avoid.

This, if not all expressed, was implicit in what he said; and if its logic were little comfort to her, she found more in a kindness she could not doubt, a sympathy which, under other circumstances, might have been the close forerunner of love, an admiration his eyes expressed as plainly as any words would have been able to do.

He left them at the frontier, when he had given what help he could, and ascertained that they would be free to go where they would in the crossing of German land. He had to report himself without delay to the headquarters of his own corps.

Would they meet again? Though they spoke few words, they were aware of a common will. But the future was hard to see. They were two among millions whose fate, whether peace or pain, would be resolved by those who ruled in the next hours.

CHAPTER LXIII.

THE Fleet Street of 1938 had many doubts, but of one thing it was sure: it was better to shout one word than to say ten in a quiet voice.

There were older journalists who could remember when it had been the custom to cover their morning placards with a dozen or twenty lines in which they would endeavour to announce all the variety of news which had been collected for their readers' pleasure during the previous day.

But now an improved technique would select one item for emphatic notice, and let the rest go.

The morning of Saturday, February 5th, 1938, brought a trouble that this method would often cause, and with an acuteness which had not been known before. There were half a dozen items of news that deserved to be shouted with cracking lungs, and it was by the malice of circumstance that they could not be distributed over a week instead of arriving at the same hour, and that they came in so barren of detail that there could be little beyond the headlines to print. For they were of a potential gravity which made it hazardous to enlarge or even comment upon them, until the facts should be more fully and clearly known.

The *Daily Record* covered the entirety of its front page with these words:

RUMOURED BURNING OF PRAGUE
REPORTED GREAT AIR BATTLES ON GERMAN FRONTIER
CZECHOSLOVAKIA DEFEATED
DRESDEN BOMBED
DECLARATION BY GERMAN GOVERNMENT

The text of the German Government's declaration shared the second page with an announcement that the Sistine Madonna, with a hundred other priceless paintings and treasures of art of less popular reputation, had been destroyed. The declaration read:

"The German Government regrets that it became necessary last evening to sever diplomatic relations with the Government of Czechoslovakia.

"Since that time, such action has been taken as will be conducive to the peace and safety of Europe, and the dignity and security of the German Reich.

"The German Government affirms its profound respect for the liberty and integrity of all neutral and friendly States.

"A further statement will be issued at noon today."

At 10:00 A.M. special editions announced that the stock exchanges of Europe were closed. An hour later it appeared that the British Cabinet had met, and that a general moratorium had been declared.

At 11:30 A.M. (Greenwich Time) there came the publication of a further manifesto by the German Government:

> "Czechoslovakia has ceased to exist. The territories of Bohemia, Moravia, and Slovakia have been restored to the German Reich, subject to such adjustments of the Hungarian and Polish boundaries as equity has required.
>
> "At an early hour this morning, Field-Marshal Vacek surrendered unconditionally to General Hoff, with the forces under his command.
>
> "The country is now quiet, with the exception of some local disturbances in its eastern districts, for the pacification of which adequate steps have been taken, that public order may be maintained."

It was no more than truth to say that, for the time at least, Czechoslovakia had ceased to resist, though existence might prove a more stubborn fact to be overcome than the German manifesto presumed.

Before morning came, Vacek had found that he had adventured that which he was powerless to carry through. It was not only that the mobility of his army had been paralysed by the loss of its nerve-centres, the depots, and junctions that the German Air Fleet had destroyed. It had become impossible for any considerable body of men or store of munitions to be assembled without a descent of German aircraft, like vultures out of the clouds, to scatter them with a rain of bombs.

Germany had gained control of the air, and the efforts of the anti-aircraft batteries, had they been twice as mobile and ten times as numerous as they were, would have been insufficient for the protection of a mechanised army, and the supplies which are essential to the maintenance of its striking power.

And it was true that Prague had ceased to exist. Its chemical devices for fighting fire had proved utterly inadequate to overcome the hundred conflagrations which had burst out in so short a time, and had been recruited continually as new bombs rained from the sky.

And, from an early hour of the night, the supply of water had failed, after the German air-fleet had made a concentrated attack upon the great pumping-station, which was built conspicuously on the river bank, as though to invite its fate.

When the fires died, as they did not wholly do for a space of days, not the commercial city alone, but all on river valley and hills which had been the beauty of Prague, was an ended dream. Cathedral, castle, and palace were broken and blackened shells. A great fragment of the castle wall, falling as it seemed in a single piece, had crashed through the roof of the ancient home of the Counts of Thun, and may have made a quicker end than would bomb or fire for those who had sheltered within its walls.

There was none living who could have told Sir Geoffrey Cullender's end. He had held his post, as he considered it his duty to do, having had no orders to withdraw, nor formal intimation that the Government to which he was accredited had removed to another place. The English flag went down in the final fire, but it had not been lowered, nor had it fled, and the omen might be taken in different ways.

But in the Europe of the coming week there would be few with leisure to ask or hearts to care how Sir Geoffrey died. Each man would have his thoughts on his own life, and perhaps on some who might be dearer than that.

CHAPTER LXIV.

MR. GANSTON was in the Prime Minister's room. The Cabinet had adjourned for a couple of hours to enable its members to deal with the departmental questions that the crisis must surely bring, and was to meet again at 4:30 P.M.

The Premier and the Foreign Secretary shared a belated lunch, and their conversation had become somewhat desultory as they relaxed from a tension which it is as impossible for the mind to maintain, at whatever need, as for an athlete to run and to never rest.

"By the way," Mr. Bewdley asked, "have you heard whether Langton got through?"

"No. There's no news yet. But the Intelligence Office had sent two rather interesting items over when I looked in on Bayford just now.

"One's from Leipzig. There's a firm of merchants there who send information over occasionally in code. It's rather cleverly done. They use a commercial code for all their own business, and if the German Intelligence Department should ever trouble to decipher it, as they easily could, and probably do at times, it's about fifty to one that they'd find nothing but legitimate business matters, of no importance at all. But if they should keep on, about every few months they might come on some words that would all be in the code book, but wouldn't seem to make sense.

"The trick is that, after a certain word, it's understood that the wire's meant for us, and then everything means something different.

"There was a wire this morning from our agent there—No. 74 they call him—which said that another man—I think he's No. 973—who's supposed to be stationed at Prague, is on his way here with military secrets too important for other methods of transit.

"Bayford was disposed to connect this with a report of something which the Germans haven't disclosed, but which is almost certainly true, that the chemical works at Leuna were blown up during the night."

"And the other item of news?"

"That's a military report which has reached us through the Italian Ministry. It's a thing, if it's true, that can't be concealed, but it's important that the present source of the information should not be guessed.

"The Germans didn't only attack from the air. They did that, right enough, even using their large airliners and other commercial craft for conveyance of troops to the centres they seized early this morning. But they also invaded the country with some huge cruiser-tanks, which avoided the main roads, where they were suspicious of mines."

"Super-tank? There's nothing very surprising in them."

"No. Then wouldn't be. They brought them out for everyone to see at the manœuvres last year. But these are something bigger than they. They call them cruisers, but they say that they look more like battleships moving on land."

"Probably exaggerated about twenty times."

"Perhaps so. But the Italian Minister believes it, and he knows the source from which the report comes."

"It seems incredible that such monsters could be secretly built."

"So it does. But when you think of what Germany did before anyone tumbled to it three years ago. Why, they had to tell us they were breaking the treaty themselves, after they'd got tired of waiting for us to find it

"It makes our agents look like fools."

"It made us look like fools ourselves, which was a good deal worse, three years ago. Do you remember how some of us used to make speeches saying that Germany wasn't armed worth mentioning, and then we had to confess in about three days that she'd got the best air-fleet in Europe, and even the best anti-aircraft batteries (though I'm not sure that we mentioned them) with gun-muzzles twenty feet long, that no one had seen them build?"

"It does make our agents look fools, all the same, if such monsters can be built and manned without suspicion being aroused."

"I don't see why I should argue that. fools are always easy to find. But we don't pay them much. And it's dangerous work to be looking round Germany now.

"Other countries execute spies during a war, but it's the best part of four years since Hitler started doing it in a time of nominal peace. He cuts their heads off, women and men, where we should give them two years, or a bit less, if we didn't let them go free

"It's been the war atmosphere there since the end of 1934, as we all know, and Germany's been like an armed camp, telling everyone how peaceful she means to be, till she feels it's the time to start, as I suppose she does now.

"And you've got to remember those autostradas that she built during 1935, following all her frontiers, except Switzerland and the sea-coast. They were made to carry something heavier than a ten-ton lorry, to get it swiftly and smoothly to any point from which they might wish to operate, and without ruining their own countryside, as these monsters would do if they had no roads in their own country fit for them to traverse. We've had warnings enough that we wouldn't see."

"Well, there's one thing sure, if they're as large as you say, they won't ship them over the North Sea, and I don't suppose they're big enough to come through with their drivers' heads out of water."

"No. We can reckon we're safe from them. I wish I felt as secure against attack from the air."

"You always have worried about that."

"So I have. With sufficient cause."

"I don't say you're wrong, although you know it's a point on which the majority of the Cabinet wouldn't agree. They'd say that there's one vital point that you overlook.

"If we had a policy of aggression, such as might bring us into single conflict with Germany any day, then it would be a plain folly to have an Air Force less than half—you will say less than a fifth—of that which Germany has.

"But that isn't the position. We don't aim at war, and if Germany should act in such a manner as to render it inevitable (you may say that she's done that now) it remains a question that affects other European nations more than ourselves.

"It's our policy to prevent war, even now, if we can; or to keep out of it if it should come.

"But if it should, and if we should be unable to stand aside, then we shall not be without strong allies; and if you count air-fleets' strength, you needn't regard ours as a separate unit, with all Germany's in the other scale.

"It would be absurd to think of us quarrelling with Germany over Czechoslovakia, and all the rest of Europe standing aside."

Mr. Ganston agreed about that. He said it would be absurd in more ways than one.

The Premier sighed, and turned the conversation to more practical issues. The British Air Force (which Herr Janda had described last week as a gallant jest) could not be changed in an hour.

Mr. Ganston showed his sense of the gravity of the position by getting up from a shortened lunch, and without indulging himself in one of that excellent brand of cigars which were always available to those who were invited to Mr. Bewdley's table.

He said: "Well, we'll meet again at four-thirty. I'll call you if anything urgent should come up earlier. I hope to get Italy's attitude clear before then. I reckon the peace of Europe depends more on that for the moment than anything else. France won't fight if she can find a way round her hands being too full, though she'll come near to choke over this pill."

For a man of his age and weight, he went briskly out being of the temperament that will react to circumstance in a buoyant way.

CHAPTER LXV.

AT half-past four the Cabinet assembled again, but Mr Ganston did not arrive as punctually as he had promised to do, and when he came he had the expression and gait of an older man than he had appeared when he had left the Premier's table scarcely an hour before.

He entered in the midst of a lively discussion between the Ministers of Transport and War concerning a proposal for the immediate closing of some of the major arterial roads to all but military or other authorised traffic, in regard to which it was clear that the former gentleman had the general sympathy of his fellow-ministers.

Mr. Ganston heard the expressions "extreme public inconvenience"—"cultivating the war mentality"—and even "such monstrous nonsense" as he entered the room.

He interrupted the discussion without ceremony, and in a voice which compelled attention: "Gentlemen, there is a more urgent matter. I have just received an ultimatum from the German Ambassador."

The words, and the gravity with which they were spoken, produced an instant silence.

Only Mr. Lloyd-Davids' combative disposition refused to accept anything at Mr. Ganston's valuation.

"I suppose," he said impatiently, "you put their backs up with that interfering message yesterday, and now they've told us to mind our own business, or take the consequence?"

Through his agile brain there passed, in that instant's space, a vision of the resignation of his blundering colleague, perhaps involving the Premier's fall, and the elevation of one more suitable to the head of a reconstructed Government.

But Mr. Ganston did not appear to resent, or even to notice, the implication of those challenging words.

He answered with a mildness amazing to those around him, who knew how swift and merciless his retorts to such provocation would often be.

"I don't think it has anything to do with last night's message. But you can put it that way if you will."

Mr. Bewdley interposed, with a note of authority in his voice which seldom heard: "If you please, gentlemen, we will here what Baron Kronin has had to say."

"He asks for an assurance of our neutrality in the event of hostile action against Germany by any Continental Power as the result of the seizure of Czechoslovakia which occurred this morning. He requires an answer by five o'clock."

"*Requires?*" Mr. Lloyd-Davids repeated the word like a protesting echo, his bellicose spirit somewhat confused in its antagonism between Mr. Ganston and the German Ambassador. "That is hardly a word which he would be likely to use, or conducive to the friendly neutrality which we might otherwise not be unwilling to give "

"Five o'clock?" Mr. Bewdley asked. "That is barely twenty minutes from now."

Mr. Ganston looked at his watch. "It is eighteen minutes, to be exact."

"And if we decline to give such an assurance, without the time which its consideration requires?"

"The omission to give the required assurance within the time stated will be accepted as a declaration of war, with its usual consequences."

The blunt statement brought a moment of amazed incredulous silence, which broke out into protests of anger or disbelief.

"He couldn't really mean that!"

"It wouldn't be a declaration of war, and it would be absurd to call it by such a name."

"It's just a damned, insolent try-on. We shall find that, if we call his bluff."

"Unless Germany's gone mad for a second time."

Mr. Bewdley, retaining an outward calmness and self-control, and disregarding the discordant voices around him asked: "Was there any threat of what those consequences would be?"

"Yes. He was quite frank. We may expect that the German air-fleets will arrive before eight tonight. I was assured that they are in overwhelming strength, and in such readiness that we could not hope for the effective interposition of any allies, if we should invoke the existing pact and they should be willing to leave their own frontiers bare. I did all I could, or I should have been here earlier, and we should have had rather more time. All I got was an assurance that it would be a necessity that the German Government would very deeply regret."

"*You mean that London would be bombed in three hours?*"

It was the voice of the Minister of Transport, loud with indignation, that interposed. It would be a serious matter for a man with a wife and her single child in a West-end flat.

The sombre gravity of Mr. Ganston's face changed to contempt: "Baron Kronin did not mention the point, or points, that the German High Command have no doubt already selected for their attack."

By this time Mr. Lloyd-Davids felt that he had given this irritating, but far from desperate, position the consideration which it required, and that his advice should not be longer withheld.

"I think," he said, with decision, "that if Germany really attaches importance to such an undertaking, it should not be refused, for which there are two excellent reasons.

"We do not desire war, and, for all we know, the declaration for which Baron Kronin asks may have the effect of causing others to pause who might otherwise bring all Europe to a final wreck.

"And if there should be such a war, we should be fortunate to be able to stand aside, as such a pledge would give us good reason to do.

"Apart from that, what could such an undertaking, even though freely given, be really worth? It could apply only to present conditions, which must alter with every hour."

There was a murmur of some approval at this advice. A voice from the end of the table said: "There's one thing clear. We can't risk being attacked tonight."

Mr. Bewdley looked dubious. He followed the processes of Mr. Lloyd-Davids' mind which he did not like. It might be unfair to say that his devices were ever dishonourable, but they too often had a facial resemblance to those that were; as though they might live in the same street. He thought of De Valera's argument that the Irish Treaty was not binding because it had been signed under the duress of a stronger Power. Had not Herr Hitler (and even Viscount Snowden in an English newspaper) argued that the Versailles Treaty was not binding on Germany for the same reason?

It was a form of argument not without force, but with some bewildering logical implications, which it would have been pleasure to analyse at a more leisurely time. But it appeared from Mr. Ganston's reply that there would be no occasion to do it now.

"The German Government seems to have observed the position in a very similar light. It asks for the surrender of guarantees. It will take over control of Gibraltar and the Suez Canal until peace shall be made secure."

Mr. Lloyd-Davids' face flushed with anger as he replied: "They can't mean that seriously. They must know that we should never agree."

"Baron Kronin seemed surprised that we should object. He observed that the whole world knows that our Empire is breaking up, and that it is a process which we do not resist; that we seem rather disposed to expedite than retard.

"He pointed out that the control of the Canal is no longer a vital need; that we are as those who hold the keys of an empty chest.

"And, in any case, he says that Germany can be trusted to give them back, they being of little value to her. But for the moment it will be to her advantage to feel that the French and Italian fleets can be confined to the Mediterranean. That alone may be enough to avert war. We are to understand that everything is being done in the cause of peace.

"Beyond that, Germany will renounce all claims upon the mandated colonies which passed under our control. We are to understand that, when she says this, she buys our neutrality at a higher price than she should be expected to pay."

Mr. Bewdley listened to this with a demeanour outwardly unmoved, but his heart shook. Was it the ultimate truth that he was the head of a nation already fallen, but unaware?

Was it best to admit that which might be plain to impartial eyes, without shedding of useless blood?

He saw, is such a swift vision as is said to come to a drowning brain, the vast emptiness of the Empire which had been won in greater, forgotten years, and for which England had ceased to care; of the stagnant birth rate of a people who said that their children's lives were beyond their means, but never shrank from the fantastic, still-growing cost of their bloody, abortive roads.

Thought is swift—but how swiftly the moments passed! He saw the millions of unconscious innocent lives which a word from him might cast to agony or to death before morning came.

Under all there was the sound of Mr. Ganston's words, with the monotony of a tolling bell: *Five to one. I believe more.*

He heard the murmur of disputatious voices around him, weak with doubt, or hard with anger, or sharp with fear, and they were like the sound of a distant sea, for this was a decision which he must make in a lonely way, with God and his own soul.

He thought of the land he loved, and asked himself if it could be true that he had brought her to this—that she must be the slave, conquered and kicked, or the sleek-fed lackey of the more virile power. Was there no better, no other choice?

Through the confusion of tongues, a clock struck.

It brought silence, out of which a voice came: "It's about three minutes fast. There's still time."

So it was. There was still time. Time for honour or shame for prudence or many deaths——

FROM THE ROBERT HALE EDITION

Prelude in Prague was written in 1935, serialised in the *Sunday Dispatch*, and then published in book form.

It is one of the most astonishingly accurate historical forecasts that have ever been written.

Appearing at a time when the English Government was assuring the country that there was nothing to fear from a disarmed and prostrate Germany, it not merely indicated the imminence and nature of the catastrophe which threatened civilisation, but showed the direction which it would take with a detailed accuracy to which there can be few if any parallels in the realm of fiction.

Its reception was curious and illuminating. On the continent it had an enormous circulation. It was translated into twelve European languages. (There were actually two separate Russian translations). A German edition was published in Paris, and was widely read by German-speaking people outside the Reich.

The German Government was furious at the too-accurate forecast of its secret plans. Its Foreign Office made protests both in London and Prague against its circulation. In Berlin a police order was issued making it a criminal offence to possess a copy.

But in Great Britain, which it had been primarily intended to warn, it was received with indifference or actual hostility. One editor objected to the appearance of such a book "when confidence was just being restored in the City." Reviewers who did not ignore it entirely professed to regard it as an idle thriller.

So we drifted into the abyss....

ABOUT THE AUTHOR

SYDNEY FOWLER WRIGHT (1874-1965) penned over seventy volumes of science fiction, fantasy, classic mysteries, historical novels, poetry, and non-fiction, many of them being published by the Borgo Press Imprint of Wildside Press. Please visit his website at:

www.sfw.org